PASSION'S MAGIC

Eventually his heart slowe[...] turned to normal. "I'm s[...] mean for that to happen."

Serena pulled her head ba[...]. "I know," she whispered. "But [...]ng, Matt. Nothing that feels so right coul[...] be wrong."

Matt swallowed heavily. That was the problem. It did feel right. Her body pressed up tight against his felt right. His lips against hers felt right. Their breaths mingling together felt right. Everything in the whole world felt right when he was holding her.

"You're so trusting, so innocent," he murmured, running a calloused thumb across her swollen lips. "I shouldn't be teaching you these things."

"Who else should teach me?" She curved her hand around his cheek. "You're the one who taught me how to ride a horse, how to shoot a gun, how to do a dozen different things. You taught me how to survive. Now teach me how to live."

Her lips captured his, and Matt succumbed to their magic . . .

JANIS REAMS HUDSON

APACHE TEMPTATION

ZEBRA BOOKS
KENSINGTON PUBLISHING CORP.

ZEBRA BOOKS are published by

Kensington Publishing Corp.
475 Park Avenue South
New York, NY 10016

First Printing: September, 1993

Printed in the United States of America

*This book is dedicated with love and
fond memories to
Dwight V. Swain, mentor, teacher, and friend.*

Land of Temptation

The desert tempts a man to harshness.
Rugged mountains can make him hard.
A vein of silver might stir his greed
while lawlessness can turn him to revenge.
But of all the temptations this land has to offer,
a beautiful woman is the strongest.
She can tempt a man to great cruelties,
or she can lure him to love.

Prologue

April 14, 1878
Triple C Ranch
Arizona Territory

The wind sent heavy black clouds tumbling across the sky until they bunched up and blocked out the sun. Matt Colton hugged Joanna to his chest and shielded her from the stinging grit that flew before the approaching storm.

He could shield her from the elements, but how could he shield her from this? How did a man explain to his three-year-old daughter about death? Her mother's death?

Pain, sharp and sickening in its intensity, knifed through him. He stared at the coffin resting on the ground next to the dark, gaping hole in the earth. He closed his burning eyes, then forced them open. If the pictures behind his lids didn't go away soon, he might never close his eyes again.

He kept seeing the ranch off in the distance over the horses' ears as he and Angela drove the wagon home from Tucson yesterday.

Yesterday? Dear God, was it only yesterday?

Then the rider appeared racing out from behind a clump of cedar. Matt could still feel Angela clutching his arm as she recognized Abraham Miller Scott, the man who had murdered her father and kidnapped her a few years ago.

If Matt closed his eyes right now, he knew he'd see Miller's gun centered on his chest. He'd see Angela— oh God, would it never stop?—he'd see Angela throwing herself between him and that bullet.

He kept telling himself the pictures weren't real, it hadn't happened. But the coffin now being lowered into the ground by his father, his brother, and his friends was real . . . too real.

Matt wasn't even aware when his stepmother took Joanna from his arms and went back to the house with the rest of the family. Somewhere in the back of his mind he registered the sudden silence, the absence of quiet sobs and sniffling.

He didn't care about the wind whipping at his back, didn't care that fat drops of rain made tiny dust clouds when they hit the ground. He didn't care about the rapid drop in temperature. He didn't care about or particularly even feel any of it. He didn't feel much of anything . . . except emptiness. And pain.

By the time he made it back to the adobe ranch house, he was soaked. He bypassed the mourners gathered in the salon and went straight to his room. Their room. If he was trying to escape his memories of Angela, he'd come to the wrong place.

He ran a trembling hand over the quilt on the bed and remembered when she'd made this quilt, the first year they were married. "Double Wedding Ring," she'd called it.

Angel.

Matt clenched his fist and turned his back on the bed. It was not a place of rest any longer; it was a torture chamber. The whole room was a torture chamber. It even smelled like her.

He swore beneath his breath and stripped off his wet clothes.

It was a different Matt Colton who entered the salon a short time later.

At the sight of him, his stepmother gasped. She took in the worn buckskins that covered him like a second skin, the six-shooter strapped to his thigh, the hilt of the knife protruding from his knee-high moccasins. He carried a bedroll and saddlebags slung carelessly over his shoulder. Her heart quailed. "Matt?"

The tremor in Daniella's voice drew her husband's attention. Travis Colton stiffened, knowing what he would find when he turned from contemplating the fire to face his son. He saw the same things Dani saw, and more. He saw death in the eyes of his oldest son—the death of one Abraham Miller Scott.

"Do you have enough money on you?" Travis asked quietly.

"I've got enough," Matt answered.

"Enough for what? Where are you going?" Daniella demanded. Then she looked into his eyes and her questions were answered. "No!" she cried. "Matt, you can't mean to go after him."

When he didn't answer, she panicked. "Travis, stop him. Matt, let the law take care of it. They'll catch

9

him—that's what the law's for."

"Where was the law yesterday?" Matt asked harshly. "What law are you talking about, anyway? The law that lets a convicted murderer escape and run loose for years? The same law that let that bastard ride up in broad daylight and murder my wife? He killed Angela. He *killed* her. If you think I'm going to wait around for the law to take care of him, you don't know me very well."

Daniella turned to her husband for help. "Travis, do something! You can't let him ride out after that madman!"

Travis looked at his son for a long moment before answering. "How can I stop him when he knows I'd do the same thing if I were in his shoes?"

Daniella's panic mounted. She swung back to Matt and tried a different tactic. "How can you hope to find him? This rain has wiped out any trail he might have left."

"I'll find him," Matt answered.

Everyone in the room heard the quiet, deadly determination in his voice, and no one doubted Matt would do what he said. Abraham Miller Scott would die. That message was clearly spoken by the gold flames blazing in Matt Colton's brown eyes.

Daniella let out a trembling sigh of defeat. She was beginning to understand what Apache women, and all other women down through the ages whose men fought and warred, must have gone through. When a man decides to face danger, it's a woman's job to help him all she can, not hinder him.

Matt had been ten when she'd married his father, but she loved Travis's son just as much as she loved the children she'd given birth to. If anything happened to him . . . she shuddered and forced the thought away.

"Give me your saddlebags," she said to Matt. She saw his doubtful look and waved it away. "It's not a trick to try to keep you here," she assured him. "But I won't let you leave without food."

When Daniella left the room, Pace, her sixteen-year-old son, followed her, then turned away from the kitchen and headed for his room.

When Daniella returned a few moments later, she nearly cried out at the sight of Matt and Travis shaking hands like two strangers. They should be hugging each other, she thought. But Matt had all his emotions bottled up tight — all except his anger and his hatred. It seemed, during these past few trying hours, that all Matt's tender feelings had died with Angela.

"Don't know when I'll be back," Matt was saying. "He's got quite a head start on me. Might take a while."

Travis took in a deep breath and nodded. "Let us hear from you, son."

Matt merely returned the nod. He took the saddlebags from Daniella's trembling fingers and kissed her on the cheek. "Thank you," he whispered. They both knew he was thanking her for much more than just the food.

All Daniella could manage past the lump in her throat was a strained, "Take care, Matt."

"G'bye, Matt," thirteen-year-old Spence and nine-year-old Jessica said in unison.

Serena, Pace's twin, held out as long as she could, then threw herself at Matt's chest and hugged him

11

tight. "Oh, Matt," she cried. "Please be careful."

"I will." Matt kissed the top of his stepsister's head. "Will you do something for me while I'm gone, Princess?"

"Anything."

"Will you look after Joanna for me? Tell her . . . tell her I love her."

"I will, Matt," Serena said, stepping out of the embrace. She gave him a trembling smile. "I'll take good care of her, I promise."

Daniella's heart contracted with pain and pride. Pain for Matt's suffering, for his leaving; pride in Serena for not adding to his problems by wailing.

Matt glanced around the room one last time, then walked out the door. The rain had stopped. Good. Maybe it hadn't completely washed out the tracks he intended to follow.

As he led his horse out of the barn, his gaze roamed over the line of trees to the south. He could almost see two lovers, himself and Angela, walking hand-in-hand beneath the branches, could almost hear her soft laughter rippling gently through the leaves. He could see her green eyes gazing up at him with love. He could hear her voice, feel her touch.

He turned his back on the memories, his face toward revenge.

He mounted up and rode west.

He didn't look back.

The family wasn't over the abruptness of Matt's leaving a few minutes later when Pace came back to the salon. At sixteen, he was lean and wiry and nearly as tall as Travis. When Daniella realized Pace was dressed much the same as Matt had been, she reeled

12

with shock.

She took a step toward him and gasped. His eyes were like hers, clear, pale blue, fringed by long black lashes. But the expression there was not hers. Nor was it the expression of her son, Pace Colton. It was the expression of the Apache warrior Fire Seeker, the half-breed adopted grandson of Cochise.

"Pace! No! I won't let—"

"Duuda', shimá," Pace interrupted. No, my mother. *"Duudaańndida.* Don't say anything." He shrugged carelessly and stepped out the front door. "Someone has to watch his back."

Before anyone could stop him, he was gone.

Travis sank heavily onto his chair, feeling every one of his fifty-six years. He knew there was no use trying to stop Pace. Nothing could reach his half-breed adopted son when Pace got that full-blooded Apache look to him. Trying to talk sense into him when he got like that was like trying to talk to a rock.

And besides, Pace was right. Matt wasn't thinking straight. He wouldn't be watching his own back. But Christ! Pace was only sixteen!

Dear God, protect my sons.

And high in the Sierra Madres of Sonora, Mexico, a wrinkled old man closed his eyes, listened to the wind, and cried.

One

June 7, 1881

It was Joanna Colton's seventh birthday, the fourth in a row without her parents. Her father had been gone since the day of her mother's funeral, just before Joanna had turned four.

Her Aunt Serena watched the party in progress, but Serena's mind wasn't on the game of blindman's buff. Her sister Jessica was in charge of the game, anyway.

Serena smiled in spite of herself. At twelve, Jessie had turned into quite the little organizer. She'd done most of the planning for this birthday party, and Serena was grateful.

Serena's mind wandered again. Where was Pace? He knew today was Joanna's birthday, damn him. Her twin brother had left two weeks ago after hearing a rumor that Matt was in Tombstone. Surely Pace had found him by now. Surely he would bring Matt home today.

Matt.

Her heart twisted at the thought of her stepbrother, Joanna's father. None of the family had seen Matt for three years. Except Pace.

Even Pace wouldn't have seen him, except he had followed Matt that day he'd set out after Angela's murderer. Pace had kept his distance, realizing Matt needed to be alone for a while. That "while" had lasted two years.

That's how long it took Matt to catch up with Abraham Miller Scott—two years. For two years Matt followed Scott and Pace followed Matt. They trailed north through Navaho country, up through Colorado and Montana, south through California's giant redwoods to San Francisco, then through Nevada and back to Arizona. They finally caught up with Scott two days into Mexico.

When Matt caught up with Scott, no one knew the exact details of what happened except Matt and Pace. When Pace came home a few weeks later, all he said was that it was over. Scott was dead.

Serena knew it hadn't been an easy death. She remembered the stories she and Pace had listened to around the campfire at night when they were children. Those stories they weren't supposed to hear. They'd heard them every time they'd gone to stay with their grandfather, Cochise.

Serena and Pace may have had to sneak out of the wickiup at night to hear those old stories, but Matt was older. He didn't have to sneak. He was permitted to listen to the tales of Spaniards torturing Apaches, Apaches torturing their own victims. He'd even seen some of it first-hand when he was younger.

No, she thought with a sigh. Abraham Miller Scott did not die an easy death. She was certain he took a long time at it.

She remembered the night just over a year ago

when she had felt it. She had been eating dinner with the family when a sudden rush of horrendous terror hit her. She had dropped her fork with a clatter and gained everyone's undivided attention while she stared at her plate in total, consuming fear.

Then, as suddenly as it came, it faded, and somehow she knew the terror was not part of anyone she loved. A moment later a feeling of such hatred swamped her that she felt sick. Somehow, piled on top of that hatred, there grew a euphoric sense of satisfaction.

It was then she had known Matt had found his prey. That feeling of hatred and satisfaction told her Abraham Miller Scott did not die an easy death, for the hatred and satisfaction, she knew, were her stepbrother's. But damn it, that was over a year ago. Where the hell was Matt?

"Rena, Rena! Come see!" Joanna cried.

Serena combed her fingers through the streak of white hair at her right temple and pulled her attention back to the birthday girl and the party in progress. "Okay, Jo, I'm coming."

"We're gonna do the piñata now! Come watch!"

Supper had been over for hours and the birthday girl lay in exhausted sleep, but Pace still wasn't back. Nor was he back the next day, or the day after. Serena paced and cursed and prayed. Where was he? What was taking so long? Had he found Matt?

Another two full agonizing weeks went by after Joanna's birthday before Pace finally rode in — alone.

"Well?" Travis demanded.

"Did you find him?" Daniella asked anxiously.

"Is he all right? Where is he?" Serena questioned.

Pace slapped the trail dust off his denim pants and slumped onto the sofa. "I found him." His voice sounded hollow, lifeless.

Serena knelt before her twin brother and studied his closed features. She searched her mind, trying to connect with his, but he was shutting her out. Serena trembled. Pace almost never shut her out. "Tell us, Pace."

"Why didn't he return with you? When's he coming home?" Daniella asked.

"He's not coming home," Pace said bluntly. "At least . . not anytime soon."

"You've never minced words before, son," Travis told him. "Don't start now."

"All right," Pace said. He took a deep breath, then let it out. "He was drunk."

"So? Why didn't you just sober him up and bring him home?"

"He didn't want to get sober. He didn't want to come home."

"What do you mean?" Serena asked. "Didn't you tell him how much we all miss him, that Joanna needs him?"

"I told him, all right," Pace said with disgust. "I told him Jo needed him. I told him about the trouble brewing on the reservation, that we needed him there. He said . . . he said Joanna's got the whole rest of the family, so she doesn't need him, and The People don't need him either."

"That doesn't sound like Matt," Daniella said, bewildered.

"It's not Matt, Mother," Pace said sadly. "Not the Matt we know, anyway."

Serena bit the inside of her jaw. Pace had never danced around a subject this way before. He'd always been famous for saying exactly what was on his mind, whether it was prudent and tactful or not. "Pace, out with it. What are you not telling us?" she demanded.

"All right." Pace pushed himself up from the sofa and faced his father. "I didn't try to sober him up because he wouldn't let me near him. He doesn't want anything to do with me or anybody else. He's too busy feeling sorry for himself to care what anybody else wants or needs."

Pace glanced at his mother, took a deep breath, then looked back at Travis. "When I said he was drunk, I didn't mean it to sound like something temporary, because it isn't. From what I heard in Tombstone, he's always drunk. I don't think he's been sober since I left him in Mexico over a year ago. Come to think of it," he said with disgust, "he wasn't sober then, either."

"Oh, my God," Daniella whispered. She went to Travis and buried her face against his shoulder. "We've got to go to him. We've got to bring him home. He needs us."

"I don't think that's such a good idea, Mother," Pace said.

"Not a good idea?" she shrieked. "You expect us to just leave him there like that? Pretend nothing's wrong? Just . . . just go on without him? What about Joanna? Is she supposed to forget she even has a father?"

"Take it easy, love," Travis said quietly. He was as

upset by the news as she was, but he wasn't ready to drag Matt home by the ear like a naughty child. And that's exactly how Matt would feel if his parents went after him, Travis knew. "He'll think we're trying to run his life. Is that what you mean, Pace?"

"I guess." Pace rubbed the back of his neck and sat down on the sofa again. "The thing is, I don't think he could take it if any more of the family showed up just now. He was pretty embarrassed when it was only me. If he saw either of you, he'd probably go into hiding somewhere and never come out."

"So we should let him drink himself to death so he won't die of embarrassment?" Daniella asked. "That's ridiculous. Nobody ever died of embarrassment."

"You're right, Mother," Serena said. "But so is Pace. Someone needs to go after him, but I think it should be me."

"No!" Daniella and Travis shouted.

"Why not?" Serena demanded.

"Tombstone is no place for a young girl alone, Rena," Travis said. "It's twice as rough as Tucson."

"Besides," Pace interrupted. "Clum's there. He's the mayor, if you can believe that."

"John P. Clum?" Serena said, her voice dripping with sarcasm. "The same John P. Clum who decided he could save the poor dumb savages from themselves by locking them all up on one reservation together and doling out tiny bits of food and clothing like he was God Almighty? That John P. Clum?"

"The same." Pace's lips twitched as he tried to hold back a grin.

"All the more reason for you not to go," Travis said. "You know what he thinks of half-breeds. You

20

won't have a minute's peace after he finds out you're in town."

"Precisely why I *should* go," Serena stated firmly. "As much as Matt loves both of you, he knows you're adults and can take care of yourselves. Even you, Mother. But as far as he's concerned, I'm just his helpless little sister. He'll be so busy trying to protect me from Clum and all the big, bad gunslingers, he won't have time to drink, much less feel sorry for himself."

An identical slow grin spread across each face in the room. Everyone remembered how protective Matt was of both his sisters.

"You're right," Pace said. Then his smile faded. "But he's . . . well, he looks different, Rena."

"How do you mean?"

Pace hesitated. "Just remember, he's been drinking for the past year. It shows, that's all."

"If you're worried about me, forget it," Serena said. "I got over that case of hero worship a long time ago."

"Did you?" Pace asked quietly.

Serena glanced at her parents, then back at Pace. "Of course," she said with a nervous laugh.

Her telltale breathlessness may have escaped their parents, but not Pace. His eyes narrowed. "Rena—"

"I'd better start packing," she said, to cut him off. "I'll have to leave early in the morning to catch the train."

Two

Serena stepped down from the stage and tried to brush at least some of the alkali dust from the skirt and sleeves of her rust plaid sateen traveling dress. The train from Tucson to Benson hadn't been bad, but the stage from Benson to Tombstone was a nightmare. Someday the idiots in charge of the railroad would surely lay track all the way to Tombstone. Serena resented having to take the stage that last twenty-five miles when a body could travel clear across the country by train.

She and the other five passengers from Benson had been packed like sardines onto the hard, unforgiving seats of the Concord. The stage had hit every single pothole along the way. The road was a sheer torture of jolts and bumps and choking dust. Walking would have been easier, and probably faster.

The exhausting journey had left her slightly less than presentable, but from what Pace had said, Matt wasn't likely to be in any condition to notice. Besides, she was too anxious to find Matt to take time checking into a hotel and cleaning up. When her bag was tossed down from the top of the stage, she carried it into the depot.

The young man behind the desk looked up from his ledger and straightened his spectacles. When he swallowed, his Adam's apple bobbed. "May I help you?" His voice cracked over the last word.

Serena smiled and asked if she could leave her bag in his office for a few hours.

The clerk scratched his head and frowned. "You're welcome to leave it here awhile, but . . . do you have someone to stay with while you're in town?"

"I'll probably take a room at one of the hotels."

The clerk shook his head. "After the fire last night, I don't know if there's a vacant hotel room in town."

"Fire?"

"I guess you haven't looked down Allen Street yet. This morning's *Epitaph* says we lost sixty-six businesses."

Serena gaped. "Sixty-six businesses in one fire?"

The clerk sent his Adam's apple up and down again. "Yes, ma'am. Stores, saloons, restaurants, offices, and three hotels. That's why I said you might not find a room. The hotels that didn't burn had to make room for everybody who ended up without one." He shook his head. "It was really awful."

Sixty-six? "Was anyone hurt?" she asked, thinking anxiously of Matt.

"George Parsons got burned up a little, helping fight the fire." The young clerk gave a negligent shrug. "The only other injury I've heard of is when some drunk had to jump out his hotel window and broke his leg. Guess we were lucky."

Lucky. What an understatement. Sixty-six businesses burned in one night, and only two injuries.

23

Serena shuddered. What an awful blow to the town. She felt for the shop owners, saloonkeepers, and others who had probably lost everything they owned in the blaze. But there was nothing she could do. The fire didn't concern her. She was here to find Matt. She left her bag with the clerk and stepped back out into the blazing sun.

After crossing the side street, she stood on the corner of Third and Allen to get her bearings. From there she saw the lingering smoke hanging over the town like doom waiting to swoop. Only the doom had obviously already swooped, even if she couldn't see the ruins yet. What she could see were numerous saloons, several hotels and restaurants, a livery, what looked like a bank, three mercantiles, a bath house, and a barber shop. Shingles over several doorways proclaimed at least a half dozen attorneys on Allen Street alone.

Allen was the main street, Pace had said. What he hadn't told her was how boisterous and lively the town was. Last night's fire apparently hadn't slowed things down. Not for a town like Tombstone. Freight wagons jammed the street two blocks down; three vegetable wagons driven by Chinese farmers rolled past her while the constant sound of hammering echoed everywhere. Tombstone, it seemed, was thriving, despite the fire.

Serena walked purposefully down the boardwalk and stopped at the first saloon she came to. This seemed like the best place to start looking for Matt. With trembling fingers, she smoothed her hair up under her hat. She'd never been inside a saloon before, never even dreamed of going into one. She stood

24

staring at the swinging half-doors for a moment, trying to work up her nerve. A glance told her several people had stopped to stare at her.

My reputation won't be worth a nickel in this town by sundown, she thought with disgust. Then she shrugged. *To hell with all of them.* If she had to go into a saloon to find Matt, then she'd do it. Who cared what anyone thought? With a deep breath, she stepped through the swinging doors.

She stopped immediately to let her eyes adjust to the dimness. All activity in the long, narrow barroom came to an abrupt halt as the men stopped their conversation, their card-playing, and their beer-sipping to stare at her.

Serena was suddenly glad to feel the weight of her mother's derringer tugging on her drawstring handbag.

As she glanced around the room, she was surprised. She'd always had the impression that saloons were dingy, dirty places filled with the dregs of society. She revised her opinion at once.

The Lucky Lady was anything but dingy. The room was dimly lit, compared to the glaring afternoon sun outside, but there was certainly nothing dingy or second-class about it. The tables and chairs were all of highly polished oak, all orderly, all clean.

And that bar — she'd never seen anything like it. At least thirty feet long and polished to a high mahogany gloss, it gleamed in the dim light. Three men leaned on it at the far end, two standing, one sitting on a padded stool. Each man had a foot resting casually on the shiny brass footrail. Behind the bar a huge mirror framed in elaborate scrollwork covered the entire wall. Row after row of spotless crystal stemware and glass mugs lined the shelf before the mirror.

There were at least a dozen patrons in the room, counting the three at the bar. Most appeared to be businessmen, to judge by their dress. A couple of cowboys sipped on their beers while three men who could only be miners played cards at a back table.

When the bartender folded his arms across his ample chest and scowled at her, Serena stopped her gawking.

"Ain't no ladies allowed in here," he said with a growl.

"Excuse me," Serena said, stepping up to the bar. "I'm looking for a man."

The bartender's face immediately cleared. His eyes roamed over her in a way that made her flesh crawl. "Well, now, that's different," he said with a grin. "We got a whole room full o' men here. I happen to have an opening for a new girl, an' you're sure pretty enough. Just take your pick, sister. You can use the last room on the right, upstairs. My take is fifty percent of whatever you make. If I don't hear no complaints about you by midnight, the job's yours. Can you deal?"

Serena felt the heat of the blush that stained her cheeks. He actually thought she . . . she was . . . she wanted to . . . In shock, she fought hysterical laughter and managed a shaky, "Uh, wh-what?"

"Deal. You know, cards—poker, blackjack."

Serena managed to regain her senses by then. She supposed she'd asked for this, coming into a saloon this way. But his assumption still angered her. "I'm sorry, but—"

"That's all right, honey. I guess it was too much to ask that a gal who looks like you could be smart enough to understand cards."

"I understand cards perfectly well, thank you," she managed between clenched teeth. "But that is entirely beside the point. I did not come here looking for a job. I came here looking for a specific man. I'm trying to locate Matt Colton."

One of the men leaning against the end of the bar chuckled at her predicament and gave her a bold wink. The man on the barstool ignored the burning match in his hand and stared at her blankly.

The bartender looked skeptical. "Now what would a pretty young thing like you be wantin' with the likes o' Colton? Why, he's meaner than a stepped-on rattlesnake. He'd chew a tiny thing like you up into a million pieces and spit you out before you knew what hit you. My advice to you is to steer clear o' him. He's just plumb bad news."

Serena clenched her teeth. "He's my brother," she ground out.

The man on the barstool straightened, his disinterested stare turning sharp with interest. The match burned down to his fingers. He winced and shook it out. Serena ignored him.

The bartender snorted. "Honey, if Matt Colton's your brother, that's your problem. Ain't seen him around lately."

Her voice said, "Thank you." Her eyes said, *Drop dead.*

She stepped back outside just as a team and wagon rattled past at top speed. Serena held her breath, waiting for the dust to settle.

Matthew Colton, you better damn well appreciate what I'm going through for you.

When she could breathe again, she walked to the next saloon with determination in every stride. This time the bartender was out on the boardwalk sweeping sawdust from in front of his door.

"Sorry, ma'am," he said, when she asked about Matt. "He hasn't been around here in at least a week. You might try across the street there." He pointed to the saloon directly opposite. "If that doesn't work, try down at the end of the block at the Last Chance."

Serena thanked him politely and hurried across the street. Her spirits rose a tiny bit. At least this second man had been nice. The first one might have been, if she'd phrased her question differently. She bit back a grin at her own stupidity in simply asking for "a man." No wonder he'd jumped to conclusions.

This third saloon destroyed her good mood. Compared to the Lucky Lady, the Watering Hole was a dump. Compared to an outhouse, it was a dump. It reeked of sour beer and sweaty bodies and lord knew what else. Every surface—tables, chairs, bar, and floor—were covered in grime. She was relieved to find out Matt was not one of their regular customers.

"Try over to the Last Chance, next block down, past the fire," the bartender advised.

Serena thanked him and stepped back outside. That's when she saw the fire damage. She shuddered. There was a gaping black hole in the middle of Tombstone. For two blocks along the north side of Allen Street, nothing stood but a few charred posts. Wispy tendrils of smoke tainted the air. The destruction flowed north along both sides of Fourth all the way up to the next street. From where Serena stood, she couldn't tell if or where the fire had spread from there.

Sixty-six businesses. It wasn't luck that there had been only two injuries. With a fire that size, it was nothing short of a miracle. Serena shuddered again, then walked on down Allen until she spotted the Last Chance near the end of the street, past the fire.

The Last Chance Saloon was every bit as fancy as the Lucky Lady, complete with velvet drapes and a crystal chandelier. But here, Serena had a surprise. She was greeted by an attractive woman, perhaps in her late twenties, dressed expensively in royal purple satin trimmed with white lace. The matching fringed hat covered in bows and flowers added just the right accent to make her highly fashionable. What startled Serena, however, was the tremendous amount of cleavage revealed by the low, scooped neckline of the dress.

The woman's mouth curled up in a surprised grin. "You must be Serena Colton. I've been expecting you."

Serena blinked. "You have?"

"Of course," the woman said.

"I'm pleased to meet you, but why should you know who I am?"

The woman laughed, a pleasant, cheerful sound. "Pace told me he had a twin sister. What he didn't tell me was how much alike the two of you look. Matt's talked so much about his family that I couldn't help but recognize you by that white streak in your hair. Although he did lead me to believe you were only twelve years old. I'm Kali Randolph."

"Pleased to meet you. You know my brothers?"

Kali laughed again. "One of them better than I should, the other not as well as I'd like."

Serena blushed and tried to stifle a giggle. "I don't think either one would want me to know which was which."

"I don't think either one would want you even talking to me, much less coming into a saloon."

Serena waved a hand in dismissal. "Pace is no prude. He wouldn't think anything of it."

"But Matt?"

"Matt will probably have a fit. Do you know where he is?"

"I might," Kali said, her look turning cautious.

Serena sobered. Kali had seemed friendly enough at first, but something had changed. "If you knew where he was, would you tell me?"

"That depends."

"On what?"

"On what you're planning to do once you find him."

"Do? I . . . don't know what you mean."

"I mean, are you going to baby him and feel sorry for him, or are you going to give him what he needs?"

"What is it you think he needs?" Serena asked.

"A swift kick in the ass."

Serena nearly strangled on her laughter. Feigning a thoughtful look of innocence, she lifted the hem of her skirt and revealed the pointed toes of her kidskin walking boots. "Do you think these will do?"

The corners of Kali's eyes crinkled with laughter. "They'll do. And so will you. Come on. I'll take you to him."

Kali grabbed her handbag and parasol from behind the polished, gleaming bar and led Serena outside. They went back the way Serena had come, then turned down a side street and nearly collided with three men engrossed in discussing the drastic results of the previous night's fire.

"Excuse us, ladies," one of them said, doffing his bowler hat.

Serena's eyes narrowed. He was attractive, with a high, smooth forehead and deep-set eyes. A thick mustache angled down on both sides of his mouth like an inverted V and emphasized his bushy goatee. Yes, he was attractive, if she didn't know who he was. But she did know, instantly.

He recognized her in the same moment. "Kali, you should be more careful about the company you keep," he said. "After all, you don't want to get a bad reputation."

Kali's brow raised in question.

The mayor of Tombstone, who Serena knew was also the editor of the *Tombstone Epitaph,* then smirked at Serena, making one side of his mustache twitch. "Why aren't you on the reservation with the rest of the squaws, half-breed?"

"Why aren't you in hell with the rest of the scum, Clum?" Serena grinned. "How about that? It even rhymes. Clum . . . scum. I like it." She nodded her head decisively.

John Clum rolled his eyes to the sky. "All the Coltons seem fairly hard to get along with," he told the men with him. "But in my experience, the females of the family are by far the worst." Then he addressed Serena with a smirk. "Saw that brother of yours last

31

week, that Fire Eater."

"Mr. Clum," Serena said as if lecturing a small child. "You know very well that Pace's Apache name is not 'Fire Eater,' it's 'Fire Seeker.' "

"Ah, yes." Clum nodded. "And what name did the Apaches give you?"

She would have walked on and ignored him at that point, but he stood directly in her path. "Up until now, they've always called me Serena. But if you don't step aside and let me pass, they'll be giving me a new name."

Clum stuck his thumb and forefinger into his vest pocket and smirked again. "And what might that be?"

"If you're lucky and I'm feeling generous, the worst they'll call me is She Who Spits in Old Agent's Face."

The two men with Clum suddenly found the toes of their boots fascinating in the extreme. Their shoulders shook with silent laughter as Clum glared at them. Kali didn't even attempt to restrain her laughter.

"One of these days that mouth of yours is going to get you into serious trouble, young lady," Clum warned Serena.

"I could say the same for you," she told him. "I don't like being called a squaw."

Clum's eyes widened, then his brows lowered. "You're half Chiricahua. You've always seemed . . . proud of that."

"Yes, Mr. Clum, I'm proud to be half Chiricahua. But a white female is called a woman. A Negro female is called a woman. A Mexican female is called a

32

woman. An Apache female is no more, no less than any other female, Mr. Clum. She's a woman, the same as they are."

No one said a word as Clum eyed Serena thoughtfully.

"Good day, Mr. Clum." Serena nodded, then stepped around him so she and Kali could be on their way.

Halfway down the block, Kali stopped and shook her head.

"What is it?" Serena asked.

"Serena Colton, I like your style."

The two young women smiled at each other for a moment, then continued down the dusty street.

The neighborhood took a dramatic turn for the worse. The buildings were all run-down, dilapidated, unpainted, some with canvas walls, others made from packing crates. Garbage lined what passed for gutters. In addition to the usual scrawny dogs who fed off town garbage, here pigs ran loose. And rats, big ones bold enough not to care that it was broad daylight and people walked the streets.

The people, too, seemed a rougher lot than those on Allen Street. There were no men in business suits and no women in nice dresses. There weren't any women in *clean* dresses.

Kali led Serena down a side alley to the back of a building that had been so haphazardly thrown together with scrap lumber that it looked like a good sneeze would topple it. There were three doors along the rear, but no windows.

Kali paused at the third door. "I don't know what you're used to, but I'm sure you're not prepared for

33

this. I . . . I should have told you right off . . ."

Serena's heart knocked against her ribs. She felt sick. What was Matt doing in a place like this? "Told me what?"

For a long moment, Kali looked everywhere but at Serena. Then she seemed to come to some sort of decision and looked Serena right in the eye. "You know about last night's fire."

Serena's heart knocked harder. "Matt's been hurt?"

"He had to jump from his hotel window. He broke his leg."

Some drunk jumped . . . "Is he all right?"

Kali grimaced. "I don't know. After Dr. Goodfellow set his leg, I took Matt back to the Last Chance with me, and put him up in my room."

Despite her concern for Matt's welfare, Serena felt herself blush at the implication in Kali's words.

"The long and short of it is, I tried to take care of him, tried to mother him, I guess. I scolded him about his drinking. He got so mad he bribed some miner into helping him leave. This is where he ended up."

Serena eyed the rickety, windowless shack and held back a shiver of distaste.

"Why don't you wait here?" Kali suggested. "If he's still in there, I'll bring him out."

Serena straightened her shoulders. "If Matt can stand it, I can stand it."

Kali studied her a long moment. "All right, but I warn you, it won't be pleasant."

Kali pushed the door open, and Serena followed her inside. A foul odor hit her in the face. Both women fumbled in their bags for perfumed handker-

34

chiefs to press against their noses. The only light in the room came through the open door and the numerous cracks in the walls. The room was tiny, filthy. Four cots, three of which were empty, left barely enough room to turn around.

Most of the smell seemed to come from the occupied cot in the far corner. As they proceeded into the room, it was impossible for Serena and Kali to keep their skirts from brushing against the disgustingly dirty blankets and walls.

"Oh, my God," Kali whispered, as she bent over the corner cot. "Can you hear me? It's me, Kali."

Serena sucked in her breath in shock, then choked on the lungful of foul air. The stranger on the bed was thin and pale, obviously ill. Where his skin wasn't covered in soot, it was a sickly yellow color beaded with sweat. Faded red longjohns, stained and singed beyond redemption, were all he wore. He hung one leg off the side of the cot and shifted restlessly, stirring up a little cloud of dust on the dirt floor. The other leg was stretched out painfully straight in a snug splint. The white bandage stood out starkly against the soot and grime.

"He's burning up with fever," Kali muttered. "If he'd gone home with Pace, like I told him to . . ."

Serena's eyes widened and darted to the man's face. His hair was soaked with sweat and plastered to his skull. His eyes were dull and lifeless, his lips caked and dry.

If it hadn't been for that scar on his cheek, Serena doubted she'd have known who he was.

It was all she could do to keep from running from the room screaming. This pitiful, run-down stranger

35

reeking with the stench of his own filth couldn't be Matt, couldn't be her stepbrother, the larger-than-life hero she'd worshipped all her life. It just couldn't.

But it was.

Three

Matt squinted at the two figures wavering above him. The curves and sweet smells told him they were women. One was only a black silhouette against the blinding light streaming in through the open door, but the other he recognized.

"Kali?" Damn, but his throat was raw. "That you?"

"It's me. Lordy, Matt, you're a mess."

Matt fumbled beneath his one ragged blanket, which was wadded up between him and the wall, and clutched his pint of whiskey. "Glad you came." It took most of his strength just to whisper the few words. "Open this for me . . . will you?"

"I think that's about the last thing you need right now," Kali said.

"Need it," he whispered hoarsely. "Come on, Kali, be a pal. Leg . . . hurts like a blue bitch." He tried to lift the bottle toward her, but couldn't. He was too weak. Damn.

"There's someone here to see you, Matt."

Matt squinted at the other figure again. "Still trying to hook me up with one of your girls?" He let out a breathless chuckle. "Give it up, Kali. I told you be-

37

fore, I don't need a woman."

Serena took a steadying breath and stepped around until the light was on her face so he could see who she was. "Aren't you even just a little bit glad to see me?"

It took considerable effort for Matt to lift his head from the bare, sweat-soaked mattress. When he finally recognized Serena, he dropped his head back and threw an arm across his eyes. "Goddamn."

"Thanks a lot. It's good to see you, too."

Matt lowered his arm and glared at her. "What the hell are you doing here? Did Pace send you? I'll kill him for this. Get out, Rena. Get out and go home. Leave me alone."

Serena took another deep breath to bolster her resolve. What she wanted to do most was cry, but any show of sympathy was the last thing in the world Matt needed from her. "See there?" She winked at Kali. "You *did* need me. I've been here only a few minutes and you've already got the strength to yell."

Matt bit back another curse and used his sudden burst of energy to uncork his bottle. He took a long pull, then sagged back against the mattress again. He barely got the cork back in the bottle when his hand went limp and his eyes slid shut.

Serena frowned. "Matt?"

"I'll be damned," Kali said. "He's passed out."

Serena sagged against the rough plank wall and fought back tears. "Dear God, he's much worse off than I thought."

"Yeah," Kali agreed. "This is the worst I've ever seen him. You gonna be all right? You handled yourself real well, but can you keep it up? He'll only feel worse if he sees you cry."

"I can handle it." Serena pushed herself from the wall. "But Kali, I've got to get him out of this place. Good Lord, how can anyone live like this?"

"I agree, but I don't know where you're going to take him. We lost three hotels last night, including the one Matt was staying in. All the others are full to bursting. Even my place is full. And after last night, he probably wouldn't stay there, anyway."

Serena shook her head. "I think what I need is someplace private. I don't think he's going to want to be around people for a while."

"What did you have in mind?"

"I don't know, unless there's an empty house around. We wouldn't need much, just one or two rooms."

"You're not going to try to take him home right away?"

"No," Serena said softly. "Not like this. He wouldn't want that. First I want to get him well and back on his feet. After that, I guess it'll be up to him."

Kali studied her thoughtfully for a moment, then said, "I think I know just the place you need, but I'm warning you, it's not much. Just an abandoned one-room adobe about an hour south of town, in the hills. And you know, don't you, getting him back on his feet isn't going to be easy?"

"I think I know, but I guess I'll find out for sure, won't I? That adobe sounds perfect. Now, how am I going to get him there?"

"That's not a problem. The saloon's got a wagon over at the livery. I'll go get it, along with a couple of men to carry Matt. Did you bring luggage with you?"

Serena nodded and told her about leaving her bag at the stage station.

"I'll pick it up in the wagon. I'll have to stop on the way back and get some supplies, too. That place out there is nothing but bare bones. I doubt if there's even a bucket to piss in."

Serena couldn't control her burst of laughter. "We can't do without that, can we?" Then her laughter faded to a wry grin. "But I don't think Matt's even going to be able to handle a bucket. I'm afraid for the next few days what he's going to need is a bedpan."

Kali's gaze narrowed and her lips twitched. "Just where would a girl like you learn about bedpans?"

"My Grandfather Jason was an invalid the last several years of his life. Bedpans are easy." Serena shrugged and grinned. "Someone else fills them up, and you empty them. Nothing to it."

Kali threw her head back and laughed. "You'll do, girl. Yes, ma'am, you'll do fine. One wagon, two men, and a bedpan, coming up."

When Kali left, Serena knelt next to Matt's cot and tenderly smoothed the wet hair from his brow. "Oh, Matt," she said with a sigh. She wished she knew if he'd passed out from the liquor or his fever, but either way, he was sicker than anyone she'd ever seen.

She chewed on her upper lip and fought back tears. Matt had always been her hero, so strong and self-assured, always there whenever anyone needed a shoulder to lean on. To see him reduced to this state tore at her heart.

This wasn't the Matt Colton she knew. This wasn't a young girl's older brother, a young woman's hero, her knight in shining armor. It wasn't the son who

40

honored his parents, nor the husband and father who worshipped his family.

This wasn't Matt Colton the rancher, respected across the territory for his strength, his wisdom, his sense of justice.

Nor was it the white-skinned, yellow-haired Apache called "Bear Killer." Never mind the bear-claw necklace and the scar on his cheek. It wasn't him.

It wasn't any of the Matts Serena knew.

Matt, Bear Killer, where are you? What are you doing to yourself?

Serena spent an eternity there, kneeling on the floor next to that dirty little cot in that dingy little room, looking down at Matt, smoothing his fevered brow. Finally, she thought she heard Kali's voice accompanied by the rumble and rattle of a wagon from down the alley.

As Serena stood up, the heel of her shoe caught on something. Bending down, she carefully felt around and came up with a torn pair of men's canvas pants. Since they were under Matt's cot, she decided to take them with her. She felt around some more, and in the far corner found a leather vest wrapped haphazardly around a pistol and holster. She claimed them, too.

Just as she heard traces jingling and horses snorting outside the door, Serena spotted a shirt she assumed was Matt's hanging on the wall above his head. His boots lay at the foot of the bed, a knife and a pair of dirty socks stuffed down inside. The fumes from the socks were enough to choke a horse.

She heard Kali's voice and took the clothes outside. "Kali, you're wonderful!" Serena exclaimed, as she squeezed the woman's hand. One side of the wagon was packed tight with pots, pans, flour, sugar, salt, ham, and dozens of other supplies.

The other side held a spotless, narrow mattress cushioned from the hard floor of the wagon by several inches of clean straw. A saddled horse—a blue roan gelding—was tied to the back, where he stood swatting flies with his tail.

"Matt's horse," Kali explained. "I won't be able to leave the wagon with you, so you'll need him."

"Thank you. I don't know what I would have done without you, Kali."

"Don't worry about it. Matt's a friend. I'd like to see him get straightened out. I happen to think you're just the one to do it."

Kali introduced her to the two men she'd brought to carry Matt. They were friends of hers, a couple of out-of-work miners named Hank and Josh. They shoved empty cots aside and lifted Matt, while Serena held his broken leg.

Halfway out the door, Matt came to. He didn't know where he was or who had him, so he began to struggle.

"Be still!"

The sharp command didn't fit with the soft feminine voice. Matt stopped struggling and squinted against the glare of the late afternoon sun. "Rena?"

"It's me, Matt. Just take it easy. We're getting you out of this place so I can take care of you."

"Put me down, goddammit. I don't need anybody taking care of me, least of all you. What I need is a drink. Where the hell's my bottle?"

"What you need is a swift kick in the pants." She

gave a sharp nod to Hank and Josh, and they placed Matt none too gently on the mattress in the wagon.

Serena tried to keep his leg from jostling, but she saw the grimace of pain cross Matt's face. She climbed in the back and tried to keep his fevered body covered with the blanket Kali had brought, while Kali sat up front with Hank and Josh.

The horses pulled the wagon with a slow walk, but the roads were deeply rutted from the recent spring rains. Every few feet, one of the wheels fell sharply into a pothole, wringing a moan from Matt. He passed out again before they even reached the edge of town.

He came to a couple of times on the way to their destination, but was unconscious again when they arrived at the abandoned adobe hut. His fever was raging and the mattress beneath him was already damp.

Kali made the others wait at the wagon while she took a broom inside. Clouds of dirt and debris billowed out the door. When she came back out a few minutes later she was grinning.

"You're in luck. This place actually has a plank floor."

This time when the men picked Matt up, they carried him mattress and all. Serena had them put him down in the corner opposite the door, next to the crude fireplace.

The fireplace wasn't the only thing that was crude. The whole structure was crude, but it would do, Serena thought. With its solid roof and walls, it provided more shelter than a wickiup would have.

The entire house, if it could be called that, consisted of one room with a fireplace, a door, and a window with warped shutters. But it was functional and private. There was a brush corral out back and a water well in front. If the roof didn't leak when it rained, she and Matt would do quite well.

"Oh, Serena, I didn't think," Kali said. "Where will you sleep?"

"Don't worry about me. I'll just pile that straw on the floor and I'll be fine. I can't thank you enough, Kali, for all your help."

"Like I said, forget it. I'll be back out in a day or two to check on you, and I'll bring more food. There's a bag of jerky somewhere among this stuff." She indicated the supplies Hank and Josh were unloading and stashing along one wall. "It'll make a decent broth for Matt until he can handle something solid."

The sun was sinking low by the time Kali and the men left for town. Serena was exhausted, but she knew her work had just begun. She heated water over a small fire and tore her oldest petticoat into strips. It was time for her first major chore, and it wasn't going to be easy.

Matt Colton was going to get a bath.

She used a knife to slice open the seams of his longjohns in order to remove them. They were so ragged and dirty and singed they weren't worth saving. She pulled them off him and tossed them in the far corner. Tomorrow she'd burn the disgusting things. She didn't dare throw them into the fireplace inside — the fumes would probably kill her.

She turned back and studied Matt's long, nude form, surprised to feel an embarrassed flush sting her cheeks. A man's nakedness was nothing new to her.

Having lived part of each year of her life with the Apaches, it would have been impossible for her to be unfamiliar with what whites considered "a man's privates." Apache men usually wore only a breechcloth.

The scant garment covered the essentials, most of the time. But when a man sat or squatted, a breechcloth tended to gap open around the legs. When he ran or the wind blew, it flapped and waved in the breeze like a woman's skirt, leaving not much to the imagination.

It was always a source of amazement and embarrassment to the Army when they hired Apache scouts and gave them uniforms to wear. The first thing an Apache did was cut the seat from the pants. He couldn't imagine why a man would want to be confined like that, and found the white man's garment much too constricting.

So even though Serena had never seen Matt before, as she had others, she shouldn't have been embarrassed by his nakedness.

Actually, she decided, she wasn't embarrassed so much by his nakedness, but by how it made her heart race. She had trouble remembering she had been raised as his sister. Yes, her racing heart and failing memory embarrassed her.

As his sister, she shouldn't have noticed that despite his current injury and fever, despite the way he'd been living the past year inside a whiskey barrel, his body was still . . . magnificent.

No. A stepsister shouldn't notice such a thing. She shouldn't notice the way those magnificent muscles still bulged and curved, creating smooth hills and valleys down his entire length. Not quite as shapely as she remembered, but still there, and still firm.

His once golden skin, now yellowed from illness, stretched tight across muscle and bone, indicating a loss of flesh. His ribs, cheekbones, and hips retained no flesh to separate them from that tight skin, which was now covered with a sheen of perspiration.

Serena let her gaze roam over him carefully. Sweat from his fever plastered his wavy blond hair to his scalp. She studied the thick straight brows above his closed lids and wondered if gold flecks still danced in those deep brown eyes.

The bear-claw necklace—the only thing he wore—had yellowed with age over the years.

She barely remembered that night in the stronghold so many years ago, when she and Pace were five and Matt was fifteen, when he had received the necklace—and the scar on his cheek. At the time, she hadn't understood what had happened, had only known Matt was hurt by a bear and her parents were very worried. Serena had tried her best to be brave and not to cry. Apache children didn't cry, and while she and Pace were in Cochise's stronghold, they were not half-breeds, they were Apaches.

But when a small child sees fear in her parents' eyes, bravery comes hard. She had somehow managed, though, because her grandfather, Cochise, had promised her Matt would be all right, and Grandfather always spoke the truth.

Matt had survived the bear attack, but not without scars. The one on his cheek was highly visible, but it was nothing compared to the scars on his chest and back.

Serena drew a finger along the bear claws. The

necklace, according to old Dee-O-Det, the shaman, would protect Matt from bears forever.

She trailed her finger down to trace one of the parallel marks that curved from his right collarbone to his left side just below his ribs. When her fingertips came in contact with his heated flesh, something happened to her.

It was like being out in the open desert with a storm approaching. The air around her seemed to crackle and snap. Her skin felt all prickly, and her fingertips tingled. Some indefinable heat flashed from his skin, through her fingers, and settled in her breasts and the juncture of her thighs. Her breathing grew labored. Her whole body trembled with unexplained excitement.

Serena gasped audibly and jerked her hand away. She spun around and faced the fire, covering her flaming cheeks with both hands, scolding herself for her foolish imagination. Such things didn't happen, not from a simple touch.

But a few minutes later, when she was washing his face and neck, she couldn't explain why she was still trembling.

Gradually she began to calm and concentrated on bathing as much of Matt as she could reach, suffering an unwanted and ridiculous clumsiness over certain parts of his body. She feared hurting his injured leg, so she didn't try turning him over to wash his back. That would have to wait.

When she had washed every place she could reach, she pulled the blanket across his hips and cut the bandages holding his splint in place. Beneath them she found a neat line of ten stitches along Matt's shin.

She wondered if the cut had come from without, or had been created by the broken bone puncturing through from inside.

Dr. Goodfellow, Kali had said. The man did neat stitches, but Serena wasn't about to trust the welfare of Matt's leg to a stranger. Any good seamstress could sew neat stitches. That didn't mean the bone was properly set. If it wasn't, Matt could be left with a permanent limp. As far as Serena was concerned, that would be unacceptable.

She poked and prodded along Matt's leg as gently as she could. If the bone was not properly aligned, maybe it wasn't too late to straighten it.

The leg was still swollen around the break, so she had to poke hard to feel the bone. She knew she was hurting him, for he moaned once and his muscles tensed.

"I'm sorry, Matt," she whispered, not taking her hands or eyes from what she was doing. "I'm hurting you, I know, but I'm almost finished." With fingers not quite as steady as they should have been, Serena felt carefully along the bone. She breathed a sigh of relief. The bone was aligned straight and true. "There," she said softly. "I'm through now."

Without thinking, she bent and placed a kiss just above his stitches. She heard his sharp intake of breath, saw and felt his entire body jerk. Her gaze flew to his face.

His fever-bright eyes were open. For a brief instant, before he could mask his expression, he stared at her with horror plainly visible.

"Did I hurt you?" she cried.

Matt clenched his fists at his sides and glanced

down his body to where her cool fingers rested on his burning flesh. He was relieved to find all but his leg covered with a blanket. That helped, but not much. He closed his eyes briefly and swallowed. "No," he whispered hoarsely. "You didn't hurt me."

Serena's gaze followed his down and then up his body, and she blushed so hard the heat from her cheeks stung her eyes. She'd seen men clad in much less than the blanket covering Matt, but she'd never seen one in *that* condition before! No wonder he was horrified. He'd just been aroused by his stepsister!

He didn't know she didn't think of him as a brother.

She remembered Kali's mutterings about Matt being too long without a woman. The best thing Serena could do right now would be to joke about his reaction, then forget it, but she couldn't. The tingling heat she'd felt in her breasts and between her legs when she'd touched his chest earlier washed over her again, and she didn't feel at all like laughing.

She felt more like crying. Yes, he was her brother. He'd steadied her steps when she learned to walk. She bit back a grin when she thought he'd probably changed her diaper a time or two. He and Mama had taught her to read. He and Dad had taught her to ride. He and Cochise had taught her to defend herself. He was her brother, but only in his mind and on paper.

The truth was, when applied to Matt, the word "brother" was only half a word. What he was was her stepbrother, by the marriage of his father to her mother, her adopted brother by law.

In her mind and heart, he'd stopped being her

49

brother when she was eight years old and had become instead her knight in shining armor. That was when she'd decided she wanted to hurry and grow up so she could marry him.

When she was ten, he'd married Angela, and Serena had given up her dreams of knights. Angela was so beautiful and kind and loving that it would have been impossible for Serena to resent her for the destruction of her dreams. Serena had loved Angela, and she'd been happy for Matt to have such a wonderful wife.

So Matt had become her brother again.

And right now he needed her as a brother needed a sister. He needed to be taken care of. He needed to be loved and coddled, or pushed and prodded, whatever it took to get him on his feet again and help him find some happiness in life.

He'd been alone for three years now, and Serena knew Matt. He wasn't meant to live alone. He had always had so much love to give those around him. Who was he giving his love to these days? Anyone? No one?

Aside from Matt, there was also Joanna to consider. She needed her father. It wasn't that the girl didn't have plenty of family around constantly showering her with love, but no one could take the place of her father. Joanna needed him, and it was time he understood that.

"Matt . . ."

Matt took a slow, deep breath and opened his eyes. Serena was looking at him anxiously. The tightening in his groin eased and he was able to smile at her. Poor girl had no idea what her soft moist lips against his leg had done to the rest of his body.

"Hold still while I rebandage your leg and get these splints back on," she cautioned. "I don't want you shifting that bone."

"Thanks, Rena," he said with a sigh. He felt his muscles relaxing now. She wasn't aware of what had happened. It was just a silly accident. Kali was right—he'd been too long without a woman. The thought made him grimace.

It had been over three years since he'd felt the pleasure of a woman's body next to his. He wasn't counting that whore in San Francisco two years ago, because there had been nothing pleasurable about her. She was nothing more than a vessel he'd emptied himself into one dark, desperate night.

That experience had made him feel as cheap as she had looked. From then on, he'd done without that particular pastime. The last pleasure he'd felt had been with Angela. Nothing had mattered since he'd lost her.

He'd been fighting a losing battle for three years, trying to forget her. Sometimes, if he could drink enough, he could go for maybe a day or two without being tortured by her memory, but she always came back to him. He hated himself for being too weak to put the past to rest. The more he hated himself, the more he drank, and the more he drank, the more he hated himself.

"Are you thirsty?"

Matt blinked and focused his gaze on Serena. She had finished with his leg and had asked him something. "Wha—yes," he said, remembering. And he was thirsty, he realized—he was parched. But he felt better than he had.

He struggled to raise himself on an elbow and reached for the tin cup Serena offered. She held it to his lips and he drank greedily, even though it was only water, then fell back to the mattress, exhausted. That simple act had sapped his strength.

"It's all right." Serena ran her cool fingers over his brow, soothing the heat and the pain there. "You'll feel better tomorrow. Sleep now, Matt."

As his eyes drifted shut, he felt her lips brush his forehead. He stiffened.

"Ssh . . . just sleep now."

The next morning Matt's fever was gone and he was in hell. How long had it been since he'd had a drink? He needed one now to clear his head. He'd had that dream again.

It was the same. It was always the same, waking up after reliving that horrible nightmare of Angela's death. Whiskey was the only thing that helped, and he was well aware that each time it took more and more whiskey. The cheaper the whiskey, the easier it was to forget.

He kept his eyes closed as the dream, the nightmare, washed over him again. Him and Angela, driving home from Tucson in the wagon. Scott, riding out from behind the brush. Angela, throwing herself in front of Matt to protect him, to take the bullet meant for him. It was always the same.

But something was different about last night's dream. When he'd gazed in horror into Angela's upturned, dying face, as he always did in the nightmare, something changed. Her green eyes, eyes like summer leaves, faded, then turned a bright sky-blue. Her yellow-gold tresses turned white at her temple, darker everywhere else, until they were black. Her beautiful, beloved features began to alter subtly, until he had found himself gazing into the face of his stepsister. Now it was Serena's face before him. It was Serena's voice whispering, "I love you, Matt." It was Serena's last breath that sounded like a soft sigh of love.

Panicked, breathing hard, Matt opened his eyes and stared blankly at the ceiling of the adobe hut. He was going crazy. God, but he needed a drink. He looked around the room and found himself alone. He spied his saddlebags a few feet away and stretched to reach them. He always kept a bottle in his saddlebags, for emergencies. This was an emergency.

Four

When Serena returned from bathing in the creek, the first thing she noticed was that Matt was awake. The second thing she noticed was that he had a bottle tilted to his lips and was guzzling like a man who'd just found water after crossing the desert.

Her gaze lit on the open saddlebag lying next to the mattress. She cursed herself for her carelessness. She should have checked the damned thing.

Matt's eyes were closed and he was making so much noise with his guzzling that he didn't know she was there. She stood quietly until he sighed, eyes still closed, and rested the bottle on his chest while he dropped his head back down onto the mattress.

When she approached his side, he opened his eyes. "Good morning," she announced with a brilliant smile.

Matt smiled in return, relieved not to get a lecture about drinking so early in the morning. Kali would have lectured. "Morning," he answered.

Then Serena's smile froze and her eyes hardened. "I'll take that." She swooped down and grabbed the bottle from his hands.

"Hey! Bring that back here, damn it."

Serena ignored him and set the bottle on a broad flat rock just outside the door.

"Rena, bring it back," Matt ordered.

She smiled slightly. "No."

Matt clenched his jaws. She didn't understand; he *needed* the whiskey. He flung back the blanket and prepared to rise, until he felt the draft of cool air across his bare skin. He quickly covered himself. A slow heat crept up his cheeks. To his chagrin, Serena's smile spread wider.

"Where the hell are my pants?"

"What pants?" she asked innocently. "You weren't wearing any when I found you."

Matt frowned. What was going on here? This wasn't like Serena at all. She'd always been the sweetest, most docile, loving, helpful child. He'd never seen this side of her before.

"Then where are my longjohns? I know I was wearing longjohns," he said, trying to gain some sort of control over the situation.

"You mean that disgustingly filthy underwear you obviously hadn't been out of in months?"

Matt eyed her with trepidation. This wasn't Rena. He must be dreaming again. What he needed was another drink. That would clear his head.

"I burned them," Rena said.

Matt blinked. "You what? You burned my underwear?"

"Yes, and I'm almost sorry I did. Three birds flew too close to the smoke and dropped dead, the smell was so bad."

"Rena!"

She just stood there, her hands on her hips and her lips pursed in a frown.

"If you burned my underwear and didn't bring my pants, what the hell am I supposed to wear?"

"You're not supposed to wear anything," she stated flatly. "You're not getting out of that bed until I say so."

"Now, wait just a min—"

"No. *You* wait just a minute. I came here for one reason, and that was to get you back on your feet. I'm not leaving until your leg is mended, your color is back to normal, your eyes lose that glaze, and you can go a day or two without a drink and not get the shakes."

Matt snorted with disgust. "So you're here to save me from my wicked ways."

"Something like that."

"And if I don't feel the need to be saved?"

"Too damn bad, buster."

Matt nearly swallowed his tongue. Serena never swore! "What's gotten into you? I've never seen you like this. You've never been mean and spiteful before, and you certainly never used to swear."

"*You* never used to wallow in self-pity and try to drink yourself to death, either," she retorted. "If you really want to kill yourself there are faster, easier ways than what you've been doing."

He felt something in his chest tighten. "Is that what you think I'm trying to do? Kill myself?"

"Isn't it?"

"No, damn it." He glared at her a moment, then closed his eyes with a heavy sigh. "No. You just don't understand."

Serena's heart softened at the pain she saw in his face. She knelt beside him and placed a hand on his arm. "You're right, I don't understand. But I'd like to."

He didn't answer, didn't look at her, didn't move. Serena decided to let it go for the moment. "Are you hungry?"

"No," he whispered, his eyes still closed.

"Can you turn over onto your stomach without hurting your leg?"

"What for?"

"So I can finish your bath I started last night. I couldn't get to your back. Once you're clean you'll feel better."

"You gave me a bath?" Matt's cheeks stung again as he wondered just how thorough that bath had been.

"You must admit you needed one. Come on. I'll help you roll over. When I'm through with your back, I'll shave you."

He ran a hand across his bristled cheeks and grimaced. "I could use a shave," he admitted.

"Then roll over and let me scrub your back first."

He did as she ordered. He turned his face to the wall, dreading the touch of her fingers, fearing his reaction. But this time it was all right. The soap and water felt good against his skin.

He must have been sicker than he'd realized, for the simple act of rolling over sapped his energy. He felt himself relaxing while she washed his back. Then he felt her pull the blanket from his hips. "Rena!"

"Oh, hush," she said with a laugh. "It isn't anything I haven't seen before."

Matt grappled for the blanket and tried to cover himself. "You go around looking at men's bare backsides these days?"

Serena jerked the blanket away and washed his lower back and clear down his legs. "Why, Matthew Colton, I do believe you're embarrassed!"

"You're damn right I am. My kid sister is treating me like I'm an infant. And you didn't answer my question, girl. Just whose bare ass have you been looking at?"

Serena laughed as she dried him and covered him again with the blanket. "Only every man who ever wore a breechcloth on a windy day, and that includes you." She felt him struggle to turn over and pushed him back down. "Just lie still." She ran her hands over his neck and shoulders. "You're too tense."

She worked at his knotted muscles for several minutes before she felt him start to relax. She kept massaging his neck, shoulders, and back until she heard the even rhythm of his breathing telling her he was asleep. Even then she was reluctant to stop touching him.

"Oh, Matt," she whispered. She caressed his shoulder slowly. "Why have you done this to yourself? Why do you drink so much?"

She was startled when he rolled over onto his back, his eyes still closed, and said, "To forget."

Thank God, she thought. At least he was willing to talk about it. She took his hand in both of hers. "Forget what?"

Matt squeezed her hand and opened his eyes. The stark pain she read in his gaze took her breath away.

"Angela." His voice shook.

"You don't mean that, Matt. You can't." She gripped his hand tighter. "She was your wife, the mother of your child. You loved her more than anything in the world. How could you hope to ever forget her? Why would you even want to?"

Matt looked at her as if she'd lost her mind. "Because she's dead!"

"Oh, Matt, I know she's dead. And I know how much you must miss her. But just because she's dead doesn't mean you should forget her. It's all right to miss her, Matt. It's all right to remember her, to think of her. She was part of you, body and soul, and you loved her. We all loved her, and we always will. No one expects you to forget her. It would be impossible. She's gone, Matt, but she lives on in you, in Joanna, in everyone whose life she touched. None of us will ever forget her."

Serena paused until he left off studying the ceiling and looked at her. "Do you understand what I'm trying to say?" she asked. "Remember when Cochise and Granddad Jason died the same day? Remember how sad we all were? Do you remember what it was that eased our pain?"

"That's the day Joanna was born," he said flatly.

"Yes. Joanna gave us something new to think about. But what also helped was that we remembered all the times we'd shared with Granddad and Grandfather, and we talked about them. And it helped. We didn't try to forget. We were just grateful for the memories they left us."

"I remember that," Matt said, studying their joined hands. "I remember I made you cry when I reminded you about the time Cochise threatened to sell you and

Pace to the Mexicans for tying his moccasins together."

"I remember." Serena smiled. "Only you said it all in Apache, and then had to explain to Angela what you'd said that had made me cry. By the time you finished describing the entire episode, we were all laughing."

"Angela never did learn to speak Apache."

Serena's heart skipped a beat at his easy comment. This just might work, if only she could keep him talking. "No," she said. "She didn't need to. She always had you to translate."

"And you. She always said she didn't know what she would have done without you that time she had to build the wickiup, right before we got married. She wouldn't have had the slightest idea what was going on if you hadn't translated for her."

"Well, you won't have to worry about Joanna needing a translator."

Matt's eyes sparked with interest at the mention of his daughter. "Tell me about her."

"Oh, Matt, I can't wait for you to see her. You'll be so proud." She threaded her fingers through his, her heart aching for all he'd missed in the last three years. "She's the most beautiful child in the world. And smart, too. She speaks three languages fluently, and she can read and write and knows her numbers. Dad swears she's a better rider than I was at that age."

Matt squeezed his eyes shut and his voice trembled with emotion. "I miss her so much, Rena."

"Which one? Joanna, or Angela?"

He squeezed her fingers so hard she thought they'd break. "Both," he croaked.

"Then hurry up and get well and come home with me. There's no need for you to miss Joanna. She's there waiting for you."

"But Angela isn't," he said harshly.

"No, Angela isn't there, she's here, Matt." Serena placed her hand over his heart. "She's right here, where she's always been, where she'll always be. That's where your comfort is, Matt, right here inside you, not in the bottom of some bottle. Look inside yourself and know that she'll always be there. And when you come home and look into Joanna's eyes, eyes the color of summer cottonwood leaves, you'll know part of Angela still lives."

The room grew quiet as the morning sun climbed higher. Matt lay with closed eyes, but Serena knew he wasn't asleep. "Get some rest," she said. She leaned down and kissed his forehead, then wrinkled her nose. "I've got to figure out a way to wash your hair. I don't know how you can stand it."

"I haven't been sober long enough to even notice," he said with a harsh laugh. Then, "Rena, where are my pants? I really do need to get up."

"I told you before, you're not getting up until I say so."

He opened his eyes and glared at her. "If I don't get up, and outside, and *soon,* you and I are both going to be pretty damned embarrassed."

Serena grinned wickedly. "We're probably both going to be embarrassed anyway. At least you will be, because you're going in this." She grabbed the bedpan and thrust it at him.

"No way, you little brat. You let me up now, and I mean it."

"Hah. You're so weak you wouldn't even make it to the door. Just use the damn bedpan." She jumped up and headed for the door to give him privacy.

"Serena, damn you!"

Laughter trailed behind her as she dashed outside into the sun.

The next morning, just before noon, Matt lay on his mattress in the corner, clutching his gut. Serena was outside somewhere, doing God knew what. Matt didn't care. He hurt too much to care. His stomach felt like there was a giant rat inside, gnawing, trying to eat and claw its way out. Matt's hands shook so bad he couldn't even wipe the sweat from his eyes.

He needed a drink.

Where had that interfering but well-meaning stepsister of his hidden his bottle? She probably put it back in his saddlebag when he was asleep. But now his saddlebag was on the other side of the room. In the shape he was in, he wasn't sure he could make it that far, but he was damn sure going to try.

He rolled over and pushed himself up on all fours, then cursed fiercely. His stomach hurt so bad he'd forgotten about his broken leg. Pain throbbed from his toes to his hip. He crawled to the wall, then braced himself and managed to stand on one leg. The rough adobe felt cool where he leaned against it to regain his breath. This was going to be harder than he'd thought.

Trembling, sweating, and aching something fierce, he managed to work his way around the wall to his saddlebags, then slumped to the floor, his injured leg extended in front of him. His breath came in harsh gasps. He fumbled with the buckles and searched first one bag, then the other.

Damn. They were empty.

He glanced out the open door to make sure Serena wasn't standing there watching him and sagged with relief. Not three feet outside the door stood a flat-topped boulder about two feet high, and on that beautiful rock sat his bottle.

Just then his luck ran out. A wagon creaked and rattled its way into the clearing, and Kali called out a greeting. Serena ran from behind the house to meet her.

Matt struggled back up and, with the help of the wall, hopped back to his bed. Christ. He needed a drink so bad he could cry. *Men don't cry, you jackass.* But then, it wasn't too long ago he'd have sworn a *man* wouldn't crawl around naked on the floor trying to find a drink of whiskey, either.

Shit, Colton, you're a sorry mess.

He pulled the blanket across his lower half just as the two women walked in. Resentment clenched his jaws. *Look at them,* he thought with disgust. Acting like they'd known each other all their lives, the best of friends, running off at the mouth like a couple of magpies while he lay there with rats gnawing at his gut.

"Matt, Kali's here," Serena announced gaily.

"I never would have known," he mumbled.

"My, my." Kali smiled and clicked her tongue. "Testy this morning, aren't we? You may not think you feel any better, honey, but you sure do look better. Imagine that. Shaved and bathed, and all in the same month. I almost didn't recognize you."

Matt's hand automatically went to his smooth cheek, then grasped the blanket again to hide his trembling. He'd forgotten Serena had shaved him yesterday. He glanced at her, then narrowed his gaze on Kali. "Just keep it up, girl."

" 'Girl'? Honey, I haven't been a girl in years, and you know it."

"Don't pay any attention to him, Kali," Serena said. "He still thinks I'm twelve years old and don't have a lick of sense. He's just mad because I took his bottle away."

"Speaking of my bottle, it's outside there on that rock. Would you get it for me, Kali? And did you happen to bring me any pants?"

With one brow raised, Kali mouthed the words "pants." Serena grinned. Kali smiled and shrugged at Matt. "Sorry. No on both counts, sweetie."

Serena stirred the coals in the fireplace. "As a matter of fact, you can take that bottle when you go, Kali." She hung the coffeepot over the small fire she had stirred to life. "If you don't, I'll just have to pour it out, and then we'll have a bunch of drunk birds flapping around the door."

She put a small chunk of wood on the fire. "Wait till you see what Kali brought, Matt. A table and chairs, and a tub."

A bleating noise blasted through the open door.

"What the hell was that?" Matt asked.

"That's the best part," Serena answered. "A goat."

"A what?"

"G-o-a-t. Goat. As in nanny. As in fresh milk. It's about time you had something in your stomach be-

64

sides rotgut whiskey."

Matt glared at Serena, then at Kali. His friend seemed to find it difficult to hold back her laughter.

"No offense intended, Kali," Serena continued. "I'm sure the Last Chance Saloon serves fine liquor, but man cannot live by booze alone. Now — why don't we bring in that table and those chairs, so we can sit down to drink our coffee?"

When the women left, Matt closed his eyes and gritted his teeth. They were having one hell of a damn good time at his expense. The more he thought about their nasty remarks, the madder he got. He heard one of them lead that damn goat around the side of the house. *Goat's milk, my ass. I'll show them.*

Adrenaline got him to his feet. Then he scooped up the blanket and wrapped it around his hips and hopped along the wall to the door. He leaned against the frame, then moaned when he saw what Serena and Kali were doing. They were unloading a crate of chickens. Goddamn chickens. What the hell were those two doing? Setting up permanent residence?

Anger at their highhanded treatment of him got him out the door and to his destination. He grabbed up the bottle and took its place on the rock, his back to the women.

Fifteen feet — that's how far he'd made it. Fifteen lousy feet, and he was so weak he was afraid he might pass out. But it was worth it. With trembling hands, he pulled the cork and raised the bottle to his mouth.

That was as far as he got.

The bottle flew from his lips and out of his hands like it had wings. It sailed through the air and crashed — painfully, Matt thought — against the hard adobe wall of the house, where it shattered into a thousand pieces. Shards of glass and amber droplets of liquid sparkled in the morning sun as they bounced off the wall and showered to the ground. A brown stain ran down the adobe, trickled into a puddle, and quickly disappeared into the thirsty earth, leaving nothing more than a spot of mud at the base of the wall.

Matt felt that overwhelming urge again to cry. He took a deep breath and forced it down, then glared at the source of his present troubles.

Serena stood before him with her feet spread wide, her hands on her hips, and her eyes matching him glare for glare.

"Damn you, Rena." Matt squeezed his eyes shut. The pain in his gut was worse than ever now. He rubbed at it with an unsteady hand.

"No. Damn you, Matt Colton," Serena said with a hiss. She grabbed his bare shoulder and shook until he opened his eyes and looked at her. "If you think I'm going to stand by and watch you slowly kill yourself, you're crazy."

"You don't understand, Rena." Each breath came hard and triggered another wrenching spasm in his stomach. It was all he could do to keep from doubling over.

Serena dropped to her knees in front of him and cupped his sweat-streaked face in her small, cool hands. Her pale blue eyes turned soft and liquid. "I do understand, Matt, at least some of it. Why can't you just tell me your stomach hurts so bad you can't stand it?"

Matt clenched his teeth and closed his eyes. Who

was he trying to kid? He knew his misery was obvious. He certainly wasn't handling himself well. He wasn't handling himself at all.

"Let me help you, Matt. Don't shut me out. Talk to me. Tell me how you're feeling. Let me help you."

He sighed and opened his eyes, ignoring the gnawing pain in his gut. He stared at the ground. "Just . . . help me back to bed."

She sighed with what was surely relief. "Wait here a minute." She ran to the wagon and came back with a pair of crutches. "Try these on for size."

Serena helped him stand, then he tucked a crutch under each arm. A couple of awkward steps took him to the door where he paused and looked back over his shoulder. He allowed a wry grin. "Thanks."

Just then, he felt the blanket start to slip. Panicked, he hurried through the door.

When Serena was halfway back to the wagon, she heard a loud clatter followed swiftly by a muffled curse. "Matt?" she called. "You all right? Need any help?"

"I'm just fine!"

Realizing he must still be embarrassed over that scene just now at the rock, Serena ignored his harsh tone and resolved to take it easy on him for a while. His ego was definitely bruised and in need of a boost. She eyed the contents of the wagon thoughtfully.

"What's that gleam in your eye for?" Kali demanded.

Serena grinned. "I've got an idea."

A few moments later, two giggling females paused outside the door and set the table on the ground. The table wasn't large enough to take up too much space

67

in the tiny hut, but it was obviously too big around to simply carry through the door.

Matt watched with a mixture of disgust and amusement as the women tried to maneuver the table past the narrow opening.

"I think it's too big, Kali."

"Hmmm. Looks like you're right."

"What do we do now?"

"I don't know. Do you have a saw? Maybe we could cut it down some."

Matt groaned and tried to control his laughter.

"No, we don't have a saw. I guess we could just leave it out here. That way, Matt could take in the fresh air and sunshine when he eats. Except when it rains, though."

"You can't do that, Serena. There's not a level spot anywhere. Your food would slide right off and you'd both starve."

Matt couldn't stand it any more. "Turn it on its side."

"On its side?" Serena whirled around to look at him. "Of course. Thanks, Matt. We should have thought of that ourselves. How silly of us."

Matt rolled his eyes. *Females*.

Serena and Kali managed, with grunts and giggles, to get the table on its side. Now the entire surface of the round table faced the narrow doorway.

"Turn it to face the other direction," Matt said with ill-concealed laughter at their inept maneuvering.

They laughed and groaned, and turned the table until all four legs pointed at the door.

"Well, what good did that do us?" Kali called to him. "It still won't fit."

"You turned it too far. Point the legs across the damn door, not at it." Matt directed, waved his arms, laughed, and swore until they finally had the table inside. "You two should never hire out as furniture movers."

"I don't know about that," Kali said. "With a little more practice, I think we could get the hang of it. Right, Serena?"

"Maybe, but it's not my idea of a good time. That thing was heavy." She braced her hands on her lower back and arched to relieve an ache.

Matt watched dumbfounded as the material of Serena's white blouse stretched tight. The third button, the one between her breasts, popped through the buttonhole and showed a brief flash of a white, lacy chemise. She turned until her profile was outlined against the open doorway and stretched her arms over her head. The silhouette of her breasts stood out sharply before Matt remembered just who he was staring at. He tore his gaze away.

She was right. He had been thinking of her as a child. He realized with a start that she wasn't twelve anymore. She wasn't even sixteen anymore. She had done some growing up while he'd been gone. He swallowed hard.

Serena and Kali went back out for the chairs, and finally the bathtub. It didn't require nearly as much maneuvering as the table had. When the tub rested alongside the fireplace, Serena began scrubbing the table while Kali carried in plates, sheets, and a second mattress so Serena wouldn't have to sleep on the straw.

Matt paid scant attention to Kali's comings and goings. His gaze kept straying to Serena as she stretched, bent, and stooped, cleaning every inch of the table, including the legs. He was fascinated by the way her blouse stretched and tightened over her shapely shoulders, narrow ribs, trim waist.

He could just picture his father standing at the front door of the house, turning away suitor after suitor. There were surely dozens of men from Tucson trying to court Serena. She was a truly beautiful girl. No — young woman.

The thought of her getting married stung. She'd leave home then to live with her husband. That old ranch house would never be the same without Serena's laughter trailing down the halls.

And who would look after Joanna for him?

Damn. Maybe that was why Rena had come. Maybe she wanted him to go home and take care of his own daughter so she could marry some man and have a home and a family of her own. She was . . . how old? Nineteen? Most girls her age were married and had one or two babies of their own.

He tried to picture the kind of man Rena would marry, but couldn't. No man was good enough for her. Who would understand the two very different heritages that meant so much to her? To retain her ties to the Chiricahua, would she have to marry into the tribe?

Matt shuddered. In the old days, even with the raiding and killing, the running and hiding, constantly fighting for mere survival, Serena might have found happiness with Chidikáágu'. Matt might have been able to be happy for her.

But not now. Not today, with a people imprisoned

on that hellhole of a reservation. Hell . . . San Carlos . . . They were the same in Matt's mind. No — Serena couldn't live like that. No one should have to live like that. Not the proud, freedom-loving Apaches, and especially not Serena.

So who, then, might she marry? Certainly not a man from Arizona, not unless she was prepared to deny her Apache heritage, which Matt knew she could never do, would never consider. But there weren't even a handful of white men in the territory who would understand the Apache side of Serena. No man he knew would even try. Apaches, Chiricahua in particular, were feared and hated with a vengeance.

A man from back East, perhaps. One who hadn't grown up watching his friends and family killed in Cochise's raids, Nana's raids, Chihuahua's, Juh's, Golthlay's raids. A man with no hatred for the Apaches.

Serena, in a city? No — not his Rena. She was strong enough to survive anything life threw at her, and she could survive life in a city. But away from the desert and mountains where she was raised, her soul would shrivel and die. Matt knew, for it was true of him, too.

No. No man was right for Serena.

The thought did nothing to comfort him.

He watched as she finished cleaning and Kali finished unloading. He let the activity wash over him and lighten his mood.

Serena poured coffee first for Matt, then for Kali and herself.

"What, no goat's milk?" Matt taunted.

71

"Don't worry," Serena replied sweetly. "Tomorrow you'll have more goat's milk than you know what to do with."

Matt rolled his eyes and groaned. "Kali, please give me a ride back to town. She's trying to kill me."

Kali laughed. "It's a crying shame she's your sister, Matt."

"I'm sure Matt agrees with you, but why is it a shame? Am I such a bad sister?"

"No, no, You're a great sister. I just happen to think you'd make him an even better wife."

Matt choked on his mouthful of coffee. "Kali!"

"Well, it's true. She's the only woman I know of, besides me, that is, who can ignore that pleading look in those big brown eyes of yours and stand up to you. That's just the kind of wife you need."

"I don't need any kind of a wife," Matt bit out.

Serena managed a composed smile despite the rapid pounding of her heart in her throat. "I think you're embarrassing him, Kali. You see, I'm not really his sister. Not the way you mean."

"I don't understand."

"I'm his stepsister. My mother was already carrying Pace and me when she met Matt's father. He married her anyway. Then, when Pace and I were born, he adopted us."

The only sound in the room was the faint crackle of burning mesquite root in the fireplace. Kali studied Serena's tight expression, then Matt's furious one.

She grinned slowly. "His stepsister?" Her chuckle started deep and low, then grew until it filled the room. "Oh, that's rich. It's perfect."

Matt glared at her. "Kali . . ."

Kali slowly calmed and pursed her lips. "All right, I'll shut up. But it really is too perfect. She's not your sister at all. I should have known."

When Kali stood and left the room, Serena followed to see her off. Kali paused before climbing onto the wagon. "If I was out of line in there, Serena, I'm sorry."

Serena forced a small laugh past the lump in her throat. "Don't worry about it. I know you didn't mean anything by it."

"Oh, but I did. You're in love with him, aren't you?"

Serena sucked in her breath sharply. "D-Don't be silly. He's my . . . brother."

"Sure he is." Kali stared at her until Serena felt like fidgeting. "Look," Kali said finally. "If I've made you uncomfortable, I'm sorry. But a blind man could see how you feel. If you ask me, which you didn't, but if you did, I'd tell you to take advantage of the situation."

"What do you mean?" Dear God . . . why had she said that? Kali was going to think . . . she'd think . . . what was the use? Kali already thought.

Was it true, Serena wondered frantically. Had her childhood infatuation and hero worship turned into something more, something bigger? Did she love him? Her mind skittered back to the night before, when she'd touched him and experienced that burst of fire in her blood. There was certainly nothing sisterly in that.

It couldn't be true. No. She couldn't be in love with him. Matt would never understand. He'd be appalled.

Her heart beat faster as she tried to force such dangerous thoughts away. She'd find a man she could really love someday, then she'd get over these confusing feelings for Matt. She'd even be able to laugh about them, someday.

But the mere thought of spending her life with another man, accepting his love, his touch, having his children, left her cold and empty, as though she'd lost something precious.

"What I mean, honey," Kali said, "is that right now he's vulnerable. He needs you. He needs somebody he can love, who'll love him back. Somebody who's good and sweet and kind, but who's also strong enough to stand beside him, not behind him, like most of these prissy-faced girls around here. Coddle him and scold him. Tempt him. Tease him, show a little skin now and then. Keep him off balance. Make him want you."

Serena wasn't as shocked as she probably should have been by Kali's advice, yet the thought of deliberately trying to ensnare Matt made her uneasy. "But Kali, that's not love, that's lust."

Kali threw back her head and laughed. "Of course it is." Then she sobered and lowered her voice. "He already loves you, silly. He's loved you all your life. You've just got to make him forget he's always thought of you as his sister. Believe me, you get a rise out of him a couple of times and he'll forget all about wanting to be your brother."

"It sounds so . . . calculating."

"Calculating as hell, honey. But if you felt this way about some other man, one you hadn't been raised with, I'd be willing to bet you'd go after him with everything you've got to get him to notice you."

74

The lone horseman, concealed by brush and mesquite on a hill overlooking the house, watched as the whore from the Last Chance drove the wagon onto the road back to town. The other woman — Colton's sister — stood in the dust, the wind whipping her skirt back against her legs, and watched the wagon until it was out of sight.

He rubbed his right thumb along the fingertips of the same hand, more from habit than for feel. The tips of his fingers felt nothing beyond a slight pressure. Feeling and texture had been burned away long ago.

What a stroke of luck, to have the sister show up. Now there they were, all alone down there, a sick, injured drunk and a helpless girl.

If the fire in town had worked, the sister wouldn't matter. It had been, he admitted with a fond smile, his best fire ever. But Colton had gotten lucky: instead of burning alive, or at least breaking his neck escaping the flames, the bastard had only broken his leg. Now the sister could be useful.

Not yet, though, he cautioned himself. Not yet . . . but soon.

Five

Serena delayed going back inside the house as long as possible. She gave the horse and goat fresh water and more feed. She turned the chickens out into the minuscule enclosure built long ago for that purpose and gave them water.

You're in love with him, aren't you?

Am I?

Don't lie.

But—

No buts.

It's true.

Yeah, and it's crazy. It's absurd. It's . . . wrong.

It's not wrong, damn it. It's . . .

Hopeless?

Hopeless.

Serena took a deep breath and cursed herself for having such ridiculous thoughts. The entire subject was beside the point. Matt would always see her as his little sister.

The goat bleated her objection to Serena's lack of attention.

"Shut up, or I'll make you go fix Matt's dinner."

The goat bleated again.

"That's what I thought."

With a smile pasted on her face, Serena forced herself back into the house. Matt needed food.

The interior was dim, compared to outdoors; it took a moment for her eyes to adjust. When she approached Matt's bed, she stumbled over his discarded crutches. She picked them up and leaned them against the wall, out of the way, then discovered blood on the lower half of one. "Matt?"

He lay with one arm across his eyes, the other across his stomach. Both fists were clenched tight; his jaw muscles worked furiously. His coffee cup, still full, sat beside the bed.

Without another word, Serena knelt and pulled the blanket back from his injured leg. Blood seeped out around his stitches, and the swelling was worse.

"Damn it, Matt, why didn't you tell me?" She set about tending his leg, probing the swollen flesh to make sure the bone was still in place.

Matt stiffened. "Where'd you learn to talk like a gutter rat, girl?"

"From a certain older brother who shall remain nameless."

"You must mean Pace. I know I never use words like that."

"Ha. The fifteen minutes Pace has on me does not qualify him as an *older* brother. If the shoe fits, Matthew . . ."

Now that she was finished poking around on his leg, he lowered his arm from his eyes and looked at her. "Am I still a brother to you, Rena?"

Serena sat back on her heels. "Don't be silly," she said

77

with a nervous laugh. "You're talking about what Kali said. Forget it. We're still the same two people we've always been."

"Are we?" He shook his head and stared at the ceiling. "I don't think so. The one you used to call brother, the one you used to tag along behind, he'd never have got himself in a mess like this."

Serena wanted to argue, but couldn't. He was right.

"And that little bright-eyed, beautiful girl, the one he used to call his princess . . ." He lowered his gaze and looked at her. "Your eyes are still bright, and you're more beautiful than ever, but you're not my little princess anymore, are you? You're all grown up now. And the tables have turned."

"What do you mean?"

"It used to be me, looking after you, taking care of you." He gave a wry grin. "Now it's the other way around."

"It's only temporary. You'll be back on your feet in no time."

"And then what? Do you drag me home by my ear?"

"I didn't come here to drag you home. I came because I thought you needed me."

Matt sighed wearily and closed his eyes.

"It's okay to need someone now and then, you know," she told him.

"Can we talk about something else?"

"Like what?"

"I don't care." He opened his eyes and studied her. "How about why you aren't married yet? You're what, nineteen? Most girls your age are married with a couple of kids already."

Serena laughed and rolled her eyes. The tension was

easing. "And just where, I ask, am I supposed to find a man that you, Pace, Mama, *and* Daddy think is good enough for me? I hear the President is already taken."

"Come on." A teasing smile curved Matt's lips. "It can't be that bad. Whatever happened to that Maichak kid, Willy? He used to hang around you all the time, if I remember correctly."

"Oh, he hung around me all the time, all right. But only so he could catch a glimpse of Angela every chance he got. Anytime she was around, he forgot I was even alive, and you know it."

"I remember that. He used to blush and stammer and knock things over whenever she came in the room. I used to want to throttle him."

Serena giggled at the memory. "You nearly did that time he spilled his tea down the front of Angela's dress, then kept trying to help her wipe it off."

Matt laughed and groaned. "I remember that. I threw him out of the house."

"And Angela got mad at you."

"That's putting it mildly. She lit into me something fierce for putting my boot to the seat of his pants."

Serena's smile mellowed. It was good to see him laugh again. If he could remember Angela with laughter, then he would heal.

"Whatever happened to him?" Matt asked, still smiling.

"His father sold their store in Tucson and they opened a new one in Prescott. I guess they're still there."

"Are you sorry?"

"Of course not. You were right when you called him a kid. He was nice, but he was just a boy. I don't intend to get serious about a boy. I'd much rather find a man."

The tension sprang up again between them then like a visible thing, without either one of them understanding why.

It was three long, awkward days before Serena finally slit open one leg of Matt's pants to make room for his splint and allowed him out of bed. She would have preferred him to keep the leg immobile for another several days, but the enforced idleness was making him irritable. And that was putting it mildly.

Every time she got near him with a bowl of broth or a cup of milk, he glared. When she changed the bandages on his leg, he refused to look at her. When she tried to get him to talk, he mumbled one-word replies at most. He was restless, short-tempered, and sick to death of lying on his back. She offered to massage his back to ease the stiffness, and he reacted as though she'd proposed something indecent. When she tried to get him into the tub so she could wash his hair, he flatly refused.

Matt took the pants eagerly and waited until Serena left before kicking off the blanket and struggling into them.

Finally . . . pants.

With his crutches, he hobbled outside for the first time since Kali's visit and sank down onto the chair Serena had brought for him. The sun and wind felt good, helped clear the cobwebs from his mind.

Serena came around the corner carrying a pick. The hefty wooden handle and shiny, sharp blade looked out of place in her delicate hands.

"What are you doing?" he asked.

"We're almost out of firewood." She approached a mesquite bush and eyed the ground until she located a section of long black root partly uncovered by the wind and recent rains.

"You can't pry that thing up. The damn pick is bigger than you are."

"Well, you can't pry it up, either, and we need wood for cooking." She hacked at the gravelly ground next to the exposed root. Once she worked the point of the pick beneath the wood, she would have to pry the root from the ground, then cut it up with an ax if it didn't break into small enough lengths on its own.

Matt flinched with each whack. "You're going to hurt yourself. Why don't you just ride into town and get someone to come out here? I'm sure Kali knows someone who'd be willing to pry and cut wood for a small fee, or even a meal."

Serena ignored him and continued hacking away at the ground. The morning sun burned through her blouse and warmed the back of her head. Her hair kept falling in her face. She stopped long enough to braid it and let the breeze dry the sweat from her brow.

A few more swings and she was finally able to work the pick beneath the root. Now for the fun part—prying the root from the ground. Already her shoulders ached and her hands felt raw. How was she ever going to finish?

Mesquite roots were hard but brittle, and they held heat nearly as well as coal. With the pick beneath the root, Serena pulled back on the handle with all her might. The soil gave up the root without too much struggle. She moved the pick down the loosened section and pried again. This time the ground wasn't so cooperative. She had to use all her strength to pry even an inch of root loose.

Then the inevitable happened. Just when Serena had nearly all her weight on the pick handle, the brittle wood snapped. She fell flat on her rear.

Matt tried hard to hide his laughter. After all, she could have been hurt. It was obvious, however, by the disgusted look on her face as she struggled to rise, that the most serious damage was to her dignity.

"Are you, uh, all right?" he ventured.

"Don't you dare laugh," she warned with narrowed eyes.

"I wouldn't," he protested, holding both hands in the air. "I swear."

Serena's expression suddenly changed from chagrin to alertness. Matt watched curiously as she scrambled up and ran into the hut. She was back a moment later and set a bucket down beside him. "There's a rider coming."

Matt looked from her to the road, then to the bucket. She nudged aside the rag that covered the bucket and revealed his Colt. Just then, Matt picked out the sound that had alerted her, a hoof striking stone.

He looked at her with surprise and admiration. "Apache ears?"

She shrugged, Matt smiled, then both turned toward the spot where the road to town emerged from the brush.

The lone rider kept his horse at a walk as he entered the clearing. "Mornin', folks." He drew his Roman-nosed dun to a halt. A fine layer of gray dust covered his black hat, morning coat, pants, and boots, muting the starkness of his white shirt. A neat black string tie held his collar tight against his throat while a shock of sandy brown hair fell from beneath his hat brim toward laughing gray eyes.

"I was up on the ridge," he said, pointing to the east, "just takin' a look around, when I spotted you folks down here." He nodded toward the pick in Serena's hands. "If you don't mind my sayin' so, looks like you could use some help there, Miz Colton."

Serena jerked, startled. "You know my name?"

"Sure do." He grinned and dismounted.

"I know you," Serena said, recognition striking her. "You were in the, ah, Lucky Lady, I believe it was, seated at the bar."

"Yes, ma'am." He doffed his hat. "Name's Caleb."

Serena smiled and extended her hand in greeting. "Pleased to meet you, Mr. Caleb."

"No mister—just Caleb." He tossed his hat onto his saddle horn, then took her hand in both of his and placed a gallant kiss on her knuckles. "And the pleasure's all mine, I assure you."

Serena forced her smile to remain in place. She'd met her share of harmless flirts before, and this man was definitely a flirt. But there was something lurking in the depths of those gray eyes that bothered her and sent a clamor of warning along her spine. Something far from harmless.

She shook her head slightly and dismissed the feeling. It was just her imagination. "This is my brother, Matt Colton," she said, by way of introduction.

Caleb rushed forward to extend his hand to Matt. "Don't get up. I can see you've had a bit of bad luck."

Matt shook the man's hand, a puzzled expression on his brow. "Have we met before? You seem familiar."

83

"We never actually met, but we've passed each other on the street a time or two, I reckon. You've probably seen me in the Lucky Lady, if you ever go there."

"That must be it. I've been there once or twice." The burning question in Matt's mind now was, what in hell had Serena been doing in the Lucky Lady? But he'd save his question for later. He didn't want to start an argument in front of a stranger.

"I can see by your leg that you're not up to choppin' wood, Colton. I'd be obliged if you'd let me do it for you. It just doesn't seem right letting a pretty little thing like your sister get blisters on those soft hands trying to do a man's work."

All the time he spoke, Caleb was removing his coat and rolling up the sleeves on his white shirt. By the time he finished, he was no longer looking at Matt, but was staring into Serena's eyes like a lovesick calf.

Matt didn't know whether to laugh or groan.

"Why, thank you, Caleb." Serena batted her lashes at him.

Matt nearly swallowed his tongue. He'd never seen Serena bat her eyes in his life.

"I don't know how we would have managed," she told Caleb, "if you hadn't come along."

Brother, was she laying it on thick. There wasn't a thing in the world Serena couldn't do when she set her mind to it. She was probably the most self-sufficient female in three territories. Matt knew, because he had helped teach her.

"Don't thank me, ma'am," Caleb said. "It's my privilege." He smiled down at her and took the pick from her hand, then turned his back and started to work.

Serena dared a glance at Matt and nearly choked

when she saw him trying to strangle his own laughter. She rolled her eyes toward heaven and shook her head.

Caleb worked tirelessly, prying up black lengths of mesquite root and cutting them into smaller pieces of firewood. Serena fetched a pail of cool water from the well and offered him a drink from the dipper. He accepted gratefully.

"Are you from around here, Mr. Caleb?" she asked.

"Just Caleb, ma'am, and no, my family's mostly scattered around. I guess we all call Tennessee home, although the only one left at the old place is Ben."

"Ben?"

"Yes'm. My older brother, Benjamin. He's tied to the land. Couldn't get him off that farm with dynamite. The rest of us, we sorta just wandered off from the place. Got itchy feet, you might say."

"Is your family a large one?"

"Naw, not really. The youngest, we all chipped in together and sent him back East to school. The oldest of us boys came out West several years ago." He dropped the dipper back into the pail and returned to chopping wood.

Serena smiled at his use of the word "boys." Caleb looked to be near thirty, around Matt's age.

"He got killed here a while back," Caleb said.

"Oh, I'm sorry. I didn't mean to pry."

Caleb stopped and smiled softly at her, transforming his otherwise plain features into what Serena considered handsome. "That's all right," he murmured.

In practically no time at all, Caleb had a respectable-sized stack of firewood piled up next to the door of the adobe. Serena urged him to stay for dinner, but he politely refused, saying he had business in town. He made his goodbyes, obviously preoccupied with whatever that business was, and rode off.

And business was exactly what had Caleb so preoccupied. The business of Serena Colton. Damn . . . he hadn't expected this. He hadn't expected to like her.

But what man could look into those pale blue eyes and not fall for her? And that hair. All that thick, glorious black hair, with that narrow white streak at her temple. He'd never seen a woman with a streak in her hair before. He had found himself wanting to release that confining braid and run his fingers through her hair and kiss the place where that streak sprouted.

Goddammit. He wasn't supposed to like her. She was only supposed to be a tool, a means to an end.

He'd just have to revise his plans. That was all there was to it. There was no reason why he shouldn't be able to figure out a way to keep her, once she'd served her purpose, was there?

Caleb began to relax. Sure, he thought . . . he just had to find a way, that was all.

The dust from Caleb's departure hadn't yet cleared when Matt pulled himself up on his crutches and followed Serena into the house.

"That was nice of him, wasn't it?" Serena asked over her shoulder as she preceded him indoors.

"Real nice," Matt said sarcastically, remembering the way the man had practically drooled over her. "I've just got one question."

"What's that?" She turned to face him with a tentative smile. This was the closest thing to a conversation the two of them had had in days. Maybe his mood was improving.

Matt narrowed his eyes and clenched his jaw, dashing Serena's hopes. "What in the hell were you doing inside the Lucky Lady?"

Serena blinked. How *dare* he take that tone with her. "I went in for a shot of rye and a quick game of black-jack when I first hit town, and the bartender offered me a job."

"*What?*"

"You mean what kind of job? What do women usually do in saloons, Matt? Don't get so upset. Your friend Kali works in a saloon. You don't seem to mind what she does for a living," she taunted.

"Kali is not my sister!" he roared.

"Neither am I!" Serena yelled back. Then, as if to take back the words, she covered her mouth with both hands and fled the room.

"Rena!"

And high in the Sierra Madres of Sonora, a wrinkled old man closed his eyes, listened to the wind, and laughed.

Six

Matt stared, stunned, as Serena ran out the door and across the clearing into the brush. He suddenly felt weak and sick, filled with self-loathing. The crutches slipped on the plank floor. He cursed and flung them against the wall, where they bounced and clattered to the floor.

He dropped onto the chair behind him and buried his face in his hands, willing himself not to throw up. He shook violently from head to toe.

First he'd lost Angela, because of a bullet meant for him. Then, because he'd felt the need for revenge, he'd lost the last three years of his daughter's life. A couple of weeks ago, when Pace had come for him, he'd seen the respect the younger man had always had for him die. In fact, it had been dead for over a year.

"Look at you. You're disgusting," Pace had sneered with contempt.

And now Rena.

What was the matter with him, he wondered as he hobbled to his bed and lay down. Why was he doing this to himself and his family? He'd lost Angela, and now he was alienating the rest of them one by one.

But he knew the answer. Deep down, he'd always known why he was doing the things he did.

It had begun with bitterness and hatred for the man who had destroyed his perfect life. And Matt's life had been perfect. A beautiful wife whom he worshipped, long days filled with warm companionship, longer nights filled with love and passion. A beautiful daughter with her mother's eyes.

Then, to have it destroyed, ripped so cruelly from his arms by that *bastard* . . .

Matt had chased the object of his hatred clear to Canada and back. When he'd caught Abe Scott in Mexico, all Matt's pent-up rage and bitterness had boiled forth. Scott took three days dying, and Matt had viciously savored every minute, every second of the man's agony.

Not until it was all over did Matt realize Pace had witnessed it all. Eighteen was too young to see the things Matt had done to his enemy, the things he'd heard about around the Apache campfires in his youth.

That's when he'd lost Pace.

Pace had ridden off with a carefully blank expression, leaving Matt alone with what was left of Abraham Miller Scott.

That was when it hit Matt just how alone he really was. He could have gone home then, but to what? To a child who wouldn't even recognize him after his two-year absence? To a bed filled with nothing but memories? To a lifetime of loneliness?

Up until then he'd been doing more than his share of drinking, but that night he had gotten serious about it. Because that was the night he admitted to himself that he was afraid. More than that—terrified. He was terrified of spending the rest of his life without that warm cocoon of love that had surrounded him for barely more than five years.

He had stumbled along the border going from cantina to cantina. Gradually he drank his way north until he hit Tombstone; that was several months ago. As near as he could remember, the day Pace left him in Mexico was the last time Matt had been sober.

Hell. If the truth were known, he didn't even remember how he'd broken his goddamn leg. And he still wanted a drink so bad he could barely stand it.

Now here he was, being looked after by a sister who didn't want him for a brother.

Rena . . . Rena. Don't you turn away from me, too.

As Matt lay there admitting his weakness, his fear, hating himself for it, he determined it was time to do something about it. It was time he took charge of his life and started acting like a man again. Serena was right—he'd been wallowing in self-pity too long.

Serena crashed blindly through the brush and rocks. Tears streamed down her cheeks. Twigs and brambles tore at her hair and clothes. She ran all the way to the creek a quarter mile from the house, where she collapsed in the sand beneath a stunted willow.

Oh God, why had she said that? Matt would never understand—never. And she could never tell him the truth. If he knew how she really felt about him, he'd die. She was his sister. She was! No matter that it was only on paper. That's how she had been raised; that's how he'd always thought of her. If he had any idea she had fallen in love with him, he'd be sickened, disgusted.

The tightness in her chest made breathing difficult. The pain behind her eyes from trying to stop the flood of tears made thinking impossible. She stifled a sob, but the one after that escaped. Giving in to them, to the tears and the pain, was a relief. She let the sobs wash over her in waves.

After a time, when she was reasonably certain she had cried herself out, she crawled to the edge of the creek and splashed cold water onto her swollen eyes and face.

Leaning back against a sandstone boulder, she wondered, *What now?* She had to pull herself together. She'd handled Matt's anger over her being in a saloon all wrong. She should have simply told him the truth and laughed it off. Instead, she'd . . . What had she done? What was Matt thinking right now?

She had to go back to him. Somehow, she had to make him forget what she'd said. He wasn't well yet, was still in considerable pain, he hadn't eaten in hours, and here she was, indulging herself, trying to flood the damned creek.

"Idiot," she hissed to herself. "He needs you right now. He doesn't need any new complications in his life. He's got enough to deal with as it is."

She traced her way back through the scrub-covered hills and across the clearing to the hut. Just inside the door, she stopped to let her eyes adjust to the dimness. Matt lay on his bed, watching her.

"Are you hungry?" she asked.

"You went to the Lucky Lady looking for me,

didn't you?"

"Yes."

"I'm sorry, Rena. I had no business yelling at you like that. I guess I was just feeling a little useless because another man had to cut my firewood. Forgive me?"

"I-I'm sorry, too, Matt. I didn't mean to say what I did." *It's the truth, but I didn't mean to say it.*

"Let's just forget it, okay?" He gave her a tentative smile.

"Okay," she said, trying to return his smile. "Are you hungry?"

"A little, if you don't have to go to a whole lot of trouble."

"It's no trouble."

"Actually, what I'd really like to do is get you to wash my hair for me."

Serena's half smile turned into a laugh. "You must really be sorry if you're going to finally let me get my hands on that hair."

"Desperate's more like it," he answered with a grimace. "It's really starting to itch."

"I don't doubt it," she said, still smiling.

She fed him first, then he was tired, so she let him nap. When he woke, she began heating water to fill the brass tub.

"What are you doing?" he asked with suspicion. "I wanted you to wash my hair, not give me a bath."

"That's what I intend to do. You can give yourself a bath."

When the water was ready, Matt demanded she turn her back while he stripped and got into the tub.

Serena quickly complied. After their recent argu-

92

ment, the last thing they needed was for her to go breathless at the sight of his nakedness. Yet if she didn't tease, he might wonder at her mood.

With her back to him, she forced a laugh. "Such modesty. I thought we'd already been through all that."

"You gonna wash my hair or not?" Matt demanded gruffly.

He sat awkwardly in the tub, his splinted leg hanging out over the side. His belligerence and embarrassment melted away, she noted, when she poured warm water over his head. She worked the soap into a lather and massaged his scalp until he moaned with pleasure. "God, but that feels good."

Serena held her breath, relishing the feel of his hair and scalp against her fingers. He leaned against the back of the tub and his head grew heavy in her hands. His eyes were closed. She wanted to close hers, too. She wanted to store up the memory of this brief, limited contact. Her fingers moved slower and slower until they stopped for a long moment. Her chest burned from lack of air.

So much for not going breathless at his nakedness. She might as well have undressed him herself, for all the good that turning her back had done. His chest and arms rose above the tub, one knee jutted free of the water, the other leg dangled outside the tub, and the water was no barrier whatsoever to the rest of him.

"Talk to me, Rena."

She jerked at the sound of his voice. "About what?" Even to herself she sounded breathless. Her fingers resumed their work.

93

"About the ranch, the family."

"What do you want to know?"

"Everything. What's been happening? How's everybody's doing?"

Serena's pulse sped. Except for asking about Joanna, this was the first time he'd asked a direct question about home since she'd been here. It was a good sign. "You won't recognize Spence and Jessie. Spence is sixteen now, you know, and nearly as tall as you and Dad. And you won't believe how much he looks like the two of you. Except for his eyes, of course—he's got Mama's eyes. He's planning on going back East next fall to school. Wants to be a doctor."

Beneath her fingers she felt Matt relax even more. His hands rested limply on a naked thigh. She had the sudden urge to replace his hands with hers, to feel for herself the taut, hair-roughened skin. She swallowed the urge and took a deep breath.

"Jessie's quite the young lady these days," she said. "Since she turned twelve this year, she's decided Mama and I should stay in our rooms and rest all day, since we're so much *older,* so we won't get in her way while she runs the house."

Matt chuckled. "Sounds like she's just as spoiled as ever."

"She certainly is, but I'm just as guilty as the rest of the family. It seems like I can never say no to her. She took it upon herself to plan Joanna's birthday party a few weeks ago," she said carefully. "She did a good job, too. Had every child from Tucson that Joanna had ever met come out for the occasion."

"Was it a good party?" Matt asked, his voice rough

94

with emotion.

"Yes, it was a very good party." *I wish you could have been there.*

Neither spoke while Serena rinsed his hair with a bucket of warm water. When she was toweling his hair dry, his voice came out muffled. "What about Dad and Dani?"

"Oh, you know them . . . they never change. They're fine. They'd have come to see you themselves, except Pace convinced them you'd appreciate a visit from them even less than one from me."

When Serena tossed the damp towel aside, it seemed the most natural thing in the world for her to reach out and scrub his back, so that's what she did. Matt was so engrossed in his own thoughts he didn't seem to notice.

"I've hurt them, haven't I?" he asked quietly. "I've hurt all of you."

Once again her fingers stilled. "No, Matt, not the way you mean, anyway. We love you. Because of that, we hurt *for* you. We don't hurt *because* of you. You know how it is. When one of us is hurting, we all hurt."

She caught herself tracing the scars along his sleek, musclebound back and reminded herself she was supposed to be washing him, not . . . petting him. Thank God he hadn't seemed to notice her behavior.

"I know I've forced myself on you, coming here like this," she told him, "but as soon as you're well I'll leave you alone, I promise. We'll all leave you alone, if that's what you want. You just do whatever you have to do. We'll understand. And if you need us, we'll be there for you. We miss you and want you

95

home, but nobody wants to pressure you into doing something you're not ready for."

She rinsed his back, then handed him the soap and left him alone to finish his bath, and hopefully, to think about what she'd said.

Later that night Serena lay in bed and listened to Matt's restless movements across the room as he tried to fall asleep. She longed to go to him and wrap her arms around him, to hold him and soothe away his pain. He was hurting, in his body and his heart, and she ached with the need to comfort him.

It was a long time before she fell asleep.

"Do you have a mirror?" Matt asked the next morning, when she came in from milking the goat.

"Why? Do I need one?"

"Hardly." He grinned. "You look terrific, girl, but I'm a mess. I need a shave." He ran his hand across his bristled cheeks and grimaced.

"I'll shave you as soon as you drink a cup of milk."

He made a face at her. "I think you're trying to drown me in that stuff. Besides, the last time you shaved me you waved the razor around so much I thought you were going to slit my throat. Only trouble was, I couldn't tell if it would have been accidental, or on purpose."

"Ha." She took on her best schoolmarm lecturing tone. "In the first place, you ungrateful clod, this milk is very good for you." She thrust a cupful into his unwilling hand. "Whether you like to admit it or not, it is helping. The pain in your stomach isn't nearly as bad as it was."

He started to speak. She cut him off. "And in the second place, sir, I don't believe you're quite steady enough to be shaving yourself."

"I'll have you know I'm as steady as a rock," he claimed indignantly.

"A rock caught in the middle of a rock slide, maybe. The way your hands are shaking, you'd probably cut your own throat. Then I'd be left with the grisly task of cleaning up the mess and informing the family of your early demise. No, thank you. At least if I'm the one who cuts your throat, I'll have no one but myself to blame for the mess and the inconvenience."

"You're all heart, you know that?"

"Thank you." She grinned at him. "I've always thought of myself as a compassionate person."

Matt groaned, then rubbed his cheeks again. "I may regret this, but all right. You can shave me again. Just be careful, would you please? I'm kind of fond of my neck just the way it is."

"Drink up. I'll be as careful as a virgin on Maiden Row."

Matt choked on a mouthful of milk and spewed it across the table. "Rena!"

She ignored him and bit back a grin while working the soap into a lather.

"Maiden Row," Matt mumbled, wiping goat's milk from his chin. "You don't even know what it is."

She arched a brow. "Of course I don't. How would I know about a street full of whorehouses right in the middle of Tucson, for heaven's sake?"

"Watch your mouth, girl."

She slapped soap precariously close to his lips

and grinned. "You watch yours, mister. Stop calling me 'girl'."

He waited until she finished lathering his face, then said, "Tell me what's been happening in Tucson. Maybe it'll take my mind off the fact that my throat's about to be slit."

"You be nice or I'll let you slit it yourself," she threatened.

"Yes, ma'am."

Serena's lips twitched with mirth. "Tucson, hmm? Well, let me think." She took the first swipe along his cheek and tried to think of what was new in town. "After the roof fell in on Mr. Levin's opera house, he decided to go into another business, so he built a combination bowling alley and shooting gallery. As if there wasn't enough shooting going on already."

She paused to wipe off the blade, then continued.

"We have an ice plant now. And a public bath house. I hear it's even got showers. The Methodists finally built a church, then the Episcopalians built one the next year. Oh, and there's a hospital, finally. It's called St. Mary's. It opened last year. Remember Bob Leatherwood?"

Matt nodded.

"Don't move your head, silly," she admonished. "Anyway, Leatherwood got himself elected mayor last year, just before the railroad came in. Imagine that. Tucson finally has a railroad. And speaking of Leatherwood and the railroad," she said with a giggle, "you won't believe what happened at the celebration the day that first train pulled in from San Francisco."

After a final swipe with the razor, she wiped the last bits of lather from his face and went to rummage

98

around in her carpetbag.

"I brought a clipping about it from the paper. Poor Leatherwood will never live this down."

"What did that idiot do now? I can't imagine him as mayor."

"Now, now, he's not a bad mayor, really. He just got a little carried away with civic pride. The day the train came in he sent telegrams out all over the country to announce the event. I mean, sending one to the governor was right. And I can even understand his sending one to the President, but—"

"The President of the United States?" Matt asked in amazement. "President Hayes?"

"Boy, you *have* been away. President Garfield—James."

Matt blinked, a mixture of shock and embarrassment in his eyes. Serena ignored it.

"Anyway, telling the President's not the worst of it. Matt, Leatherwood sent one of those telegrams to the Pope."

Matt laughed until he choked. "The Pope." He pressed a hand to his side and laughed even harder. "I can just see it. 'Dear Holiness, the train finally got here.' God, the gall it must have taken." Matt whooped and laughed until tears streamed down his cheeks.

Serena laughed with him. Her heart lurched at the boyish glee on his face. It was the first time he had smiled since she'd come to Tombstone.

When he finally calmed down, she went on. "You haven't heard the best of it yet."

"Oh, no," he said wiping the tears from his eyes. "There's more?"

"Is there ever. Dad and a couple of men from town thought the wire to the Pope was a bit much, so they bribed the telegraph operator out of sending it. Then they drafted a reply of their own. I brought the clipping so I could read it to you." She forced the laughter from her voice and took on a serious tone as she read the copy of the telegram.

" 'His Holiness the Pope acknowledges with appreciation receipt of your telegram informing him that the ancient city of Tucson at last has been connected by rail with the outside world. He sends his benediction, but for his own satisfaction would ask, where in hell is Tucson?' "

Matt burst out laughing again, a full-throated roaring laugh. In between her own giggles, Serena said, "It's signed 'Antonelli'."

"Oh, Lord. I can't picture Dad having anything to do with that telegram."

Serena just grinned at him.

"Did he really?"

"I don't know how much of it he composed, but I saw the original, and the whole thing was in his handwriting."

Matt held his sides and laughed again. "What did Leatherwood say?"

"By the time somebody read the thing to the entire town in the middle of the celebration that night, Leatherwood and everybody else there was so drunk, no one even questioned it."

"That sounds like Bob," he said. "He should have stuck to shoveling manure and stayed out of politics."

* * *

The laughter they shared over the absurd telegram set the tone for the days that followed. Serena pushed her longings aside and concentrated on taking Matt's mind off his troubles. They were like two children again, except that it had never been quite this good between them before.

In the past, Matt had always been in charge, responsible for her welfare when they were together. When she'd first arrived in Tombstone, the situation had been just the opposite. Now it had changed again. It was more even, more balanced. Matt helped her as much as his broken leg allowed, then he stood back and let her do what she had to do.

Serena fed him, always badgering him to eat more. She poured milk down him until he swore it was coming out his ears. She teased him and laughed with him, but when that certain faraway look came over his face, she learned to ease off and give him the privacy he needed.

Their relationship had changed. It pleased Serena and puzzled Matt. No longer were they older brother and younger sister. Matt was amazed to realize they had somehow become equals, friends—the very best of friends.

He'd had other female friends. Dani had been his best friend since she'd married his father, when Matt was ten years old. Then came Angela, but that was different. In addition to the love they shared, they both honestly liked each other, but from the very beginning their relationship had been too intense for mere friendship.

And Kali. She was his friend.

But Rena was . . . different, special. She was

softer, yet somehow stronger than most women, easier to be with, fun. She let him be himself, with no lectures, at least not lately, on what he should and shouldn't do. Except when it came to the welfare of his leg . . . or his stomach, he thought wryly.

He'd never admit it in a million years, but he was actually starting to like that damned goat's milk.

"You just washed my hair yesterday," Matt said, eyeing Serena while she dragged the brass tub before the fireplace and began filling it with hot water.

"This isn't for you, it's for me," she said, trying to keep the quiver from her voice. She'd been very careful so far not to do anything even remotely connected with the teasing and tempting Kali had recommended. But that cold creek was about to get the best of her. Matt would just have to turn his back or go outside, she determined.

Matt swallowed, suddenly uncomfortable in the closeness of the small room. He tried to shrug off his unease. "So you're after a hot bath, huh?"

"Yes. The creek is freezing, there's a storm brewing to the southwest, and I feel like I need a good soak. I hope you don't mind," she said tentatively.

A devil pricked him. His unease evaporated. "Why should I mind?"

She narrowed her eyes at the teasing in his voice.

Matt grinned. He was about to give her a dose of her own medicine. "As you said to me," he continued, "it won't be anything I haven't seen before."

"Matt!"

He laughed at the shock and denial on her face.

"There's not a man alive who's ever seen me naked, least of all you!"

"Oh, but you're wrong," he taunted. "Not only have I *see* you, I've even kissed your bare bottom."

"You have not!" she shrieked.

"More than once," he stated emphatically. "The first time I did it, you were about a week old." The look on her face was priceless. "Not only that," he continued relentlessly, "I used to bury my face in your belly and make growling noises. Of course, I did the same thing to Pace, but he doubled up his fist and hit me in the eye. You, on the other hand, loved it."

"Well," she said flippantly, a telltale blush staining her cheeks, "you've never seen me take a bath, and I don't intend for you to start now, so would you mind turning your back while I undress?"

"But I *have* seen you take a bath. In fact, I even gave you one once, the night Spence was born. You were three years old. I was pretty good at it."

"Ha," she declared. "What were you, thirteen? Experienced man of the world. You should have been ashamed of yourself, taking advantage of a helpless young girl that way."

Sweat popped out along Matt's upper lip. Good God. What the hell was he doing, sitting here teasing her about giving her a bath when she was getting ready to—

One of her moccasins hit the floor. He gulped. She was—

The second moccasin hit the floor. He jerked. His heart thundered in his ears.

She reached around to unbutton her skirt.

Matt grabbed his crutches and stumped out of the

room like his tail was on fire. He knew his face damn sure was.

Serena sighed and closed her eyes. Damn. Why did she do that? *Because you wanted him to stay,* said a nasty little voice in the back of her brain. *You wanted him to watch you undress. You wanted him to see you as a woman.*

Tears stung her eyes. She walked slowly over to the door and closed it, then finished undressing. Thunder rumbled in the distance.

Perfect, she thought. Let it rain. It would match her mood.

Matt crashed through the brush in the dark on his unsteady crutches. The only thought he gave to the occasional flashes of lightning was that they helped him see where he was going. Not that it mattered. He didn't have the slightest idea where he was headed, except that he knew he was running away.

One minute he'd been innocently teasing her, and the next, he'd caught himself staring at that half-breed skin of hers glowing golden copper in the lamplight, her pale blue eyes with their thick black lashes. Her dark moist lips.

Sweet Jesus, he'd definitely been without a woman too long if he could feel what he'd just felt for his own sister.

Is she really your sister?
Yes, damn it. Yes.

104

Seven

Serena tied her hair up to keep it dry, then stepped into the tub. As the warm water seeped into her pores, her bones, she forgot everything. Oh, it was heavenly. It was heavenly not to think, but only to feel. Her muscles quivered, then relaxed one by one. Steam wafted upward to curl the little tendrils of hair around her face.

After several minutes of sheer physical pleasure, Serena forced herself to sit up and wash. She scrubbed her face and neck. Then, after rinsing the suds away, she paused to listen.

Thunder.

Suddenly she began to hurry, her leisurely bath cut short by the threat of rain. Matt would be back any second, and she didn't want to be caught like this.

Yes, you do.

Shut up. No, I don't.

And she wasn't. By the time she had donned her white cotton nightgown, Matt wasn't back yet. Just as she belted her robe the rain hit. Thunder and lightning crashed all around. Rain gushed down in torrents, poured as if someone were dumping buckets of water onto a tiny anthill.

Serena went to the door, thinking to open it in case Matt needed the light to guide him home. As she lifted the latch, a gust of wind tore the door from her hands and crashed it against the wall, sending a sheet of water with it. In less than a second, Serena and half the room were soaked. She had to get behind the door and push in order to close it against the raging storm.

Matt.

Surely he'd been able to take shelter somewhere, she hoped. But the way the wind was whipping the rain around, she knew standing under a tree, what few there were in these hills, wouldn't keep him dry in the least, but would only increase his chances of getting struck by lightning.

She closed her eyes and offered a quick prayer.

After changing into a dry dress, she paced before the fireplace, willing Matt to come through the door. A few minutes later she cocked her head to one side and listened. Something was different. The rain sounded . . . strange. Harder. The tone and rhythm of the storm had changed. A full minute later, she realized what she was hearing: hail.

Serena groaned and cursed herself. Why did she have to pick tonight to take a bath? Why had she teased Matt, making him think she was going to undress in front of him? If she'd just asked him to turn his back, he'd be inside right now, instead of out there Lord knew where, being pounded by thousands of ice balls.

The next twenty minutes were sheer torture. She'd never known it to hail so long. *Oh, Matt.*

As abruptly as it had hit, the storm stopped. After

106

the hail, there was nothing. No sound, no movement, no wind. Serena grabbed the lantern and was out the door in a flash. Then she came to an abrupt halt, her feet shifting on the uneven ground. She stared, stunned. A blanket of white covered the ground. From pea-sized to plum-sized, hailstones lay in ankle-deep piles. She'd never seen such a thing!

In the few seconds she spent staring, she felt the cold of the icy balls seep through her moccasins.

"Matt!" she cried, holding the lantern aloft. "Matt! Where are you?"

No answer.

"Matt! Matt!"

Out of sheer habit, she let her feet carry her across the clearing and down the path toward the creek. She kept calling his name and tried desperately to hold back her panic. It wouldn't do to lose her head now. Matt needed her.

The lantern cast eerie shadows among the brush and scrub. Serena's own shadow bobbed and stretched across the hail-covered path. With every step she took, hailstones shifted beneath her feet, making walking difficult.

The creek was swollen and raging from the sudden downpour. There was no sign of Matt. Why had she thought he'd be here? He could be anywhere. God! He could have fallen in the water and been washed downstream! *"Matt!"*

Her foot struck something beneath the cover of white. The hail shifted along a five-foot line out in front of her. Scraping the hail away, she uncovered one of Matt's crutches. Her mouth went dry. *"Matt!"*

She swung the lantern around, searching frantically for any sign of him. The roar from the angry creek drowned out her cry. Stumbling, she ran along the water's edge, ignoring the tingling warning of approaching numbness in her toes.

A long dark shape stretched out along the ground ahead. A rock? A log? In her haste to reach it, she tripped on a hidden rock and thrust one hand out to catch herself as she tried desperately to hang onto the lantern.

She made it to the dark shape. It was Matt. She'd found him, thank God. She dropped to her knees beside him, ignoring the sharp stab of icy hail beneath her. He was freezing cold, soaked to the bone, and unconscious. With her heart thundering, Serena rolled him over and cradled his head in her lap, crying his name over and over.

He came to with a groan and tried to raise his head, then let it fall back to her lap. "Rena?"

"It's me, Matt. Are you all right?" she asked, her nerves screaming in protest. He didn't need this. On top of everything else, he didn't need an illness or another injury. And it was her fault.

"I . . . lost a crutch . . . then I . . . fell. Must have . . . hit my head." His teeth were chattering so hard she could barely understand him. And he was shivering. "C-cold."

"You've got to get up, Matt. We've got to get you inside where it's warm."

He struggled to sit up. "Wa-warm?"

"Yes, it's warm in the house. Let me help you up."

She scrambled around underneath the hail and found the other crutch that had gotten him this far. When he was finally balanced precariously on one

108

crutch, she quickly retrieved the one she'd tripped over and got it beneath his other arm before he could fall.

For the first few shaky steps, she had to help him maneuver the crutches while she held the lantern out in front of him. He was finally able to propel himself forward, but the going was extremely slow. Twice she had to thrust herself under his arm when a crutch slipped on the hail.

It was the longest trip of Serena's life, not to mention Matt's, she was sure. By the time they reached the adobe, Matt could do no more than lean on his crutches and shake. She had no idea what held him upright. She left him propped against the table while she tore through the room. Somehow she managed to drag the brass tub, still half full of water, to one side. She drew Matt's mattress near the hearth, tossed more wood on the fire, and gathered every blanket in the room.

When she stripped Matt's cold, wet clothes from him, he made no protest. His skin felt like ice, his face was gray and haggard, and his lips held a blue tinge. He was shivering uncontrollably.

She wrapped him in a blanket and got him onto the mattress. Then she began to rub him briskly all over. The only sounds in the room were the crackling fire, her gasping breath, and Matt's chattering teeth.

He was so cold, too cold to help himself. She had to do something. She wished now that she hadn't broken that bottle of whiskey; maybe it would have helped warm him. She tried to get hot coffee down him, but most of it ran down his neck.

There was something she could do, though. She

could warm him with her own heat. But if he ever found out — well, he just wouldn't find out, that was all. *She* certainly wasn't going to tell him, and he was out now, so he'd never know the difference, except he'd be warm.

The hem of her dress was cold and wet from trailing in the hail. The bodice and skirt were, too, from her fall near the creek. Her nightgown and robe lay in a rain-drenched puddle where she had left them by the door. That left her chemise. How its ruffled hem remained dry when the lace trim on her drawers was damp was beyond her.

She stripped off everything but her chemise and, without giving herself time to think, crawled beneath Matt's blanket and curled up against his side.

She gasped at the contact with his frigid skin. With a deep breath, she pressed herself against his length.

Even as cold as he was, touching him felt so good. For this brief time, she could hold him. She could run her hand across his chest and arms and feel the strength of him. She could study his face at length. If she wanted, she could even place a kiss on those beautiful, cold lips.

She wanted.

And she did. She savored every moment of it, vowing to leave his side as soon as he warmed.

Gradually, his muscles relaxed and his teeth stopped chattering. Only an occasional shudder disturbed him now, and his skin began to warm to her touch.

Serena breathed easier, then easier still. The night had taken its toll on her. The hot bath, followed by her anxiety and near panic, then the struggle getting

110

Matt home, had sapped her strength. Now that she knew he was going to be all right, she could relax.

Matt opened his eyes. The sun wasn't up yet, but the room was getting light. The fire in the hearth was no more than a few glowing embers. He closed his eyes again. In that fuzzy stage of near-sleep, he rolled away from the meager warmth of the fireplace and turned toward that other, softer warmth pressed against his side. His restless hand roamed over soft fabric covering softer flesh, around curves, down valleys, up hills, until he cupped a firm, full breast.

He was dreaming. He had to be dreaming. He hadn't felt anything so good since—*don't think about it,* his mind warned, and he didn't. He was asleep anyway, and this wasn't real, so why not just enjoy it?

He ran his thumb back and forth and felt the nipple pucker and harden beneath some soft, thin material that barely separated his fingers from the flesh beneath. His body responded with a hardening of its own. Heat, fire swept through him. Blood rushed to his loins. He groaned with satisfaction. It felt so damned good to respond to a woman. Why had he denied himself this pleasure for so long?

Still befuddled by sleep, he wondered vaguely whose breast filled his hand. Where had she come from? What was she doing in his bed? Then he stopped caring. He bent and buried his face between the soft, firm breasts, letting his hand wander down narrow ribs and past a narrower waist to gently flaring hips. The woman's low moan of pleasure raised his temperature another notch.

With his lips, he trailed a path across a lace-covered collarbone until he found the bare flesh of her throat. There he dipped his tongue like a hummingbird stealing nectar from a flower and felt her pulse race. Sweet. She smelled so sweet, tasted so sweet.

She moved beneath him and his heart thundered. He trailed his hand to her firm belly and couldn't remember the last time he'd felt so alive. Every nerve in his body tingled with anticipation.

Mouth and tongue took a downward path until he buried his face in the deep valley between her breasts again. Lips and teeth nipped up one mound at a time, stopping at the crest of each to tease the turgid buds and suck on their sweetness . . . such sweetness, even through the fabric.

The woman beneath him gasped. Her hands clutched his head, but only to hold him closer. Someone moaned. He wasn't sure who, and he didn't care.

He trailed hot, wet kisses up her chest and neck and along her jaw, and settled his mouth on her eagerly parted lips. He eased his tongue in. She pulled hers away shyly. When he retreated, she didn't follow.

Through the fog of lust in his brain, Matt realized that her body knew all the right moves, her hands knew to touch that place on his neck and drive him wild, but her mouth was inexperienced. He cupped her breast and opened his eyes a fraction, peering through his lashes, awake now, trying to discern just who this enchanting creature was.

Her eyes were closed. He kissed her again, teasing with his tongue. He was so close to her that her features were a blur. There was nothing he could even focus on except for her temple, where a white streak—

Jesus God Almighty!

Matt jerked away, his whole body rigid with shock, his gut churning in horror at what he'd nearly done.

Serena whimpered in protest at the sudden loss of the warm hand on her breast and the moist, hungry lips on hers. In that hazy, dreamlike state halfway between sleep and wakefulness, she groped blindly for her mysterious dream lover.

"No!"

The harsh voice startled her awake. She blinked at Matt in confusion. Comprehension came quickly. She bit back a sob. She'd never seen such a look of revulsion on a man's face in her life. He looked like he was going to be sick, and she felt like it. "Matt . . . I—"

"No! Rena, don't say anything. I'm sorry. God, I'm so sorry. I didn't know . . . I was asleep, and—"

"It's all right." Serena lowered her eyelids to hide the sudden gathering of tears. She rolled away from him and sat up, hugging herself against a sudden chill. "I . . . that is, you were so cold . . . last night. You couldn't stop shivering. I had to warm you. I guess I . . . fell asleep."

"Damn, Rena." Matt clenched his eyes shut to block out the sight of her thick black curls tumbling around her shoulders in disarray and the look of pain and betrayal on her face. "You should have let me freeze," he said harshly.

"It's all right, Matt. Just forget about it. Nothing happened."

"Nothing happened?" He laughed harshly. "Noth-

113

ing happened. I just damned near raped my own sister."

Serena reached out a hand to touch him. "Oh, Matt—"

"No! Don't touch me!"

Serena didn't know whether to laugh or cry over the irony of a thirty-year-old man begging a nineteen-year-old virgin not to touch him.

"Listen to me." She took a deep breath to calm her rapid pulse. It didn't help. "I said it once in anger, I'll say it again, this time calmly and with no malice." The directness of her gaze prevented him from looking away. "I am not your sister."

Things were never the same between them after that. Matt retreated to some private corner of his mind and would have nothing to do with her. If she was in the house, he went outside. When she went out, he came back in. He spent nearly all his time either stumping his way through the hills alone or feigning sleep indoors.

One night at supper, Serena handed him his plate and their fingers accidentally touched. Matt jerked away as if he'd been burned. The tin plate hit the floor; food scattered everywhere. Matt stared blankly at the mess while Serena choked back tears of frustration and cleaned it up. She refilled his plate and slammed it down on the table before him, nearly spilling the food again.

Neither said so much as a single word.

Serena had her own problems to contend with. Before that accursed storm hit, her longing for Matt had been a longing of the heart and soul. But since that night another more disturbing longing had awakened — the longing of the flesh.

Not an hour went by that she didn't recall the feel of his hands on her body, the long, hard length of him pressed against her, his lips teasing her breasts and mouth, the pressure of his hot, hard arousal against her thigh. And every time she saw him or thought of him, the juices of her body flowed to that secret, dark place between her legs and set up a throbbing like she'd never known before. Her nipples puckered and her lips tingled.

And he acted like he wished a hole would open up in the ground and swallow one of them — probably her.

Why did her mother have to marry Travis Colton? Why did Travis have to adopt her and Pace? Why did she and Matt have to be raised as brother and sister when she wanted something else entirely?

Foolish questions, she scolded to herself. Foolish questions from a foolish heart. But she couldn't stop her heart from wanting him. She didn't even know how to try.

"What are you doing with that?"

The sound of Matt's voice startled her, nearly making her drop the razor. It was the first time he'd spoken to her except in answer to a direct question in days.

"I'm going to shave you."

"I'm growing a beard."

"So I noticed. You're starting to look like a derelict

again."

She approached the bed where he lay and knelt beside him. The shaving brush rattled in the mug as she whipped up a lather. A few moments later, she reached toward his face with the razor. That she was slightly unsteady was an understatement. Matt grabbed her wrist and stared at her trembling fingers. She was shaking every bit as badly as he had been in the beginning.

"I was drunk for the past year. What's your excuse?"

Serena stared at the long blunt fingers next to her smaller tapered ones and didn't answer.

"You're terrified of me, aren't you?"

She jerked her head up and stared at him in surprise. Or shock. "Of course not. Why should I be?"

"I think we both know the answer to that."

"Oh, come off it, Matt." She yanked her hand free. "So you kissed me. Big deal."

"I did a damn sight more than that, or don't you remember?"

She closed her eyes and sighed. "I remember." She looked at him again. "What I'd like to know is who you blame the most, yourself or me?"

He sat up abruptly. "I don't blame you for any of it."

"Then why have you been treating me like I've got the plague?" she cried, her anger matching his. "I don't bite, I won't contaminate you, and I promise I'll try real hard not to attack you."

"You're angry."

"No kidding."

"I'm sorry."

116

"Would you stop apologizing?" she shrieked. "You were half asleep and you felt a nearly naked woman pressed up against you. It was a perfectly normal reaction."

"Not when the woman is your—not when she's someone you've always thought of as your sister."

"And not when you still think of her as a little girl, right? Well, let me set the record straight." She slammed down the razor and wiped her hands on a towel, then looked him in the eye. "That was no little girl in bed with you the other night. Since you don't seem to have noticed, I happen to be a woman, not a child. I stopped thinking of you as my brother when I was eight years old."

She got up and rummaged through her carpetbag. "And furthermore," she said, pulling out a small mirror on a stand and crossing back to his side, "I *liked* what happened between us the other night." She dropped the mirror in his lap, tossed her head defiantly, and marched out the door.

Let him think about that for a while. She stomped off to the brush corral, kicking dirt with every step until her moccasined toe connected with a rock by mistake.

Cursing under her breath, she picked up a piece of burlap and started rubbing down Matt's horse. Gradually, her anger drained away to be replaced by sadness. She'd always known she'd never have Matt. She'd had more of him, felt closer to him these last few weeks than she'd ever dared hope. She should be willing to settle for that. It should be enough. But it wasn't—it wasn't nearly enough.

He'd been miserable when she'd found him. Then,

for a while, he'd seemed carefree and happy. Now he was miserable again, and this time it was her fault. She should never have crawled under that blanket with him. To him, pneumonia would have been preferable to his present feelings of self-loathing and guilt.

She finished grooming the gelding, then gave him, the chickens, and the goat fresh water. After searching for eggs and finding none, she finally headed back to the house. A sad little chuckle escaped her. She couldn't decide who she felt sorrier for, Matt or herself.

When she stepped around the corner of the house, she came to an abrupt halt. Matt was outside, leaning against the adobe wall, a crutch tucked up negligently under each arm. But it was a different Matt from the one she'd been seeing lately.

Spit-shined—that was the word that came to mind. And gorgeous. He wore a clean shirt tucked into dust-free trousers. Where had he come up with a clean shirt? The bear-claw necklace teased from the open vee of his collar. He wore a boot on one foot and a sock—a clean sock—on the other. His hair was neatly combed and damp around the edges, and he'd shaved.

And he looked so damned good. She leaned toward him, but her feet stayed glued to the spot. What could she say to him after that last parting shot? What was he thinking?

Matt pulled slowly from the wall and made his way toward her. He stopped a few feet away, his dark, troubled gaze locked with hers.

The silence—or what passed for silence, consider-

118

ing the horse, the goat, a dozen cackling hens, and countless birds — was broken by the jingle of a harness and a feminine voice calling out, "Hello!" Kali's voice.

Matt closed his eyes briefly in frustration, then scowled when he saw Kali wasn't alone. Next to her on the padded leather seat of the shiny black buggy sat the man called Caleb.

Kali pulled the buggy to a halt beside the house and called out, "Thought you two might be getting bored out here, so we decided to visit." She secured the reins and, without waiting for Caleb's help, climbed down from the buggy.

With her hands on her hips, Kali watched Matt and Serena approach. "Well, you look like a new man, Matthew."

"Why, thank you kindly, ma'am," Matt drawled with exaggeration. "You look pretty nice yourself, if I may be so bold." He swept a crutch out before him with a flourish.

"You, sir," she purred, flicking a long, elegant finger against his nose, "may be as bold as you please."

Serena gritted her teeth and swallowed painfully. Was this why Matt couldn't see her as a woman? Was his mind already on Kali? And was Matt the first brother Kali had mentioned, the one she knew better than she should?

No wonder Matt couldn't take his eyes off the woman. She was stunning. The yellow satin dress draped over her hourglass figure breathed coolness on this hot morning. Silk daisies trimmed the low, scooped neckline and framed the upper half of her breasts in open invitation. Her auburn hair was

119

curled artfully atop her head, crowned with a frilly yellow hat bearing more silk daisies.

She wore powder and rouge on her face. Her brows and lashes, above laughing black eyes, were artificially darkened, but on Kali, the look was glamorous rather than cheap.

Serena cringed inwardly, comparing her own appearance to Kali's and coming up severely short. She had on one of Pace's old white shirts with the sleeves rolled up to her elbows. Her drab gray skirt was covered with horsehair and dirt. Her hair hung loose down her back and over her shoulders. She definitely felt dowdy.

But she'd be darned if she'd act like it. She nodded to Kali, then stepped past the woman and extended her hand. "Caleb," she said with a warm smile. "What a pleasant surprise. How nice to see you again."

Serena watched Caleb kiss her hand and missed Matt's scowl, but Kali saw it and smiled to herself. That was definitely not brotherly concern she saw in his eyes.

"I hope you two haven't eaten yet," she said, digging around beneath the buggy seat and piling items into Caleb's arms. "We've brought a picnic."

They spread a quilt beneath the outstretched limbs of the Arizona white oak a dozen yards from the house. Kali emptied the baskets of fried chicken, potato salad, corn on the cob, freshly baked bread, juicy dill pickles, hard-boiled eggs, cherry pie, apple pie, and china, silver, and crystal. She even brought two bottles of wine.

Throughout the meal, Kali had a hard time controlling the urge to laugh. Caleb couldn't seem to keep his eyes off Serena, or his hands, for that matter. Every time he brushed against the girl accidentally or touched her on purpose, Matt's scowl grew more fierce. Kali half expected him to leap up any minute and throttle poor Caleb.

Since no one else seemed to have anything to say, Kali kept up a running monologue to fill the silence. She paid particular attention to the fact that Serena and Matt refused even to acknowledge each other's presence.

Kali filled Matt and Serena in on everything that had happened in town and abroad. On July 2 some attorney in Washington named Guiteau had shot President Garfield, but the president had survived — for now.

"Closer to home," she said, "I guess you've heard about the Indian raids."

"What raids?" Matt and Serena demanded.

Aha, Kali thought. *Now* she had their attention. "That old renegade Nana is at it again, terrorizing everybody for five hundred miles. Why, in the last two weeks alone he's stolen over a hundred horses."

"How many men ride with him?" Matt asked sharply.

Kali grimaced. "I knew you'd ask that." She heaved a sigh. "No more than a handful. A dozen at most."

"Well, then," Caleb said. "Why hasn't the army put a stop to it?"

Serena's lips twitched. "I imagine they've tried. How many troops are after him?" she asked Kali.

Kali heaved another sigh. It was embarrassing. Downright embarrassing. "Around a thousand."

Matt hooted.

Serena flashed a glare his way. "It's not funny. It will only cause more trouble at the reservation."

"You're not kidding," Kali told them. "The way I hear it, the Army's afraid Nana will ride in and break all the Chiricahua out of San Carlos. They've sent in hundreds of extra troops."

"Yes," Serena said. "And that's got The People stirred up."

"How bad?" Matt asked.

"Bad enough that they've started listening to an old White Mountain shaman called Nocadelklinny, who says he can raise enough dead warriors from the grave to rid the world of all white men."

Matt pursed his lips and whistled.

Serena leaned toward him. "Maybe when you're well you could find Nana, talk some sense into him. If he backs off, maybe the Army will, too."

Matt snorted. "I doubt it. Besides, that old war horse would just as soon skewer me as look at me. I'd do more good at San Carlos."

"You're right. He never did like you." Serena frowned. "Maybe Pace and I could get him to—"

"No!" Matt cried. "Absolutely not. You go anywhere near Nana and his renegades, girl, and I'll tan your hide."

"You and what army, buster?"

Matt made as if to rise.

Kali bit back a grin and put a hand on Matt's chest. "Now, children, no squabbling. It's much too nice a day. Besides, poor Caleb hasn't got a clue to what you're talking about."

To forestall further argument, Kali dished out more

potato salad and changed the subject. With a combination of relish and horror—she still didn't know how she felt about it—she told them about Tombstone's Independence Day celebration. When she mentioned the holiday, Matt and Serena both looked blank. It was plain to Kali that neither had realized the date had come and gone. She was sure they weren't even listening when she told them about the town's historical first hanging in the afternoon and the spectacular fireworks that night.

"The next day," Kali said, "Doc Holliday got himself arrested and tried for killing that stage driver, Kinnear, during the holdup last March. Doc's . . . ahem, *wife,* Big-Nosed Kate Elder, testified Doc had bragged about the holdup and the shooting. Doc swore he'd been playing cards over in Charleston that day, and Wyatt Earp backed him up. Doc was acquitted."

The others only half listened to her, but Kali didn't care. "Just the other day, Kate got soused—again— and Virgil Earp arrested her. She had to pay a twelve-dollar-and-fifty-cent fine for drunken and disorderly conduct. Served the old biddy right, turning on Doc the way she did. She left town the day after Virgil turned her loose. Good riddance, I say."

Everyone was so preoccupied with private thoughts—Matt trying not to look at Serena, Serena trying not to look at Matt, and Caleb trying not to take his eyes off Serena—that Kali was able to orchestrate the entire afternoon like a symphony conductor leading a Sunday concert. Before anyone realized how it had happened, Caleb and Serena were off for a walk in the hills and Kali and Matt were left alone.

"He's a nice-looking man, don't you think?" Kali asked innocently, staring after the departing couple.

"I wouldn't know."

"Well, take it from a woman who appreciates a nice-looking man—he is."

"If you say so." With each passing moment, the crease between Matt's eyes grew deeper.

"He seems respectable enough, and I understand he's got some money. Serena could do a lot worse for herself."

Matt's eyebrows nearly touched his hairline, he had them raised so high.

"Don't look at me like that," Kali cried. "She's well past marriageable age, you know. You can't expect her to remain your little sister forever."

Another furrow appeared in his brow.

"And it's plain as the nose on your face that Caleb adores her," Kali went on relentlessly.

Matt lowered his gaze, afraid to let Kali see how her words troubled him. What the hell was taking those two so long, anyway? What was so fascinating about the damned hills? What were they doing that they couldn't do right there in front of him?

As various possibilities came to mind, he squeezed his hand around a chicken bone. It snapped in two.

Kali bit back another grin. His sister, indeed. Kali would bet good money that with the close living arrangements, with them isolated out here away from town, and with Serena's having to take care of Matt, the two were starting to forget whose mother was married to whose father.

By the time Caleb and Serena returned to the clearing, Matt was ready to explode. It didn't help his mood one damn bit to see Serena's hand casually grasping the inside of Caleb's elbow, or the teasing smile she flashed her escort.

With her free hand, she patted Caleb's shoulder. "Just keep walking," she said cheerfully. "I told you there was nothing to worry about."

Only then did Matt notice the peculiar look on Caleb's face. Tense, wary. Lips thinned and white. Beads of sweat along his brow and temples.

"Matt," Serena called. "You have a visitor."

Matt cocked his head and realized there was too much shuffling and crunching of gravel for the footsteps of only Serena and Caleb. Behind the two, a dark shape rustled out of the brush. Matt grinned. "Hello, *shash*."

The young brown bear on all fours following Caleb and Serena gave a snort and grunt.

Caleb flinched.

"It's all right," Serena crooned. "It's just here to see Matt."

Matt threw back his head and laughed until his sides ached. Once he calmed, he eyed Serena's escort. "How'd you like your chaperon, Caleb?"

"Call it off, Matt," Serena said. Her eyes shot fire at him.

Matt laughed harder.

"It's not funny. Get rid of the damn bear."

Beside Matt, Kali made a strangling sound. "I've heard about it for years," she said in awe, "but I never believed it."

"Believe it," Serena said with disgust. "Everywhere Matt goes, a bear shows up." To Caleb, she said, "Not to harm anyone, unless they threaten Matt.

Since the time he killed a bear when he was fifteen, they follow him all over. The old shaman calls them Matt's guardians."

The bear shuffled past a petrified Caleb and an irritated Serena and sniffed Matt's shoulder.

"Good, *shash*," Matt said. "Thank you. Now go on. *Núúghuyáhah*."

As if understanding Matt's command, the bear gave a final sniff, then turned and lumbered off over the hill.

Caleb swallowed, then visibly relaxed. "I've shot a bear or two, but I never had one follow me around like a tame dog."

Serena gave Caleb's arm a last pat, then turned loose of him. "Matt didn't shoot his bear. It attacked him when he was trapped in a rock slide. All Matt had was a knife."

If Matt didn't know she was madder than hell at him, he would have sworn her voice held a hint of pride.

Eight

"That was nice," Serena said, watching the buggy carry Caleb and Kali back to town.

Matt ground his teeth. Nice? *Nice?* He swung around to face her. "I'll just bet it was."

"What's that supposed to mean?"

"Didn't your mother ever tell you what can happen when you tease a man like that?"

"Tease?" she shrieked. "I did not—"

"You had him wrapped right around your little finger. Every time you batted those big blue eyes, he practically drooled."

"You're crazy."

"You're the one who's crazy, Serena, leading on a cheap tinhorn like that." He took a step toward her. "Haven't you got any sense at all?"

Serena held her ground. With hands on hips, she glared up at him. "Why is it you call me Serena only when you're angry?"

"A man like him expects to get all that's offered to him. From where I sat, you offered him plenty."

"I did no such thing, and you know it. What's the matter with you, anyway?"

"Me?" he cried. "What the hell's the matter with *you?"*

"There's nothing in the world the matter with me. Just because you see a skinny little kid with pigtails when you look at me doesn't mean everybody else does. Caleb happens to think I'm a lovely young woman."

Matt swung a step closer. "Did he say that?"

"As a matter of fact, he did."

"He's faster than I gave him credit for. He's already started with his line of sweet little lies."

Serena narrowed her eyes and clenched her jaw. "Lies?" she ground out. "Lies, you say?" She advanced until she stood nose-to-nose with him. "Not too many days ago, *brother,* you called me beautiful. Were you lying, or is it only other men who lie? Make up your mind, Matt. You can't have it both ways." She turned and took a step toward the house.

"Wait." Matt grabbed for her. She spun away and he missed. "Rena, wait."

She glared at him over her shoulder. "What now?"

He cleared his throat nervously, looked down at the ground, then back up. "We . . . need to talk."

She studied him a moment, then said in a lifeless voice, "It appears to me we've both said enough." She turned away and walked off into the hills. Again.

When had she become such a coward, she wondered. This was her second trek through the brush today. She couldn't keep running away like this. But what was she supposed to say to him? It's all right, Matt, I'll be your little sister?

No, she couldn't do that. She could never be his sister again after the night of the storm. She remembered every vivid detail of that night, from the shock of his icy skin against her when she crawled beneath his blanket, to that last scorching kiss before he pulled away in horror.

She remembered the way his tongue, firm and hot and sleek, had searched out the hidden corners of her mouth and stroked her own tongue to life until the two were dancing together to the beat of some inner, unknown rhythm.

And his hands, rough and calloused, had set her skin on fire with their heated touch. She remembered the exquisite sensations his lips created when they surrounded the tip of her breast. She'd been more than half asleep at the time, but she remembered.

The mere thought of his touch turned both nipples to hard nubs that stood out like pebbles against the soft, worn cotton of her shirt. Liquid heat pooled in that secret place between her legs. Her knees turned weak.

Oh, Matt.

She sucked her lower lip between her teeth and tried to force away the ache of wanting him. So this was what it was like to want a man. The terrible craving for his touch swirled around her and settled in the pit of her stomach like a rock. A hot, heavy rock.

Wanting him was madness, and she had to stop. Matt would never feel the way she did. To him, she was a little sister, whether she wanted to be or not, and there didn't seem to be a whole lot she could do about it.

Tempt him, Kali had said. *Make him want you.*
How?

Serena didn't know the first thing about how to entice a man. Even if she did, she knew she couldn't do it. If she succeeded in making Matt want her, it would destroy him. He already carried so much guilt, about Angela's death, about leaving his daughter and family, about his drinking . . . Serena just couldn't add to that.

And his wanting her would add to it. He would feel so guilty for wanting his *sister*, it would tear him apart.

Tearing him apart was the last thing in the world she wanted. She wanted to see him whole and happy again. She wanted to hear him laugh and see the flecks of gold sparkle in his coffee-brown eyes. She wanted to hear him whistle between curses while he worked with the horses at the ranch. She wanted to see the pride in his eyes as he watched his daughter grow up.

His happiness was her happiness. Her needs were nothing compared to his. His biggest need was someone to love. He needed a wife. Matt wasn't meant to live alone, even in the midst of a large family. He had such a loving, giving nature, he would shrivel up and die without someone to spend it on.

Serena wondered if she had the strength to slip back into the role of sister and watch him someday take a wife. And someday he would, she knew.

No. She wasn't that strong. It was one thing to be ten years old and watch him marry Angela. But now, when she knew the feel of his lips and the touch of his hands . . . No. She knew most of her strengths and weaknesses, and she knew she wouldn't be able to stand it.

Nonsense, an inner voice cried. *You can stand*

*whatever you have to. If you love him as much as you
think you do, as much as you say you do, his happiness is more important than yours.*

Serena wrapped her arms around the trunk of a
cottonwood near the creek and pressed her face
against the rough bark. "What am I going to do?" she
moaned. Tears stung her eyes and flowed down her
cheeks unheeded. "Is it true? Can only one of us ever
be happy? Oh, Matt, I love you."

Angry now, she pushed herself away from the tree
and wiped her sleeve across her face. This wasn't getting her anywhere. The first thing she had to do was
make some sort of peace with Matt. They couldn't go
on snapping at each other this way.

She hesitated by the tree and decided that making
peace with Matt was the second thing she had to do.
First, she had to sit down a minute and rest. She was
used to all manner of physical activity, but not this
constant emotional strain. Her argument with Matt
this morning, then having to be nice to Caleb when
all she wanted to do was hit something—how dare
Matt accuse her of teasing Caleb?—then another argument with Matt . . . she felt drained.

Matt leaned on his crutches and watched Serena
run off—again. Damn. Couldn't that girl stand still
and finish a discussion without running off to hide all
the time? He closed his eyes in frustration.

Actually, he didn't really blame her for running
out. If he hadn't been hampered by his damned
crutches, he might have tried it himself a time or two.
As a matter of fact, he did do it himself once, the

131

night of the storm.

At the reminder of that night, he swore. Even now, the thought of her silky skin, her warm, responsive body, and her willing lips sent his blood soaring and caused a tightness below his belt.

You bastard. She's your sister.

Is she?

Yes, damn you.

He swore again, then stomped his way into the house to get out of the sun. That's what it was—too much sun. That's why he was able to forget for long moments just who she was.

The crutches made a thumping noise against the plank flooring. He paced back and forth, *thump, step, thump, step.* In another week or so, the damned leg would be healed and he could get the hell out of there and away from her.

But, if he went home, she'd be there.

He paced back and forth until he rubbed blisters under his arms, but gradually he began to calm. What had possessed him to yell at her that way about Caleb? He knew she hadn't encouraged the man. She'd barely looked at him, except when the two of them had gone for a walk.

What did they do out there in the hills for so long? Talk? Laugh? Hold hands? *Kiss?*

A shudder ran through him at the thought of another man tasting those sweet lips, teaching her how to kiss and please him. He managed to convince himself for a few minutes that the only reason that thought disturbed him so much was because of the brotherly protectiveness he felt for her.

Serena was a young girl on the verge of womanhood, already in possession of a woman's body. She had no idea of the effect she had on men, the power she could wield if she only knew how.

Matt glanced out the open doorway toward the path Serena had taken and was startled to see the sky turning dark. The sun was down and the light was almost gone. Where was she? In another few minutes she wouldn't be able to see to find her way home. Was she lost? Hurt?

Serena wouldn't get lost. He knew better than that. She knew more about how to survive on her own than most men. Cochise and he himself had seen to that.

Something must have happened to her. Suddenly frantic, he lit the lantern, tossed one crutch aside so he could carry the lantern, and took off as fast as he could into the hills.

"Serena!" he called. "Rena? Answer me! Where are you?"

If she was sitting on a rock somewhere still sulking, he'd wring her neck for scaring him this way. Yet even as he felt his anger swell, he hoped to God she *was* sitting on a rock somewhere nearby. It was so much better than the alternatives that haunted his mind.

It was almost completely dark when he found her near the creek, curled up in a ball at the base of a cottonwood. "Rena!" He nearly tore the ground up with his crutch, getting to her. "Rena!"

Dear God, please let her be all right.

Matt flung his crutch aside and dropped to the ground in front of her, holding the lantern high to look for injuries. He reached out a trembling hand and smoothed the hair back from her face. Thank God she was still breathing.

133

Serena nuzzled her face into the palm of his hand. "Matt," she whispered.

"Rena, where are you hurt?"

"Matt?" Her eyelids fluttered, then she gazed up at him in confusion. "What is it? What's wrong?"

Matt ran his hands down her arms and legs. "Is it your head?" he asked. "Did you hit your head?"

She blinked slowly. "What are you talking about?" She stretched her arms above her head and yawned, and then her eyes opened wide. "Oh. Good heavens. I must have fallen asleep."

"What?" Matt roared, raising up on his knees to tower over her. "You mean I've been pacing the floor for hours, wondering where the hell you were, and you've been asleep? Thinking you were so mad at me you just took off and left without a word, and you've been *asleep?* I rubbed blisters in my goddamn armpit rushing out here to save you from Lord knows what kind of disaster, and you've been *asleep?*"

Serena blinked again, amazed by his outburst. "You really thought I'd just leave, without telling you?"

"You scared ten years off my life, woman. I oughtta turn you over my knee and blister your rear."

"There you go again," Serena said wearily. "First you call me a woman, then you threaten to treat me like a child."

"Rena, so help me—"

"I'm sorry." She placed her fingers over his lips and had to ignore the rush of heat caused by the simple contact. "Both for what I just said, and for worrying you. Don't be angry, Matt, please. I hate it when we fight."

134

Matt slumped down against the tree near Serena's head and took several deep breaths. She sat up beside him and he took her hand in his. "I hate it, too," he confessed. "I'm sorry I yelled. I seem to be doing a lot of that lately. But I was worried when you didn't come back."

Serena leaned over and kissed his cheek. "Thank you."

"For what?" he asked, startled by the kiss.

"For worrying about me. For coming to find me."

He had a peculiar look on his face when he answered, "Isn't that what big brothers are for?"

Her smile was only slightly unsteady when she replied, "Right."

The next few days were calmer than the ones up to and including the day of the picnic. The easy, comfortable camaraderie, which they'd shared before the storm, was missing, but neither of them mentioned it. On the surface, everything was smooth.

They went through their daily routines carefully, deliberately. On the outside, everything was normal. But Matt did not ask her to shave him, and she didn't offer. When she served a meal, she placed his plate on the table rather than handing it to him. When he saw the tired slump of her shoulders at the end of the day, he wanted to massage them, but didn't offer.

Beneath the surface, tensions ran high. The hot, dry days and the too-warm nights contributed to Matt's edginess, an edginess he did his best to conceal.

Serena was so wrapped up in her own misery she

wouldn't have noticed anyway. She concentrated all her energies on being friendly and polite, and talking only about safe subjects like the weather or what to fix for supper. Inside she was so miserable it was a real effort to keep from crying.

If only she hadn't fallen asleep the night she'd warmed his cold flesh with her body, they wouldn't now be acting like polite strangers. She might have been able to go on indefinitely with her girlish longings tucked safely away in her heart.

She sighed heavily. She'd been doing a lot of that lately . . . sighing. She tossed down the shirt she'd been mending and wiped the perspiration from her brow. It was too hot to work, especially indoors. Not a breath of air stirred in the tiny house, but outside there was at least a breeze.

After telling Matt she was going for a walk, she headed for the creek. When she got there, the water proved to be too much of a temptation. As heedless as a child, she tossed her clothes over the nearest bush and spent the next hour lying in the knee-deep water.

She faced the sky with her feet against a small boulder and her head pointing upstream. The slow-moving water caressed her from head to toe as it passed on its way through the hills to the San Pedro, a lover stroking her, bidding her farewell.

The water buoyed her as it swept around and beneath her. It parted at the top of her head and swirled around her, taking turns with the sun and the air at teasing and touching her breasts and stomach and thighs bobbing in and out of the water.

And that's how Matt found her.

It had been lonely at the house without her, and it

had seemed twice as hot after she left. He'd left his shirt draped on a bush and headed toward the stream, expecting to catch her dangling her toes in the water.

The first thing he saw was her clothes — all of them — scattered on the bushes. Instantly he had turned to leave, not wanting to impose.

Not much, you lowlife bastard.

He turned, intending to go, and there she was, stretched out in the water, eyes closed, body laid out for all the world to see — for him to see.

His mouth went dry and his arms refused to move the crutches. He drank in every inch of her skin greedily. When his gaze finally reached her face, the breath left his lungs. She was watching him.

Serena blinked slowly, at first doubting what she saw. Matt stood on the bank, devouring her with his gaze. She might not be an experienced woman-of-the-world, but she knew a look of hunger when she saw it. She couldn't have moved just then if her life had depended on it.

She gazed at him just as greedily as he stared at her. Weeks of supporting his weight on crutches had brought back the muscles of his chest and shoulders. Her eyes slid hungrily over the curves and bulges usually hidden beneath his shirt. She longed to run her fingers through the golden curls on his chest, to follow them down to where they narrowed to a thin line and disappeared beneath his belt.

She studied every inch of his tanned flesh. She visually traced the scars on his chest, put there years ago by the bear. She knew there were matching scars on his back. Her gaze traced the final scar, the one on his cheek, then traveled to meet his eyes.

137

Their gazes locked. For one brief instant, their minds touched. Hers rushed forward eagerly. His retreated in panic.

Pulled by the magnetism of his eyes, Serena slowly rose from the water.

Matt tried to leave. He really tried.

But he couldn't.

Her long, wet hair plastered itself to her back and shoulders, draping down and clinging to her breasts, where it parted to reveal dark nipples, shriveled and hardened from the cold water. Crystal water droplets slid down golden bronze breasts to fall from the dusky peaks, drawing Matt's gaze like a beggar to a feast.

Tempting. So damn tempting. His breath rasped in his throat. His heartbeat thundered in his ears.

He took a hesitant step toward her, then stiffened. "No!" He squeezed his eyes shut and turned his back. A deep shudder ripped through him. He forced himself to head for the house. If he could have run, he would have. He had to get away from her. If he didn't, he knew he'd do something unforgivable, something horrible, something forbidden.

Serena's dry, burning eyes were open wide. She stared at the streaks of moonlight on the wall next to her head, not daring to close her eyes. If she closed them, she'd see Matt turning his back on her and walking away . . . again. He did it only once, but in her mind it kept happening over and over every time she closed her eyes.

He wanted her. This afternoon at the creek, he had

138

wanted her. The way a man wants a woman. When their eyes had met, he knew then that she wanted him. She should be glad it happened, but she wasn't. He hated himself for what he was feeling. His body and his mind were at war, while his heart still grieved for Angela.

Serena buried her face in the pillow to stifle a moan. She didn't want him fighting himself; she wanted him to be at ease. In her heart, she knew she could give him the peace and happiness he needed, if only he would let her.

There didn't seem to be much chance of that, though. Ever since she had returned from the creek, he'd refused to even look at her. When she tried to talk to him, he walked away. She cooked a meal, more out of habit than hunger, and he refused to eat.

Now he was outside somewhere. It was late, the moon rode high, but he wouldn't go to bed in the same room with her. He was out there sleeping on the ground, if he slept at all.

Oh, God. Was what she wanted so terrible? So wrong? *It can't be wrong,* her heart cried. There had to be a way! There just had to. She loved him so much.

The tears she'd been holding back all day suddenly gushed forth and soaked her pillow where she hid her face. She couldn't let him hear her crying, but she couldn't hold back the tears or sobs that shook her shoulders and stole her breath.

A warm hand closed around her upper arm, heating her skin through the thin cotton of her nightgown. She flinched.

"Rena?" Matt's voice was husky as he knelt beside

139

her. "Rena, don't cry."

His tender request had the opposite effect, and she only cried harder.

He lowered himself to her side and took her gently in his arms. She melted against the comfort of his broad, bare chest and wrapped her arms around him.

He buried his face in her hair and murmured, "Don't cry anymore, please, Rena. I can't stand it when you cry."

Her tears finally stopped, and Matt stroked her back and kissed the top of her head. His hand continued its lazy, comforting rhythm up and down her spine while his lips traveled down her brow to sip the tears from her eyes, then her cheeks.

Serena tilted her head back until his lips hovered over hers. His eyes were no more than dark pools in his shadowed face. She wanted him to kiss her so badly that a tiny whimper escaped her throat.

His arms tightened around her, crushing her aching breasts against his tear-soaked chest. "This is wrong," he whispered hoarsely, his lips only a breath away from hers. "I know it's wrong, but . . . God help me, Rena . . . I have to do this."

Neither was prepared for the sudden spark that shot through them when their lips only barely touched. Matt drew back sharply and sucked in his breath. Then, in the next instant, his lips lowered to hers with a will of their own.

At first it was a tentative touching of lip to lip, a gentle, beautiful hello, miraculous, wonderful, soothing. But soon it was not enough. Matt's tongue drew a line between her lips and she eagerly opened them for him. He dipped into her mouth and tasted every surface. His tongue tutored hers, slowly, carefully, until the kiss deepened. Hands clutched, heads tilted, lungs heaved, hearts pounded.

Serena was floating on air, drifting on a sea of sensation she never knew existed. Every nerve in her body screamed out the rightness of what he was doing to her. She tingled from head to toe and never wanted it to stop. When Matt tore his mouth away, she cried out in protest.

Matt pushed her head down to his shoulder and held it there. He was stunned. He'd never expected to feel this way again after losing Angela. Rena's response to him excited him beyond all reason.

Eventually his heart slowed and his breathing returned to normal. "I'm sorry, Rena. I . . . didn't mean for that to happen."

Serena pulled her head back to look at him. "I know," she whispered. "But it's not wrong, Matt. Nothing that feels so right could ever be wrong."

Matt swallowed heavily. That was the problem — it did feel right. Her body pressed up tight against his felt right. His lips against hers felt right. Their breaths mingling together felt right. Everything in the whole world felt right when he was holding her.

Yet it was wrong.

"You're so trusting, so innocent," he murmured, running a calloused thumb across her swollen lips. "I shouldn't be teaching you these things."

"Who else should teach me?" She curved her hand around his cheek. "You're the one who taught me how to ride a horse, how to shoot a gun, how to do a dozen different things. You taught me how to survive. Now teach me how to live."

Her lips captured his and Matt succumbed to their magic.

Serena's emotions nearly overwhelmed her as she clung to him. She scarcely knew when he rolled her onto her back. She arched against him, trying to get closer, wishing she could somehow crawl inside his skin and become part of him. When his hand cupped her breast, she moaned and arched herself more fully into his palm.

Her response nearly drove Matt out of his mind. He tore his mouth free and trailed hot, moist kisses down her neck and over the mound of flesh that begged for his lips. He closed his mouth over nightgown and nipple.

When he sucked the hard nub into his hot, wet mouth, Serena's back rose clear off the mattress. She cried out his name and clung to him, one hand on the back of his head to hold him closer.

Silver threads connected her breasts and the juncture of her thighs, and Matt was pulling them, plucking them, with every move of his mouth on her nipple. She thrust herself against his hips in an unconscious effort to end the torment she never wanted to end.

She moved so provocatively against him that he groaned. Her hands, first fluttering across his back, then clutching his shoulders, did wild things to his heartbeat, to his mind. He sipped at her breast again before moving up to recapture her lips in a kiss hungrier, hotter than the one before.

He rolled onto his back and took her with him, their lips still seared together. She fit perfectly in the cradle of his hips. He moved beneath her and she answered by pressing herself more firmly into his loins. His hips taught hers the ancient rhythm, as old as time itself, shared by lovers since the first dawn.

But soon it became too much. And not enough. Matt felt his control slipping away faster and faster. With what little remained of his sanity, he tore his mouth from hers and forced her head down to his shoulder again. With his other hand, he pressed her hips firmly against his to still her erotic movements that drove him wild.

"Don't move," he gasped.

She squirmed beneath his hand.

"For God's sake, Rena, don't move, or I'm liable to disgrace us both."

It wasn't his words that stilled her hips, for she barely heard them over her own labored breathing and pounding heart. It was the ragged edge of hysteria she felt in his shaking hands that penetrated the fog of passion in her brain.

For a long time neither of them moved, except to gasp for air. Finally their heartbeats slowed and their breath came easier as the storm of emotions subsided.

"Rena?" he whispered. "Are you all right?" His hand trembled when he smoothed the hair from her face.

She raised her head and looked at him. The moon had moved, now bathing their faces in pale light. Matt saw the look of total wonder in her eyes. "God, don't look at me like that."

She traced a finger across his full lower lip. "I can't help it," she breathed. "I didn't know . . . it would be like this."

"I know you didn't. You shouldn't know it now," he said, squeezing his eyes shut. "Not with me." It was a long moment before he could look at her.

Her wide gaze searched his face, then a wicked smile teased her lips. "You'd rather I learned from someone else?"

The mere thought of Rena with some other man was enough to choke him. Matt tightened his arms around her, nearly cutting off her breath, and pushed her head back to his shoulder. "No!" The word felt as if it were torn from somewhere deep inside him.

God help him. What was he going to do now?

Nine

Serena ran her fingers lovingly over the indentation in the pillow where Matt's head had lain. Her eyes drifted closed as she relived the sensations his touch had created last night in the moonlight. She unfolded them one by one, secret treasures she would cherish for the rest of her life. Precious memories of the man she loved.

The smell of coffee sailed through the open door on the morning breeze. They'd been doing their cooking outdoors since the weather had warmed up.

Serena threw back the covers with a burst of energy and climbed from the bed. She was suddenly starved for the sight of him. But what a mess she was! She didn't want him to see her like this.

She splashed cold water on her face and dressed carefully in a blue cotton dress with a scooped neck and elbow-length sleeves. The snug waist emphasized her breasts and the pale color matched her eyes. She'd always been told she looked good in this dress.

With trembling fingers she brushed her hair, then coiled it at the back of her head. She stepped into a pair of soft kid slippers, ran her hands nervously down the front of her dress, and walked outside.

"What are you doing?" she cried.

Matt didn't look up. He was seated on the flat rock, unwrapping the bandages holding his splint in place. "What's it look like?" he said gruffly.

Serena rushed to his side and put her hand on his shoulder. He stiffened, then shrugged her hand off. "Don't."

A shaft of pain shot through her. She backed away and closed her eyes. After all that had happened, all they had shared last night, nothing had changed. She read him like a book. He blamed himself for everything and felt guilty as hell for letting last night happen in the first place.

Her heart pounded, her hands trembled. She had to bite her tongue to keep from screaming. *Can't you see how much I love you? How much you need me? How right we are together?*

But he didn't see it. Wouldn't.

As calmly as she could, keeping her gaze lowered, she knelt before him. "Let me do it," she said, brushing his hands away.

"I can do it."

"I know you can. But I don't trust your judgment on whether or not it's healed."

With swift, efficient movements, she finished unwinding the bandage and removed the splints, then the second bandage next to his skin that kept the splints from rubbing him raw. She'd removed his stitches weeks ago and the cut was no more than a faint scar.

His skin felt warm and vibrant to her touch. At the first contact of her fingers against his flesh, Matt stiffened. She knew she hadn't hurt him, but if he was that stiff to start with, how would she know if she did hurt him? She probed along his shinbone. "How does that feel?"

"Like you're trying to gouge a hole in me."

"Does it hurt?"

"No."

The bone beneath her fingers felt whole and smooth and straight. "All right, stand up. But don't put any weight on this leg 'til I tell you. Use a crutch."

He did as she ordered, gradually putting more and more weight on the leg while she felt where the break had been. When his weight was equally distributed on both legs, she stood back. "Does it hurt?"

He looked over her shoulder, at the ground—anywhere but in her eyes. "No."

"Would you tell me if it did?"

His gaze jerked to her face as a guilty flush stained his cheeks. "It's . . . uh . . . a little weak, that's all."

"Keep a crutch handy 'til your leg feels stronger. And for goodness sake, take it easy. The splint really should stay on another couple of weeks." She turned and started for the house. She had to get away from him. The distance he'd put between them this morning was tearing her apart. He was so aloof, so cold. He wasn't the same man who held her last night.

They should have awakened together in each other's arms. There should have been good morning kisses and touches and sighs. There should have been tenderness and sweet words.

"Rena?"

She halted and held her breath. She didn't turn around. "Yes?"

"We need to talk."

147

She clasped her hands at her waist to still their trembling. "If it's about last night, I know what you're going to say."

"Do you?"

"Yes." She turned then and faced him. "You're going to tell me how wrong it was, that it shouldn't have happened."

"I'm . . . glad you understand."

"I understand," she said. "But that doesn't mean I like it, or that I agree with you. You woke up this morning consumed with guilt because sometime during the night you managed to convince yourself you'd been seducing your little sister. And if you dare say you're sorry one more time, I'll scream."

She felt his gaze on her like a warm caress. Like a soft goodbye.

"You're an incredible woman, Rena. Last night was . . . well, to be honest, I felt things last night I never thought I'd feel again, never wanted to feel again. It was good. It was wonderful. For any other two people in the world it would have been perfect. But not for us, Serena."

His voice turned rough. "It's not right for you and me to feel things like that for each other. Nothing could ever come of it. We'd only end up destroying ourselves, as well as the rest of the family. I can't let that happen. I don't ever want to be the cause of your pain."

"You think what you're saying right now doesn't hurt?"

"Better now, like this, than to let things go any further."

Serena bowed her head and took a deep breath, then

148

looked him in the eye. "Okay, you've had your say. Now it's my turn. I think you believe everything you've just said. And if that's the way you feel, then that's the way it'll be. But I think you'd be saying the same thing no matter who you were with last night. I think you've decided that if you can't have Angela, then you don't need anybody."

"This has nothing to do with — "

"I say it does," Serena interrupted, taking a step toward him. "I know how much you loved her, Matt. And I can only imagine what it was like for you to lose her. But you can't spend the rest of your life alone, living on memories."

She took a shallow breath, all her lungs would allow. "Memories can't hold you in the night and keep you warm. You can't reach out and touch them when you're lonely. They won't laugh with you or cry with you or make that empty feeling in the bottom of your heart go away. If you can think of me only as your sister, there's nothing I can do about it. But if not me, then find someone else, Matt. Find someone to share your life with before all that love you have trapped inside you shrivels up and turns you into a bitter old man."

Matt looked away to hide his discomfort. Some of her words struck a little too close to home to suit him. When he looked back, she was gone. He sat down again to take the weight off his leg. He wished he could get Serena off his mind as easily.

What was she suggesting? That she spend the rest of her life with him? Did she fancy herself in love with him? Impossible. She was too young to have feelings like that.

149

You weren't, at nineteen. That's when you met Angela.

That's different.

Angela was only seventeen. You never thought she was too young.

That's different.

If it were anyone else but Rena . . .

Hell. Who was he trying to kid? He wasn't ready for another woman in his life. Never would be. No one could take Angela's place. No one.

But if he were any other man . . .

She came outside just then and he took in the perfection of her face, the temptation of her lips. With her beauty, her generous, loving nature, she could tempt a man to do just about anything. Some other man, anyway. But not him. No. Not him.

Then he noticed she had changed clothes. The blue dress she'd been wearing was replaced by a white blouse and brown skirt. She wore a low-crowned, broad-brimmed hat, and boots instead of her usual moccasins or the slippers she'd had on earlier. In one hand she carried her bulging carpetbag. Her face was carefully, deliberately blank.

Matt felt a tightening in his chest. "Going somewhere?"

Serena paused and looked at him. "I'm going home. I'll send Kali out with the wagon to pick you up. I'll have her bring a cane, so you can get rid of those crutches. Your horse will be at the livery."

"Just like that? You're leaving? I thought you came here to talk me into going home."

"I came here to get you on your feet. You're on your feet. You'll come home when you're ready."

150

Serena turned away and walked around the corner of the house toward the lean-to and makeshift corral. She refused Matt's help with saddling the horse and shortening the stirrups.

"Rena, don't go . . . at least, not like this."

She gave him a wry smile. "Don't go away angry and hurt, just go away? Is that what you mean?"

"I've hurt you," he said quietly. "I never meant to do that."

"I know, Matt. Don't worry about it. I'll be fine."

She tied the carpetbag behind the saddle and checked the cinch one more time. With eyes stinging, she hiked her skirt, revealing the pants she wore underneath, and swung astride into Matt's saddle. She had to swallow twice past the lump in her throat to get her voice to work. "There's plenty of food inside if Kali doesn't make it out 'til tomorrow," she said, without looking at him. "And Matt?"

"Yeah?" He couldn't keep the dismal tone from his voice.

"When you get ready to come home," she said, still not looking at him, "just send word ahead and I'll . . . go visit friends in town, or something."

"There's no need for that, Rena."

"Maybe, maybe not." She looked at him them. "All I know is that I came here to make you feel better, and I've only made you miserable. I don't want my presence at home to keep you away from Joanna. She needs you a lot more than she needs me."

"Rena—"

"Goodbye, Matt." She kicked the blue roan gelding, and he sprang from his haunches into a trot across the clearing and down the trail toward town.

151

Dust swirled in the horse's wake and clung to the thin film of sweat on Matt's skin as he watched Serena disappear.

"Damn."

The little adobe shack wasn't the same after Serena left. At times it took on the proportions of a huge cave, its emptiness rolling on forever. At other times it shrank to claustrophobic proportions, and Matt found he had to go outside to breathe.

But at any time, anywhere he looked, he saw Serena. She was there before the darkened fireplace, or curled up asleep on her now empty mattress, or sitting across the table from him, or outside, trying to chop wood. Or at the creek, lying naked in the crystal-clear water.

Matt cursed vividly, trying to banish the pictures and the feelings they roused in him.

The nightmare came again that night, for the first time in weeks. Angela laughed beside him on the wagon seat. Abe Scott rode out from the trees and pointed his gun. Angela threw herself in front of Matt. Scott fired. Angela crumpled against Matt's chest.

Then, as happened that last time, Angela's features changed, and it was Serena who lay dying in his arms, whispering, "I love you."

Matt came awake with a start. "No!" Sweat soaked his body. His lungs struggled for air. He tossed off the blanket and staggered outside.

It was nearly noon the next day before Kali showed up with the wagon. Hank and Josh rode in a few seconds later.

"About time you got here," Matt growled.

"My, my, aren't we testy this morning?" Kali said with her brows raised. She nodded to Hank and Josh. The two dismounted and began loading everything from the house into the wagon.

"Serena said you could use this." Kali threw a man's walking cane more or less directly at Matt's head.

Matt jerked and caught it just before it bounced off his face. "What's eating you?" he demanded.

"Humph."

Matt shook his head, then went to help Hank and Josh finish loading. After crating up the chickens and tying the goat to the back of the wagon, Matt took the reins from Kali and headed the wagon toward town.

Matt gave the blue roan a final pat and stepped out of the stall. Serena was as good as her word. Horse and tack had been right where she'd promised — at the OK Corral. But then, he'd known they would be.

He left by way of Allen Street and ignored the burned-out ruins that stretched more than a block beyond the livery. Not much "ruins" left, actually. The air rang with the sounds of hammers and saws. The rebuilding was well under way. Matt wondered if the town would think to do anything about the lack of available water should something else catch on fire.

He stepped incautiously around a stack of lumber and was rewarded with a shaft of pain up his shin. He cursed sharply. He'd forgotten to pamper the damned leg. He could practically hear Serena scolding him.

He gripped the cane tighter and led with it.

The next unburned building he came to housed the Crystal Palace. Matt stopped there for lunch. Afterward he walked the streets, visiting saloons and friends. If he was honest, he'd admit to himself he knew the saloons a hell of a lot better than he did the people.

He wasn't sure he was ready for that much honesty.

He didn't feel like talking. What he wanted was a drink. Damn. But he wouldn't.

A shudder ripped through him at the thought of what he'd gone through to dry out — what Serena had gone through. What she had put him through.

No. No drink. He wouldn't endure that again. Not by choice.

It was dark before he realized it. How long had he been walking around aimlessly? Three hours? Four? He couldn't remember. Each hour seemed like the last.

What was he doing here anyway, he wondered. Marking time. For what? But he knew the answer. He was ready to go home, but he wasn't ready to face Serena. What would he say to her? How should he act?

The questions were always the same. The answers were never there.

After dinner, he wandered into the Last Chance for a game of poker.

Kali greeted him at the door with a frown. "You still in town?"

Matt glared at her. "Nice to see you, too." He took an empty chair at a back table and waited for the current poker hand to end. Kali had pestered him all the way back to town that morning about his going home. He might be a lot more inclined to comply, except for her damned belligerent attitude.

He won a moderately large pot in his first round, then lost a few dollars in the next. That was usually the

154

way it went for him. Because he didn't really need the money and wasn't a serious gambler, he nearly always came out ahead. It was the poor slob who bet his last dollar trying to win enough to feed his family who usually lost.

Matt was bored. If he stayed in Tombstone, it would be the same thing night after night. The same lifeless faces, the same raucous laughter from Kali's same girls, the same stale, smoke-filled air, so thick you burned your eyes and lungs just thinking about it.

With a grunt of disgust, he threw in his hand and headed for the door. Just as he reached it, the door swung in and Caleb nearly stumbled into Matt. It was the first time they'd seen each other since the day of the picnic.

"Howdy, Colton," Caleb said casually. "See you're up on your feet. How's the leg?"

"Fine."

"Noticed your sister left town this morning."

Matt grunted and tried to step past Caleb to reach the door.

"By the way," Caleb said. "I hope you don't mind, but I thought I'd go calling on Serena in a few days. I'd like to see more of her."

Matt had an immediate flash of Serena lying in the shallow water of the stream. *I'd like to see more of her.* He clenched his fists and turned back toward Caleb. "Just what do you mean by that?" he demanded.

An expression suspiciously like a smirk crossed Caleb's face before he took on a look of total innocence. "Why, just that I'd like to spend more time with her . . . get to know her. She's a beautiful woman."

Matt didn't think about what he did next. An unconscious effort sent one foot back a half step and his right fist plowing into Caleb's mouth.

Caleb staggered into the bar and slid to the floor, a stunned look on his face.

"You keep the hell away from Serena. No cheap tinhorn drifter is fit to wipe her feet." Matt spun toward the door.

"Matt?" Kali called.

He stopped halfway through the door and glared back.

"Where are you going?" Kali asked sweetly, a secretive, satisfied smile playing on her lips.

"Home, damn it."

Ten

"Faster! Faster, Uncle Pace!" Joanna screamed, as Pace ran his horse directly at her.

Serena grinned at Joanna's look of total concentration. The child might consider it just a game or a trick, but Joanna knew Pace expected the best from her, and she would give it.

In the past year, Pace had taken it upon himself to teach Joanna everything the girl could learn about riding. The feat they practiced now was one Grandfather Cochise had taught the twins years ago. To Joanna it might be a game, but to the Apaches, the ability to jump onto a running horse could mean the difference between life and death.

Pace galloped toward the child at an all-out run. When he neared, he leaned down and extended his arm to her. Joanna's concentration was fierce as the dust swirled and the pounding hooves came closer. Her eyes were riveted on her uncle's arm. At just the right moment, she jumped into the air, wrapped both arms around his, and sailed up, up, up. Her short legs spread wide. Her skirt, with boys' pants underneath, flapped in the wind. With a half-shout, half-grunt, she landed with a jolt right behind Pace on the horse's rump.

Pace swung the horse wide and headed back toward Serena. He let out a shrill, spine-chilling Apache victory cry. Serena laughed and answered with one of her own, then Joanna's youthful voice chimed in, too.

"Sounds like a bunch of wild Indians around here."

Serena froze. Her heart missed a beat. She, Pace, and Joanna all turned toward the sound of the deep voice.

Pace grinned. "Well, it's about time."

Serena smiled nervously and wiped her suddenly sweating palms on her dusty skirt. She glanced from Matt to Joanna. The girl's wide-eyed look of wonder, of yearning, tugged at Serena's heart. But when Joanna clung to Pace's waist without moving, Serena grew concerned. "Jo?"

Joanna hugged Pace's back and stared at the man approaching them. He looked like . . . *Oh. Oh!* Heart pounding, she jerked into sudden motion. She scrambled down Pace's leg as if it were a ladder, then ran to Serena and clutched her aunt's arm with both hands.

"Is it him?" she demanded breathlessly. "It's him, isn't it! He came . . . just like you said he would." She couldn't take her gaze off the tall, blond-headed man who watched her from a few feet away. It had to be him. It *had* to be! The scar . . . the bear claws around his neck. It had to be him.

Joanna didn't wait for an answer. She stepped forward hesitantly, suddenly more afraid than she'd been since the day he'd left home, all those years ago, when she was little. "Did . . . did you come to see me?"

The big man with the scar on his cheek just like

Grandpa's knelt before her. His eyes looked shiny. "Of course I did, Pumpkin," he said hoarsely. "Aren't you my favorite girl?"

Joanna blinked. A tear ran down her cheek. She swiped at it with the back of her hand. It was him! It was! Everybody called her Pumpkin, but only her daddy had ever called her his favorite girl. Her voice cracked when she answered the way she always had, before he went away. "You m-mean . . . ex-cept for . . . Mama?"

Matt's own eyes filled then. He hadn't expected her to remember that. He forced his response past the lump in his throat. "Except for Mama."

He held out his arms, and Joanna threw herself at his chest. "You came! Oh, Daddy, Daddy, you came home!"

Matt closed his eyes and hugged her to him, his heart cracking at all the missed hugs, the missed years. Tears flowed freely down his cheeks.

The rest of the day and evening turned into a celebration. The whole family went wild with joy at Matt's return. Travis got emotional; Daniella cried. Jessica, the little organizer, made certain everyone had a chance to hug the prodigal. Spence, the future doctor of the family, actually tossed his beloved books aside for the entire evening, although he did, much to his parents' secret amusement, question Matt thoroughly on the condition of his newly healed leg.

Through it all, Matt and Joanna clung to each other as if afraid to let go.

Serena watched with a bright smile pasted on her

face. Her cheeks hurt from forcing the expression to remain in place, when what she really wanted was to hide in her room and cry.

She was overjoyed and thankful Matt was home. The light in their parents' eyes, not to mention Joanna's, made whatever she was feeling seem insignificant. But where did his homecoming leave her?

In Tombstone, Matt had needed her. Now he didn't. In the two days she'd been back, her parents had constantly needed her reassurances that he was all right, that he would be coming home. Now they didn't. For the past three years, Joanna had needed her. Now she wouldn't.

Serena had never felt so adrift and alone in her life. She shouldn't feel this way, she knew she shouldn't, but she couldn't help it. When Matt carried Joanna off to bed, Serena slipped out of the salon and made her way to her own room, where she quietly buried her face in her pillow and wept.

"Come on, Pumpkin," Matt said softly to his yawning daughter. "Let's get you to bed."

"She's in your old room, Matt," Dani informed him. "Yours is now the next door down the hall."

Matt closed his eyes and breathed a silent thank-you. He hadn't thought of having to sleep in the room he had shared with Angela, but he was grateful someone else had. He wasn't sure he could have handled sleeping there. Just entering the room was going to be bad enough.

But when Joanna opened the door and led him in, it wasn't bad at all. The room looked totally different

160

from when he and Angela had shared it. It was now a little girl's room, complete with ribbons and lace and bright yellow ruffles hanging from a canopied bed he'd never seen before.

"Where's Rena?" Joanna asked, peering back down the hall.

"I imagine she's still in the salon with the others."

"But she has to tuck me in." Wide green eyes stared up at him expectantly.

Matt suffered a sudden attack of nerves. It had been years since he'd helped his daughter get ready for bed. He'd forgotten what to do. Finding Serena seemed like a much easier task. "Would you like me to go get her?"

Joanna smiled shyly and nodded.

"You get ready for bed and I'll go find Rena."

But Serena wasn't in the salon with the others. He checked the study and then the courtyard before heading for her bedroom. He knocked softly on the closed door. "Rena?"

Serena stiffened. She hurriedly wiped the remainder of her tears away. What did he want?

"Joanna says you're supposed to tuck her in," Matt called through the door.

Serena sagged with a mixture of relief and disappointment. He hadn't come to see her, after all. Joanna had sent him. "I'm coming."

She opened her door and crossed the hall into Joanna's room, barely looking at Matt. Tucking Joanna into bed was something she'd been doing every night for three years. It was a ritual they shared, a nightly hugging and kissing and prayers. No matter what happened during the day, they could always count on those few minutes together.

But things were different now, with Matt home. Suddenly Serena felt like an intruder, as if she didn't belong to this intimate goodnight scene. She felt even more awkward when Joanna insisted Matt sit next to Serena on the edge of the bed.

The mattress sagged under his weight. Serena leaned forward to keep from touching him while Joanna said her prayers.

"Now I lay me down to sleep, I pray the Lord my soul to keep. If I should die before I wake, I pray the Lord my soul to take. And God," Joanna added, her hands clasped tightly together, "thank you for letting my daddy come home. Amen."

"Goodnight, sweetheart." Serena kissed Joanna and gave her a hug. Then fled.

After swallowing the giant lump in his throat, Matt kissed and hugged his daughter, turned out the lamp, and caught up with Serena in the hall. He took her by the arm and turned her toward the courtyard. "Walk with me a minute?" he asked.

Serena fought a shiver and kept her gaze lowered. She didn't want him to see what his touch did to her. He led her to a stone bench in the dark courtyard and pulled her down beside him. The night was warm, the air still. Matt dropped her arm and propped both elbows on his knees, then turned his head to look at her.

"Do you know," he said softly, "that the only thing you've said to me since I got home is 'I'm coming,' and even that was through a closed door."

"I-I didn't . . . realize. I'm sorry." Her mouth felt dry and her heart pounded. He sat so close she could feel the heat from his body. "Welcome home, Matt."

"Do you really mean that?"

162

"Of course I mean it." She tried to meet his gaze, but couldn't. "This is your home. Where else should you be?"

"But?"

Somewhere in the hills beyond the creek a coyote howled. "But what?"

"You don't seem very glad to see me."

"It's not that," she said quickly. "It's just . . . I thought you were going to write first," she blurted.

"So you could leave? So I wouldn't have to face you? This is your home, too, Rena. You shouldn't have to leave because of me."

Serena scuffed a shoe along the smooth stone beneath her feet and turned her face away from his piercing gaze. "I just thought you'd be more comfortable if I wasn't here, that's all."

"Why do I get the impression you're suddenly a lot more uncomfortable than I am? Are you afraid of me, Rena? Are you afraid that what happened that last night in Tombstone might happen again?"

He was blaming himself again, and she couldn't stand that. She placed a hand on his arm and her eyes found his through the darkness. "No, Matt, I'm not afraid of that, or of you. I know you'd never hurt me."

Matt dropped his head and stared at the ground. "I think I already have."

"No!" she said sharply. She squeezed his arm until he looked at her. "Listen to me. That night in Tombstone . . . it wasn't something you did, or something I did. It just . . . happened. And it happened to both of us."

"But it shouldn't have happened at all, damn it!" He jerked his arm free of her hold and stood with his back

163

to her. "I should have stopped it. I *could* have stopped it, but . . ."

Serena had to clasp her hands together to keep from reaching out to touch him. She forced her voice to remain steady. "You talk like you're the only one who was there. I was there, too, Matt. There were two of us in that bed. I may be inexperienced, but I'm not entirely stupid. I knew what was happening. I could have stopped it, too."

He whirled to face her. "Then for God's sake, why didn't you?"

Serena jumped to her feet. "A minute ago you were blaming yourself. Now you're blaming me. This whole thing is ridiculous! If it bothers you so much to think of me as a woman, then don't, damn it. We'll both just forget the entire thing and pretend it never happened. I'll be what you want me to be. In public, in front of the family, I'll be your *sister.*"

Her outburst stunned him. She spit the word "sister" out as though it were something foul. She stood before him, breasts heaving, eyes snapping, and it was all Matt could do to keep from crushing her to his chest.

He was crazy; that was the only answer. He must be insane to want her so much. He fought back the urge to kiss her, but he couldn't stop his question. "And in private?"

"There'll be no private," she hissed. "Not for us. Not for brother and sister. I wouldn't dream of compromising your high moral standards by tempting you beyond your endurance."

Serena stalked past him and headed into the house, ignoring his plea to stop. Her back was as rigid as a fence post until she was behind her closed door.

* * *

Matt appeared more than a little leery the next morning when Serena greeted him at the breakfast table with a brilliant smile. She steeled her nerves for the performance of her life. He wanted a sister; that's what he'd get.

"Morning, Matt," she said with forced brightness that sounded almost normal. "Did you sleep well your first night home?"

He sat down across the table from her and Joanna. "Fine." He narrowed his gaze at her. Serena could almost feel him trying to gauge her mood.

Jessica was the last to arrive. She sat between Matt and Spence with a breathless apology for being late. Platters heaped with eggs and ham made their way around the table, followed by baskets of biscuits, boats of gravy, and bowls of fresh fruit and preserves.

Joanna watched her father sip his coffee and sat a little straighter in her chair. "I'm a big girl now, Daddy," she blurted.

Serena steeled her heart against the tender look on Matt's face as he smiled at the little girl who sat on two pillows so she could reach her plate.

"You sure are, Pumpkin," he said.

"Then how come I can't drink coffee, like you?"

Matt's lips twitched. "You don't like milk?"

"Milk's for babies," Joanna said with disgust.

He pursed his lips a moment, then reached out and switched his cup of coffee with her glass of milk. "Is that better?"

Joanna's eyes grew big and round as she stared with awe at the steaming cup of coffee next to her plate. "You mean it? I can drink it?"

165

"Sure," he said easily. "But I'll warn you, it's not near as good as milk. And it's real hot, so you'll have to be careful." He took a long drink of milk and let out a satisfied sigh. "Oh, yeah," he said. "That's much better than coffee."

Liar, Serena thought, suddenly amused. She *knew* how much he hated milk.

Joanna eyed him skeptically. "You like milk?"

"Sure I do. When I was sick, your Aunt Rena gave me milk every day."

"And it made you get better?"

"Yep."

"But you're not sick now, are you?"

"No. Now I drink it just because I like it."

It was all Serena could do to keep a straight face.

"How about you?" Matt asked his daughter. "How do you like your coffee?"

Joanna picked up her cup carefully with both hands and blew on the steamy liquid. She took a hesitant sip, then shuddered and returned the cup to its saucer. "Yuck! That's terrible."

The adults choked back their laughter, but Jessica spoke up. "That's what I say, Jo. I don't know how anybody can stand the stuff. I'd rather drink mud."

Joanna wrinkled her nose and pushed the cup away. She watched her father take another drink of her milk. The plea was plain on her face.

"You wanna share?" Matt asked.

Joanna did indeed want to share the milk, rather than drink the coffee. A few minutes later, she was the first one finished eating and asked to be excused.

When she was gone, Serena turned on Matt and fought to keep from laughing. "You should be

166

ashamed of yourself, lying to a child that way."

"Who, me?" he asked innocently. "I never lie."

"You do, too, you rat. I had to force that milk down you, and you know it."

"I never said I didn't like milk. If you'd been paying attention, the only thing I complained about was the quantity. You tried to drown me in the stuff."

"I did not," she protested.

"Five glasses a day is drowning, Rena."

Travis threw back his head and laughed. "Five a day?"

"You really did try to drown him, didn't you?" Pace added.

Serena narrowed her gaze at Matt in mock anger. "Jessie, I can't reach that far. Would you please slap your brother for me?"

Jessica grinned up at Matt and said, "Sure thing." Then her left hand shot out and slapped Spence on the arm.

Laughter spread around the table. Spence never even looked up. He had his nose buried in a history of Julius Caesar and was oblivious to everything around him.

Serena did all right for the rest of the day. She managed to keep away from Matt as much as possible, getting near him only at mealtime. But during supper, trouble started. She'd been watching Matt when she thought he wasn't looking, but he caught her at it. When she passed him the potatoes, their gazes locked. When their fingers accidentally touched, they both reacted as if they'd been stung.

Serena jerked her hand away from the bowl and glanced quickly around the table to see if anyone noticed their behavior. Her gaze collided with Pace's as he scowled at her. His thoughts flew into her brain.

Tell me what my eyes see is not true.

I don't know what you're talking about.

His touch makes you tremble!

Serena glanced to the end of the table, relieved to see her mother in conversation with Spence. Sometimes her mother could pick up on the thoughts the twins flung at each other, but only if she concentrated. *You're mistaken,* she told Pace in her head.

You love him! Pace's thoughts dripped with outrage.

Serena glared at him. *Leave me alone. It's none of your business.*

Daniella might not have been paying attention, but Matt was. He didn't know what they said to each other, but he knew Pace was angry, and he had the uneasy feeling it had something to do with him. He was certain a few moments later when Pace turned to glare at him with cold blue eyes. Dani's eyes. Serena's eyes.

Serena escaped the table as soon as politely possible and headed for her room, but she wasn't fast enough. Matt caught her in the hall and stopped her.

"What's going on, Rena?"

She tried to tug her arm free of his grasp, but he held on. "I don't know what you mean."

"What's Pace so upset about?"

"Is he upset?"

"Don't lie. The two of you nearly set the table on fire. If looks could kill, I'd be dead from the one he gave me."

"I didn't tell him anything, if that's what you're worried about."

Matt sighed with frustration. "I never thought that."

"Would you let go of my arm, please?"

"Sorry." He released her, then paused. "Joanna will want you to tuck her in soon."

"I've been putting her to bed every night for over three years. It's not something I'm likely to forget."

"I didn't mean it like that."

But Serena didn't answer. She went into her room and shut the door behind her.

She'd been doing a lot of that lately.

Later that night, after kissing Joanna good night while Matt watched, Serena tried to escape to her room again, but Joanna stopped her cold at the door.

"Good night, Daddy," the child said, as Matt hugged her. Then she called to Serena at the door. "Good night, Mama."

Serena felt the blood drain from her face. A giant fist squeezed the breath from her lungs. Never in her life had she wanted to run and hide like she did just then. But she couldn't. This was something that had to be straightened out now. It wasn't fair to anyone to let the girl get away with such a thing.

Serena crossed the room slowly and knelt beside the bed. When she reached a trembling hand to brush a strand of hair from Joanna's face, her shoulder brushed Matt's knee. She flinched at the contact.

"You shouldn't call me that, Pumpkin." Her voice shook with emotion as she struggled to keep from weeping.

"Why not?"

"You know why not, Joanna. I love you very much,

169

but I'm not your mother, I'm your aunt."

"Don't you wanna be my mother?"

It was a long minute before Serena could speak past the huge lump in her throat. "It's not a question of what I want, sweetheart, or even what you want. It's just the way things are."

"But—"

"That's enough, Joanna," Matt interrupted softly. "It's time you were asleep. We'll talk about this another time." When he leaned down to kiss Joanna's cheek, Serena stood and fled as fast as her trembling legs would carry her.

She dashed down the hall and out into the empty courtyard until she stumbled into the peach tree in the far corner. She clutched at it desperately as anguish overwhelmed her. One sob after another escaped her tortured throat.

And that's how Matt found her a few minutes later, clinging to the tree, crying against the rough bark. He pulled her away and turned her into his chest. When her arms crept around his waist, a multitude of feelings washed over him. He felt sympathy for the pain she was experiencing, and an overwhelming desire to protect her and make her pain go away. There was no lust in him as he held her trembling body next to his, but there was something warmer, softer, stronger . . . scarier.

"Don't cry, Rena," he said roughly. He tightened his arms around her. "She didn't mean to hurt you. She doesn't understand."

"And you do?" Serena asked, her voice breaking on a sob.

"I think so." She tried to pull away, but he held her,

one hand pressing her head against his shoulder. "You've been mother and father both to her, as well as aunt, for three years. It's only natural you'd come to think of her as yours."

"Oh, Matt, I swear . . . I swear she's never called me that before. I'd never have let her call me that."

"I know, I know." Another sob shook her. Matt pressed his lips against her hair. "You'll never lose her, Rena, I promise you that. I'd never separate the two of you. Don't cry anymore, honey. I can't stand it when you cry."

His arms were so strong, his breath against her face so warm. Finally she began to relax in his embrace. When his lips touched her forehead, she sighed and closed her eyes. Then he began kissing the tears from her lashes and cheeks. As his lips neared hers, her heart pounded and her knees started shaking.

She had promised herself she wouldn't let this happen again. She wouldn't get close enough to let him kiss her. But as his lips hovered over hers . . . *Just this once. Only once.*

Serena raised her face and opened her lips to his. The kiss was so tender that fresh tears seeped from beneath her lashes and a soft whimper escaped her throat.

"Shh," he whispered against her lips. "It's all right. Shh." His lips nipped softly at hers, then sipped the new tears from her cheeks. He pressed her head back against his shoulder. "Come on. I'll walk you to your room."

He kept his arm around her shoulders and walked her to her door. There, he cupped her face in both hands and brushed his lips across her forehead. "Get

171

some sleep, sweetheart."

Serena waited until he'd gone to his room and closed his door before she went into her own room. She touched her fingers to lips that still tingled from his kiss. The tears started again. They didn't stop until sometime after she fell asleep.

Eleven

Serena thanked Pace for hitching the gray mare to the buggy.

"You gonna be all right?" he demanded.

"I'm fine, Pace. I'm just going to visit Sylvia for a while, that's all." She knew her sudden departure troubled Pace, but her mind was too filled with her own problems to worry about his. "I'll be back in a week or two. I'll leave the horse and buggy at Leatherwood's Livery in case Mama wants to send someone for it."

A few minutes later, Serena was down the road and out of sight of the house. She wiped impatiently at the tears stinging her eyes. She was being a coward again, running away like this. It made her angry with herself. Grandfather Cochise would be ashamed of her. She could hear his voice on the morning breeze.

"You cannot run from pain, *bizáayéń,* little one, for it will follow wherever you go. To run from it is to acknowledge it, to admit it is more powerful than you. To acknowledge pain and give in to it is to allow it to control you. Pain is like fear. It happens, but you must never let it show. Pain and fear are your enemies. The *Chidikáágu'* do not run from their enemies, granddaughter."

Yes, Grandfather would be ashamed of her. She was half Chiricahua, and the Chiricahua did not run from pain. But she kept her face to the west and urged the horse on toward Tucson. She wasn't really running from the pain, anyway, she decided, because it was still with her, and would be. She was running from the source of the pain—Matt. And Joanna.

Serena might have been all right, might have been able to deal with Joanna calling her "Mama," if Matt hadn't been so . . . so sympathetic and understanding, so tender and caring. If he'd just left her alone, she might have been able to stand it.

If. What was the use in "if"? He hadn't left her alone. He had shown his brotherly concern, followed by a not-so-brotherly yet passionless kiss, and here she was, on the road to Tucson, running away.

The sun crept over the mountains at her back and cast long shadows before her. Some distance up the road, light flashed off metal. Serena soon realized a rider was coming her way. She reached into her drawstring bag next to her on the seat and checked her derringer to be sure it was loaded. A rider this far from town, this early in the morning, could spell trouble.

She was relieved a few minutes later when the rider came closer and she recognized Caleb. Relieved, but surprised, and more than a little puzzled. She pulled on the reins to slow the mare as Caleb turned his gelding and rode beside the buggy.

"Good morning!" he said, doffing his hat. "Would you believe you're just the person I was coming to see?"

At this hour? "Not really," she said, smiling.

His face took on a look of mock dismay. He held his hat over his heart. "Oh, but it's true." Eyes twinkling,

174

he settled the dusty brown Stetson back on his head. "Is it all right if I tie my horse on behind and ride with you a spell?"

"Where've you been?" Travis asked, when Pace finally showed up for breakfast. "Where's Rena?"

Keeping his gaze lowered, Pace sat down and began filling his plate. "I was just hitching up the buggy for her. She's headed into town for a couple of weeks to stay with the Ortegas."

Matt slammed his fork down beside his plate. "She's *what?*" he demanded.

Pace raised his gaze to his brother slowly. When he spoke, his soft voice carried a hint of steel. "You heard me."

Daniella set down her cup of coffee carefully. "She didn't say anything to us about staying in town." She looked to Travis for confirmation. He shook his head.

Pace glared at Matt. "It was a sudden decision."

"Damn that girl," Matt muttered. "How long ago did she leave?"

"About a half hour," Pace said, lowering his gaze to his plate again.

Matt excused himself and rushed from the room.

Pace's face turned to stone as he rose to follow. His mother stopped him with a hand on his arm. At the look of fury in his eyes, she let go of him. "What's going on?" she demanded.

"Trouble, that's what."

Pace caught up with Matt just inside the barn. He grabbed the older, larger man by the shoulder and spun him around. A hard right to the jaw took Matt completely by surprise. He staggered backward and stared at Pace in total amazement.

Raised as brothers, the two had naturally had their share of disagreements over the years, but they had never struck each other in anger. Never.

"Are you crazy? What the hell was that for?" Matt demanded.

"*Shilghúkéne,*" Pace said with a snarl.

"*Your* sister? I was under the impression she was *my* sister, too."

"Not to hear her tell it."

A cold feeling of dread washed over Matt. "You got something to say, *shik' is,* brother, then say it."

"I say you're not going after her."

"The hell I'm not. I'm damn sick and tired of having her run off and hide every time something upsets her. She and I have unfinished business to discuss." He wasn't sure just how he would handle that business. He intended to talk to Joanna himself about her calling Rena her mother. He couldn't let Serena leave this way. He couldn't let her hurt.

"Leave her alone, goddammit. You know good and well the only time she runs and hides, as you put it, is when she hurts so much she can't take any more." Pace glared at the brother he'd always looked up to, the brother he'd always trusted, and felt the rage and betrayal well up in his chest. "What did you do to her this time, damn you?"

Matt's face looked like it was carved from granite, except for the muscle twitching along his jaw. The scar on his cheek turned red. His gaze wouldn't meet Pace's.

"Christ!" Pace cried. "I should have known better than to let her go to Tombstone. She never did have any sense when it came to you."

"What are you talking about?"

"Don't play dumb with me. You know damn well she thinks she's in love with you."

The look of stunned horror on Matt's face, his sudden pallor, brought a sharp bark of harsh laughter from Pace. "You didn't know!" he crowed. "The great know-it-all Matt Colton can't tell when a girl's in love with him. Well, what do you know about that?"

"No!" Matt protested. "You're wrong. She can't be."

"I wish to hell I was. She's had her sights set on you since we were kids. I thought everything was going to be fine when Angela came along. And it was, 'til Tombstone."

Matt turned and headed for his saddle. "I've got to talk to her."

"Don't, Matt. Leave it be. What are you planning to do, ride up to her and ask her if it's true? Leave her alone. Give her some time to herself. She's spent the last three years looking after Joanna like the girl was her own. Then she spent weeks with you in Tombstone. She hasn't had one minute to herself since she was sixteen. Give her a little room, Matt. Besides," he added, "you'll only embarrass her if she finds out you know."

Matt gripped the saddle until his knuckles turned white. It was all he could do to keep his voice steady when he said, "I can't let her hurt because of me, Pace. I can't."

"I don't know what's been going on between you two, if anything, but give her a few days, at least. And for God's sake, when she comes home, don't tell her what I've said."

"Thanks," Matt said sarcastically. "But I'm not quite that stupid, little brother. I think you're just trying to save your own hide."

"Damn right," Pace said with a tight grin. "She finds out I opened my mouth, she'd make what you did to Scott look like some sort of beauty treatment compared with what she'd do to me."

Matt purposely let the mention of Abe Scott distract him. He'd never talked with Pace about what happened down in Mexico, and it was long past time he did. "About Scott."

"What about him?"

"I . . . I'm sorry you had to see all that," Matt said with a wave of his hand. "I shouldn't have . . ."

"Shouldn't have what? You don't mean you shouldn't have killed the bastard?" Pace demanded. "Everything you did, he had coming to him, and more."

Matt shook his head. "I shouldn't have done it in front of you."

"Hell, Matt, what does that have to do with anything? The only thing you shouldn't have done was let that buzzard bait off so damn easy."

Easy? Good God. And here he'd been thinking for months that what Pace had seen in the hidden canyon had upset him. Matt shook his head again.

"Like I said," Pace muttered. "Serena will make all that look tame if she knows I've opened my mouth."

"Just why did you tell me?"

A cold, hostile mask settled over Pace's face. If it weren't for the blue eyes, Matt would have sworn he was looking at a full-blooded, hate-filled Chiricahua warrior.

"So there wouldn't be any more scenes like the one last night out in the courtyard, you bastard."

* * *

Serena would rather have avoided having Caleb join her at all, much less ride with her in the buggy, but she merely shrugged. What could it hurt? Maybe he was just the thing she needed to take her mind off her troubles. He was friendly, cheerful, and totally harmless.

"You'll have to get back on your horse before we reach town," she warned him jokingly. "After all, a single girl has her reputation to uphold. If we were seen together in this buggy, the gossip would start before we passed the first house. By the end of the day the whole town would have us marching down the aisle within the week."

Caleb laughed and joined her on the padded leather seat. "Actually, I really was looking for you," he said, taking the reins from her hands and urging the horse forward.

"Why?"

"You left Tombstone so sudden-like, then, the next day, Matt did the same thing. I guess I just wanted to make sure everything was all right."

"Thank you for your concern, Caleb. I appreciate it, and I'm sure Matt does, too, but everything's fine. I hate it that you made such a long trip just because of us."

"It was worth it." He gave her a smile. "I got to see you, didn't I?"

Serena cocked her head and looked at him in confusion. He was starting to sound almost forward. That was something new. Had he just been on his best behavior in Tombstone? Or had she somehow mistakenly encouraged him?

"Besides," he said, "my business in Tombstone was finished. It was time to move on."

The buggy rattled on down the road, dust curling up

in plumes behind it. The sun rose higher. Caleb plied Serena with questions about Tucson. It was a full minute after he pulled off the road and headed for the trees before she realized what he'd done.

She tensed. "What are you doing?" she asked sharply.

"There's something over here I want to show you. It's not far."

"Caleb, I seriously doubt there's anything in this entire territory you could show me that I haven't already seen at least a dozen times. I'd appreciate it if you'd turn around and get back on the road. I have an appointment in town. I don't want to be late."

"In a minute," he said easily.

"Give me the reins, Caleb."

He only smiled and kept driving. Irritated, but not yet angry or frightened, Serena made a sudden grab for the reins.

Caleb, however, was faster. He grabbed both her hands in one of his. "Just take it easy. We're almost there."

He drove the buggy in a straight line due south from the road. Serena knew that if she'd been looking behind her, the road would have disappeared several minutes ago.

Anger simmered in her veins. Just who did he think he was, dragging her off this way? And what kind of idiot was she to have allowed it?

He hadn't said anything in quite a while, and that worried her. So did the confident look on his face. Her anger slowly seeped away, to be replaced by a strong sense of unease.

This is ridiculous, she chided herself. *Toss him out on his ear and turn this damned buggy around.*

180

Just then it seemed that Caleb was willing to cooperate with her wishes, for he guided the buggy around a scraggly clump of cedars and pulled to a halt. He reached across her and tied the reins to the whip, which still rested in its socket near Serena's right knee.

Good, she thought, as he stepped down from the buggy. She reached for the reins herself, intent on getting out of these trees, away from Caleb, and back on the road.

Caleb leaned into the buggy and placed a hand boldly on her left knee. "Leave them," he said, indicating the reins.

The look she gave him as she glanced up from where his hand now squeezed her thigh was cold enough to freeze milk. She'd used that look before on men, always with the results she desired.

But not this time. Caleb's eyes blazed and his lips parted in a leering grin. His face took on characteristics she'd never noticed before. He'd always been polite, friendly, and smiling. There was nothing polite or friendly about this smile, however. Suddenly he looked hard, determined . . . dangerous.

Serena's throat tightened. There was something going on here — something she didn't understand, didn't want to understand. It was past time to leave.

Without warning, she knocked his hand from her leg and reached again for the reins. Again she wasn't fast enough. Caleb grabbed her by the arm and yanked her across the seat until her face was only inches from his. "I said, leave them."

He stepped back and jerked her hard. As he did, she reached with her free hand for something to hang on to, but caught only her drawstring purse. She managed to loosen the opening and slip her hand inside the bag. Gritting her teeth in determination, she clasped her hand around the cool, smooth butt of her mother's two-shot derringer.

Her thigh hit the front wheel hard. She winced. But she couldn't grab the seat with her free hand, couldn't stop him from pulling her out of the buggy without letting go of the gun. That she refused to do. When her feet finally hit the ground, he jerked on her arm again and she stumbled into him. The back of her skirt ripped where it snagged on the wheel.

"What the hell do you think you're doing?" she demanded.

Caleb's grin broadened. "I've got some unfinished business in these parts, and you're gonna help me finish it."

She shook her right hand twice and the purse fell away. "That's what you think, mister." She swung the little double-barrelled pistol up to point directly in his face.

For one brief instant, Caleb froze, his eyes wide with disbelief. Then in a flash, his hand came up with a chopping blow to her wrist. Serena's hand flew up. The gun discharged, the bullet whizzing harmlessly into the air.

Her hand felt numb and her wrist ached something fierce, but she kept a deadly grip on the derringer. One shot wasted. The next one had to count.

When she brought the gun back down, Caleb released her other arm and grabbed her wrist with both hands. They struggled, but she was no match for his strength. He squeezed until she cried out in pain, then he squeezed some more. She never even felt her finger pull the trigger, but the gun went off, the shot embedding itself into the trunk of the nearest tree.

He released her then and grinned. He knew the gun was empty. The fool thought that meant the fight was over. *The hell it is.* Serena had no intention of giving up simply because she was out of bullets. She raised her arm back and swung. He ducked. The blow she aimed at his temple landed on the top of his head instead.

Caleb cursed, then grabbed a handful of hair beneath the brim of her bonnet and yanked. Serena winced and gritted her teeth. Her breath came in hard gasps, but fear and anger lent her strength. She whacked him on the wrist bone with her gun.

He yowled and released her hair immediately to grasp his wrist. The grin had long since disappeared from his face.

As he advanced on her, Serena stepped back. "Keep away," she warned.

His grin returned, evil and menacing. He took another step forward.

Serena backed up again and felt the buggy wheel through the back of her skirt. If she could distract him, get him off guard for just a second, she might have enough time to reach the whip on the far side of the buggy. Maybe.

Caleb chuckled. "I've got you now, girl." He took another step forward.

One more step, and he'd be close enough to grab her! Just as he shifted his weight to step again, Serena reared back and threw the derringer at his head.

Her action took him by surprise. The little gun struck him hard on the cheek, just below his eye. The skin broke. Blood trickled down his face. His bellow of pain and rage echoed on the still morning air.

Taking her chance, Serena spun and stretched past

183

the front wheel, across the floorboard, until her fingers brushed the whip just below where the reins were tied. She'd have to free the knot in order to get it. Her fingers fumbled, tugging on the knot, trying to loosen it.

The mare, nervous over all the commotion, tried to sidestep between the buggy shafts. The whole buggy jerked and shuddered. Serena's fingers slipped from the knot. A fingernail tore loose. She swore and reached again, only to be yanked backward by a pair of hard hands on her waist. Backward, into a hard, broad chest. When her head snapped and caught him in the chin, Serena and Caleb both grunted.

Caleb dragged her away from the buggy once more while she squirmed and fought him all the way. He managed to turn her around in his arms.

That was his mistake.

With no second thought, Serena raised her knee in a swift, sharp thrust and caught him right between the legs.

Caleb screamed like a woman and thrust her roughly away.

She stumbled and fell, landing in a heap of skirts and petticoats near his feet. He crouched before her, his face pale and twisted in a grimace of pain, his hands holding his crotch, his eyes glazed.

Serena grinned in triumph, and let her gaze fall from his as she struggled to rise.

And that was her mistake.

With a roar of rage, Caleb dealt her a vicious backhand across the face. Her head snapped back. She hit the ground hard. Her breath whooshed out. Blackness crept in until only two tiny pinpoints of light remained. When her vision cleared, she was staring down the barrel of a .45 caliber double-action Colt Thunderer—the same gun used these days by the United States Army. The hammer was back. The finger on the trigger was sweaty and tight.

Serena froze. Her eyes widened, her mouth dried up, and her heart pounded its way into her throat.

"Don't move." Caleb straightened slightly, his breath still coming in short gasps. "I like a little fight in a woman, but girl, you've got more than your fair share. Must be all that Apache blood, huh?"

She felt her heart slide back down into her chest. If he wanted to talk, then he wasn't ready to kill her . . . yet. But she'd be damned if she'd let the bastard see her fear. She raised her gaze slowly to his and took a short breath. "That Apache blood will see you dead for this."

Maybe it was the calm, matter-of-fact tone in her voice, the confident tilt of her chin, or the ice and fire that glowed in her pale blue eyes. Maybe it was the slight smile on her lush lips; Caleb wasn't exactly sure. But something sent a cold shaft of foreboding stabbing through his gut. A faint shadow passed before his eyes, then the brightness of the day returned, making him feel foolish for his fear.

"Get up," he growled.

Serena clenched her fists. "Why should I?" If she got up now, he'd see how badly she was trembling. She couldn't let him see her fear. It would be another weapon in his hands to be used against her at his will. "If you're going to kill me anyway, why should I do what you say?"

"I might kill you," he said with a nod. "Maybe. Eventually. But I really don't want to. Not yet. But if you don't do like I say, I *will* shoot you. Not bad enough to kill you, though. Just bad enough to make you wish I had. Now, get up."

Serena paled at his threat. The strange light in his eyes told her he was just crazy enough to do what he said. She pushed herself to her feet, slowly, deliberately, her eyes locked on his. His hand snaked out and yanked the bonnet from her head.

"Take off that dress," he ordered.

Her eyes widened. Did he mean to rape her? *I'll die first,* she thought.

When she didn't move to obey him, he forced his fingers inside the neckline of her dress and ripped it open clear to her waist. Serena gasped.

"Take it off, goddammit!"

To give herself time to think, she did as he demanded. She had to find a way either to get free, or to force him to kill her. She would not be raped. Not while she lived.

When her trembling fingers had discarded the dress, he motioned to her petticoats with the end of his gun. She untied them and let them fall to the ground. Wearing nothing but camisole, drawers, stockings, and shoes, she stepped out of the pile of white ruffles and gray serge. Caleb reached to the ground behind him and tossed a saddlebag at her feet, the gun still pointed at her. His suddenly hot eyes devoured her.

"There's clothes in there." He nodded toward the saddlebag. "Put them on."

His gaze raked her from head to toe, making her feel naked . . . dirty. Cold. Minutes ago, she had been warm. Now her fingers felt like ice. She tried to control her shaking as she fought the buckle of the saddlebag. When she finally had it open and had pulled out the contents, she couldn't hide her surprise. A clean neatly folded shirt and pair of pants, large enough for two of her.

"Not exactly the latest fashion, which I'm sure you're used to," he told her with a sneer. "But adequate covering for those lovely limbs of yours. Put them on."

The shirtsleeves were so long she had to roll them up four turns just to find her hands. The pants, too, had to be rolled before she could take a step. Caleb tossed her a length of rope to use as a belt to hold the pants up.

While she dressed, she darted nervous glances at her captor. If not murder or rape, what was he after? He never took his eyes or his gun off her for a second. She tried to act unconcerned when he circled behind her. As soon as she knotted the rope at her waist, he grabbed both her arms from behind and tied her hands with rope that felt like it was embedded with cholla spines.

In the next instant she found herself facedown in the dirt. Her breath left her in an audible rush. Caleb tied her feet together at the ankles. Bound tight, trussed up like a Christmas goose, all Serena could do was watch while Caleb made ready to leave.

He backed the buggy between the cedars, then camouflaged the back of it with cedar branches he must have cut earlier. Her heart knocked against her ribs at the realization that this was obviously no spur-of-the-moment abduction. He'd planned it all out. And she'd fallen into his hands like a ripe plum. She felt like an idiot. A scared idiot.

Caleb unhitched the gray Triple C mare from the buggy. Next, he produced a worn, beat-up saddle from behind the trees and a brand new bridle from the canvas bag hanging from his saddle horn.

After saddling the mare, he untied Serena's feet. Before she could stand, he grasped her firmly around the waist and hoisted her into the saddle. His hands squeezed painfully, then rose to cup her breasts. Serena sat ramrod straight and slowly turned her head to glare down her nose at him. She knew he must feel her trembling, but she refused to acknowledge it.

His hands drifted down her ribs and belly to her thighs. A puzzling look of sadness crossed his face, making her wonder what went through his mind.

She tried to reason with him calmly. "Don't do this, Caleb. Let me go."

He stepped back and gave her a narrowed look.

Serena was tempted to give the horse a kick and make a break for it. But the saddle was too large and unfamiliar, too smooth and slippery, her feet didn't reach the stirrups, and her hands were still tied behind her back. She'd never be able to stay mounted. Bareback, she might have chanced it.

Then, as if he'd read her mind, Caleb tied her reins to the back of his saddle. If she'd had a chance at all, it was gone.

Caleb looped a rope around one of her ankles and ran it under the horse's belly to her other ankle. Serena cursed silently. She was trapped. Damn! If the mare stumbled and fell, Serena would go down with her and be crushed.

When Caleb freed Serena's hands, then retied them to the saddle horn, she at least had the illusion of being somewhat in control, false though she knew that illusion was.

She kept her voice low and reasonable when she asked, "Why are you doing this?"

At first she thought he would ignore her, but then he

finally said, "It's nothing personal. I told you—it's just business."

Inside her head, she was screaming her fear and shrieking her rage, but outside she was calm. "What could I possibly have to do with your business? What kind of business requires you to abduct me?"

This time he did ignore her. He gathered his belongings and loaded them onto the back of his horse. Just before mounting, he grabbed Serena's hair, twisted it into a knot on top of her head, and crammed a lopsided, beat-up sombrero down on top. When he tightened the strap beneath her chin, his fingers trailed along her jaw in a light caress. "So soft and beautiful," he whispered.

A cold shiver ran down Serena's spine.

A moment later Caleb mounted and kicked his horse into a gallop, leading the way south.

Always south.

South down the Santa Cruz Valley, but not by way of the usual trail. He kept to the brush as much as possible, avoiding the occasional ranch and any travelers he spotted.

Serena tried to keep her mind off her physical discomfort, but it wasn't an easy thing to do. She hadn't slept much last night, so she was tired. Her arms, her back, and her backside were killing her. With her feet tied the way they were, she couldn't bend her knees or reach the stirrups. All she could do was bounce painfully in the saddle. With her hands tied to the horn, she couldn't brush the loose strand of hair out of her eyes. And damn it, her nose itched.

Yet if she didn't let herself think about discomfort, the only thing left to consider was her terror. It rose within her.

She choked it down. She couldn't afford to let fear take over and cloud her mind. She had to stay calm. And sharp.

Where was he taking her? And why? He avoided the trail as though he wanted their passage to go unnoticed, yet he rode at a speed that raised a dust cloud plainly visible to anyone who cared to look. And he made no attempt at all to cover their tracks.

They stopped only briefly to rest and water the horses, but Caleb made no move to untie Serena. She was forced to stay mounted, her hands and feet and rear growing more numb by the hour.

When they made camp just after sundown, she was forced to eat the jerky and hardtack he tossed at her while her hands remained bound. He had even retied her feet.

Would he come at her now?

Serena watched his every move, sure he would lunge at her or grab her any moment. But he didn't. He stared at the fire between them and ate without looking at her. The flames seemed to mesmerize him. His gaze appeared . . . longing. He looked like a young boy on the verge of manhood who'd just discovered the most beautiful woman he'd ever seen. During the entire meal, Caleb didn't blink. Not once.

After eating, he rolled a smoke and leaned back against his grounded saddle, a satisfied grin on his face.

When he spoke, Serena jumped. It was the first time he'd spoken in hours. "The way I figure it," he said, his grin spreading wider across his sweat-streaked face, "your family's probably worried by now, it being dark and you not home yet." He rubbed his hand along his whisker-stubbled jaw and grinned wider.

190

"Matt Colton, I've got you now," he said with relish. "Come sunup, if not sooner," he said to Serena, "that brother of yours will probably ride into Tucson looking for you. Take him a while to figure out you're not there."

He poked a stick in the fire until it caught, then held it up, twisting it back and forth, watching the flames eat down the dried wood toward his fingers.

"It'll take him a while longer to spot where the buggy left the road. Probably be late in the afternoon before he picks up our trail."

A bare second before the flames would have singed his fingertips, he grinned and tossed the stick into the fire.

Serena watched him closely, each flick of eyelid, each twitch of muscle. Something in his face confused her. Was it confidence? Satisfaction? Shouldn't he be worried about being followed? If she read his expression correctly . . .

Her eyes widened in disbelief. "You *want* him to follow?"

His grin broadened yet again and his eyes flared.

"Are you crazy? Don't you know he'll kill you for this?"

Caleb laughed. The sound bordered on madness and sent shivers down Serena's spine.

"All we have to do is stay ahead of him," he said. "That'll be easy with the head start we've got. He'll follow. He'll follow until I've got him right where I want him."

Serena swallowed to moisten her mouth. "And where might that be?" she asked as casually as possible.

"Just a little place I've got picked out south of here."

"South. Mexico, maybe?" He didn't respond, just kept grinning at her. "So you want to get Matt to Mexico, and you're using me as bait, is that it?"

"You got it, sister."

Serena allowed a smile to curve her lips. "I hate to be the one to tell you this, but there's a tiny little flaw in your plans."

"I doubt that."

"Oh, but there is," she assured him brightly. "It's quite simple, really. He won't come."

Caleb hooted with laughter. "Nice try, Miss Colton. He won't come. Ha! I kidnap his sister, and he won't come? Who're you trying to kid, girl? I've never seen a more protective, possessive brother in my life than Matt Colton. If looks could kill, I'd have been dead the first time I got within ten feet of you. He dotes on you." He sipped his coffee, then bobbed his head up and down. "He'll come."

Serena kept the smile on her lips. "No, he won't."

Caleb started to speak, but she held up her bound hands to interrupt him. "Not because he isn't protective of me. You're right about that. If he knew I was missing, he'd surely come. But you should have asked me how long I was planning to be away from home before you cooked up this little scheme."

His eyes narrowed as the grin slowly slipped away. "What are you talking about?"

"No one will know I'm missing for a week, maybe two." She leaned against the boulder behind her, her smile held in place by sheer will. "You see, I'm afraid we had a little . . . family disagreement. I left to spend some time with friends in town." Was she putting her head in a noose, telling him this? If he thought her useful as bait for Matt, he might not harm her — yet. But if she had no more use, then what?

She straightened her shoulders. Whatever would happen would happen. But first she wanted to see the look on his face when he realized his plan had failed. "My friends in town of course, didn't know I was coming, so no one will even miss me for days and days."

"You lie!" he yelled. "You're just trying to trick me, to get me off-guard so he can sneak up on me."

"Why would I lie about it? I want him to come, probably as badly as you do." She let her smile slip and gave rein to anger. "I want him to catch you. I want to watch while he peels the hide off your bones." She stopped and forced a calming breath into her lungs. "But he won't come. Do you hear me? He won't come."

"Shut up!" Caleb jumped to his feet. The low fire between them cast red lights and black shadows across his features. As he skirted the fire and came toward her, she half expected to see horns on his head, so evil did he look just then.

But there were no horns. Only a man. A big, angry man with a half-mad light in his cold eyes. He paced back and forth in front of her.

"If he'd just been a little bit drunker that night in Tombstone," Caleb muttered, "he'd never have made it out that damn window and I wouldn't have to be going through this now. The fire would have taken care of him like it should have."

Serena straightened, her heart thudding. "Fire?"

"He's got the devil's own luck. My biggest, best fire yet, and all the bastard gets is a broken leg."

Good God, he didn't mean — "The fire that burned half the town?"

Caleb gave her a disgusted look. "Yeah, half the

town, but it missed the one person it was intended for, dammit."

Horror filled her throat. "You started the fire in Tombstone? To kill Matt?"

His eyes took on a faraway look. "You should have seen it. If you'd come a day earlier you would have. It was really something. So hot, so alive, so beautiful."

He's crazy.

His gaze focused on her sharply. " 'Course, your goddamn brother got away. This is his fault, you know. If he'd died like he was supposed to, I wouldn't have to use you to get to him. But he'll come."

With hard, jerky motions, Caleb bent and untied Serena's feet, then grabbed her arm, dragged her across the little clearing, and tossed her at the base of a scrub oak. He used the rope that had been around her ankles and secured her bound hands tightly against the rough, flaking bark.

He left her there. While he kicked dirt onto the fire, he cast her a hate-filled look over his shoulder. "He'll come, damn you. He'll come."

But now he wasn't so sure. It seemed like she spoke the truth. *Damn her.* She was ruining all his plans!

He tossed himself onto his bedroll and stared at her through the darkness. His original plan hadn't had anything to do with Serena, only Matt Colton. He had to kill Matt Colton. And he would, by God!

But then he'd seen Serena and decided to use her to get to Matt, a good plan. Only thing was, this second plan of his would see Serena tortured and dead. He wasn't so sure he wanted to do that anymore.

She was so beautiful, so proud and courageous. For someone like her to die the way he'd intended — no. He wouldn't do it.

Couldn't. He wanted her for himself.

Now, wouldn't that get ol' Colton's goat? What if the bastard came after his sister only to find she'd fallen in love with her captor?

'Course, she wasn't in love with him. Probably never would be. A rich rancher's daughter like her, and him just a poor dirt farmer. But rancher's daughter or not, she was still just a half-breed. A half-breed Apache. Not a popular thing to be in this part of the country.

If he changed his tactics, played up to her, she just might be grateful for his attention. He could take her back to Tennessee. Nobody cared much one way or the other about Apaches back there. Nobody even had to know she was Apache. She ought to like that.

He clenched his fists at his sides. He couldn't go home until Matt Colton was dead. He needed a way to make the man come to him, but he was no longer eager to harm Serena in the process.

But Colton didn't have to know that! All he had to do was *think* Caleb would kill her.

Or *had* killed her. That was it!

A new plan formed in his mind. Of course, he might need a little help, but then, that's what that greasy little Mex fellow was for. Pablo would do anything for a little spending money.

Caleb relaxed his hands and allowed a smile to spread. He would kill Matt Colton and have Serena all to himself. This was even better than his other plans. Things were going to work out just fine.

He took a deep, satisfying breath and drifted off to sleep. He dreamed of Serena.

"Where's Aunt Rena, Daddy? Isn't she going to tuck me in tonight?"

Matt straightened the covers beneath Joanna's chin. "No, Pumpkin, she went to Tucson this morning."

"Will she be home tomorrow?"

"I don't think so."

And she wasn't. Nor was she home the day after, or the day after that. Each night Matt found himself echoing Joanna's plea. Each day was longer than the previous one. Where was Serena? What was she doing? Was she crying? Because of him?

A couple of weeks, Pace had said. A couple of weeks.

Twelve

Serena vowed that if she made it out of this alive, she would never let herself get so soft and out of shape again. That first day on the trail with Caleb had been exhausting. The second was torture. The third, just as bad. But by the fourth day her muscles had begun to firm up, and now, eight days after she'd left home for Tucson, staying in the saddle all day was no hardship at all. It would have been even easier, however, if her hands and feet weren't tied.

What *was* hard was knowing she had no choice in what was happening to her, not tied up the way she was. But she watched, and waited. If her chance came, she would take it.

The sun had beat down on Serena and Caleb without mercy from the clear blue Arizona sky. Now it hung motionless hour after hour over the high Mexican desert.

After crossing the border, Caleb had turned east. Conversation between them had been practically nonexistent for days. Each night, Serena had waited with dread for him to force himself on her, but he'd made no such move. Was she truly only bait to draw Matt?

After days of purposely avoiding all contact with other people, Caleb now led her straight toward two Mexican riders approaching from behind a jagged boulder. Serena straightened in the saddle, her senses alert.

Caleb greeted one of the men with familiarity, calling him Pablo and demanding to know who the second man was.

"Es mi hermano," Pablo said.

Caleb seemed satisfied that the second man was Pablo's brother and motioned for Pablo to lead the way.

The way was slow and tortuous. They entered a virtual jungle of cholla and Spanish dagger, with an occasional organ pipe and a few barrel cacti scattered about. The vicious plants gave way here and there to black, porous lava, jagged, uneven, and treacherous, left by some ancient volcano.

The narrow trail twisted and turned, backtracking on itself, sometimes stopping altogether at a solid wall of cactus or lava, forcing the riders to back their horses carefully to another opening. Caleb swore colorfully at the sharp needles that seemed to jump out and stab him. The Mexicans didn't appear to be bothered, and Serena knew enough to lean away. Their calmness only added to Caleb's growing anger.

Time in that cholla forest stood still. It seemed they would never find their way through that maze of black rock and man-eating plants. Caleb kept demanding to know how much farther. Pablo kept shrugging his shoulders and swearing, "Not much, *señor.*"

How much farther to what? Serena wondered. What were they doing in this prickly place? Surely they could have gone around it.

Then something tickled the back of her mind. Some

memory. A story she'd once heard. *No! Not once, but heard many times!* Heard over Apache campfires in her childhood. She knew now where they were headed.

Canyon de los Embudos, the Canyon of Tricksters. Canyon of Deceptions. Thirty miles below the Arizona border. Guarded by miles of cholla forest, with false, dead-end trails to trap the uninitiated. Old Chihuahua's favorite hideout, before he went to the reservation.

Serena wondered what accident had led Pablo to discover the way into the canyon. She had heard the entrance was well hidden, disguised by a huge tumble of boulders. Anyone fool enough to come through all the cactus was likely to ride right past the narrow cut. A mere slice in the rocks led the way down to the clear pool surrounded by sycamores and willows on the canyon floor.

Of course, Chihuahua wouldn't be there now. But wouldn't Caleb be surprised if old Nana and his warriors popped up from behind the rocks?

Late in the afternoon, Pablo finally led the way behind the guardian boulder and down the steep path to the canyon floor. He chose a campsite along the edge of the pool, beneath an overhang of lava. A thick stand of willows surrounded the clearing.

Caleb untied Serena from the saddle and lifted her to the ground. Her skin shrank from his touch. He left her sitting with her back to a tree, her hands still tied together, while he led the two Mexicans aside. They were too far away for Serena to make out their words.

When they came back, Caleb jerked the sombrero from Serena's head and combed her hair out with his fingers. He clasped her by the jaw and forced her head around, pointing to the streak of white at her temple.

None of the men spoke. Serena held her breath, straining to keep from jerking from Caleb's grasp.

"Can you do it?" Caleb asked Pablo.

Pablo fidgeted with the end of his drooping mustache, his eyes narrowed in thought. "*Sí.*" He nodded slowly. "*Sí,* I can do it."

Caleb turned loose of Serena and walked to his horse.

Serena worked her jaw to ease the ache caused by his tight grip. She'd be bruised, she knew.

Caleb pulled a leather pouch from his saddlebag, then led the men off again. A few minutes later, the two Mexicans mounted and headed out of the canyon, leaving Serena and Caleb alone.

When he returned to her side, he checked her bonds. The slight tug he gave the rope tore another scab loose from her wrist. She bit the inside of her cheek to keep from crying out. To take her mind off the pain, she said, "Your friends didn't stay long."

Caleb presented her with what she read as a smile of satisfaction. "No," he said. "They didn't."

When he didn't volunteer any further information, Serena kept quiet. The day, and then the night, passed uneventfully. Then more days and nights. He'd finally begun to untie her during the day, when he could watch her. Her wrists, hands, and feet silently thanked him. So did her mind. Now she could think about escaping.

But he never gave her the chance. When she was untied, he watched her every movement. When he left to hunt for game, or when he slept, he tied her to a tree.

After about a week, Serena decided Caleb was much too sure of himself. It was time to give him something to worry about. That evening, over roasted rabbit, she said, "Interesting spot you've picked to lead Matt to. Do you still think he'll come?"

Caleb just smiled. A secretive smile. An I-know-something-you-don't-know smile.

"I can assure you," Serena went on, "he won't come. But that doesn't mean someone else won't."

"Someone else? And who might this 'someone else' be?"

Serena smiled. "For some odd reason, you seem to think Matt's the only relative I have. You forget about the other half of my family."

"What other half?" he asked, his eyes narrowing.

"The half that roams this part of the country raiding and killing everything in sight."

"If you're tryin' to scare me with stories about bloodthirsty Apaches, forget it. Even I know all the Apaches are cooped up on reservations nowadays."

"All?" Serena raised a brow as she spoke, and her lips quirked. "Now, where in the world would you hear a whopper like that? You've heard how nervous the Army is these days, with Nana running loose."

"Why should that worry me? Everybody knows he's in Arizona. In case you haven't noticed, we're in Mexico. Besides, I don't believe half of what I hear about him. People are jumping at shadows. One old man with a handful of followers can't be that dangerous."

Serena smiled wider. "Don't kid yourself. That old man is as dangerous as they come. And just to give you warning, should he by chance show up, he happens to be a personal friend of my mother's, and therefore, of mine."

Caleb laughed outright. "Your mother! Next thing you'll be telling me is she's the one who's going to rescue you."

201

Serena let the smile fade from her lips. "For your sake, you'd better hope she doesn't. Have you never heard the legend of Woman of Magic?"

Caleb paused with his coffee cup halfway to his lips, then set the cup back down. "Who hasn't? She's that white woman the Apaches all treat like she's some kind of goddess. You're not trying to tell me she's—"

"My mother. Yes."

"I'm shaking in my boots."

"You should be," she said softly. "The other thing you should know is about this nice little canyon you've chosen to hide in. Do you know what they call this place?"

"Sure. Canyon de los Embudos."

"That's right," she said. "As far as it goes. Canyon of Tricksters. Canyon of Deceptions. But it happens to be a favorite hideout of the Apaches, because it's so hard to find. What do you suppose will happen if Nana and his men, or some other band of Apaches rides down into this canyon and finds you holding me captive?"

Caleb stared at her a long moment, then took a sip of coffee. "Glad you warned me. Tomorrow I'll start scouting for another way out of here, while you stay tied to that tree."

Serena tossed a rabbit bone into the fire and smiled at him again. "You can scout all you want. You won't find another way out. The Apaches have their own name for this place. Cos-codee."

"Which means?"

"No escape."

The name wasn't accurate, of course. There was another way out. Serena had heard about the secret Coscodee Pass up on the cedar ledge at the far end of the

202

canyon. She'd also heard it was ten times more difficult to locate than the way they'd come in. But only the Apaches knew of its existence. If and when her chance for escape came, that's where she'd head. The trail from there led to Pa-Gotzin-Kay, another Apache hideout higher in the Sierra Madres, but only a half day away.

And Pa-Gotzin-Kay wasn't deserted, Serena knew. Back when the government had decided to do away with the Chiricahua Reservation in the Dragoons shortly after Cochise's death, Tahza, the new chief, had agreed to move to the new reservation at San Carlos. But he'd heard terrible things about disease and starvation among the Indians there. He didn't want his wife and young son to live in a place like that, so he sent them with another thirty to forty members of his band to an ancient Apache hideout, Pa-Gotzin-Kay.

Those escapees, including Dee-O-Det, Cochise's old shaman, still lived there in secrecy. Serena remembered hearing that Tom Jeffords, Indian agent at the time, had helped in the endeavor. When Nod-ah-Sti, Tahza's wife, took her son, Niño, plus Dee-O-Det and the others, to Mexico, Jeffords destroyed the records of the Chiricahua Reservation. No one at San Carlos knew the names of those who fled. Subsequent agents referred to them as the Nameless Ones, when they referred to them at all. But these days, the government never even admitted the existence of a free band of Apaches living peacefully in the Sierra Madres, not raiding or killing, but raising their own food and minding their own business.

Of course, "free" was a relative term. They weren't free to come and go as they pleased, but were forced to sneak in and out of the area so no one would learn the location of the stronghold.

They weren't even free to keep dogs to warn of the approach of strangers. Barking dogs meant men were near, and the clear mountain air carried the barking for miles. Dogs would alert the Mexicans to the Apaches presence.

No, no dogs. Only old men, women, and children trying to survive on their own.

Nod-ah-Sti was one of Serena's best friends. Serena would be welcome at Pa-Gotzin-Kay. If she could get away from Caleb.

True to his word, Caleb left Serena tied firmly to a tree the next morning and went off searching for a back door to the canyon. When he failed to find one, he searched again the next day. And the next.

By the end of the week, he decided maybe Serena was right. Maybe there wasn't any way out but the way they'd come in.

Late in the afternoon they heard riders approaching. Before Serena could cry out to whomever was coming, Caleb thrust a greasy handkerchief into her mouth and tied it in place with his bandana. He tied her to a tree, then crouched behind another, rifle in hand, sweat pouring down his face.

Serena held her breath, waiting to see who came. A moment later her shoulders slumped when Pablo and his brother rode into view.

Caleb rushed out to greet them. "Did you do it? Is it done?"

"*Sí, señor,* it is done."

"No trouble?"

Pablo shook his head and grinned. "No trouble."

Caleb visibly relaxed. "Good." He reached into his

saddlebag and pulled out a small leather pouch. When he tossed it to Pablo, it clinked. "Swap one of your horses for this one," he said, indicating the gray mare from the Triple C. "Then head on up to Fronteras, or wherever you like. And *amigo,* thanks."

"De nada, señor. Adiós."

Pablo stripped the saddle from his shaggy brown mustang and placed it on the mare, then he and his brother rode out of the canyon. As soon as they were gone, Caleb began breaking camp.

"We're leaving?" Serena asked, when he removed the gag from her mouth. "I thought you were convinced Matt would come here. I thought that was the whole idea."

Caleb paused in rolling his bedroll and looked at her. A new look that she couldn't quite read filled his eyes. "It doesn't matter anymore," he said. "I've changed my mind. I can kill Matt Colton anytime I want. Right now I've got other things I'd rather do. I know he won't come after you now. I've seen to it."

Serena grew cautious and tried to hide the worry eating at her. "What do you mean?"

"I mean he won't come now. There's no reason for him to. He thinks you're dead. No one will come for you. They can't possibly deny the proof I sent them."

Her mouth went dry. "What proof?"

He didn't answer.

"Have you considered that if my family thinks you've killed me, nothing on earth will stop them from tracking you down?"

Caleb just shook his head as though the idea were absurd.

"And it won't be just Matt you'll have to worry about. He's not my only brother, you know. I have two others. And a very protective father, not to mention my mother, plus all the manpower the Triple C possesses."

She watched with grim satisfaction as Caleb glanced sharply from side to side, as if he would deny her words.

"Of course, one of my brothers is half Chiricahua, like me. I suppose he'll let Uncle Naiche know what's happened. Did you ever hear of Naiche? He's Cochise's son — chief of the Chidikáágu'. Chiricahua, to you. I happen to be his favorite niece." Despite her fear-dried throat, she managed a forced laugh. "Could be because I'm his only niece, but then, this just may be the excuse he's been looking for to bust off the reservation. I wonder what he'd do to you if he caught you."

Caleb tied his bedroll behind his saddle with jerky motions, his jaw clenched tight. "He couldn't do any worse to me than your brother did to my brother."

A prickly feeling ran up Serena's arms. "What are you talking about?"

"Did you know I had a brother?"

"You mentioned one at home and another off at school somewhere."

"I also mentioned my oldest brother. The one who came west and was killed. Murdered. He wasn't much to brag about, but he was my brother. He didn't deserve what Matt Colton did to him. Nobody deserves that. Not even a stinking rattler."

A hard knot tightened in the pit of Serena's stomach. She didn't want to know what he was talking about. She didn't want to know who his brother was, how he died, or what that had to do with Matt. She didn't want to know. But she did know.

206

Caleb rambled while he saddled her horse. "We're one of those alphabetical families. You know the kind, where each kid's name starts with the next letter of the alphabet. Ma wanted to be sure we at least knew our ABCs. She didn't get very far, though, before she died. Davy, he's the youngest. Then there's me. Ben's next to oldest. It was the oldest one who came west several years ago. Ma always said the West was wild and dangerous. She didn't know how right she was. Did I tell you my oldest brother's name?"

His gaze locked on hers, and she saw terrible things there. Deadly determination . . . pain. Fear. Hate.

"Abraham Miller Scott." She didn't realize she'd spoken aloud the name that was a curse in her home, until she saw Caleb's nod of satisfaction.

"I see you've heard of him. Heard what your brother did to him. Now Matt Colton is going to pay. He thinks I've done to you what he did to Abe, and he's going to be eaten alive by it. Because he'll know it's because of him. Because of what he did to Abe."

Serena's heart pounded. Her hands shook. How could he know what Matt did to Abe Scott? Even the family didn't know. Not exactly, anyway. Pace was the only one besides Matt who knew, and Pace wasn't talking.

She licked her lips nervously. "Just what is it you think Matt did to your brother?"

"Look at you," he said. "You know what he did to him. I can see it in your eyes. From the description I had, I'd say he learned a few things from the Apache half of your family. You know how long it took my brother to die? Do you?" he yelled. His hatred for Matt, plus horror over his brother's death, shot from his too-bright eyes.

Then his eyes narrowed. "You didn't think anybody knew, did you? Well, I know, goddammit. It happened right here. Right here!" He shouted and pointed at the ground between his feet. "But your brother wasn't as careful as he thought. Someone was hidden in the brush, right up there on that rim, watching the whole thing. He came to me and told me all about it."

A shudder ran visibly through him. "God," he cried. "The things he did. It was inhuman, what your brother did to mine. Four days. It lasted four days, before Abe finally died. Christ. I'd rather be burned alive!"

"You keep on with this, and you just might get your wish," Serena warned. "Let me go, Caleb. Give me a horse and just let me go. I promise, no one will come after you. It'll be over. Just let me go."

"Never," he said in a hard, determined voice. "Like I said, you're only a tool in all this. I don't want to kill you, but you give me any trouble and I will. Matt Colton's gotta pay for what he did. And I'm the one who's gonna see to it."

Serena shook her head. "It'll never happen, you know. He'll catch you. And he'll give you plenty of time to regret what you've done before he lets you die. Just like your brother."

Caleb finished packing the skillet, tin plates, and cups, then turned back to her. "What I don't understand is why. Why did he do it? Why would one man do that to another?"

She stared at him, stunned. "You don't know?" Her voice came out in a croak. "You came halfway across the country to avenge your brother's death, and you don't even know why he was killed? Is it possible you don't know what kind of man Abraham Miller Scott was?" she shrieked.

"Well, let me tell you," she went on, warming to her subject. "Nearly ten years ago, he murdered a man. The man had just buried his wife and was standing over her grave when your *brother* bushwhacked him. The man's daughter saw it all. Later, she married Matt. A few months after that, your dear *brother* kidnapped her. She was carrying Matt's child. Your brother hit her in the stomach with a chair. She lost the baby and nearly died."

Serena forced down the bile that rose at the memories. "He was arrested, stood trial, and was sentenced to hang. But first they had to send him back East someplace, where he was wanted for other crimes. Sometime after that he managed to escape. Your brother was a real charmer."

"You're lying."

"Three years ago," she continued, "Abe rode down on Matt and Angela while they were coming home from town, and he shot her. He killed my brother's wife! The dirty, no-good son of a bitch deserved everything Matt did to him, and more! And you're going to get the same, if you don't let me go."

"You're lying, I say. Just trying to save your own skin. I don't believe a goddamn word."

"Yes, you do. I see it in your eyes. You know it's true."

Caleb jerked her up and slammed her into the saddle. "Shut up." He tied her hands to the horn, finished tying her feet, then mounted and led them out of the canyon.

It took him hours, a half-dozen false turns, and several vicious cuts from the cacti to lead them out of the cholla forest. When the mass of cactus and lava finally thinned, he turned south.

Serena glanced over her shoulder and saw the tracks left by Pablo and his brother as those two had headed north.

Where was Caleb taking her now? She should have kept her mouth shut. At least Matt might have known to look for her at Cos-codee.

Would she ever see Matt again? Or anyone, for that matter? A chill crept through her limbs as she admitted to herself that Caleb was more than a little crazed by his quest for revenge. What would he do to her? Would she be able to fight him?

As the days passed slowly, Matt grew increasingly restless and irritable. He needed to talk to Serena. He didn't have the faintest idea what he would say, he just needed to be able to look into her eyes, to know what she was thinking, to see her, to hear her laugh again.

A couple of weeks, Pace had said.

Matt would never survive. He was already going slowly out of his mind with worry, and she'd been gone only four days. He swore under his breath. Damn it, he'd waited long enough.

The next morning Matt was in the saddle and riding for Tucson before the sun was fully up. He couldn't let things slide any longer. He had to talk to Rena.

Matt hadn't been in Tucson for three years. Under different circumstances, he'd have ridden right through the middle of town and stopped along the street a dozen times to renew old acquaintances. But not today. He skirted the edge of town and came to the Ortega house by the back way.

210

Miguel Emilio Ortega made his fortune when the territory was young by freighting otherwise unattainable goods up from Sonora and Chihuahua. When his only daughter, Sylvia, brought home the pretty little blue-eyed Colton girl and announced that Serena was now her very best friend, Don Miguel was pleased to have a connection with the wealthy and powerful Colton family.

Pleased until he found out, weeks later, that his daughter's best friend was a half-breed Apache. The revelation of that particular fact nearly gave him a stroke, for his freighters had been fighting every step of the way against losing their goods and their very lives to the marauding bands of cutthroat Apaches for years. That Serena considered Cochise her grandfather only made matters worse.

But unlike Ortega's successful attempts to defend his merchandise, he lost the battle to keep what he then called "the little savage" from his home. Even at that age, when Serena Colton chose to put forth the effort, which was seldom, she could charm the skin off a snake. She didn't usually bother to dissuade people of their prejudices, but Sylvia had begged her to make friends with her father. It hadn't taken Serena long to have the man eating out of the palm of her hand. Don Miguel had been a good friend of the Coltons ever since.

But neither he nor his daughter had seen Serena since the day she'd come home from Tombstone a week ago. The news sent a prickle of unease down Matt's spine. He was further disturbed to learn that Serena had not mentioned that she planned to come for a visit in the near future.

Had Pace misunderstood where Serena was going?

Then another possibility occurred. Pace could have lied to keep Matt from finding her.

Matt paid brief visits to a few more of Serena's friends, using the excuse that he'd just gotten home and wanted to let her know he was back. But no one had seen her. Her buggy was not at the livery, where she should have left it.

Matt was beginning to believe Serena hadn't come to Tucson at all. When he noticed clouds building in the west, he headed for home. He couldn't wait to get his hands on Pace.

That Pace had lied to him was the only possibility Matt allowed himself to consider. If Pace hadn't lied, that meant either Serena had lied to Pace, or something had happened to her. Matt couldn't even consider either idea.

If she lied to Pace, then she had taken off for parts unknown. That would have been a little more likely if she'd been on horseback, but not in the buggy.

And if she really had intended to go to Sylvia's, then why wasn't she there?

No. Pace had lied.

By the time Matt stomped into the house just ahead of the storm, he was as furious as the black, rolling clouds outside.

He found Pace, Dani, and his father in the study. Ignoring his parents, Matt crossed to the sofa and lifted Pace by the front of his shirt. "All right, goddamn you, where is she?"

"Matt!" Travis and Dani cried in shock.

"What's gotten into you?" Travis demanded.

"Watch your language," Dani ordered. "And while

212

you're at it, put your brother down."

Matt dropped Pace and leaned over him, fists clenched, jaw twitching. "She's not at the Ortegas'. Where is she?"

"Serena's not at the Ortegas'?" Dani asked.

"How do you know?" Pace demanded.

"Because I just came from there. They weren't expecting her, they haven't seen her. You lied to me. Where is she?"

Pace sprang from the sofa and stood nose-to-nose with Matt. "I may be a lot of things, *brother,* but I'm not a liar. You ever call me that again, I'll —"

"That's enough. Both of you." Travis came from behind his desk and stood before them. "Now, what's all this about?"

While Matt explained where he'd gone that morning looking for Serena, he watched Pace's face. When he realized Pace had not been lying, Matt's insides tied themselves into knots.

"Oh, my God," Dani whispered.

Travis put his arm around her. "Now, don't start worrying for nothing, love."

"But she wouldn't just run off, Travis. It's not like her."

"I don't know," Pace said thoughtfully. "As upset as she was."

"Upset? About what?" Travis asked.

"Ask him," Pace said, nodding at Matt with narrowed eyes.

Matt tossed Pace an irritated glance, then sighed.

"Matt?" Dani asked. "What happened? Why was she upset?"

"It was Joanna," Matt said wearily, rubbing the back of his neck. "When Rena tucked her in the other

213

night, Joanna called her . . . Mama."

"Oh, no," Dani moaned. "I was afraid something like this would happen. They've been so close, those two. Inseparable. I should have done something. I should have—"

"Hush, love," Travis said, squeezing her arm. "There wasn't anything you could have done short of shipping one of them off. The problem right now is to find Serena. We'll take some men and head out at first light. Wherever she is, we'll find her."

Travis led Dani from the room, and Pace started to follow. He paused in the doorway and glanced back at Matt. "There's more to this than you're telling, isn't there?"

"If there is, it's none of your business."

"I'll make it my business if anything's happened to my sister because of you."

"*Your* sister? What the hell is she to me?"

"That's what I'd like to know."

Thirteen

Caleb and Serena were three days out of Cos-codee when Caleb stopped unexpectedly in the middle of the afternoon and jerked Serena from the saddle. He carried her off the trail into the deep woods and, without a word, gagged her and left her tied to a tree.

Serena wanted to demand he tell her what was happening, what he was doing, but she kept quiet. He was starting to make her more nervous than ever.

When they left Cos-codee, he'd been the nervous one. Nervous and irritable. But the farther they got from that place, the more relaxed and confident he'd become.

And he'd started touching her. Fingers through her hair, a knuckle brushing lightly across her cheek, hands that lingered too long on her waist when he lifted her down from the saddle. Little touches. Some made to look like accidents. But he grew bolder, more deliberate every day. He made her flesh crawl.

Then there were his eyes. At Tombstone, they'd been laughing eyes, pleasant, full of gaiety. Bright, twinkling gray. When he'd first kidnapped her, they were cold and hard as granite. At Cos-codee, they were troubled and dark, like thunderclouds.

But now when he looked at her, his eyes were different. She'd never seen gray and thought of heat before. Yet whenever he turned his gaze on her, she saw hot gray. Hot, devouring, and . . . hungry.

Serena shuddered in the afternoon heat. When she had finally decided he wasn't going to rape her, that's when he started undressing her with his eyes. If she didn't escape soon, he'd be doing it with his hands!

Footsteps crackled across gravel and dead leaves. Serena stiffened. He was coming back.

Looking excited and eager, Caleb bent beneath the low branches and squatted next to Serena. His hot gaze raked her from head to toe. One hand settled boldly on her thigh and squeezed slightly. It was all Serena could do to keep from shrieking and kicking, but she was determined to hide her fear and revulsion. She had to stay calm.

Don't let him know he's getting to you.

She did her best to present a demeanor of cool, haughty disinterest.

Caleb grinned, then winked, as if sharing a humorous secret. After giving her thigh a final squeeze, he removed her gag and worked on the knot that bound her to the tree.

"We're almost there," he said casually. "Bet you'll be glad to get off that horse and under a roof for a while."

"Almost where? What roof?" Serena demanded.

"Well, it's not much of a roof, really, but it'll do for now."

"Where are we?" She knew, but she wondered if he did. It seemed foolish on his part to hide her out only a day's ride from the Arizona border.

At least, she *thought* they were a day's ride from the border. When they had headed south from Cos-codee, they hit the down-Bavispe and followed it west past the

216

Rio Agua Prieta junction to the up-Bavispe. Then they'd cut northwest and crossed another river. If Serena's calculations were correct, that crossing was due south of Fronteras.

Unless she'd lost all sense of direction, they were now in the Cananea Hills, barely a day's ride south of Naco Springs, which was on the border. Did Caleb know they were that close to Arizona? To her family?

Caleb tossed Serena back onto the horse, then grabbed her reins, mounted, and headed out at a walk. He didn't tie her feet. Her hands, although tied together, were, for once, not tied to the saddle horn.

If only she had the reins! Or no reins at all! She could kick the horse and guide it with her knees. At least she'd have a chance at freedom.

But with the reins in his hand, it was useless. Even if he dropped them, she'd never be able to retrieve them with her hands tied. And she had no desire to attempt a run for it with those long reins trailing down between her mount's hooves, tangling around his legs, tripping him. It was a long shot at best, and the odds were stacked too high against her. She would have to wait for another chance.

Caleb led the way to a narrow, rocky streambed. The August rains were late this year. The stream was only a small trickle of moisture across the gravel.

The horses didn't care for the small shifting rocks beneath their hooves, preferring instead the hard, dry banks on either side. But Caleb kept them in the streambed and headed north. He was, at last, apparently trying to hide their tracks.

Serena smiled to herself. He'd made no attempt to hide their tracks before. They'd left a trail a blind man could follow. This morning, in a fit of inspiration, he'd tried to wipe out the signs of their camp.

Serena had bitten her tongue to keep from laughing out loud. He'd kicked the rocks away that had circled the fire, then tossed two handfuls of dirt over the ashes, covering them haphazardly. Next, he'd picked up a loose, dead tree branch and scratched it around on the ground. An inexperienced child would still be able to tell where the fire had been and see the footprints and hoofmarks beneath the scratches.

For a man so bent on revenge — murder, kidnapping, and Lord knew what else — he was remarkably naive about the signs he left of his passing.

Serena flinched inwardly. He wasn't used to this sort of thing. Taking a hostage and covering his trail. No, he wasn't an experienced, trail-hardened criminal. He was plenty competent at getting them where he wanted to go but he certainly wasn't used to hiding his tracks.

He wasn't cut out for this kind of life. He wasn't mean enough or hard enough or cold enough. He scared too easily at stories about vengeful Apaches. He was trying to avenge the honor of a dishonorable brother.

And he was going to get himself killed.

Serena flexed her fingers and stared at his back, her jaw hardening. She wouldn't waste her sympathy on Caleb Miller Scott. He didn't deserve it. He'd taken her from her home and family against her will, kept her tied hand and foot for two weeks, and he wanted to kill Matt. He deserved whatever happened to him.

The streambed they followed seemed to end as the ground rose before a sheer rock wall ahead. But Caleb led them through a narrow, slanted cut in the rock and into a small box canyon.

Scrub oak, cedars, and junipers dotted the canyon floor and clung precariously here and there along the vertical rock walls. The stream widened near its source—a spring-fed pool at the far end of the canyon. A half-dozen cottonwoods shaded the pool.

A dozen yards off stood a cabin. As they approached, Serena glanced around, searching out a potential hiding place to use should she happen to get loose. The canyon didn't offer much in the way of opportunity, unless she could climb up to one of those ledges along the walls. The ledges were narrow, but a deep shadow now and then indicated the possibility of a cave or two, or at least a crevice.

The cabin was made from discarded packing crates and looked like a pebble tossed against it would send it crashing. It was tiny, maybe eight-by-eight. No windows and only one door, but enough gaps where the pieces of crates didn't meet to let in plenty of air. And rain. And scorpions, rats, snakes, or anything else that might want to walk, crawl, or slither in.

When Caleb took her inside, she was surprised to find a scarred, flimsy table, one intact chair and pieces of others, a tin pail, and most amazing of all, a small rock-and-mud fireplace on the far wall. The shack also boasted at least a year's worth of dust. Rat droppings covered every surface. Dead leaves and an occasional bone from some unfortunate animal littered the hard-packed dirt floor.

"It's not exactly what you're used to, I'm sure. But we'll clean it up a bit and it'll do."

Do for what? Serena wondered, but she didn't ask. She was too busy being relieved at having her hands at last untied. They were half numb and a little swollen. Her wrists would bear scars for months.

* * *

Caleb took another pull on the bottle of cheap, burning whiskey. He was drunk, and he knew it.

Drinking wasn't something he normally did a lot. Neither was kidnapping beautiful young women. He and Ben had usually left that sort of thing to Abe.

Abe. The oldest brother. The firstborn.

Caleb took another drink, frowning at how little was left in the bottle, and remembered. He remembered Ma, with her face black and blue from Pa's fists. Abe had worn his share of bruises, too, as had Ben and Caleb and Davy. But mostly it was Ma and Abe. Ben, Caleb, and Davy had been the lucky ones; Abe had protected them as much as possible from Pa. He'd taken more than a few beatings on himself to spare his younger brothers. And he'd been a grown man at the time.

The only thing that had kept Abe from fighting back was Ma. She'd have cried her eyes out if any of her boys had struck Pa. And Pa would have made damn sure Ma heard about it.

Everything changed that day the old man knocked her down and she hit her head on that rock. Abe was the one who'd found her, dead.

Abe had gone for Pa's throat with both hands. Caleb could honestly say he and Ben wouldn't have lifted a finger to interfere. They hadn't, either, until three neighbor men rode up. It had taken all five—both brothers and the neighbors—to pull Abe off. By then, Pa wasn't breathing.

Then one of the neighbors—Caleb couldn't recall which one—mentioned going for the sheriff. Abe had lit out.

Damn shame he hadn't stuck around. After he left, Ben led the neighbors to Ma's body.

There wasn't a one among those three men who hadn't

been on the receiving end of Pa's foul temper at one time or another. Yet Ma, well, everybody had liked Ma. She'd nursed their wives and kids through every kind of sickness and injury.

The men decided then and there that they had never been to the Scott farm that day. They agreed to be deaf, dumb, and blind to what had happened to Pa.

Only trouble was, no sooner had they cleared out than Ben discovered Pa wasn't quite dead. The old bastard. He was *supposed* to be dead, damn him.

Ben brought the shotgun from the house. "I'll finish him off."

"No." Caleb shook his head. "Too many questions."

"You got a better idea?"

Caleb had grinned. "An unfortunate accident."

The smell of coal oil tickled Caleb's memory. The fire had devoured first the straw, then the dry old barn, and Pa along with it. God, what a blaze that had been. One of Caleb's best. He got hard just thinking about it.

He shook his head and blinked away the memories. If he didn't get ahold of himself, he'd start thinking about fires and end up burning down the damn shack just to see the blaze reach to the sky.

After that, they only kept track of Abe by rumor. He was out there somewhere thinking the law was on his tail for killing Pa. Yet the rumors they heard about Abe were bad. It seemed like killing Pa, like he thought he'd done, set something loose inside him. Something mean.

In the far corner of the cabin, Serena sighed and shifted beneath her thin blanket. Caleb knew she wasn't asleep. He could see the reflection of the fire in the narrow slits of her eyes.

Lord, she was beautiful. Even after the way he'd treated her for the past weeks, keeping her tied up and all, she was still the most beautiful woman he'd ever seen.

He shifted against the sudden tightening in his pants.

Goddammit, Abe, what have you got me into? I owe you so much. Ben and Davy and I all do. But was Serena telling the truth? Oh, I know you kidnapped that woman all those years ago, but did you come back later and kill her? Is that why you're dead now? Is that why I'm here in this hovel, holding Serena against her will, hating her family but wanting her? Damn you, Abe!

And he did want her. He'd wanted her from the first time he'd seen her, standing in that damned saloon looking so prim and proper, asking about her brother.

But he'd never raped a woman before, and he knew if he was to have her, it would have to be rape.

Or would it? She'd been nice to him at Tombstone. She'd even said she liked him. Maybe, if he was nice to her now, she'd like him again.

He lowered the level of whiskey in the bottle another inch, then stared into the fire, letting the dancing flames soothe him. He'd never be able to let Serena go. Not after kidnapping her. He knew, too, he'd never be able to kill her. Even if he hated her, he couldn't kill her. And he sure as hell didn't hate her.

He wanted her. And he wanted her to want him. They could go somewhere back East, where her Apache blood wouldn't mean much, where nobody knew them. Maybe he could even take her to the farm. Ben would like her. Ben's wife might appreciate having another woman around to help with the chores.

That was it! All he had to do was make her love him. He'd gotten his revenge on Matt Colton by making him think his sister was dead. He'd paid his debt to Abe. It was time to think of himself. And Serena.

One last pull, and the whiskey bottle was empty. It

222

landed on the dirt floor with a muted thud. Even the crackling and hissing of the fire sounded muted as blood rushed to his groin and roared in his ears.

In his mind, he rose from the rickety chair with masculine grace and strode slowly to Serena's side. He knelt next to her and ran a finger across her perfect cheek.

In reality, when he stood, his foot wrapped around the leg of the chair and he stumbled. He shook himself loose. The chair and table crashed to the floor.

Serena flinched. For one long second, her heart stopped. Then it pounded so hard it threatened to burst through the wall of her chest. He was coming! He'd left her alone for more than two weeks, but now he was coming.

With her hands tied over her head to a corner post of the shack, there was nothing she could do to stop him. She was utterly, terrifyingly, helpless. Fear left a metallic taste in her dry mouth. Her muscles knotted. Her breath refused to come.

Caleb's large, dirty hand reached down and yanked the blanket from her. She wanted to cringe away, to scream and cry. But she didn't. She refused to let him see her terror. She forced her eyes to meet his, but his were glazed, unfocused. He rubbed his crotch with one hand and ripped her shirt open with the other. Her flesh tried to shrink and disappear.

Caleb said nothing. He worked his mouth and rubbed his crotch and stared. Then he reached for her. Dirty, broken fingernails dug into the tender flesh of her breast.

As her stomach threatened to erupt, Serena swallowed hard.

Is this what you felt, Mama? This terror, this degradation? This horror? Oh God, Mama! How did you stand it? How will I stand it?

"That's it, little sister, just lie there. I like my women willing." He used both hands to work at removing her pants.

Serena fought the panic that threatened to overwhelm her, and lost. She shrieked and squirmed and kicked, trying to defeat the hands that were even now tugging her pants down around her thighs.

Caleb got the pants as far as her knees, then had to throw one leg across both of hers to still her thrashing. Damn, but she felt good beneath him. If only she would lie still.

When she kept squirming beneath him, he forgot any intention of trying to woo her. He was going to take her, by God, and there wasn't a damn thing she could do about it.

He tightened his hands around her waist until Serena was sure he would squeeze her to death. Still, she kept struggling. It wasn't in her nature to give up, and she was too scared to just lie there and let him have his way.

"Be still!" he shouted, his whiskey breath gagging her.

He buried his face between her breasts and thrust the hard proof of his arousal against her thigh. She tried to jerk away, but his weight held her down. His rough beard scraped the delicate skin of her breasts. When his tongue came out and swiped a nipple, she gagged again. She was going to be sick.

His hands, rough and hurting, roamed over her body, leaving her no secrets, no dignity. She'd never known anything so horrible in her life as this beast pawing at her. Heart thundering, bile rising in her throat, she pulled on the rope above her until her wrists were raw. It made no difference. She was firmly trapped.

Caleb grew tired of her thrashing and sank his teeth into her breast. That ought to keep her still, by God.

Serena gasped at the pain and lay perfectly still, except for the heaving of her chest, the cringing of her flesh, and the sickness in her gut.

One hard, unrelenting hand dived down between her legs. She screamed. His other hand struck her across the face, cutting her scream in half.

The terror and shame, combined with the probing, hurtful fingers between her legs and the smell of his fetid breath, were more than Serena's stomach could stand. Its contents burned a path up her throat.

At the strangled sound she made, Caleb turned his face toward hers and laid his head on her bare stomach. She raised her shoulders from the ground. Caleb grinned, then thrust his fingers deeper inside her dry, unwilling body.

Fourteen

The morning after Matt's fruitless trip to Tucson, an even dozen men, under the direction of Travis Colton, fanned out on either side of the road to town, searching for any trace of Serena's passing. Anything at all out of the ordinary. They stretched out in a long line, each man keeping the next in sight.

The three Trevino brothers, Carlos, Benito, and Jorge, had lived and worked on the Triple C since it was built. The bright-eyed oldest daughter of the Coltons was special to each of them, as she was to the other hands who had volunteered to search.

They were a hard-eyed, tight-lipped group, each man a good tracker in his own right. If Serena had left the road before reaching Tucson, they would find her trail. Of course, it would have been easier if several days hadn't passed since she'd left, and if they hadn't had that toad-strangler of a storm last night.

Travis himself took the road, eyeing every inch on both sides for any sign. Fifty yards to his left, Pace scanned every tree, every bush and cactus, every scraggly blade of grass. To Pace's left rode fifteen-year-old Spencer.

Spence hung back, going slower than the others. He

wasn't as experienced, and was being especially careful so as not to miss something. No one had asked him to come, but he had put down his books — a rare occurrence — and demanded his place among the men. Like the rest of the Coltons, Spence had a strong sense of family. There wasn't anything he wouldn't do for any of them.

That was the main reason he had decided to study medicine. At first he had thought of law, but lawyers were a dime a dozen. Arizona was lousy with them.

Besides, a lawyer wouldn't be able to help Spence's father if he suffered a stroke the way Granddad Jason had when Spence was a kid. But a doctor could. Maybe. If he was good enough.

A lawyer couldn't have saved Angela. A lawyer couldn't ease pain, bind wounds, or bring new life into the world.

No, Spence didn't want to be a lawyer. He was going to be a doctor. The best damned doctor this territory had ever seen. *Then* he would be able to help his family. He would do anything for his family. He would do whatever he could to take that look of helpless terror from his mother's eyes.

So he had put down his books to ride with the men. He wasn't as good a tracker as the others, but he wasn't bad, either. Growing up in a house full of Apaches, he couldn't help but know more about tracking than the average citizen.

Fifty yards to the right of the road, Matt wasn't thinking about Spence or anyone. Only Serena. Pace said he had watched her leave, so they knew she had headed toward town. But somewhere along the way, she had seemingly just disappeared.

Rena was much too responsible to have run off, so what had happened? There was no reason for her to leave the road, yet she must have. There was absolutely nothing between the ranch and town. No neighbors of any kind. Not even a water hole. And she was too experienced to have had trouble with the horse.

The remaining possibilities sent sharp pain stabbing in Matt's chest.

But his imaginings were absurd. The bandits who occasionally flooded across the border and terrorized the valley hadn't raided this close to Tucson in twenty years.

Of course, Tucson itself was a favorite haven of the dregs of society. The town literally crawled with everything from petty thieves to cutthroat murderers.

Matt tried to block out pictures of Serena in the hands of scum like that, yet he forced himself to admit it was a very real possibility.

But, his mind argued, there was no reason for outlaws to take this road. It led nowhere except to the Triple C.

Matt forced the unsettling thoughts away. Serena had to be all right. She had to be. If anything terrible had happened to her, Pace and Dani would have felt something, wouldn't they? *He* would have felt something.

The thought startled him, but as he turned it over in his mind, he knew it was true. If something had happened to Rena, he would have known. That emptiness she had so recently filled would have swallowed him whole.

He didn't even want to consider what his new awareness meant.

The line of men swept all the way to town without finding a single trace of Serena's passage. They gathered at the edge of Tucson, then broke up and searched every square foot of town for a glimpse of Serena, the buggy, or the gray mare.

They found nothing.

The next morning, they all switched places, so no man would cover the same ground he'd covered yesterday. They pulled in their ranks, riding at twenty-five-yard intervals.

The tension built in each man as the day wore on. If they didn't find something before they reached the ranch, where would they look next? How would they ever find her?

Matt's eyes burned so badly with fatigue he was afraid he would miss something important. Hell. Who knew what he might have missed already? If he had crossed a set of railroad tracks in the past two hours, he probably wouldn't have seen them.

He pulled his horse to a halt and rubbed his eyes. "Christ," he muttered. It had to be here. Some trace, some sign . . . something. She had to have left the road. He didn't know where, or why, but she *must* have left the road.

He blinked and focused on the flattened bush beside him. *Flattened?* He stared at it a long moment, then slowly dismounted. On either side of him, Benito Trevino and Tinker Williamson saw and drew their horses to a halt.

Matt knelt in the gray dirt and studied the bush. That storm could easily have flattened it, yet the ones next to it, no bigger, no sturdier, stood upright. The only hoofprints in the immediate area were his, so that ruled out one of their own men having trampled it.

One twig lying on the ground had a break in it. Matt carefully reached out and lifted the clump of stems next to the broken one. Those stems had evidently been beaten down by the rain, because underneath, protected from the downpour by the covering, lay a single track — a wheel track.

Matt pulled his pistol and fired three quick shots. The signal brought the other riders at a gallop.

All except Spence. He was the last rider in line on the south end of the search. He heard the shots, but ignored them. He'd been following a series of broken shrubs for several yards, wanting to make certain of what he'd found before signaling the others. The line of broken shrubs led straight into a thick clump of cedars and brambles.

The wall of green he faced looked impenetrable. If that was the remains of a wagon or buggy track he'd been following, it couldn't possibly have gone through there. He dismounted, picked up a rock, and tossed it through the cedar branches. It struck something and gave back a hollow thud. Not the dull sound of a rock hitting a tree or the ground, but a rock hitting a board.

Excited now, yet cautious, afraid of what he might find, he pushed a branch aside. Amazingly, it fell to the ground. He touched more branches. They, too, fell. Spence peered through the new opening and took in a sharp breath as he stared at the back end of the family buggy.

For one brief instant, he panicked. He couldn't see inside the buggy. What if Rena was in there? Fear shook him from head to toe. He took a deep breath to calm himself. It didn't help. Another branch fell beside him. A blue jay screeched and darted away. Spence jerked like he'd been shot. Any more sudden sounds, and he just might piss in his pants.

Ready, should anyone jump out of the surrounding brush, he stepped back several paces and fired off three rounds.

Matt froze at the sound of the signal. He glanced around the circle of men. "Spence," he said under his breath, naming the only one who wasn't there.

All the men jerked into action at once, mounting up and riding toward the sound of the signal. For one brief second, Matt, Pace, and Travis read the mixture of hope and fear in each others' eyes. Had Spence found a sign? Or had he found . . . Rena?

Nerves screaming, Matt kicked his blue roan into a gallop and gripped the reins tight to still his shaking.

Had Spence found her? Her . . . body?

No. She wasn't dead. He wouldn't, *couldn't* let himself believe she was dead.

He beat his father and Pace to the clearing by two lengths. There, he got a firm grip on himself and dismounted. He couldn't panic now. He had to keep his head. Looking around, he took in details.

An old campsite indicated someone had waited, hidden, for several days. One man, one horse. Then the buggy had come, and two horses had left. One had been range-fed. The other had recently eaten grain.

Matt nudged the grain-filled droppings with the toe of his boot. He looked to Pace.

Pace nodded. "The gray mare I hitched was grain-fed."

Matt forced himself toward the buggy.

Serena's handbag lay on the ground beside the left front wheel. Her carpetbag was still inside, on the floorboard. Nothing in the bag seemed to have been disturbed. Then there was the dress. Matt felt ice form in his veins as he fingered the gray serge material that lay in a torn heap on the buggy floor.

"She was wearing that the day she left the house," Pace said.

Benito, the oldest of the Trevino brothers and foreman of the Triple C, cleared his throat then hesitated. "Señor Travis," he began reluctantly. "Is it possible . . . well . . .

231

that the *señorita* knew this man was here, met him, and . . ."

"And ran off with him?" Spence finished for him.

No. Matt knew better.

"If she did," Pace said, "she didn't leave willingly." With his pocketknife, he dug a slug from the trunk of a tree. "This came from her derringer, that little one of Mother's Rena carries when she travels."

"Who?" Matt whispered. "And why?" He shook his head. "I don't believe she came here and met someone. He had to have met her on the road and forced her here. Any tracks would have been long gone. It's a miracle we found this at all, this far from the road. You did good, Spence. Damn good."

Travis squeezed Spence's shoulder. "You sure did, son. We're proud of you."

Spence nodded, swallowed, and blushed.

"Now," Travis said grimly. "After a week of wind, followed by that goddamn storm, tracking Serena and whoever took her is going to be damn near impossible."

"But at least we know she's alive," Spence offered.

Benito said what no one else wanted to, but what they all were thinking. "She was alive when they left here, seven days ago."

"She's alive!" Matt refused to acknowledge any other possibility.

"I pray this is true," Benito said fervently.

"She's alive," Pace said calmly. He closed his eyes and took in a slow breath, searching inside himself for that special bond he and Serena had always shared. He reached for her voice, but it wasn't there. But there was no emptiness, no gaping hole in his soul, as he knew there would be if she were dead. "She's out there, somewhere. And she's alive."

232

That was good enough for Matt. He *knew* she was alive. She had to be.

When Pace opened his eyes, Matt met his gaze, then gave a sharp nod. "How much grain did you feed the mare?"

"More than that," Pace said, indicating the pile of broken manure at Matt's feet.

"Pair up in twos, spread out, and zigzag toward the south," Matt told the men. "That horse had at least one more dump of grain left in her, and she had to shit again sometime. Find it."

The men began to mount up, but Travis stopped them. "There's only about an hour of light left. We wouldn't get far enough today to make any difference, and we didn't bring enough supplies. We'll go home, each man will load a full pack of provisions, and we'll head out at dawn."

Matt started to protest at what he considered an unnecessary delay, but he knew his father was right. And there was Dani. She'd be crazy with worry by now. She would need all of them with her when she learned what they'd found.

They rode in at dusk. In minutes Dani had a hot meal ready for her family. A similar meal awaited the returning ranch hands at the cook shack.

Jessica and Joanna were sent to bed while Travis explained to Dani what the men found. Pace went to organize supplies for the search. They had no idea how long they'd be out, so he also arranged for a chuck wagon to follow them. The rest of the family gathered in Travis's study.

By the time Pace had left the study, there wasn't much left for anyone to say. Spence finally went to bed. Matt watched his stepmother pace the floor, his thoughts even

233

more tortured than hers. He blamed himself for whatever was happening to Serena.

Travis sat at his desk and idly sorted through the mail he'd picked up in Tucson but hadn't looked at yet. There was a new contract from the Army for beef for the reservation, and a letter from his old friend, Cal. Cal's letters always made him smile, but Travis wasn't in the mood to be cheered just then. He had another letter, this one from Washington, regarding the meeting he was trying to arrange with the president to discuss the deplorable conditions the Apaches were forced to endure at San Carlos. Since Garfield was shot last month, Travis didn't hold out much hope for the meeting.

Also in the mail was a package for Matt. "Here." Travis tossed the leather bundle marked "personal" to his son.

Matt welcomed the distraction from his tormenting thoughts and studied the package. No return address. Who did he know who would send him a personal package? The rawhide string was knotted tightly, so he pulled his knife from his belt and cut it. The end flap came open. Matt held the package up and dumped the contents onto his lap.

His sharp cry split the air as he stared at the hideous thing that fell out. He went light-headed. His stomach heaved to his throat.

Travis saw it at the same time Dani did. He barely made it to her side before her eyes rolled back in her head and her knees gave way beneath her.

The grisly thing in Matt's lap was a scalp, a fairly fresh one. With black hair. And a white streak where the right temple should be.

Fifteen

Pace was just entering the room when Matt flung his head back and roared in anguish and disbelief. The gruesome thing lying across Matt's thighs brought a look of surprise, then puzzlement to Pace's face. "Now, why do you suppose someone would go to all that trouble just to make us think Serena was dead?"

Dani's eyes fluttered open to stare at Pace.

"Are you crazy?" Travis demanded, his face grief stricken, his arms around his wife. "That . . . that's your . . . sister's . . ." He couldn't bring himself to finish.

Matt watched Pace closely. Anything to keep from looking at the thing in his lap. Pace seemed so sure. Matt had never known Pace to be mistaken when it came to anything to do with his twin. His teeth clenched tight, Matt worked up the nerve to touch the long black and white hair lying across his thighs. As he fingered it, his eyes widened and his heart pounded with excitement. "No," he cried. "It's not Rena's!"

"God knows," Travis said, his voice shaking with emotion, "I don't want it to be hers, but are you both blind? Who else has hair like that?"

"I don't know." Matt shook his head. "But it's not Rena's. It's too . . . coarse, too thin, too curly. Rena's hair is softer, thicker. Straighter."

Pace glared at Matt. "Just how the hell do you know how soft and thick my sister's hair is?"

"*Your* sister?"

"Yes, damn you, *my* sister."

Matt grinned. "Thanks. I'll remind you of that one day."

Pace lunged at Matt and reached for his throat. Matt grunted at the impact, surprised by Pace's strength. The kid was growing up. Matt had once been able to throw him off easily, but not anymore.

"Stop it!" Dani pulled free of Travis's arms and thrust herself between her son and her stepson. Pace backed off instantly. Matt sat where he was and rubbed his bruised throat.

"I don't know what's going on between you two," Dani said angrily, "and right now I don't care. We've got more important things to consider. When Serena is home and safe, you two can tear each other to pieces if you want."

Matt cringed inwardly. He hated to upset Dani for any reason, and she was under so much strain right now that he was ashamed for adding to her trouble. He lowered his gaze and caught a glimpse of something white on the floor next to his foot. He reached down and picked up the folded piece of paper.

It was a note. It must have fallen out of the pouch when he and Pace struggled.

"Read it," Travis ordered.

"It says . . ." *God. No.* That light-headed feeling threatened to send him to the floor. " 'A sister for a brother. She died the way he did — slowly, and with much pain. Her screams now echo across this canyon with his.' " The paper rattled as Matt's hand shook. "It's signed . . . 'Caleb Miller Scott.' "

"Oh, my God," Dani whispered.

"Abe Scott's brother?" Travis asked, dazed.

"Apparently so." Matt swore viciously. "I should have known! Goddammit! I should have known it was too much of a coincidence."

"What are you talking about?" Pace demanded. "You know this bastard?"

Matt closed his eyes and swallowed. "Rena and I met him in Tombstone. We knew him only as Caleb. But his eyes . . . God, I should have known those eyes. He said he wanted to come calling on Rena. Goddamn, I should have known."

Behind his closed lids, Matt saw once again Abe Scott riding from behind the trees. He shook the vision away. No time for that now. Angela was dead. Abe Scott was dead.

And now Caleb Scott had Serena.

Matt made himself read the note again. "Well, we can call off the search."

"But you said she was alive." Travis's voice shook. "You said that . . . thing . . . wasn't hers."

"It's *not* hers, Dad. She's alive, and now I know where he's holding her."

Pace nodded. "Cos-codee."

Dani frowned. "Chihuahua's old hideout in Mexico?"

"That's where we caught up with Scott two years ago. He got himself trapped in there. Didn't know there was a back way out."

"But there isn't a back way out," Dani protested. "That's why it's called Cos-codee, 'No Escape'."

"Around the point, on the back side, there's a pass up on the cedar ledge. It's just wide enough to lead a horse through, as long as both you and your horse aren't too wide. A loaded pack mule would never make it."

237

* * *

Later that evening, when it was finally settled that Matt and Pace would ride out at first light, the two men sat with their parents in the salon. Matt watched as Pace stared broodingly at the floor.

Suddenly Pace jerked, spilling part of his drink. He turned abruptly and stared hard at his mother, something dark and unreadable in his eyes.

Matt tensed. Something was happening. Something was wrong. "Pace?"

"Do you feel it?" Pace asked his mother.

But Dani didn't hear her son, much less answer him. She sprang upright in her chair. Her glass of sherry fell from her fingers as her eyes glazed over. A deep moan of anguish rose from the depths of her soul. "Nooooo!"

Pace jerked again. With a look of revulsion, he brushed frantically and repeatedly at his chest. "He's touching her. Oh, God, I can feel him touching her!"

Pace's body became Serena's. He could feel the cruel hands grasping at her, pinching, hurting, as he tried in vain to brush them away.

Matt met his father's gaze. Each understood what was happening, though it had never happened before. Pace was feeling on his body what Dani was seeing in her mind.

Travis had never tried to free his wife from one of her visions before, but this time he had to. He couldn't let her see whatever was happening to her daughter. If his suspicions were correct . . . The blood in his veins turned to ice. He shook with horror. He couldn't let her see!

"Dani!" He grasped her shoulders and shook her. "Dani! No! You have to stop!"

Amazingly, he got through to her. Her eyes focused

238

abruptly on him. "Travis! He's—he's—oh, God!" Tears gushed down her face as she trembled violently in his arms. "My baby, Travis! He's . . . raping my baby!"

Travis tightened his embrace and buried his face in her hair, wetting it with his own tears. He'd never felt so totally helpless in his life.

Something deep inside Matt twisted. With a gut-wrenching sense of dread, he forced his gaze back to Pace.

Suddenly Pace stiffened. "Serenaaaa!" Breathing heavily, he jerked to his feet and stumbled toward the empty fireplace. He leaned against the mantel with outstretched arms, his head thrown back, eyes squeezed shut. His face was that of a man suffering the worst torture imaginable.

Matt wanted to scream. He wanted to kill.

A moment later, gasping for breath, Pace sprinted from the room. Matt followed as Pace threw open the front door with a bang and dropped to his knees just beyond, where he promptly heaved the contents of his stomach into the flowerbed.

Matt felt his stomach churn with the knowledge of what had just happened to Serena. As he turned away and walked to his room, his rage increased with each step, even as his vision blurred. He nursed the rage. It grew hotter and more powerful until it glowed white-hot in the pit of his stomach and threatened to consume him.

In his room, with the door closed, he sat on the edge of his bed and gripped the mattress to keep from screaming.

Soon, too soon, anger faded. Pain and guilt took its place.

Rena! Rena, I'm so sorry. Forgive me. I should never have come home. I should never have let you stay in

Tombstone. I should have known who Caleb was. I should have killed him. I should never have hurt you. I should never have touched you. I should never have held you, kissed you.

I should never have let you out of my sight.

Then slowly, selfishly, the unbidden thought came, *I should have loved you while I had the chance.*

He pushed the thought away. It was wrong! She was his sister, for Christsake!

No, she isn't, whispered a devil in the back of his mind. Her mother was only his stepmother. Her father was some unknown Apache rapist. He and Serena weren't actually related at all—not by blood.

But they were related by law, and by love, and by virtue of having been raised as brother and sister since the day she was born.

He remembered the day she was born as if it were yesterday. God almighty. He had been nearly eleven. Even if they'd been raised as strangers and only just recently met, he was too damned old for her.

His mind told him it was wrong, but his heart, and his body, too, he admitted, told him it was right. All the things he'd felt for her since she'd found him in Tombstone rolled over him, enveloped him, and not one of those feelings had anything to do with brother and sister. They were feelings a man had for a woman—the woman he wanted.

Now, because of his own foolishness in refusing to recognize the truth sooner, she was out there somewhere, being tormented . . . because of him.

He'd heard of women who'd been raped and could never stand the touch of a man afterward. Dani had been that way for a while, when he'd first known her. Would that happen to Rena?

The thought crept forward again. *I should have loved her while I had the chance.* If he had, he could have given her pleasure like she never knew existed. He could have introduced her slowly and gently to the physical side of love. She'd wanted him, he knew that. And he'd wanted her — still did.

But it was too late.

He'd been so worried about what was right and what was wrong, and now all Serena would know of lovemaking would be violence and pain and fear. It was something she might never get over.

Any way he looked at it, Serena's pain was because of him. Caleb Scott was out to get even for the death of his brother. Serena had fallen into the bastard's grasp because she was running away from the pain Matt had inflicted on her.

With effort, Matt pushed the thoughts away. If he expected to find her, he had to get some sleep first. And he *would* find her . . . or die trying.

He lay in the dark for hours, trying to keep his mind blank, before he finally fell asleep. It seemed like only minutes later when he woke and cried out, cold sweat streaming down his heaving chest from a nightmare. The images kept playing over and over in his head of Caleb Scott forcing his way between Serena's soft thighs and thrusting brutally into her virgin flesh.

Even though they weren't related by blood, Matt and Pace looked so much alike the next morning it was uncanny. One face was slightly darker than the other, with black hair surrounding it instead of blond. But their features, usually so different, looked as though they had been chiseled from the same piece of stone. Jaws were rigid, chins prominent and determined. Their eyes, one pair brown, the other blue, were filled with cold, hard purpose. With death.

Travis Colton stood with his arm supporting his wife in the predawn light and eyed his two oldest sons, one of his body, the other of his heart. No words were spoken. No words were needed. Be she alive or dead, they would find Serena and bring her home.

And Caleb Miller Scott would die a slow, painful death.

It was hours before either Matt or Pace spoke, but when they were finally forced to slow the horses for a breather, Matt asked the question that had tormented him all night. "Is she alive?"

Pace took a slow, deep breath and kept his gaze on the trail. "She's alive."

The reassurance those words should have brought didn't come. "Are you sure? Can you see her? Can you hear her, Pace?"

Pace shook his head in frustration. "No. I can only hear her when she wants me to . . . when she thinks of me. I only know that she's alive." He swallowed heavily. "She *is* alive."

Matt might have been a tad more reassured if Pace hadn't felt the need to repeat himself. Was he reiterating something he felt, something he knew, or something he only hoped for?

They didn't stop long enough to prepare a meal until the next night. While Matt heated beans in a skillet over the small fire, Pace went to the nearby stream to wash up. When he came back, carrying his shirt in his hand, Matt stared curiously at his stepbrother's smooth, bronze chest covered in bruises. "What happened to you?"

Pace followed Matt's gaze and looked down at his own chest. His eyes widened, then closed tightly. A look of pain briefly crossed his face before he schooled his expression into a hard mask. With jerky movements, he put his shirt back on and buttoned it. "They're Rena's."

Matt started to ask what he meant, then stopped. Their gazes locked, each man torn at the thought of other bruises, on other parts of Serena's body.

Matt's voice echoed like cold steel. "As soon as the moon rises, we ride."

Pace merely nodded his agreement.

They continued south along the old Gila Trail. Just past Tubac, about twenty miles north of the Mexican border, the trail angled southeast, then due east. Day after day the hot August sun beat down, only to rise again in waves of heat from the dry, baked earth. They kept to the Gila Trail until it crossed the Rio Agua Prieta, where they turned south.

At this time of year, the only hint that a river ever flowed down the dry wash was an occasional muddy spot. Once in a while, a small trickle of moisture seeped down from the rocks along the east bank.

When they were in sight of the junction of the Rio Agua Prieta, such as it was, and the down-Bavispe, they cut eastward across the canyon and waited until dark to move on.

They were close now. After six rugged days and several nights in the saddle, Matt felt his weariness slide away with the knowledge that tonight he would have Serena at his side.

A half-moon gave them ample light as they rode to within a mile of the hidden valley known to Apaches as Cos-codee, to Mexicans as Cañon de los Embudos. Matt and Pace hid their horses and went the rest of the way on foot, sliding silently, fluidly, from shadow to shadow until they reached the rocky crevice marking the entrance to the ancient hideout.

Beyond that point, they were even more careful not to make a sound that would give them away. They wanted no announcement of their arrival.

They split up and went in opposite directions. Each would cover half the area. They would meet at the base of the cedar ledge, which led to the secret Cos-codee Pass.

Matt cursed the still night. A constant whisper and rustle of wind through the cedars would have helped disguise any sound he or Pace might be clumsy enough to make. He wasn't worried that Scott would hear them—he and Pace had both been trained by the best Apache warriors. It was the horses, with their much sharper hearing, who might betray their presence.

If there were any horses. If Scott hadn't already fled, which was highly possible. He had plainly given Matt his location. The man had to know Matt would come after him. Would he be here, waiting? Was Serena still with him? Was she still alive?

If she wasn't . . . Matt's blood turned to ice in his veins. If Serena was dead, he would find Caleb Scott, no matter how long it took. And when he did, he would make what he'd done to Abe Scott look like a friendly handshake compared with what he'd do this time.

In fact, the bastard had a long, slow death coming, even if Serena was alive. He was a yellow-livered coward who preyed on an innocent woman instead of confronting the man he was really after. Scum like that didn't deserve an easy death.

There was no hint of another person in the hideout as

Matt made his way toward the back ledge. Disappointment and frustration ate at him.

As he waited at the appointed spot for Pace, he realized that in all the commotion over Serena's disappearance and the arrival of the scalp, it hadn't occurred to him to wonder how Caleb Scott even knew of this place, or what had happened to Abe here.

How *had* he known?

His thoughts were interrupted as Pace stepped out of the shadows and joined him. With silent hand signals, they determined Cos-codee was empty. No Scott. No Serena.

Matt and Pace agreed to camp back where they'd left their horses so as not to disturb anything they might have missed in the hideout. They would come back in the daylight and go over every inch of the place. They would search for any clue that Serena had actually been there, any trace of a trail leading away from the hidden canyon.

The only things they managed to find in the canyon the next morning were the cold, week-old ashes of a campfire, and a nearby clearing where horses had been picketed. At the entrance, where the rock jutted up from the ground to conceal the canyon, they followed the faint trail through the lava and cactus. Faint, but not faint enough for just Scott and Serena to have come and gone. Too many tracks for just them.

At the edge of the lava Matt and Pace found more than they wanted. They found two separate trails leading away in opposite directions. Both trails were cold.

"We'll each take a trail," Matt said, with a calm he didn't feel. Scott had to be at the end of one of the trails. And hopefully, Serena. "Whoever runs into a dead end comes back here and follows the other trail. Agreed?"

As it seemed their only choice, Pace agreed. It was inconceivable to him that Scott would head back toward Arizona, so he chose the trail heading east into the Sierra Madres.

Having no reason to object, Matt went along with Pace's choice.

But the tracks Pace followed didn't head east for long. By the first afternoon, the trail began to wind and curve through dry canyons and across high ridges.

Whoever he was following had not bothered to conceal their tracks. Either they were confident that no one would follow, or they hoped someone would, or they simply didn't care.

The morning of the third day found Pace staring with frustration at the dusty little town of Fronteras. He'd chosen the wrong set of tracks for finding Serena. Surely Scott wouldn't have brought her to a town. So who was he following? What did they have to do with Serena?

He didn't have answers to those questions, but he fully intended to before the day was out. He glanced down to make sure he wore nothing to identify himself as an Apache. His people were hated here just as much as they were above the border. But with his hair only reaching his collar, he could pass for Mexican—except for his eyes. No one would know his heritage. Everyone for miles around had skin as dark or darker than his.

Satisfied with his appearance, he concentrated on finding the two riders he'd been trailing for three days. They could be long gone by now.

When he rode past a small cantina halfway down the dusty street, he gripped his reins tight and felt his heart pound. It had been much easier than he'd anticipated. One of the horses tied to the hitching rail in front of the cantina was a gray mare with a familiar brand, the brand of the Triple C. It was the horse Pace had hitched to the buggy for Serena the morning she left for Tucson.

He dismounted and tied his horse to the hitching rail across the street. He entered the cantina. *"Una cerveza, por favor."*

Warm beer in hand, Pace sat before the filmy fly-specked window in the cantina and watched the street. He settled down to sip and wait.

While Pace waited for the rider of the Triple C horse to appear, Matt was in the Cananea Hills, about a day's ride south of Naco Springs. His gelding's ears pricked forward. Matt drew to a halt. Then he heard it, too — a man-sound. The sharp ring of an ax on wood.

This was it. He was close. Matt could feel Serena. She was near, reaching out to him.

He tethered his horse in a thick clump of cedar and juniper. He removed his spurs and exchanged his boots for knee-high, tab-toed *kébans,* the moccasins worn by the Chiricahua. He tucked his pant legs inside. After checking his pistols, he tested the wicked, gleaming blade of his bowie knife. It was sharp and ready to bite. He slipped it back into the sheath on his belt.

Heart pounding, Matt moved slowly, stealthily. Now was not the time to send any animals scampering or frighten the birds into giving away his approach. The steady, hollow ring of the ax was his signal beacon as he crept forward. The ground ahead rose sharply. Matt angled to the right and discovered a narrow cut in the rock — the opening to a small box canyon. Scrub oak, cedar, and juniper clung precariously to the vertical rock walls and dotted the canyon floor.

The sun flashed briefly off something metal. In the next instant the ringing of the ax echoed, pure and sweet

247

in the still, clear air. Matt peered through evergreen branches and steeled himself for the sight of his quarry.

And it was him — Caleb Miller Scott.

It was ironic, Matt thought grimly, that chopping wood was the excuse Scott had used to enter their lives, because it was going to be one of the last things the bastard ever did. He'd announced his presence with it here just as surely as he had in Tombstone, and it was going to be the death of him.

Matt backed away from the mouth of the canyon and made his way around and up, careful not to dislodge any rocks or snap any twigs. He concealed himself along the rim of the canyon and studied the area closely. Near the highest wall, at the back, stood a crudely built shack whose door faced the canyon mouth. It was a stroke of luck that there were no windows on the side facing Matt — not that he intended to be seen anyway.

There was no sign of Serena, except that there were two horses browsing on the sparse grass inside a brush corral. But she was down there. He could feel her presence as strongly as he felt the sun beating down and burning his back through the fabric of his shirt. She was down there.

Matt forced himself to concentrate. He studied every inch of the steep slope before him, which led to the canyon floor, and planned each step he would take when darkness came.

Sixteen

Serena came awake slowly, unwilling to leave the oblivion of sleep. Her gritty eyes felt like they'd been sewn shut. To open them would surely tear out a thousand stitches.

Her nose twitched. Meat. Roasting meat. Her mouth watered. Her stomach cramped. He was cooking again. Damn him.

On the trail, Caleb had been perfectly content with beans and jerky. But in the week they'd been at the shack, he'd made sure fresh meat roasted in the fireplace every night. Just so she could smell it.

How much longer could she go without food? She hadn't been permitted anything but an occasional sip of water—just enough to keep her alive—since the night he'd tried to rape her.

"You'll come around," he had said the next day. "You'll come around when you get hungry enough. You don't eat 'til you give me what I want."

At the memory of that night, a shudder ripped through her weak limbs. He hadn't tried anything since then. But what he had done was perhaps just as bad. He had taken her clothes and blanket and left her lying on the hard dirt floor, naked, tied by her hands to a slat in the wall. And he had not allowed her to eat so much as a bite.

Some of her Apache ancestors had gone without food for days on end and survived. But that didn't make it any easier on her. By her best guess, this was her fifth day without food. Her fifth day of starvation. Her fifth day to smell fresh meat roasting over the fire only a few feet away.

Her fifth day to lie naked before his hated, hungry gaze. To look in his eyes, she could almost believe he was the one going without food. But his hunger wasn't for food—it was for her.

He'd said he wouldn't try to force her again. When she was ready to cooperate, she could eat.

Serena wasn't sure she was strong enough for the test ahead. Could she just lie there and allow herself to starve to death? Even if he grew lax and left her untied, she doubted she had the strength to escape. But to just let herself die?

Her only alternative—the only way to survive—was to give in. To let him use her body.

To be held down and forcibly raped was one thing. To give in, to agree to what he wanted, even though it was still brought about by force—the threat of starvation—was something else. She might have been able to live with the former. The shame of submitting to him in order to fill her stomach was something she didn't think she could survive.

Dear God, what was she going to do? A few more days, and the choice would no longer be hers. She couldn't last much longer without food.

Caleb kicked the door open and sauntered in with an armload of firewood. He stacked the pieces near the fireplace and fed one to the small blaze beneath his spitted rabbit. When he stood, his gaze raked her naked form.

Let him look. Serena was past caring.

When he'd first taken her clothes, she'd spent all her time and most of her energy curling up into a ball to hide as much of herself from his eyes as possible. Now she didn't bother. She didn't have the strength for it anymore.

Caleb threw back his head and laughed. "Hungry, little sister?" he asked with a snort.

Yes, damn you. Yes, I'm hungry, she thought. But she kept silent. Talking took energy.

Caleb turned and checked the meat. Deciding it was done, he pulled it off the spit and dropped it directly onto the table. No plate, no nothing. Just juicy meat on a bare, dirty table.

Serena used some of her precious store of energy to roll to her side and face the wall. It was either that, or watch him eat. Even this way, it was bad enough. He made sure she heard everything he did. He chewed with his mouth open, smacked his lips, licked his fingers, and punctuated every swallow with a loud, satisfied "Aah!" or a grotesque belch. It was almost more than she could bear.

She concentrated on staring through the crack in the wall. She had no idea of the time, just that it was dark out. The only light came from the small fire behind her and a lantern perched on a rickety shelf over the fireplace.

She forced her ears to pick out night sounds and ignore Caleb's tactics. Frogs sang somewhere close by. Water must be near. Maybe there was a pond at the head of that little creek she'd seen the day they'd arrived.

Somewhere behind the shack a horse snorted. An occasional rustle in the nearby underbrush indicated small animals about at night. Rats, maybe. Or more rabbits.

Then, into the night came another sound, one that comforted her. It was the soft coo of a mourning dove. *Ooah-ooo-oo-oo*. A sound of home. Serena smiled sadly. She doubted she'd ever see home again now.

She listened for the call to repeat, or be answered by a mate. The calls always came in twos or threes. Strange time for a dove to be calling. They were usually active only during the day. Except, of course, when she was growing up. Then she'd heard them at night quite often, when Matt was teaching Pace Apache signals.

The thought made her stiffen. She forced herself to relax and wait. The soft call was not repeated.

For the first time in days, hope flared in her heart. That was no mourning dove out there! It was Matt or Pace. She knew it, felt it. She searched her inner mind for some message, some sign that would tell her it was Pace. Nothing came. Then she knew: it was Matt. He'd found her. *Thank God.*

If she hadn't had her back turned to Caleb just then, she would have given everything away by the tears of joy in her eyes and the trembling smile on her lips. It took her a moment to compose herself. She had to get Caleb to untie her. She had to have her hands free in case Matt needed her help.

She rolled slowly on to her back and turned her head to look at Caleb. Her gaze settled involuntarily on his greasy lips as they smacked another bite of rabbit.

Her stomach clenched.

Only one thing would make him untie her. She looked up at the ceiling and focused on a star peering through one of the numerous holes above her. *God, give me strength.*

"Caleb?" Her voice came out in a soft croak. She cleared her throat and tried again, louder. "Caleb?"

Caleb blinked at the sound of her voice. She hadn't spoken a word in days. He let the half-eaten rabbit leg dangle from his greasy fingers. "Yeah?" he said, around a mouthful of meat.

Serena worked her mouth to try to bring moisture to her tongue. "I'll make a deal with you."

Caleb laughed and took another bite of meat. "I'll bet you will. What kind of deal did you have in mind?"

Her empty stomach quivered at the sound of his noisy chewing. She tried to slow the rapid beat of her heart. Matt was near. He was coming for her. She had to get free and distract Caleb so Matt could make his move.

And what if that really is a bird out there? a voice in the back of her head asked.

If it was a bird instead of Matt, she'd be committing herself with her next words. Her entire body trembled at the thought.

But it *was* Matt. She knew it was. She just couldn't be wrong. She licked her dry, cracked lips and forced her voice to work again. "I'll do what you want, but—"

"No buts, little sister. You do what I want, or you don't eat. That's the deal."

Serena glanced at him, then away. "I only meant to say that I'm so weak . . . if I could just have something to eat, just a little bit. And my hands are numb. If you'd untie my hands and let me eat something, I'd . . . I'd—"

"You'd what?"

She glanced at him again and shivered. She read victory and lust in his narrowed gray eyes. *Oh God, oh God, oh God* . . . "I'd . . . be . . . grateful."

Caleb tossed the half-eaten rabbit leg onto the table, then sat back and folded his arms, ignoring the grease on his hands. His lips parted in a wide, knowing grin. His eyes . . . his eyes made her shiver.

"How grateful?"

Serena swallowed hard and stared at the ceiling again. Was she making a mistake? She'd heard no other sounds from outside. The frogs still sang, the horses snorted and stomped occasionally. No sound gave away the presence of a man creeping through the shadows.

But then, Matt wouldn't be so foolish as to give himself away. If it really was Matt.

It is Matt. I know it is. It has to be.

She swallowed again. "Real grateful," she whispered, her voice shaking with uncertainty. She held her breath, waiting for Caleb's response.

As he stood, the chair scraped across the dirt floor. Serena flinched. He walked slowly around the table—stalked, actually, like a hunter closing in on his trapped prey—and stood looming over her, his very nearness making her stomach churn. He stooped; she flinched again. Instead of grabbing her, though, he pulled a knife from his boot and straightened, his gaze locking with hers.

Along the edge of her vision, Serena saw him toy with the blade. Her nerves stretched to the breaking point. When she thought she couldn't take any more, he reached down and cut her wrists free.

She lay still for a long time letting the blood carry life and pain to her stiff fingers. When she slowly brought her arms down to her sides for the first time in days, her tortured muscles screamed. She knew her arms were at her sides—she could see them. But they felt like they were still stretched above her head.

She was so slow in sitting up that Caleb lost patience. His goal was in sight, and he was tired of waiting. He tucked the knife back inside his boot, then grabbed her roughly by both arms and hauled her to her feet. She scarcely felt his fingers digging into her half-dead flesh.

But the sudden shift from prone to upright made the blood rush from her head. Her weakened legs refused to hold her. She stumbled against the rough planks of the wall, scraping the skin on one cheek and both palms. Despite her determination to not give Caleb the satisfaction of knowing her pain, she cried out.

Caleb ignored her plight and jerked her toward the table, then shoved her down onto the chair. When he let go, she swayed and had to grip the edge of the table to keep from sliding to the floor. The chair was rough and hard against her bare flesh.

"There," he said with satisfaction, a hint of warning in his voice. "Now eat."

The smell of roasted rabbit rose from only inches away and assaulted her senses. Her mouth watered, even as her stomach protested the strong smell. She stared at the remains of the carcass and wondered if she'd be able to chew, much less swallow.

"What are you waiting for?" Caleb demanded. "I said eat."

Serena leaned against the table and forced one trembling hand toward the greasy meat before her. Where was Matt? If that was him out there, he should have been here by now! Had she been mistaken? Could she have imagined that solitary birdcall?

If she was wrong, the mistake was going to cost her more than she was willing to pay.

In that instant, she knew she'd rather starve than give in to Caleb Scott's demands. She prayed fervently it wouldn't come to that. She wasn't eager to die, but Coltons did not knuckle under to threats. Neither did

Apaches. And Serena was both.

The meat was slippery to her stiff fingers. It took three tries to tear off a small piece. Caleb watched her every move like the vulture he was.

She held the meat in her mouth a moment without chewing, to savor the juicy flavor. But as she swallowed and began chewing, the sliver of meat seemed to grow inside her mouth. It got bigger and bigger. Her jaws locked. Her stomach quivered, begging for more as the juice hit bottom, but the piece in her mouth just kept growing until she gagged on the sheer size of it.

With a strangled cough, she spit the meat out onto the table, amazed to find it to be the same small sliver she'd put in her mouth only a moment ago.

From across the table, Caleb scowled. He stepped around and stood next to her with a threatening gesture. "You eat, and eat now, or I'll cram that meat down your throat, sister."

Terror shook her like a hound shakes a rat. *Matt, are you here?*

When Caleb made as if to reach for her, she quickly tore off another small bite of meat. She couldn't force herself to try the same piece again.

This time she started chewing as soon as the meat touched her lips, and it seemed to work. She swallowed, then waited a moment to make sure it was going to stay down.

"Could I have some water, please?"

Talking made her throat hurt, but she wanted to keep Caleb distracted. She was almost surprised when he merely grunted and turned away. He stooped over, only three feet from where she sat, and reached for the canteen atop the small woodpile. His fingers brushed the strap. Before he could grasp it and straighten, a thunderous crash shook the entire cabin. Caleb and Serena jerked as one and faced the door.

But the door wasn't there. It lay in pieces on the floor, clouds of dirt billowing up from where it had landed.

In its place stood Matt Colton.

For one sharp instant all three of them froze.

Serena's heart filled with joy and love. He'd come for her! Matt had searched and found her!

Matt's heart filled with hate. He forced himself to keep his eyes on Caleb Miller Scott, when they wanted to settle on Serena.

Caleb's entire being filled with sheer terror. The man before him was a savage. He had the look of a marauding Apache, despite his blond hair. A bandana, folded into a narrow strip wrapped around his forehead, held his hair back from his hard, chiseled face.

The broad, bare chest heaved like an open taunt. The bear-claw necklace told of the savage ruthlessness Caleb knew the man possessed. Buckskin pants were tucked into the tops of knee-high moccasins. The well-worn holster tied down to his thigh was empty.

Caleb stared, mesmerized for an instant by the gaping black bore of the double-action Colt .45 that seemed a part of Matt Colton's hand.

Caleb tore his gaze away and looked up at Colton's face. Death looked back at him — slow, terrible, brown-eyed death.

With a speed born of desperation, Caleb grabbed Serena to his chest, shielding himself from the silent menace at the door.

Serena's cry of alarm stilled the faint movement of Matt's finger on the well-worn trigger. His jaws clenched and his nostrils flared. Hatred bunched in his gut. "Is that all the men in your family know how to do, hurt women? Don't you ever fight men? Or are you too afraid?"

Caleb was most definitely afraid. Sheer panic registered in his eyes. Then something else flashed there: determination. With a hint of resignation. The latter was a puzzle Matt didn't take the time to solve. He couldn't afford to take his eyes off his opponent for a second, even though he longed to reassure Serena with a look or a word.

But when Caleb's eyes widened, Matt involuntarily looked down. Serena lay slumped over Caleb's arm. The man thrust her aside with a growl. When she hit the floor, she cried out, then scrambled on hands and knees to the wall.

Caleb didn't hesitate. While Colton's eyes were on Serena, Caleb drew his Smith & Wesson. But he wasn't fast enough to draw down on a man whose pistol was already out and aimed. Even if the man was temporarily distracted.

Matt squeezed the trigger almost without thinking.

Caleb's hand exploded in pain. The gun flew from his grasp and bounced off the wall behind him. Blood sprayed his face. Fiery pain shot up his arm.

Now it would come. Colton would kill him, here and now. At least it would be quick. Just a bullet, probably in the chest, maybe the head. Could be worse.

But Matt Colton didn't shoot.

What kind of man was this? He had Caleb right where he wanted him, unarmed, at the end of his gun. But instead of firing, Colton holstered the pistol. Caleb stared in confusion.

Then, with strong, sure movements, Colton worked the buckle at his waist and tossed the holster and gun behind him, out the door, and growled, "I'm going to kill

258

you with my bare hands, you bastard."

Caleb's heart thundered in his chest. His fear somehow did not lessen. This threat was just as deadly as the .45, only not as swift, not as clean.

His right hand was growing numb. But what did it matter? He was as good as dead.

Then something tickled the back of his mind, some dark advantage he possessed but couldn't remember. A forgotten ace up his sleeve. But what was it?

Colton advanced slowly into the room. With a growl, Caleb flung the table aside and launched himself through the air to land with his hands clutching Colton's throat. Both men went down under the impact.

Serena pulled herself up from the floor and leaned, panting, against the wall. She stared wide-eyed at the jumbled mass of arms and legs thrashing in a cloud of dust near the doorway.

Didn't Caleb realize that even if he weren't wounded, he wouldn't stand a chance against Matt? Matt was going to kill him. And Serena, no matter how hard she tried, could not work up any regret over the thought.

But the fight wasn't as uneven as Serena had thought. Desperation lent Caleb strength. His right hand was a bloody mess, but he packed a powerful punch with his left.

Matt caught the fist flush in the mouth. Pain exploded. His head snapped back and struck the dirt floor with an audible thud, jarring his teeth. Blood trickled from a cut in his lip. Caleb was all over him then. Knees and boots and elbows and fists struck and gouged from one end of Matt's body to the other. He was stunned by the ferocity of the attack.

Matt worked a knee up into Caleb's stomach and shoved, bringing his foot up as Caleb rose above him.

The man sailed over Matt's head and landed on his back, just outside the doorway. Matt gained a temporary breather. He rolled to his knees and waited, letting his breath come back.

Caleb pulled himself up from the ground and shook his head. Droplets of sweat sprinkled down around him. Matt regained his breath and rose to his feet. Caleb roared with rage. He lowered his head and charged, butting Matt in the chest.

Matt's breath left him in a grunt of pain. He scrambled backward for purchase, trying to stay on his feet. Just before he hit the wall, he gained his balance and struck out with a hard right, taking Caleb in the left eye. Blood spurted from the deep gash left there.

Caleb dodged the next blow and landed one of his own in Matt's shoulder, barely fazing him. Matt swung again, his breath whistling through his teeth. This time his punch landed squarely on Caleb's jaw, spinning the man completely around.

Caleb came back swinging. Matt ducked right and stepped out away from the wall. He circled until Caleb crouched with his back to the fireplace. Matt landed three blows to his one.

Both men fought for breath as well as victory. Suddenly Caleb stepped inside Matt's reach and wrapped both arms around Matt's chest. The fierceness of the hug brought a groan to Matt's lips. He raised his hands and slapped his open palms sharply against Caleb's ears.

Caleb released Matt and grabbed his ears, his face twisting in a grimace of pain. The sudden concussion of Matt's blow left him momentarily stunned. Matt didn't wait. He moved in, driving one fist after the other into the man's belly.

Staggering backward, Caleb crossed his arms to ward

off the blows. His head struck the rickety shelf over the fireplace. The lantern wobbled precariously, danced toward the very edge, then settled in place.

Caleb swung a hard left. Matt dodged and stepped back. Something akin to pleasant surprise flickered in Caleb's eyes. Like he'd just realized an easy way out of this mess.

Like hell, you bastard, Matt thought grimly. He moved in to finish him off. Instead of swinging back or raising his arms in defense, Caleb's left hand darted in and out of his pants pocket. Firelight flickered off metal.

Matt recognized it at once. He heard Serena gasp as she, too, recognized her own derringer.

Seventeen

Caleb raised the little gun swiftly.

Matt countered just as fast. With his right hand, he grabbed Caleb's wrist and forced the gun up to point at the ceiling. With his left hand he made a sharp jab to Caleb's chin.

Caleb's head snapped. The back of his neck hit the shelf. His head struck the lantern, shattering the glass globe. The lamp base fell on its side. Oil ran from the reservoir onto Caleb's already greasy, oily hair.

Matt watched, stunned, as one entire half of Caleb's head burst into flames.

Serena screamed from her corner.

The acrid odor of burning hair filled the room.

Caleb screamed. Flames raced down the side of his face to his shoulder, his chest, engulfing him in a wavering sheet of fire. He kept on screaming. Then, as if suddenly realizing exactly what was happening, he wrenched his arm from Matt's grasp and staggered blindly out the door, his screams growing more shrill with each step.

Matt and Serena gaped at each other, shocked. Matt had wanted to kill the bastard, slowly. But to see a man burn alive was somehow different — terrible.

"My God!" Serena cried when she finally found her voice.

Matt suddenly snapped to. The shack was in flames! The dry, flimsy walls caught fire like dead leaves. He swooped down and grabbed Serena to his chest, cringing at how frail she felt, and dashed out the door. On the way, he managed to kick his holstered gun away from the door of the cabin.

He sat Serena down a safe distance from the fire and picked up his gun.

"No." Serena clasped his arm.

Matt looked down at her, his breath still coming hard. "I came to kill him, Rena."

"He's as good as dead already," she cried.

Caleb's shrill screams grew weaker in the night. Rena was right. No one could live through being burned like that.

A moment later the screaming stopped.

Matt dropped to his knees beside Serena. He followed her gaze and watched the shack collapse in upon itself. Dry and brittle, it was only a matter of moments for it was entirely consumed. The fire managed to burn itself out before it could leap out of the clearing and spread to the rest of the small canyon.

Serena huddled next to Matt, shaking violently from all that had happened. He knelt beside her, uncertain what to do.

She stared up at him, her eyes wide and glassy. "He's dead."

"He's dead," Matt answered grimly. "I'll finish with him tomorrow."

Serena frowned. "You mean bury him?"

"Among other things," he said through stiff lips.

"What other things?"

"Never mind," Matt said. "We've got to get you some clothes."

Serena's eyes narrowed. "Don't change the subject. What 'other things'?"

Matt cursed beneath his breath. "You don't think I'm going to let the bastard meet his maker with all his body parts still attached, after what he's done to you?"

She shook her head and reached for his arm. "It isn't necessary."

"Maybe not, but he's damn sure got it coming."

"No, he doesn't, Matt. That's what I'm trying to tell you — he didn't do anything to deserve that."

Matt shifted from his knees to sit down next to her. One large hand cupped her bruised, dirty cheek. "It's all right, Rena. You don't need to deny it. Dani saw what happened."

Serena gasped. Her hold on his arm tightened. "No!"

"Yes." He stroked her cheek. "Dani saw, and Pace felt. So there's no need to deny it. You'll forget, in time. You'll get over all this."

By now, the shack was nothing but glowing embers and rising trails of smoke. Serena tried to make Matt understand. "I don't know what Mama saw or Pace felt. But Matt, you have to believe me. The worst thing he did was starve me for the last several days."

"Rena —"

"I mean it, Matt," she cried earnestly. "I'll admit he did try once. That must have been what Mama saw. I even remember thinking about her at the time. But Matt, he never finished, and he never tried again. That's why he wouldn't feed me. He wanted me to *let* him. He didn't want to try to force me again."

Matt looked at her skeptically. "If he tried, what made him stop? Am I supposed to believe you *talked* him out of raping you?"

Serena grimaced and looked away. "I did worse than that — I got sick and threw up all over him."

Dumbfounded, Matt stared at her a long moment. Then he threw back his head, and his full-throated laughter boomed along the canyon walls. Still laughing, he reached out and pulled her onto his lap and hugged her fiercely. Giddy with relief, he laughed until his sides ached.

Serena sagged against his chest, reveling in the warm strength of his arms. Arms she had despaired of ever feeling again.

Oh, Matt.

He had come for her, saved her. Tears stung her eyes.

But he was still laughing. She pushed back from his chest and pursed her lips. "Frankly," she said, "I don't see what's so funny."

In between fresh bursts of laughter, Matt said, "I've never heard of a more effective way of cooling a man's . . . ardor."

When his laughter finally died, he rose to his feet with her in his arms. "Let's get some food into you before you faint. How long's it been since you've eaten?"

"A while," was all she said.

Matt stopped and looked down at her. The moonlight bathed her face with a soft glow. "How long?" he demanded.

"I'm . . . not sure. Four days, I think."

Matt groaned and tightened his hold on her, crushing her against his chest. "Oh, Rena," he moaned. "It's all my fault. I'm so sorry, sweetheart. So sorry."

"Hush," she told him. "It's not your fault. It's *his* fault. He did this, not you."

"But he only took you in the first place to get back at

me. Rena, Caleb was Abe Scott's brother. That's why he kidnapped you."

Using very nearly the last of her strength, Serena reached up and brushed his cheek with her fingers. "I know. He told me."

Matt fought the guilt and remorse that threatened to overwhelm him. When he had a better grip on himself, he started walking again. "Did he happen to tell you how he even knew who I was and what happened to his brother?"

"I wondered about that myself. Someone saw you from the rim of the canyon."

Matt carried Serena to a cave halfway up the far wall of the canyon. He'd brought his bedroll, saddlebags, and canteen down from the ridge and spent the afternoon in its dim coolness, watching his quarry chop wood.

At the abrupt change from hot August night to cool, damp cave, Serena shivered in Matt's arms. Matt fumbled in the darkness until he found a blanket. He wrapped her snugly and sat her against the wall. She shivered again at the loss of his arms.

He started a fire, then pulled a strip of jerky from his saddlebag.

"Lord. I never thought I'd be glad to eat jerky."

"I hate to disappoint you, but I don't think your stomach could take this stuff as is."

Matt proceeded to tear the jerky into small chunks and drop it into a skillet of water, which he set on a flat rock at the edge of the fire. Serena knew he was right. The broth alone would do her more good than large hunks of dried meat hitting her empty stomach. But the waiting would be agony. The one bite of rabbit had merely increased her hunger.

Matt saw the wistful look on her face and gave her a hard biscuit to chew on while she waited. It disappeared in no time.

"How about a bath?" he suggested.

Serena grimaced. "You think I need one?"

"Yes," he said with a laugh. "I think you most definitely do."

Serena couldn't agree more. She'd been smelling herself for so many days, she no longer noticed her own odor. But Matt surely must. She wanted nothing more than to scrub away the filth of her ordeal. But her strength was gone, and she didn't want Matt to know just how weak she really was. He would only make a fuss . . . and blame himself.

"I'd rather eat first."

Matt knelt beside her and rested a hand on her shoulder. He winced at the frailness he felt there. "I know you're hungry. But it'll be a while before that's ready," he said, nodding to the skillet. "Come on. A bath will feel good, and it'll make the time pass. I'll help you." He went to his saddlebag and fished around. "I even have soap."

When he returned and picked her up, she was too weak to argue, and had the sinking feeling he knew it, too. He carried her back outside, where the warm air felt good against her chilled cheeks.

By the time they reached the canyon floor, her head rolled against his shoulder. "Matt?" she whispered.

"What, sweetheart?"

"I . . . can't do it."

"Can't do what?"

"Take a bath. I'm too . . . tired."

Matt pressed his lips to her forehead. "I know, sweetheart. Don't worry. I'll take care of you. Just rest."

"Where are we going?"

"That stream that runs the length of the canyon comes from a pool at the north end. That's where I'm taking you. Don't talk now, just rest."

He walked on, surefooted in the darkness, cradling his precious burden carefully against his chest. She was so thin, so weak. God, but he wished Caleb Scott was still alive, so he could kill him with his bare hands!

"Matt?"

"Hmm?"

"Thank you."

"You're welcome. But what for?"

"For coming after me. For finding me. For saving me."

Matt walked on in silence, unable to speak past the lump in his throat. There was no way in hell he could have *not* come after her. The thoughts that filled his mind during the past weeks hadn't been thoughts of a brother for his sister. They'd been the thoughts of a man whose woman had been torn from his side. Those kinds of thoughts, that kind of anguish, were familiar to him.

Yet he was still confused. It was hard to let go of the past, and he had two pasts to cope with. The one with Angela as his love, his wife, and the one with a sister named Serena. He no longer knew what to do, what to think, what to feel. What was right, and what was wrong. He only knew that Serena felt good in his arms. Good, and right.

When he reached the sparse grass at the edge of the pool, he lowered Serena to the ground. Moonlight sparkled on the still water and turned her face a pale, milky white. Gazing down at her familiar features, a fierce longing engulfed him. A longing to hold and protect her, to see her smile again, hear her laugh. To spend his days, and yes, his nights, too, by her side.

He pulled off his moccasins, then started to remove his pants, but stopped. Even dirty and bruised as she was, the sight of her was enough to start a tightening in his loins.

He removed the buckskins, but left his underwear on.

When he lifted Serena from the blanket, he had to shake her awake. Her eyes came open with a snap. Even in the darkness, he could read the fear. "Ssh," he whispered. "It's all right. It's only me."

"Matt?"

"That's right. We're getting into the water now. It's spring fed, so it'll be cold."

She nodded her understanding, and he walked into the pool. At its deepest spot, it came only to his thighs. He knelt and lowered Serena carefully. Ice-cold water caressed her feet, then her backside. She gasped.

When the water was up to her neck, Serena sighed. "Feels so good," she whispered. She rolled her head back and let herself float in Matt's arms. A few moments later, he pulled her toward the edge of the pool so she could sit on the sandy bottom while he bathed her.

Matt hadn't been so gentle and careful since he'd bathed his daughter when she was a baby. Angela had laughed at his care, swearing to him that Joanna wouldn't break.

"She's a Colton," Angela had told him. "Coltons don't break."

Strange, he thought, brushing soap-slicked fingers down Serena's cool arm. It didn't hurt so much now to think of Angela. For a moment, the thought panicked him. Then he relaxed. From somewhere deep inside came the knowledge that Angela didn't want her memory to hurt him. She had never wanted anything to hurt him.

For as long as he lived, he would never forget Angela and the love they shared. She would always be a part of him, just as Joanna would always be part of them both.

But as the soap slid off his fingers, so did the grief slip out of his heart. He was ready to live again. And yes, he admitted, even love again. It was time.

Beneath his hands, Serena sighed. Careful of her bruises, he washed her from head to toe and tried to ignore the feel of her flesh against his fingers. Yet even in her present state, battered, exhausted, starved, she was beautiful to touch, beautiful to look at.

The cold spring water did nothing to lessen his response. *Right here, right now, I want her.* And the wanting felt good.

Never mind that the timing was wrong, that he wouldn't give in to the heat raging in his blood. It was enough just then to feel aroused without the guilt that had consumed him in Tombstone.

How wise Rena had been, how right, when she had reminded him so bluntly that no matter how they were raised, she and Matt were not brother and sister.

Tomorrow, or as soon as she was rested, they would talk. Tonight, he would take care of her and remind her she was safe. Her ordeal was over.

It took two soapings before he was satisfied that her hair was as clean as it should be. After rinsing her thoroughly, he lifted her from the water and wrapped her in the blanket once more.

He stepped behind a bush and traded his wet underwear for dry buckskins, then put on his moccasins. He returned to her side and lifted her in his arms. "Feel better?" he asked.

Serena closed her eyes and sighed. "Nothing in the world could possibly feel better."

Matt chuckled deep in his throat. "That's what you think, girl."

Serena's eyes popped open. All thoughts of fatigue and hunger fled as she looked into his shadowed eyes. Was that a suggestive tone in his voice? He couldn't possibly have meant what she thought he meant, could he? He had never talked to her like that before. Since she'd found him in Tombstone, their entire relationship had been one of her pursuing him, and him not only denying it, but running like a scared rabbit.

Now it sounded like — like she didn't know what. At the very least, he was loosening up around her. Or had she misread him?

She watched the smile die on his mouth. With lips still parted, he slowly lowered his face to hers. She waited breathlessly as, inch by inch, he came closer. The first touch of his lips on hers was feather light. Her heart slammed against her ribs. Then, when her lips parted in response, he kissed her fully. It was the most tender, most soul-shattering kiss imaginable. Hot tingles raced down her arms and legs.

It ended all too soon, as far as Serena was concerned, but her heart filled with hope. He had made the first move this time. He had kissed her. It was a beginning, more of a beginning than she thought she would ever have.

Her spirits soared. A slow smile spread across her face. "Maybe you're right. Maybe there *is* something better than a bath."

"You think so?" he asked with a grin. "You must mean food. Let's go get you fed."

Matt carried her back to the cave, where he gave her a cup of broth containing chunks of softened jerky.

Serena's shrunken stomach could hold only about half of what Matt gave her. While he held her on his lap and combed the tangles from her hair, she fell asleep.

He held her against his chest, her head on his shoulder, and ran his fingers from her scalp clear down to the ends of her silky hair. Again and again his fingers threaded through the long black tresses with the white streak, lift-

271

ing them to the heat of the fire. He tried not to remember that sharp stab of terror he had felt when the black and white scalp had landed in his lap.

Trying not to remember didn't help. He clenched his fist around a handful of hair and pressed it against his lips. With eyes squeezed shut, he kept feeling the terror, seeing that scalp again and again. *Thank God, thank God it hadn't been hers.*

When her hair was dry, he laid her on his bedroll spread out beside the fire. Before drawing the blanket up, he gave in to the need to simply look at her.

The bruises on her golden skin appalled him. When he'd first seen her lying naked in the cabin he had thought most of what covered her was dirt, but he'd been wrong. A smudge of purple discolored one cheek. Finger-sized bruises marked her upper arms, her waist, her thighs, her breasts.

What set his blood to boiling, what made him wish once again that Scott was still alive so Matt could strangle him slowly, were the teeth marks forming twin curved lines above and below one dusky nipple.

As he covered her with the blanket, his hands shook.

Matt was still awake several hours later, staring out the mouth of the cave into the darkness, when Serena began thrashing and moaning in her sleep, fighting to throw off her blanket.

He'd let the fire burn down, and all that remained were glowing coals. In the dim light, he knelt beside her and touched a hand to her bare shoulder.

She came awake with a start, a soundless scream working her throat.

"It's all right," he said quickly. "It's only me, sweetheart. You were having a bad dream, that's all."

Serena couldn't control the shudder that ripped through her from head to toe, nor the fierce pounding of her heart. She looked up at Matt, his face bathed in the orange-red glow of the dying embers, and felt tears sting her eyes. With a silent plea, she leaned up and reached her arms out to him. "Oh, Matt, hold me. Please hold me."

When his arms came around her, she gasped at the warmth of his bare chest against her naked breasts. God, he felt so good.

"Ssh. It's okay. I'll hold you," he crooned softly.

It was an effort for Matt to speak at all with her cold-hardened nipples drilling little holes in his chest and the feel of her long, silky hair beneath his hands. Beneath the hair draped across her shoulders, his calloused fingers touched soft, bare skin.

She trembled and let out a sob. Matt tightened his arms around her.

"Make it go away, Matt," she whispered against his shoulder. "Make it go away."

Her hot tears burned his skin. His own stung his eyes. "I will, Rena, I promise. Just tell me what it is, and I'll make it go away."

She cried softly against his shoulder. It was a long time before she spoke, then her words came slowly, haltingly, as if she had trouble getting them out.

"It's . . . him. His touch. In my sleep, I feel his hands on me, and I can't stand it! I can't! Make it stop, Matt, please. Make it go away."

Her tearful plea pierced his heart and brought a lump to his throat. He lowered her to the bedroll and lay down next to her. "Ssh," he whispered. He sipped hot tears from her cheeks. "It'll be all right, honey."

God, please let it be all right, he prayed. After all she had been through in the past weeks, would she ever get

273

over it, ever forget it? *Please let her forget. Help me help her.*

Not knowing what else to do, Matt trailed tiny kisses across her face until her tears stopped. She lay on her back and he on his side, barely touching her with his body. He raised up on one elbow and leaned over her face. "Look at me, Rena. Open your eyes."

Shimmering pools of blue blinked up at him. Such trusting eyes. He lowered his mouth to hers. Just before their lips met, he whispered, "Keep your eyes open."

Serena tried. She really did. But when the gentle, tender kiss turned heated, her lids grew heavy. Warmth filled her veins as his tongue stroked hers. Emotions held in check for weeks burst forth, making her head reel with pleasure.

When he tore his mouth away, they were both gasping for air. "Kiss me again," she begged. "I can forget everything when you kiss me."

He obliged her with a kiss so searing it made her squirm. A heaviness throbbed low in her belly. She tried to turn toward him, but his hands on her shoulders stopped her. He drew back slightly, not breaking the kiss, but lessening its intensity.

When he raised his head, he smiled and whispered, "You closed your eyes."

Her eyes fluttered open, and she answered his smile. "I know."

Matt's smile slowly died. "Keep them open, Rena. I'm going to touch you." He stroked her bruised cheek with one finger. "I'm going to wipe away his touch with mine." He lightly kissed the cheek, then pulled back and looked at her, his eyes dark and serious. "Keep them open and look at my face. Know it's *me* touching you. Just me. No one else."

274

His lips followed his fingers across her shoulder and down one arm until he had touched and kissed every bruise in his path. His voice, his words, hypnotized her. She watched his face and saw his pained expression when he reached the teeth marks on her breast.

He traced the bruises with his fingers. "See? It's just me. There's nothing left but my touch. Mine is the only touch you'll remember."

Slowly, deliberately, he lowered his head. Her pulse raced. His tongue traced the same path his fingers had followed. Then his lips settled over her nipple and she gasped. Heat rushed through her veins and centered where his lips met her flesh. *Yes,* she thought fiercely. *Yours is the touch I'll remember for the rest of my life. No one but you will ever touch me again.*

Serena grasped the bedroll beneath her with both hands to keep from touching him. She was afraid to move, afraid the magic spell he wove would be broken. Afraid he would remember she was only a little sister to him.

His fingers and lips touched every inch of her arms and torso, down to her stomach. When he bypassed the place that throbbed for his touch the most and stroked his way down her thighs, she groaned aloud.

He touched and kissed his way down one thigh and up the other, then buried his face in the tight black curls at the juncture of her legs. His hot breath drew a moan from deep within her. She couldn't help but move her hips against him.

His head came up slowly, then his gaze locked with hers. "No touch but mine. Not ever."

Eighteen

Matt watched every flicker of her expression as he explored the silken secrets of her body. Her bright blue eyes darkened until they were almost black. Her mouth parted, gasping for breath. Was that her heartbeat or his, thundering in his ears?

She groaned.

He got harder. Her response triggered an excitement beyond any he'd ever known. She came alive at his touch. The little whimpering sounds in her throat made his blood heat. The darker her eyes turned, the faster he breathed. She was like liquid fire in his arms. He bit the inside of his jaw to keep from whispering words that would shock her, hot words of need and want and sex. Words he wouldn't be able to take back.

He couldn't tell her how he felt. He couldn't show her, either, by burying himself deep inside her, so deep he could never be separated from her. So deep she would never again know the kind of fear she had lived with these past weeks.

He couldn't give her that. All he could give her was this.

Serena's very bones seemed to melt beneath his touch. His hand . . . oh, God, what he was doing to her with his hand. Could a person die from such exquisite pleasure? If so, she didn't care.

Her hips raised and rotated with no direction from her mind. Her mind had ceased to function.

Matt's voice was hoarse and strained in her ear. "That's it, honey. Just let it happen. Look in my eyes and let it happen."

Serena felt the throbbing between her legs grow. The pressure built until she whimpered with want of something she didn't fully understand. But she never took her eyes from his. She strained upward with her hips, pushing against his hand, harder . . . harder. Climbing. Striving. Turning into a mass of wild, burning sensation.

Feelings, both emotional and physical, tore through her. Feelings so powerful, so out of her control, that for a moment fear threatened to douse the fire. Then she blinked, and Matt's face came back into focus. The fear melted into nothing, leaving her soaring free and high on the headiness of his touch.

Then came an explosion within her body that ripped her loose from the world. She half rose from the ground with a cry, her eyes widening as a thousand stars burst around her. Brown eyes became the center of her scattering universe.

With his mouth against hers, Matt caught her cry and shuddered as she fell apart in his arms. The urge to take her then and there rode him hard, so hard that for a moment he thought he would lose the battle he fought.

Then he felt tears trickle down her cheeks to his lips. He sipped and tasted salt. God, what had he done? "Rena, Rena, I didn't mean to make you cry."

Beneath his lips, her cheek flexed. A smile?

"I didn't know I was crying," she whispered.

Matt raised his head. The look in her eyes took his

breath away. She wasn't hurt or angry or humiliated. She was none of the things he had feared her tears meant. She was . . . she was . . . the only word he could think of was "glowing." Her eyes, her smile, her whole face glowed with physical satisfaction, with the new knowledge of her body he had given her, and with an emotion so deep, so obvious, and so pointedly directed at him, he felt humbled. And scared. It was the look of a woman in love.

"Rena, I—"

"No." She put her fingers over his lips. "Thank you." She closed her eyes and replaced her fingers with her mouth. The softness of her mouth and the heat in his veins would not let Matt resist. He closed his eyes and kissed her back.

When they surfaced for air, Matt found himself on his back with Serena draped across his chest, one of her legs tucked between his.

"Thank you," she said again. "I knew it had to be good, but I had no idea anything could be so beautiful."

He smiled sadly and held her close. "I know you didn't. I'm not sure you should now. At least, not with me."

"We're not back to that again, are we? We've had this conversation before. If not with you," she said, running her hand through the hair on his chest, tracing a scar, "then with whom am I supposed to be like this? Name him. Name the man I'm supposed to share myself with."

Name the man. The thought had Matt grinding his teeth. She was playing him like a fish, and they both knew it. He would kill any man who touched her. By the grin on her face, she knew that, too. "Stop teasing me."

Her grin faded, and her look turned bold. Deliberate. "I'm not teasing. I'm trying to get you to admit you don't want another man touching me. Surely you weren't being my brother just now." She moved against him, her knee against his groin.

Matt squeezed his eyes shut and nearly groaned aloud. His arousal leaped in response to her touch. *"No."* The word came out through clenched teeth.

"That's good. Because you know I could never let another man near me. Not now, not ever. I belong to you. Just as you belong to me." She rubbed a palm down his chest toward his waist, then paused.

Matt sucked in a sharp breath. "Rena, no." Between her knee, her hand, and her words, she was killing him. He pushed her knee away and covered his face with a bent arm.

"You gave me so much a few minutes ago." Her knee brushed his groin again. "Why didn't you give me this?"

He brushed her knee away without looking at her. "Don't."

His voice sounded so cold and stiff, Serena almost relented. But the hardness below his waist was still there. She could see it straining against his buckskins. "You gave me such pleasure, Matt. I only want to do the same for you. Show me what to do."

"You're not ready for this, Rena."

Not ready? "How can you say that?"

Finally he took his arm from his face and looked at her. "You're too . . . vulnerable right now. You've been kidnapped, abused . . ." He traced the raw flesh on her wrist. The gentleness of his touch, the pain in his eyes, made her want to weep.

"The bastard nearly raped you, damn it," he said fiercely. "You need time to get past that."

Serena's heart rate doubled. He wasn't saying no! He wasn't telling her how wrong he was for her, or she for him! "How — " She had to stop and swallow. "How much time?"

He met her gaze with a head-on directness that took her breath away. "In a few days, when you're rested and feeling better, we'll talk."

She swallowed again. "Do you mean it?"

After a long pause, he gave her a nod.

Her heart leaped. She wanted to shout for joy. *Oh, Matt, I love you.* But she didn't say the words. Not yet. She didn't want to send him running, or make him push her away again.

But neither did she want to let him forget this night. If only he would cooperate. "All right, we'll talk later. But for now, I can't leave you wanting."

The touch of her hand through his pants took Matt completely by surprise. Every muscle in his body tensed and jerked. But when he reached down, instead of flinging her hand away, he covered it with his own and thrust upward with his hips.

Ah, God. He ground his teeth together. He had to stop this. It was crazy. It was dangerous. But knowing that didn't help. Her response to his touch moments ago had driven him nearly over the edge. Her fulfillment left him wanting, panting for that same state of mindlessness. He had wanted nothing more than to lose himself in her hot, dark depths.

But he couldn't. Not here, not now, when she was so vulnerable. So he had settled for giving her pleasure and denying his body what it craved.

Now, here she was, wanting to pleasure him. That she was willing to do this took his breath away. That she *was* doing it nearly stopped his heart. Never had a woman's touch affected him so thoroughly. Common sense fled as her fingers tightened through the buckskin. His fingers clamped around hers.

"Like this?" she whispered.

He groaned. "Yes!" He couldn't stop her now if he tried. "Oh God, yes."

When she took her hand away, it was all he could do to keep from whimpering. She had changed her mind. He squeezed his eyes shut, determined to somehow live through the pain.

In the next instant, soft, warm fingers worked their way beneath the waist of his pants and grasped him fully, firmly, flesh to flesh.

Serena was enthralled with the feel of him. He was the hardest steel sheathed in the smoothest, softest velvet. Steel that pulsed and throbbed with a life of its own.

Matt's eyes flew open in shock just in time to see her lowering her lips to his. Her kiss was tentative at first, then bolder as she drew on the response he could not hold back. He was lost. He closed his eyes and groaned. He clenched his fists to keep from flinging her on her back and plunging into her.

"Tell me what to do, Matt," she whispered against his lips. "Show me." Her fingers tightened around him, making him gasp in tortured pleasure.

His mind, his control snapped. He fumbled with one hand to unlace his buckskins. With his other hand, he held her tightly by the waist, afraid she might disappear, that this was only a dream that would blow away like smoke on the wind.

But Serena wasn't going anywhere. She wasn't about to let go of this sense of power his response gave her. She knew instinctively that while she held him in her hand, he would promise anything, do anything she asked. She buried her lips in the crisp blond curls on his chest to keep from asking. To keep from demanding that he love her the way she loved him.

The opened pants gave her freer access to him. She

loosened her grip and ran her fingers lightly from base to tip and back again, wrenching another groan from deep in his chest.

Her teasing drove Matt right over the edge of sanity. He wrapped his fingers around hers and guided her hand up and down his length, tighter, harder, faster. Faster still, until, with a deep moan, he rolled over, away from her, and thrust his hips to the ground. Her hand still gripped him; his still gripped hers.

Serena lay sprawled across his bare back with her arm disappearing round his waist. Her hand felt crushed, trapped as it was, with his, between the ground and his body. But she didn't care. She trailed hot, moist kisses along the scars on his back. Knowing what she knew now, she sensed he was near the end of his journey to the far side of the stars.

The next time, she determined, they would travel together as one.

Suddenly Matt stiffened beneath her with one final, forceful thrust. His tortured cry echoed forever along the walls of the small cave and down into Serena's very soul.

It was a long time before he raised enough to remove their hands from beneath him, longer still before his breathing returned to normal. Serena stroked and kissed his smooth, hard back. She couldn't stop touching him.

Finally he moaned and rolled to his side, his back to her, and fumbled with the laces on his pants. When he turned to face her, he kept his gaze lowered.

"I'm sorry," he said stiffly. "I haven't lost control like that since I was fourteen years old."

Serena bit back a giggle. "Is that the time Mary Beth Sloan's father caught you and her up in the hayloft?"

His shocked gaze flew to her face and narrowed with a threat. "Where did you hear a story like that? You were barely out of diapers."

"Ah, so it's true, then," she said with mock seriousness.

Instead of answering, he kissed her, a soft, slow kiss that took her breath away. They both forgot all about Mary Beth Sloan.

Serena curled up against his side like a nesting bird. Matt covered them both with the blanket. For a night that had begun as a nightmare, it was ending like her fondest dream. Matt was holding her in his arms. What they had just shared was the most beautiful thing in the world. It was between a man and a woman. There was no trace of the brother left in him, thank God.

"It's hard to imagine there's anything better than this," she said with a sudden smile. "Better than what you gave me, what you let me give you."

"What makes you think there is?"

Serena leaned up on an elbow and grinned at him. "Matthew, I may be inexperienced, but it seems to me that for what we did tonight, a person wouldn't necessarily need a partner. It has to be better the other way, or men and women wouldn't put up with each other."

His chest rumbled with deep laughter as he tugged her back down to his side. "You're outrageous. Shut up and go to sleep, woman."

Serena hugged him close and smiled to herself. *I love you, Matt Colton. One day soon, you'll admit you love me, too.*

Matt closed his eyes with a tired, satisfied sigh and acknowledged how right he felt with Serena's naked body resting against his. He wasn't sure where tonight would lead them, if anywhere. He only knew that the grief and guilt and loneliness he'd lived with for so long were gone. Washed away by her tender trust. Burned away by her touch, her kiss.

Angela's face suddenly appeared behind his closed lids. But still he felt no guilt or grief. He felt only her approval and encouragement.

Angela would always be part of him, held in a special place of her own in his heart. But it was time to get on with his life, time to make a new start. For himself, and for Joanna. For the first time in years, he felt free to do just that.

Matt woke at dawn to the exquisite pleasure of Serena draped across his chest, with his arms holding her in place. God, but she was sweet to hold. So sweet, and he had almost lost her, almost never known the peace she brought him with her touch, her kiss. The thrills and pleasures they had shared last night.

A shudder tore through him at what might have happened had he not arrived when he had last night.

He blanked out the thought and, with a reluctance so great it surprised him, pulled himself from her arms. She slept on soundly. He was glad. He had a chore to perform that was better done without her watching. He had to bury the bastard down in the canyon.

As gray light filtered into the shallow cave, he saw again the dark shadows beneath Serena's eyes, the bruises on her flesh, the scabs and rope burns on her wrists.

Yes, by God, he would bury Caleb Scott. He only wished the son of a bitch was still alive while he did it.

The cool morning air raised goosebumps on his arms. Matt tugged the blanket over Serena's shoulders and up to her chin. "Stay warm, sweetheart, and sleep," he whispered.

After donning his shirt, moccasins, Colt, and knife, Matt checked his Winchester and left it lying at the edge of the blanket, within easy reach for Serena. Next to it he placed the drawstring bag of clothes he had brought for her from home.

Then he made his way silently out of the cave and over the canyon rim to where he had hidden his horse. In less than an hour he was riding up the gravel creekbed and through the entrance to the canyon.

It took him less than five minutes to realize he had no body to bury: Caleb Miller Scott was gone.

Matt swore long and hard at his own carelessness. He should have gone after the bastard last night and finished him off. But Serena had asked him to stay with her. Matt had not been strong enough to resist her plea.

Stupid fool. Now look what's happened.

Then he told himself to relax. Scott's horse was still in the canyon. The man had been burned beyond endurance. He couldn't have gotten far. And he couldn't, with the injuries he had suffered, have lasted the night.

Yet Matt spent half the morning searching up and down the creek and couldn't find a trace of Scott's passing. Frustrated and more angry with himself than he ever remembered being, he headed back to Serena. He had left her alone long enough.

Up in the rocks near the canyon entrance, one good eye, half blurred with pain, watched the rider below. The other eye didn't work at all. Wouldn't open. It seemed . . . sealed shut. Melted. Like hot wax.

The brain behind the eye thought it should know the man in buckskins and moccasins, but the agony of burned flesh wouldn't let it concentrate.

Hate. The man below generated so much hate inside him it seemed to radiate off the very rocks, like heat. *Like fire.*

Why so much hate? Why did it taste so bitter, feel so strong? And where was the woman? There should be a woman, shouldn't there?

Later. Knowledge would come later. The hate would become clear when memory returned. Thinking hurt too much. For now, get away. *Get away. Hide.* Yes. Hide. Then, rest. Blessed, sweet, sweet rest.

There would be time enough later for hate.

The cave was too small to hold its coolness against the midday heat. Serena woke alone and hot. The blanket smelled like Matt. She missed him sharply. Where was he? She had obviously slept half the day away.

Then she remembered. He had to bury Caleb. She shivered despite the heat. The sight of Matt's Winchester beside the blanket comforted her. She reached for the drawstring bag next to the gun. The contents made her smile at both his thoughtfulness and his typical male forgetfulness. He had included a dress, a pair of shoes, and the silver-handled hairbrush from the top of her dresser at home. He had not, however, remembered to include underwear.

She took a deep breath and stared out into the brilliant daylight. She was free of Caleb and his threats; she had her own clothes to wear; she was with Matt; and as soon as she could wolf down a biscuit or two, she wouldn't even be hungry. Life was perfect.

At least, for a minute. Until she was buttoning her yellow gingham dress and felt the prickling along her spine, the raising of the fine hairs on the back of her neck. What was it? Something, some feeling pushed at her, growing stronger by the second.

She shivered again. Then it hit her. A wall of hate so solid, so terrifying it threatened to buckle her knees.

Who? Where? What was happening?

She spun around with jerky movements, searching every inch of the small cave. No one was there. With her gaze trained on the entrance, she reached for Matt's Winchester. Her hands trembled violently.

Still the emotion threatened to suffocate her. Where did it come from? Whose was it? Who hated so strongly she could feel it pressing against her from all sides?

Then she knew. *Caleb.*

Oh, God, he was alive!

She squeezed her eyes shut and gripped the rifle harder, feeling the smooth wooden stock slip along her sweaty palms, telling herself she had to be wrong. No one could live through having so much of his body burned so severely. It was impossible. Her last sight of him had been of his hair, half his face, one arm, and part of his chest and back engulfed in flames.

And my derringer in his hand. With one shot left.

"Matt!" Her heart quivered. Where was Matt?

She dashed toward the ledge.

"Rena?"

She squeaked with fright.

Matt grabbed her by the shoulders. "Rena, what's wrong?"

She wanted to slump against him in relief. He was all right. He was there with her, safe and sound. But the relief wouldn't come, only the fierce, consuming hate. She shuddered. "He's still alive."

Matt let go of her and turned his head a little, watching her warily out of one eye. "Who's still alive?"

"Don't give me that. This is *me* you're talking to. You didn't bury him, did you?"

Matt took the rifle from her clenched fists and propped it against the wall.

"You didn't bury him because he wasn't there. He's *not dead.*"

"Rena—"

"Don't bother lying to me," she said. "It's *me,* Matt. I knew the day, the *minute* you found Abe Scott. I could feel his fear, smell it, taste it. At first I thought it was yours, but then I knew. Just as I know today."

"What do you know today?"

She swallowed hard. "Hate."

Matt ran his hands up and down her arms and frowned. "What are you talking about?"

"Caleb Scott's hate for you, maybe for me, too, I don't know. But I feel it, strong, right here inside me." A shudder ripped through her. "All around me."

"Rena." Matt pulled her into his arms. The feel of him, his heat, his scent, pushed away the hate, sent it running.

"It's all right, sweetheart. He can't hurt you, not again. I swear he'll never hurt you again."

Serena pushed away from him, surprised to feel wetness on her cheeks. She swiped at the tears she hadn't realized she'd shed. "It's not me, you dolt, it's you. *You're* the one he's been after all this time. It's *you* he'll come for."

"No, hush." He pulled her into his arms again. "Even if you're right and he's still alive, he can't last long. You saw the shape he was in."

She shivered.

Matt held her tighter. "He's gone, Rena. He'll be dead by nightfall, if he's not already."

She started to speak, but he stopped her. "Don't worry. I don't plan to leave anything to chance. Not where you're concerned. I'll find him. I'll make sure he can't hurt you or anyone ever again. I swear, sweetheart. I swear."

* * *

Matt couldn't resume his search for Caleb that day. Serena was so exhausted all she could manage was to eat and sleep. He refused to leave her alone while she was asleep and vulnerable. If she said she felt Caleb Scott was still alive, then Scott was still alive.

But not for long. If Matt didn't find him dead, he'd find him alive. And he would kill the bastard.

As it turned out, he didn't have to. A cougar beat him to it.

The next afternoon, when Serena was alert enough to take care of herself, Matt left her with a kiss — one meant to comfort her, but that ended up curling his toes — and went in search of Caleb Scott. It took only a few minutes to find the spot where Caleb had, incredibly, dragged himself up into the rocks at the canyon entrance. The man had more grit than Matt had given him credit for, to have even lived through such severe burns long enough to get away, much less to drag himself up into the rocks.

But the bloody streaks across the limestone and granite atop the ridge told Matt he wouldn't have to worry about Caleb Scott any longer.

A cougar — a big one, at least seven feet, judging by the size of the tracks left in Caleb's blood — had dragged Caleb to a deep crevice. Or rather, had dragged Caleb's body. No sign of struggle marked the trail. Sometime the day before, the cat had dragged a dead body, not a live man.

Bloody smears streaked down the sheer rock wall of the crevice as far into the darkness below as Matt could see. He didn't need to descend to make sure his prey was dead. If the bloody drag marks hadn't told him, the smell coming from the crevice would have — the sickening sweet odor of rotting flesh.

Would the smell be so strong this soon?

Yes. In this heat, yes.

"Good riddance, you bastard."

Still shaken from the hatred that had nearly overwhelmed her the day before, Serena paced the small cave and waited for Matt. He would probably be gone for hours, she knew, but she couldn't sit still. Not that she didn't feel rested or refreshed from all the sleep she'd had the day before, she just had too much nervous energy to rest until Matt returned.

He made it back sooner than she'd thought he would. His grim expression sent a chill of foreboding down her spine. "You didn't find him."

Matt shook his head. "I found him. He's dead."

"You're sure?"

He gave her a crooked half-grin and pulled her into his arms. "I'm sure. He can't bother us again."

Serena let out a tense breath and relaxed against him. But Matt was not relaxed. She felt his tautness in every muscle. She pushed back and looked up at him. "What aren't you telling me?"

He let out a sigh that echoed with exhaustion or frustration, she couldn't tell which.

"Riders are coming." When she didn't say anything, but only looked at him, he added, "About an hour away. It's the family."

"The family?"

"Pace and Dad and Dani, plus Carlos and Jorge."

Serena swallowed. "All of them?"

Matt nodded, his eyes locked on hers.

"So soon?" she whispered.

They stared at each other a long moment, then Matt grabbed her swiftly to his chest and kissed her, a hard, urgent, desperate kiss. He told her with his mouth, his hands, and his body, that he wasn't ready to share her with the rest of the family. Not yet. He wanted her to himself.

He tore his mouth away and fought for breath. Serena tried to pull him back. "No." He held her away. "Before they get here, there's something I need to ask you."

"What is it?"

He squeezed her shoulders and inhaled deeply. "In Tombstone, one day when you were mad at me — which was often," he added with a little half-smile, "you said something I've been wondering about ever since. You said you hadn't thought of me as your brother since you were eight years old. What did you mean?"

Serena lowered her gaze and gave a shaky laugh. "Oh, that."

Matt raised her chin with a fingertip until she looked at him again. "Tell me, please?"

Serena slipped out of his hold and stepped to the mouth of the cave. "Remember the squirrel's nest?" She smiled at him over her shoulder.

He frowned and shook his head.

"You and Pace and I were in the Dragoons, with The People. Grandfather Cochise wanted fresh blueberries, so I went to find some. I spotted a squirrel's nest near the top of a big old cottonwood up the creek and got a little sidetracked. I only wanted a peek, just to see if there were any babies. I managed to get myself good and stuck."

She laughed softly. "I was up there for hours, convinced no one would ever find me. Then, near dark, you came. I was never so glad to see anyone in my whole life. I looked down and there you were, standing tall and straight so far below me."

Serena looked at him and laughed again. "When you told me to jump, I got so mad I tried to spit in your face. I squirmed around and ended up dangling from that old branch by my hands. I felt like I was at least a mile above the ground."

"I remember now," Matt said with a soft smile.

"When the branch started to crack, you told me to let go. I thought for sure you were trying to get me killed," she said. "But you just stood there beneath me, your arms held out, and said, 'Jump, Rena. I'll catch you.' You said you wouldn't let me fall, you wouldn't let me get hurt."

She was quiet for a long time. "I don't get it," Matt said. "What has that got to do with you not thinking of me as a brother anymore?"

Serena glanced at him, then stared back out at the canyon. "It was what happened to me when I let go of that branch and you caught me."

Matt placed a hand on her shoulder, forcing her to turn and face him. "What happened?"

She looked up at him with wry amusement. "I developed a terminal case of hero worship. I decided right then and there that I was in love with you. Even though I didn't really know what it meant, I decided you were going to be my mate. Letting go of that dream was the hardest thing I've ever had to do."

She watched Matt's face, but couldn't read his expression.

"But did you let go of it, Rena?"

She smiled softly. "The day you married Angela."

Matt frowned and looked away. "You were what, ten then? It must have hurt."

"It did," she said, her smile still in place. It was her turn now to force him to look at her. "But Matt, I did let go of my dream. Angela made me see that you shouldn't have to wait for me to grow up before you took a wife. And she was right. She was so beautiful, so kind to me. I think I loved her almost as much as you did."

Matt stepped away and walked past her to stand in the sun on the ledge. "It was all nonsense, you know. You were just a kid."

"Yes, I was a kid. But to me it wasn't nonsense."

"You had a crush on me. You outgrew it."

"It was more than that, and I didn't outgrow it. I put it away."

"For good?" he asked, his gaze trained on the mouth of the canyon.

"I thought so." She stared at his rigid back for a moment before continuing. "I was happy for you and Angela and Joanna. Even after Angela died, I still thought of you as her husband. I was content with that."

Matt spun on her then, his face a mask of furious frustration. "Then what the hell is going on?" he demanded. "What the hell changed when you came to Tombstone?"

"It's simple." She raised her chin a notch. Her voice, when it came, was sure and steady. "I fell in love with you."

Matt stood still as a fencepost and stared at her a long moment. Finally, he spun away and spoke over his shoulder. "Stay here. I'll be back."

Shocked and hurt, Serena couldn't move. No acknowledgment, no look, no nothing. Just a curt "Stay here," and he was gone. She bared her deepest feelings to him, and he walked away.

It was all she could do to keep from screaming at his back. But no. *Let him go,* she thought. *Give him room to breathe, time to think.*

At the bottom of the trail, Matt stopped and leaned against the rock wall. He turned his face up to the sun and closed his eyes.

I fell in love with you.

His heart picked up speed. His kid sister thought she was in love with him.

No. That wasn't the childish voice of the little shadow who used to trail around behind him. It was the voice of a beautiful young woman, a passionate woman, who was old enough to know her own mind.

So Pace had been right after all. Serena loved him.

That explained all the questions that had been haunting him for so long. It explained how easily he'd managed to hurt her so many times without meaning to. It explained why she pursued him one moment, ran from him in the next.

And he'd left her standing there in that cave without a word. What must she be thinking? He turned to go back to her, but a flash of light from down the canyon caught his eye. Sunlight on metal. Matt stiffened. Pace wouldn't be so careless as to give away his presence like that. Neither would Dad or Dani.

But then, Pace had a way of knowing things other people didn't know. Like when trouble was brewing on the reservation, even though he was miles or days away, or when things were peaceful. When a man would back down, or when he wouldn't. When it was safe to enter a box canyon, or when it wasn't. That was Pace's gift: he knew things.

Reluctant to have his time alone with Rena come to an end, Matt nevertheless strode forward to greet the family.

He paused a moment later, out of sight, to listen. Only one rider. Had he missed something when he'd spotted the wagon and riders from up on the rim? Was someone else coming besides them?

The shrill screech of an owl pierced the midday stillness.

An owl at noon. Real subtle, Pace.

Matt stepped from behind his cover and met Pace on the edge of the clearing, near where the shack had stood.

Pace glanced around, noting the scattered ashes, the pile of burned rubble. No Serena. From the calm look on Matt's face, he knew she had to be near, and safe. "Where is she?"

"Resting. In a cave up the wall." Matt indicated the general direction with a nod. "Dad and Dani?"

"Right behind me." Pace turned in the saddle and gave three short, piercing whistles. Seconds later, Matt heard the creak and groan of a wagon rattling its way through the narrow canyon opening. A plume of dust rose in its wake.

Pace scanned the clearing again. "Scott?"

"Dead."

"I trust he didn't go fast, or easy."

Matt remembered burning hair and flesh, bloody tracks, paw prints. "Slow, and very hard. But it was an accident."

The sun burned down from overhead. The air still smelled of ashes. Pace dismounted. While they waited for their parents, Matt told him about the fight and how Scott had died.

Pace wore a look of fury on his face. He ignored the wagon that pulled to a halt behind him. "You mean he went in one piece?"

Matt greeted his parents with a nod. When he spoke, his words were addressed to all of them. "There was no reason to cut him up."

"No reason?" Pace's eyes flared and he took a step toward Matt.

"He didn't rape her."

"But I saw it," Dani cried from her seat on the wagon.

295

Travis reached over and grasped her hand.

"And I felt it," Pace said with a growl.

"Oh, he tried," Matt said. "But he didn't make it."

"But how — what happened?" Travis demanded.

Matt looked back at Pace and fought a grin. "Remember when you fed the bushes that night?"

Pace nodded. That was a night he wasn't likely to forget for a long time. "If you'd felt what I did, you'd have been sick, too."

"I'm sure I would have. But if you were feeling what Rena felt, then it wasn't necessarily you who got sick."

"What the hell are you talking about?"

"Scott didn't finish on her because she threw up in his face. You can imagine the effect that had on him."

The chorus of relieved sighs and occasional chuckles was interrupted by a heart-stopping shriek.

The hair on Matt's nape stood on end. "Rena!" He whirled and raced for the canyon wall.

Nineteen

Serena grew tired of waiting. Her family was down there, and she wanted to see them. Stepping carefully on the rocks, she started down the steep path that zigzagged its way to the canyon floor. But all the care in the world couldn't make up for the inappropriateness of the slippers Matt had brought with her dress. They weren't made for climbing around on broken rocks and loose gravel. About halfway down the narrow trail she slipped, landed hard on her rear, and tumbled over the edge. Her heart lodged somewhere in her throat.

She was going to die.

Her scream ripped her throat raw and stole her breath. Stark terror blackened the world and tasted like copper on her tongue as she plummeted toward the jagged, broken boulder more than twenty feet below the ledge.

Something huge and solid slammed into her stomach. Her lungs collapsed. Pain exploded in her chest and stomach.

Her heart beat so hard and so fast for a moment she feared it had stopped altogether. Panic like she'd never known before held her in such a tight grip, it took her a long moment to realize she wasn't dead. A twisted, scraggly cedar had saved her.

She went limp with relief.

The tree grew straight out from the wall for about three feet before its branches curved upward toward the sky. The horizontal section had caught her in the stomach. It knocked the wind from her, but it broke her fall.

From far off, she thought she heard her name called out. The world dimmed as she fought desperately for air. With every painful gasp, the skinny tree swayed and bobbed and threatened to tear loose from the wall.

When she finally drew a decent breath, the blackness faded and her vision cleared. She became aware of a knot in the trunk of the tree that dug painfully into her stomach. Holding on with both hands, she tried to lever herself toward the base of the tree and the doubtful security of the rock wall.

The tree objected to her weight and movement. Loose dirt and gravel trickled from a crevice. A root popped loose. Serena froze. Sweat poured down her face and between her breasts. Her mouth dried and her hands shook.

From somewhere below came a loud crashing through the trees and brush. "Rena!"

Serena twisted her neck and tried to see. "Matt?"

"What the—"

"Are you all right?" Pace demanded.

"Oh, sure," she called down. "I just thought I'd hang around awhile. Get me down from here!"

"Rena, it's Dad," Travis called. "Just hold on, baby. We'll get a rope and climb up to you."

Another root broke free of the wall. The tree jerked downward with an ominous cracking sound.

"There's no time for that, Dad." Matt started up the rocky incline, scrambling for hand- and footholds. Above him, the tree let out another crack.

"Hurry!" Serena cried.

Five more feet, and Matt heaved himself up onto the broken boulder directly beneath Serena. "I'm here," he called. "Just slide off the tree and hang by your hands. I'm right beneath you."

Serena clenched her teeth and forced herself to do as he'd said. The rough dry bark tore at her dress and hands. Chunks came loose in her grasp and crumbled beneath her fingers.

"That's good," Matt called. "Now, move to your left a bit."

She glanced down at him, standing there a good fifteen feet below her. But he wasn't directly below her. Directly below her was a deep black hole between the boulder and the rock wall. She squeezed her eyes shut and fought the jellylike trembling in her bones. But shutting her eyes scared her as much as anything else, so she forced them open.

Her palms grew sweaty as she inched her way sideways. More bark came off, leaving her grasping slick, smooth trunk. The farther she got from the wall, the more the tree sagged and swayed, and her with it.

"Okay," Matt called. "That's far enough. Just let go. I'll catch you."

His words whirled her back through time. Suddenly she was a child of eight again, stuck up in that tree.

"I won't let you fall. Just let go, Rena."

Serena blinked and came back to the present. She looked down at him standing there with his arms held out to her. His eyes flicked down the length of her, then he smiled. "Come on."

Heart thundering in her chest, she took a deep breath and squeezed her eyes shut again. For this she didn't want to see. There was only one thing to do. With a shrill Apache battle cry, she let go of the tree. Air rushed past her face and billowed her skirt. A second later, she landed squarely, safely in Matt's arms.

Matt staggered backward at the impact of her weight, but managed to keep his balance. He held her tightly in his arms and breathed a silent prayer of thanks for her safety. Oblivious to the rest of the family, Matt buried his face in the curve where her neck joined her shoulder and felt his heart start beating again. "You all right?"

"I am now," she murmured. "We're being watched, Matt. Put me down. I'm heavy."

Matt pulled his head back and grinned at her, his back to the others. "You're right. You didn't weigh this much when you were eight years old."

Serena gave him a mock glare and punched him in the shoulder.

He laughed. Then, for her ears alone, he whispered, "But at least you wore underwear then."

Serena's eyes popped wide open and her face caught fire. The dirty rotten polecat. While she'd been dangling from that damned tree, in fear for her very life, he'd been standing down here looking up her dress! "You— You—" She couldn't think of a name bad enough to call him.

Matt threw back his head and laughed again. "Watch out. We'd have some heavy explaining to do if I had to kiss you to shut you up."

Serena beat her fists against his shoulders. "Put me down, you . . . you lecher," she hissed.

"But I like holding you."

Something in his voice made her pause. Her fists halted in midair. He spoke the words easily, sincerely, and with tenderness. A tenderness matched by his soft smile and warm, glowing eyes. As if of their own accord, her arms slipped around his neck. A new, exciting breathlessness

300

seized her, and her lips parted. "Matt," she whispered with longing.

He lowered his head a fraction, then stopped. "Later. We've got company."

Matt straightened, then turned and carried Serena to the edge of the rock. Travis came forward to take her so Matt could climb down more easily, but Matt ignored his father's outstretched arms and held her carefully while he scrambled down on his own.

Once on the ground, Matt released her legs and steadied her as she stood. He kept one arm around her shoulders until Travis swooped her up in his big, strong embrace.

"Princess," Travis said with feeling, "we were so worried about you. Are you sure you're all right?"

Tears formed in Serena's eyes. She rested her head on her father's broad chest. "I'm fine now, Dad." Then she felt another hand on her shoulder. "Mama! Oh, Mama, I'm so glad to see you."

Serena blinked tears away and hugged her mother. When she stepped back, Pace was there. She kissed him on the cheek. "Thank you for coming for me." She searched her mind for some response from him, and found nothing. Puzzled, and a little hurt by his stony silence, she stepped back. His face was expressionless.

"Rena," Matt said coming up behind her. "I think you'd better sit down and rest. You're still weak."

"I thought you said she was all right," Travis said.

"I never said she was all right. I said he didn't rape her. The other thing he didn't do was feed her."

"I'm fine now. Really," Serena protested.

Matt ignored her protests and tried to lead her to a fallen log to sit. She pulled away from him. "Just because you look like my father doesn't mean I'll do what you say."

Daniella's lips twitched. Serena might have just been through the worst ordeal of her life, but there wasn't much to worry about if she felt good enough to sass Matt.

"Sit down," Matt said, grabbing her again and pushing her down until she sat on the log.

Pace tucked his thumbs through the beltloops of his denims and sauntered up to join the others around the log. He let out a snort of disgust. "Look at them. If she was still a virgin when he got here," he said coldly, nodding toward Matt, "I'll bet she isn't now."

A stunned silence fell across the group like a hammer blow. All eyes turned to stare at Pace. Serena gasped and sprang to her feet. She ignored the hand Matt placed on her shoulder. "That's the most ridiculous thing I've ever heard!"

"Is it, now?" Pace stared at her a moment, then turned cold, blue eyes on Matt, who glared back at him.

Daniella looked at her son, aghast at his behavior. "Pace!"

"What the hell is that supposed to mean?" Travis demanded. "That's sick."

Serena bit back a cry. It wasn't sick! What she felt for Matt, what he might feel for her, was good and right.

"What's gotten into you?" Travis demanded of Pace.

Pace's hard gaze flashed to his parents, then back to Matt. "Into me? Look at him. He can't keep his hands off her."

The others looked. Matt's hand tightened on Serena's shoulder. Serena pulled out of his grasp. "You don't know what you're talking about," she said to Pace. "He wouldn't have me if I tore off all my clothes and threw myself at him."

Travis and Daniella stiffened.

Pace sneered at Serena. "A lot you know."

302

"I ought to know, damn you." She spared a quick glance for her parents, then glared at Pace. "It so happens I've tried it. More than once."

"Serena!" her parents cried.

On her shoulder, Matt's fingers dug in. She ignored him and faced Pace with a small, harsh laugh. "Don't look so surprised, Pace. You've always known how I felt."

Then she turned to her parents. They stood there, shocked. "And don't either of you go blaming Matt. He had no idea how I felt about him until just recently. Believe me, he resisted my advances admirably."

Matt didn't know whether to laugh, cry, or strangle Serena. He was still feeling his way through his new relationship with her, still wondering exactly where it would lead, wondering just how serious Rena's feelings for him were. He wasn't ready to deal with how the family felt about them becoming a couple. If that's what he and she were doing.

On the other hand, if left to his own devices Matt would never have been able to come up with a way to tell his father and Dani about the new turn of events. Rena had, bless her stubborn little head, solved that problem.

And created a whole new set of problems, if the looks shooting between Dani, his father, and Pace were anything to judge by.

And high in the Sierra Madres of Sonora, a wrinkled old man closed his eyes, listened to the wind, and chuckled.

Long before the next morning, Serena regretted her outburst. Not because she didn't want the family to know how she felt about Matt — she was in love with him. She didn't care if the whole world knew. Pace had always known. If Matt returned any of her feelings — and she knew he felt something other than brotherly affection for her — then she *wanted* her parents to know. But she hadn't counted on how they and Pace would treat Matt.

She was furious — livid! — at the way her father and Pace watched every move Matt made. If Matt got within ten feet of her, Pace placed himself between them, or Travis sent Matt on some errand.

And Serena's mother wasn't any help at all. While she did not constantly toss malevolent looks in Matt's direction, she blithely set about preparing a meal and ignored the tension in the air.

Serena went to her mother's side. "You haven't said much."

Daniella looked up briefly, then returned her gaze to the quail on the spit over the fire. "What is there for me to say? You're old enough to know your own mind."

"Would you mind repeating that to Pace and Daddy? If their looks get any colder, Matt's liable to freeze in his tracks."

"Matt's a grown man, Serena — he can take care of himself."

Frustrated and dissatisfied with her mother's attitude, Serena left her alone and paced along the edge of the clearing. A few minutes later, she saw Matt saddling his horse. Before she could get near him, Pace was at her side. She ignored him and asked Matt, "Where are you going?"

Matt hooked the stirrup over the saddle horn and tightened the cinch, keeping his gaze on his task the whole time. "Going to bring in Carlos and Jorge."

"Another errand to keep you away from me?"

Beside her, Pace stiffened.

304

Matt shrugged without looking at her.

"I'm sorry," she whispered.

Matt's hands froze. "For what?"

"For the way these two . . ." She shot Pace a dirty look. ". . . *imbeciles* are treating you. You haven't done anything to deserve this."

Pace grunted. "Not for lack of trying, I'll bet."

Serena whirled on her twin, nearly choking on anger. "Shut up! Just shut up and get your foul mouth and your dirty mind away from me!"

Matt watched the blood drain from Pace's dark, fierce face and felt sick to his stomach. No two people in the world were closer than the twins. They were so close they didn't need words most of the time to talk to each other. Matt, in his weakness for Rena, was destroying that.

He closed his eyes and rested his forehead against the saddle. What had he done by giving in to these new feelings for Rena? What in God's name had he done?

"You let him come between us?" Pace said to Serena.

"It's not him," Serena cried, "it's *you*. You make what I feel for Matt sound dirty and wrong, and it's not. You know it's not, Pace. Don't do this to Matt. Don't hurt me this way."

"I'm not hurting you," Pace said. "You're hurting yourself. You always have, when it came to him. He'll hurt you, too."

Matt straightened and jerked his head around. Hurt Rena? He would die before he would intentionally hurt Rena. Surely Pace knew that.

"He's a grown man," Pace told her. "You're just a kid."

"So much younger than you," Serena tossed back.

"I don't doubt he'll take whatever you offer him, but he'll get tired of you fast enough. Then where will you be?"

"Rena's right, Pace," Matt said. "You do have a dirty mind."

"What's going on over here?" Travis's voice boomed beside them. "I thought you were going out to bring in Carlos and Jorge, like I asked," he said to Matt.

"You mean, like you *ordered*," Serena said.

"You stay out of this," Travis told her.

"I will not."

"Ride, Matt."

Matt gave his father a hard look. "You gonna browbeat her while I'm gone?"

Travis looked outraged. "What the hell kind of question is that?"

"Don't worry about me, Matt," Serena said. "I can take care of myself."

Matt ignored Serena and answered his father. "Pretty damned pertinent, if you ask me."

"*Im*pertinent, you mean," Travis said. "You're my son. You don't tell me how to deal with my own daughter."

Matt gave his father a level look. "Yes, I'm your son. And she's your daughter. But she's not my sister."

Serena felt a fluttering sensation in her chest.

Daniella pushed her way past Travis to Matt's side. "Ride on out and get Carlos and Jorge." She stretched onto tiptoes and kissed Matt on the cheek. "Supper will be ready by the time you get back."

Matt looked into Dani's bright blue eyes, just one of the gifts she'd given to Pace and Serena, and saw the calm strength there. She hadn't said much all afternoon about his and Rena's new relationship. She hadn't hovered over Rena or tossed Matt dirty looks the way his father and Pace had. She was obviously reserving judgment.

306

Matt gave her a nod. Maybe while he was gone she could calm everyone down.

No one calmed down. Jorge and Carlos were obviously nervous at the tension and undercurrents evident around the campfire that night. Serena bitterly regretted her earlier outburst that had started all this. But then, Pace was the one who'd really started it, with his nasty comments about Matt.

Still, she knew he thought he was looking out for her best interests. She just wished he would give her enough credit to know what those were for herself.

"Notice you got the buggy horse back," Matt said to Pace. "Where'd you find her?"

Pace smiled grimly. "Fronteras."

"You found Pablo?" Serena asked.

The grin widened. "I found him."

"Who's Pablo?" Travis demanded.

"The one who sent Matt the scalp," Pace answered.

Serena's mouth went dry. "Scalp? What scalp?"

Matt frowned at Pace while he answered Serena. "Just a little message Caleb presumably paid Pablo to send, trying to convince me you were dead."

A chill raced down Serena's spine. "So that's what he meant," she whispered. "He surely didn't expect you to fall for it. Nobody else in the world has hair like this." She tugged on her white streak.

From the corner of her eye, she saw a shudder rip through her mother.

Matt cocked his head at Pace. "Just how did they do that?"

"How did they do what?" Serena asked, a sense of dread crawling up her arms.

"Took them several tries to get the one they sent you."

Daniella raised a hand to her mouth. "You mean they—"

"I'm sure you don't want to hear this, Mother," Pace said.

"No." She swallowed. "I want to know exactly what happened, how they could have made it look . . . like . . ."

Serena's stomach clenched. Her family had been sent a scalp that looked like hers! *Oh, God, how they must have hurt.*

Pace looked to his father. Travis gave him a reluctant nod. "Go ahead. We might as well hear the worst."

With grim, clipped words, Pace told how Pablo and his brother had bragged about the way they'd scalped a Mexican woman, then tried to bleach a strip of her hair white. But the streak turned out red rather than white, and they knew that wouldn't work.

With no more thought than they would give to an old pair of boots, the two men then took another scalp and tried again. This time the streak turned yellow. Still not good enough, they knew.

"They finally got smart," Pace said. "They found a white-headed old man and died his hair black except for the streak. Came out just the way they wanted, so they scalped him."

"Madre de Dios," Carlos muttered.

"How—" Daniella cleared her throat and started over. "How did you get them to tell you all this?"

"Don't worry, Mother, I leave the torture to Matt. All I had to do was furnish the tequila and start asking questions. And speaking of torture," Pace said to Matt, "you had a witness at Cos-codee the day you caught up with Abe Scott."

Matt raised a brow.

"Good ol' Pablo was up on the rim. Apparently saw the whole thing. He had met Scott a time or two, so he sent word to Caleb. That's how Caleb knew about Abe, about Cos-codee."

Matt held Pace's gaze and took a slow sip of coffee, then balanced the cup on his knee. "Where's Pablo now?"

Pace gave a nonchalant shrug and said, *Équusdi.*"

Serena tensed. Beside her, her mother paled.

"How did he die?" Matt asked softly.

Pace gave another shrug. "From trying to breathe through a slit throat."

"Pace," Daniella cried. "You didn't!"

"You better have," Matt muttered.

Pace stood and stretched like a lazy cat. "Think I'll turn in."

"Pablo's brother?" Matt called to Pace.

Pace grinned over his shoulder at Matt. "The ailment ran in the family."

Twenty

Pain bit deep and sharp and woke him. Fierce, hot pain. Burning. Like fire.

Fire.

In that instant, memory rushed in, and Caleb Scott knew who and where he was, how he got there. And he knew hate, hate so powerful it cleared the vision in the one good eye he had left.

Dim light glowed from somewhere above, telling him that out in the world, the sun was shining. Daytime. How long had he been in this pit? How many days since he had wakened to find himself falling, bouncing down the sheer rock walls with the triumphant roar of the cat in his ears?

Matt Colton had done this to him. Matt Colton. Damn the bastard! "He's killed me, sure as he killed Abe." Just as slowly, just as painfully, Caleb was going to die. He knew it. He lay burned, broken, and bleeding in a stench-filled den somewhere in the bowels of the rocky canyon wall. And any minute, the cougar would return.

He wouldn't think of it. He would think of the woman. Serena. Calm, beautiful Serena. She had been weakening. Had Colton not shown up when he did, Serena would have been Caleb's. He would have buried his flesh in hers and she would have welcomed him. She would have loved him.

Just one more thing Matt Colton had taken from him.

Colton had taken everything. He'd taken Abe, wiped him off the face of the earth. He'd taken the revenge Caleb had lived for. He'd taken Serena, Caleb's freedom, and now, his very life.

Goddamn you, Matt Colton. I'll be waiting for you in hell.

A snuffling sound echoed in the hidden cave and sent icy fingers of terror down Caleb's spine. The cat was back. Female, Caleb remembered. Her sagging tits told of a recent litter.

The sweat of fear rolled down his face and nearly blinded him. A mother cat with a hungry litter somewhere close. And Caleb Scott stretched out before her like a pig on a platter. A big platter. His body broken and useless, his strength gone.

The cat licked her lips and showed her teeth. A low rumbling came from her throat.

Caleb shook so hard he heard his bones rattle.

No. Not bones. Something else, something important. But what?

He tried to raise his head, but couldn't.

The rattling grew louder, taunting him. It was important, he knew. Something in him, on him, near him. He couldn't tell.

The cat sniffed his foot.

He jerked.

She sniffed his ankle, his calf.

"No! Goddamn it, no!" Gagging on the stench of fear — his — and rotting flesh — from the mangled carcass in the corner — Caleb tried to move away.

The cat leveled hungry yellow eyes on him. She put a giant paw on his thigh and let out a howl so sharp and loud that dirt sifted down from overhead.

With his one good arm, Caleb frantically swiped the dirt from his one good eye. Something hard and cold hit him in the nose.

Serena's derringer. He blinked. There it was, the little two-shot pistol, right there in his hand. It must have been there all along, since he'd pulled it on Colton. His mind was suddenly so clear and calm, he knew instinctively he was saved the horror of watching himself being eaten alive, limb by limb, bite by bite, by the devil incarnate disguised as a cougar.

He knew, because he remembered. The derringer had one shot left. Only one, but one would be enough. One little .22 slug to the brain, and Caleb would be free of the teeth even now reaching for his bloody thigh. Free of the fear, the horror.

Free.

With the last of his strength and no regrets, he raised the pistol slowly, carefully. His finger was sure and oddly strong on the trigger. He squeezed.

The shot echoed through the cavern and erupted from the crevice overhead like lava spewing from a volcano.

At the abrupt rend in the silence, birds squawked and flapped away. Small animals raced for cover.

And somewhere across the canyon, a bear threw his head to the sky and roared.

For Serena, the trip home was a nightmare. The tension in the air crackled like lightning. Even her mother got caught up in it, no longer able to keep her serene attitude. Pace couldn't speak to Matt without snarling. Travis couldn't look at Matt without frowning. It was enough to

312

make Serena want to cry.

And both Pace and her father were treating her as if she were some hothouse flower that might wilt at the slightest inconvenience.

"Ride in the wagon, Serena. You're still too weak to handle a horse."

"Sleep next to your mother, Serena, in case you need anything during the night."

"Let me help you up, Serena."

"Let me help you down, Serena."

It was enough to make her grind her teeth to keep from screaming. When they crossed the border into Arizona, they were still at it.

"Let me help you down, Serena." Her father reached his arms up to lift her from the wagon, where she had ridden most of the day to pacify him.

"I can get down just fine, thank you." The sharpness in her voice was something she could no longer control. She didn't bother trying.

"I know you can, honey. I just want to help."

The hurt in her father's voice made her feel small and petty. She fought the feeling. "I appreciate it," she told him, "but I'm starting to feel like I'm smothering with all this attention. Please, Dad, stop hovering."

Travis sighed, shook his head, and walked away.

Serena was halfway over the side of the wagon, one foot on the back wheel, when Pace ran up.

"Here, Rena, let me help you."

She ground her teeth. "I don't need any help, thank you."

"Well, pardon the hell out of me for offering," he said, before stomping off in a huff.

Matt came next.

"Don't you dare offer to help me down, or I swear, I'll

313

spit in your face."

"Not me." Matt raised both hands in defense. "I wouldn't think of it."

Serena finally made it to the ground beside Matt and shook the dust from her skirt. "Thank you. I appreciate it." She tossed her father and Pace a glare.

"They getting to you?"

"That's putting it mildly."

"They're only acting this way because they love you."

Serena whirled on him. "Don't you *dare* take up for them. They love you, too, and look how they're treating you!" She glanced up at him and knew instantly she shouldn't have.

This was the first time they'd been within yards of each other without an immediate audience since Pace and their parents had arrived in the canyon. It was the closest she'd been to him since he'd carried her away from her near-fatal fall from the ledge.

She wanted to touch him so badly. She wanted to lean against him, feel his arms around her, feel his lips on hers. *Oh, Matt.*

"Don't look at me like that," he said softly, his brown eyes flaring with heat. "I mean it, Rena. If you think what you said that day in the canyon shocked them, that was nothing compared to how shocked they'll be with what I'll do right here and now if you don't stop looking at me that way."

Serena sucked in a sharp breath. The images his words conjured made her knees go weak. "Matt."

"Rena, don't."

"What are we going to do?"

Matt fought for the strength to resist the plea in her eyes. He fought the need to pull her to him and hold her close. With a deep breath, he stepped back and looked up

314

at the sky. It was the same color as her eyes. "We're going to give everyone a chance to calm down and get used to the idea of you and me."

"And then?"

"And then we're going to make damn sure of my feelings and yours before we take this . . . whatever it is between us, one step further."

"What are your feelings, Matt? You've never said."

The quiver in her voice made him face her again. The anguish in her eyes made him ache. "I'm still . . . trying to understand, myself. But one thing I do know, whatever we decide will be between you and me. The others have nothing to say about it."

"Nothing to say? Matt, this whole family is already tearing itself apart because I couldn't keep my feelings to myself, couldn't keep my mouth shut. I don't want them to hate you because of me."

"Ah, Rena." He couldn't stop himself from pulling her into his arms and holding her close. "It'll work out, you'll see. This family's too strong to fall apart. What I feel for you, what we can have together, is too strong for them to stop us if we don't let them. Trust me, Rena," he said softly. "Trust me."

Serena clung to him, savoring the shelter of his embrace. "They're watching," she whispered.

"Let them."

She wanted to melt into him, become part of him so no one could separate them. Footsteps crunching on gravel told her it couldn't be. Not here, not now.

"What's wrong with her?" Travis demanded.

Serena squeezed Matt once, then stepped back.

Matt refused to drop his arms as though he'd been caught doing something he shouldn't. He kept them loosely around Rena's shoulders. "Nothing's wrong."

From out of nowhere, Pace grabbed Serena's arm and jerked her from Matt's embrace. "Then leave her the hell alone, you bastard."

"Damn you!" Serena swung her fist against Pace's jaw. Pain shot up her arm at the impact.

Pace reeled from the blow, stunned.

The fire of righteous anger heated Serena's blood. "Don't you ever, *ever* do that again," she told him. "I am *not* some mindless ragdoll to be tossed and jerked around. You remember that, *shilghúkéne*. You stick your nose in my business again, I'm going to cut it off. *K'eedaashnndi,*" she repeated in Apache.

"You threaten me? You—"

"No. *Bíni'*. Stop, stop!" Matt could not watch Serena and Pace fight because of him. He simply couldn't. They were saying and doing things they didn't mean, because of him. How long before they both turned on him, blaming him for coming between them, hating him for destroying their closeness? Matt shivered at the thought. He clamped an arm around each one's head and a hand over each mouth and held them tight. "Stop it, both of you."

Pace stood stock still. Matt could feel every muscle in the young man's body quivering with rage.

With her eyes full of outrage, Serena squealed behind Matt's hand.

"I know," Matt told her. "I know, but stop. Please." He pulled them both against him and rested his head between theirs. "Please don't do this to yourselves, to each other."

When he released them, they both started to speak. Nearly trembling with rage at them, at himself, at the whole damn world, Matt raised his hand. "No! Rena, Pace is only acting like an overbearing ass because he loves you. He thinks he's protecting you from me, that I'll hurt you."

Pace made a snarling sound. Matt turned on him. "I know it's not her you're angry with. You want a piece of my hide, you come get it any time. Just stop ripping at her for whatever it is you think I've done."

Pace snarled again and raised a fist.

"Don't!" Matt squeezed his eyes shut. "Please, please don't let me come between you two."

After the wearing tensions of the day, Daniella couldn't sleep. Judging from the restless rustlings around her in the dark, no one else was having much luck, either—except Serena. Daniella ached with each sleepy whimper from her daughter's throat. Dreams shouldn't be painful. After what her daughter had been through these past few weeks, plus the sharp friction now among the men, Daniella could well imagine what tormented Serena's sleep.

As a family, the Coltons had weathered every crisis they had faced and come out stronger each time. But never had they torn at each other the way they had on this trip.

Pace's anger she understood. It was anger bred by a pain he refused to admit. His twin sister was a woman now, with a woman's needs, a woman's wants. She was growing away from the close bond the two had shared since before their birth. She was turning to another man.

How long would it take Pace to understand his own heart? How much pain would he inflict on himself and those around him until he came to terms with losing a part of himself?

Then there was Travis. His initial reaction hadn't surprised Daniella. She, too, had been shocked by the idea of Matt and Serena as anything other than brother and sister. But that had lasted only a second.

She wondered why Travis hadn't realized, as she had,

317

that no amount of disapproval would change the feelings Matt and Serena had for each other. Serena's feelings ran deep, Daniella knew. It was Matt's she wasn't sure about.

She didn't for a minute believe he would toy with Serena's affections. She thought maybe, though, that even Matt wasn't sure of his feelings.

What worried Daniella about Travis was that he should've understood by now what she herself had realized almost immediately. That Serena, raised half-white, half-Chiricahua, would never be happy with a man who didn't completely understand both sides of her heritage. For Serena, Matt was the only man.

Beside her, Travis shifted beneath the blanket and pulled her closer. She took comfort from his warmth and sought a way to make him understand how right Matt and Serena could be for each other. If only the family would give them a chance.

A few feet away, Serena shifted abruptly. Something in her dream must have wakened her.

The restless movements from Pace and Matt stilled. Daniella could almost hear them listening to Serena rise from her blankets and walk silently away from camp.

Travis moved as if to follow. Daniella threaded her fingers through his and squeezed his hand. She, too, hurt for their daughter. But she suspected Serena had had enough family interference for one night.

Let her go, love, she thought to Travis.

As though he heard her, or at least understood the tightening of her fingers on his, he let out a breath and relaxed.

Then Matt got up, pulled on his boots, and followed Serena. Daniella made no attempt to stop him.

But when Pace rose a moment later and started past her after the other two, Daniella reached out and grabbed

318

him by the ankle none too gently. With sharp hand signals, she motioned him back to his blankets.

Pace loomed over her in the darkness a long moment before complying. His anger and frustration vibrated silently through the darkness.

"Couldn't sleep?"

Serena jumped and nearly screamed. She had been so immersed in her own thoughts she hadn't heard Matt approach. Now he stood so close beside her she could feel his heat. She took a step away. "I slept for a while."

"What's wrong?"

She shook her head. What could she say? She couldn't tell him about the dream—no, the nightmare—that had wakened her.

Fear shivered down her arms. The fear and guilt of watching her entire family destroy itself because of her feelings for Matt. She took a deep breath of cool night air, hoping to chase the remnants of the nightmare away, knowing how easily it could all come true.

"Rena?"

"Nothing's wrong."

"If you're worried about Dad and Pace, don't be."

"Don't be? With the way they treat you?"

"I'm a big boy. I can take care of myself."

Serena shook her head back and studied the stars. "You certainly don't seem to be taking any of this too seriously. Don't you mind that because of me they're treating you like a leper?"

"I figured you were blaming yourself."

"Any reason why I shouldn't? If I had kept my head when I was in Tombstone, none of this would be happening."

"Maybe you're right. But then I wouldn't be feeling like a human being for the first time in years, either," he said softly. With a hand to her cheek, he turned her face toward his. "I wouldn't be standing here remembering what it's like to hold you, wanting to hold you again so bad I ache with it, and relishing the ache because wanting you makes me feel so damned alive. Take the credit, Rena, not the blame."

The thought of him holding her, of him *aching* to hold her, turned her knees to water. It was all she could do to keep from rubbing her cheek against his palm, then turning and placing her lips there.

"You're trembling."

What could she say? He was right.

"Are you cold?"

"No." If her answer came too fast, if her head jerked free of his hand, it was out of desperation. If he thought she was cold, he might put an arm around her. If he touched her again she would fall apart. "I'm afraid, Matt."

"Not of me. You can't be afraid of me."

She stared at the different shades of black across the land. She stared at the sky, the stars. Anything to keep from turning and throwing herself into his arms. "I'm afraid they'll keep on blaming you and you'll grow to hate me for it."

This time his soft laughter was tinged with sadness. "You must think I'm one shallow bastard if my feelings for you can be swayed by a few harsh looks."

Serena squeezed her eyes shut. "You know I don't think that."

"You said you loved me, Serena. Have you changed your mind?"

"No," she cried softly.

"Then will you have a little faith, give us a chance to work things out before you start imagining all sorts of horrible things? For me, Rena. For us."

Us. Would there be an *us?* she wondered. She knew his feelings for her weren't as strong as hers for him. He'd never said he loved her. Yet all he was asking for was her faith. How could she possibly deny him that? "All right," she whispered. "I'll try."

Matt breathed a sigh of relief. Still, he couldn't let go of his worry completely. Since Tombstone, she had been adamant that she was — or could be — the woman for him. Now, when he was just beginning to realize how right she was, he felt her slipping away.

For his own sanity, he couldn't let her go. Not like this. Not simply because the family disapproved. He understood her loyalty to the others. He knew she would cut out her own heart to keep from hurting one of them. Would she cut out his, too?

He wanted to hold her, to reassure them both that what they felt was too important, too right to give up, but he didn't dare. He could feel three distinct sets of eyes drilling into his back that very moment. And if he held her, he would kiss her. If he kissed her there, in the quiet darkness of the night, he feared he wouldn't be able to stop. And the eyes would see.

"It's time for me to relieve Carlos," he said. "I'll see you in the morning. Get some sleep."

But Serena didn't get any more sleep that night. Judging by the mood around the campfire the next morning, neither did anyone else. The situation did not improve as the day progressed. Her father glared at Matt, Matt glared back, and Daniella pursed her lips and stared at the horizon toward home.

Something new was going on in Pace's mind, though. Serena watched him pull more and more into himself all morning. By the time her father called a halt at noon, Pace seemed practically oblivious to his surroundings.

After the nooning, Pace was the first to mount. "I'm going to San Carlos," he said.

"Now?" Travis asked. "Why?"

Pace frowned and shook his head. "I don't know. Something . . . something is wrong."

Serena tried to catch Pace's glance, but he wouldn't look her way. She searched her mind for his private voice, the one he shared only with her, but it wasn't there.

"What is it you think is wrong?" Matt asked Pace.

Pace shrugged, something obviously more important on his mind than his animosity toward Matt. "I don't know. Maybe nothing. I just . . . have this feeling."

No one tried to talk Pace out of heading for the reservation. If he had a feeling something was wrong, then something was most assuredly wrong. The only debate came about his riding alone into possible trouble.

Matt knew he should offer to ride with him. Trouble or not, it was past time Matt renewed his old ties among The People. He hadn't seen them since before Angela's death.

The sharp pain, the stark, black emptiness he expected at the reminder of Angela, didn't engulf him. Instead, he felt a dull ache inside, smoothed over by years of warm memories.

He had Rena to thank for that. How long would he have wallowed in his grief and self-pity had she not come and jerked him out of it?

Neither Rena nor Angela would forgive him for staying away from The People so long. He would never forgive himself. Especially not if there was trouble he might be able to help ease. And trouble aside, he missed his friends. He missed Shanta and Chee's companionship around the fire at night, missed Dee-O-Det's stories of the ancient ones, his humor, his wisdom.

Matt missed the old days of hunting through the woods and canyons of the Dragoons, or the pine forests of the Chiricahua Mountains, with Hal-Say.

Those times, like Hal-Say himself, were gone. Another void in Matt's life. Hal-Say had been Matt's "second father," Huera his "second mother." Both had died shortly after being moved from the Chiricahua Reservation in the Dragoons to the dry, dusty San Carlos Agency on the White Mountain Reservation.

How many others had died since being forced onto Hell's Forty Acres?

He should go. He should ride with Pace to San Carlos.

But as much as the old ties called him, Matt still wanted to go home to Joanna and the ranch. He wanted to spend time with his daughter, with Rena, his parents, the ranch hands he'd known since childhood.

Still, if there was trouble at San Carlos . . .

His father must have read Matt's mind. "Why don't you go with him?" Travis suggested.

"I was just thinking the same thing," Matt said.

"No." Pace shook his head.

Matt could almost see the conflict in Pace's eyes. Pace would love to get Matt away from Rena, Matt knew. But for some reason, Pace obviously did not want Matt with him on this trip.

"You've been away too long," Pace told him. "Friend or not, your skin is white, and The People's mood is ugly. Even Mother might have trouble right now."

Even Mother? Shock held Matt silent. Since she was adopted into the tribe by Cochise himself some twenty years ago, Woman of Magic had been considered by every

Chiricahua as one of them. For her to be unwelcome was unheard of. "It's that bad?"

"It's not good. Not since the Army started surrounding the place with troops to keep Nana from riding in and breaking everyone out."

Travis gave a snort. "As if The People needed Nana or anyone else to break them out."

"As if any number of soldiers could keep them in," Rena added.

Travis and Rena were right. All the troops would accomplish would be to stir up The People, frighten them with threats of arrest, make them angry. Maybe Matt *should* go, see if he could do anything to help ease the situation. The older warriors would not necessarily listen to Pace. But then, they wouldn't necessarily listen to Matt, either. They might, however, listen to Dani. And if the Army would listen to any Colton, which was doubtful, Travis had the best chance there.

But in the end, Pace rode alone for San Carlos. If he thought the family could help, he would send word.

Serena breathed a selfish sigh of relief. She would lay down her life for The People if the need arose. But she did not want Matt riding off alone with Pace, no matter how he might be able to help at the reservation. The relationship between the two was strained enough. Because of her.

Matt's relationship with his own father was in trouble. Again because of her.

The family was tearing itself apart because she hadn't been able to keep her feelings for Matt under control. What was she to do? Could the balance in their family life be restored somehow?

For the rest of the trip home, Serena worried about it. By the time they reached the ranch, she could see only one possible solution. Unless she was willing to watch Matt become more and more estranged from his father and Pace, Serena would have to end things between her and Matt before they went any farther.

The mere thought of never again tasting Matt's kiss, feeling his arms around her, of never knowing what it was like to love him and be loved by him, had her crying herself to sleep her first night home.

But she couldn't see any other way to bring Matt and the rest of the family back together again.

That night in her room, she vowed to talk to Matt the next day and tell him what she had decided.

Serena never got the chance. At breakfast the next morning, Tomás, who had spent the night in Tucson, rode in with a telegram from Pace that sent the whole family reeling.

As Travis read the message silently, his brow folded into deep creases and his mouth turned down hard at the corners.

"What is it?" Daniella asked. "What's wrong?"

Travis handed her the telegram, and she read aloud: " 'I have seen my grandfather. Come. Pace.' "

Matt stared sharply at Daniella. "What the—"

"Nocadelklinny," Serena whispered in shock.

"Don't be ridiculous," Travis said. "You don't believe that old shaman can raise the dead any more than the rest of us do."

"Neither does Pace," Serena shot back. "So explain that telegram."

He couldn't, and Serena knew it. That Pace had seen his grandfather was inexplicable.

Daniella pushed back her chair. "We ride."

No one argued or questioned. They would ride to San Carlos at once. As they stared at each other around the breakfast table for a final stunned moment, each one had the same thought.

Pace had seen his grandfather, Cochise.

Cochise, who had been dead more than six years.

Twenty-one

The San Carlos area of the White Mountain Reservation was everything Matt remembered it to be. Flat, barren, and hotter than the fires of hell. The stiff, searing wind carried with it a stinging grit that sheared off any plant that dared stick its head up out of the cracked, sunbaked ground. Nothing grew along this stretch of the Gila River. Not plants, not animals. Certainly not people.

Actually, that wasn't entirely true, Matt admitted. Some things did thrive at San Carlos — things like rocks and heat, cactus, rattlesnakes, and insects, especially the biting kind.

But no game, no edible plants.

The Chiricahua were dying here, from disease, from starvation, from loss of freedom and loss of hope. From broken hearts and broken spirits.

The political situation only compounded the problems. The brilliant plan to put all the area Indians on one reservation did not take into account that most of the tribes were fierce rivals, if not downright enemies. Add to that the usual compliment of corrupt, incompetent agents, conflict between civil and military authorities, white settlers with an eye to the more habitable parts of the reservation, and the current troop buildup of alarming proportions, and what chance did The People have of a decent life?

Hell's Forty Acres.

Matt wanted to weep at the injustice of it all.

But there was no time for tears. From the minute Matt and the others reached San Carlos and found it deserted of all the Apaches, there was no time for anything but action. No time to consider why Rena seemed to be purposely keeping him at a distance. No time to convince his father that Matt was the right man, the only man for Rena.

Matt firmly believed that now, in his heart, in his mind. Rena was his. And he was hers. He knew now he was in love with her. Why it had taken him so long to realize it, he didn't know.

But there wasn't even time enough to tell her how he felt. On the trail from home they were never left alone, not for a minute. At San Carlos, time flashed by in a blur of tension and fear.

The wickiups around San Carlos were empty because The People had gone to Cibecue Creek to meet with other tribes. That in itself was alarming, as there wasn't a tribe on the reservation that called the Chiricahua friend.

At Cibecue Creek, the Coltons found total chaos, along with an unprecedented alliance between the Chiricahua and all the other tribes represented at the gathering. The Army had decided Nocadelklinny's antiwhite preaching was a threat. They were, for once, quite possibly right, Matt thought. No one since Cochise had exercised enough influence to bring warring tribes together the way this old man had.

Mere hours before the Coltons had arrived, Colonel Carr and his troops had been sent to arrest the shaman.

The Indians, including the Apache scouts formerly loyal to the Army, had protested vigorously.

In the ensuing fighting Nocadelklinny had been shot and killed. The Army claimed it was an accident. The Apaches said otherwise and took up arms.

The old woman telling the tale moaned. "He made the dead walk again. For that, Los Goddammies have killed him, and now our men go to fight."

"Fight? Where?" Daniella demanded.

"Tl'ók'al'íí."

Matt's stomach tightened. Good God. The warriors, scouts included, had taken up arms and headed for Fort Apache.

"Shit," Travis said between clenched teeth.

Yes, Matt thought. Shit.

Daniella's face paled. "Pace. Where is Pace?"

"I do not know this Pace," the old woman said.

"My son. *Shiye'.* He is called Fire Seeker. Do you know of him?"

" *'Au.* I know of the young warrior of whom you speak. He rides for the fort with Geronimo."

Matt's stomach clenched. "Shit."

It was dark by the time they neared Fort Apache, dark but for the lights inside the buildings at the fort, and the quarter moon playing tag with scattered clouds that would bring no rain. Empty but for the feel of a hundred eyes piercing the darkness. Silent but for the drums and chants and shouts of war Matt imagined from memories of the old days.

But the sounds were only in his mind. The night was quiet.

They drew their horses to a halt on the low rise south-

329

west of the fort. The land seemed empty of people, but Matt knew better. The Apaches were masters at concealing themselves. The scattering of rocks, cactus, and sparse brush could, and probably did at that moment, hide dozens of warriors.

A figure emerged silently out of the darkness.

Pace. Wearing moccasins, a breechcloth, a headband, and nothing else. Except the carbine in his hand and the knife at his waist.

Not Pace. Matt had seen that look in his brother's eyes before. This was Fire Seeker, Apache warrior.

Dani leaped from her horse, with Travis close on her heels. "What are you *doing?*" she hissed to Pace.

"Trying to stop a war. What took you so long? They won't listen to me. Come," he told her.

She stepped forward. When Travis made to follow, Pace held a hand out to stop him. "No, Dad. Don't come."

"Where she goes, I go."

Still mounted, Matt gripped his reins in a tight fist. He heard the steel in his father's voice. He prayed Pace would heed it.

"You can't help," Pace told Travis.

"She doesn't go alone."

And that was that. Travis would go. But when Serena dismounted and stepped forward as if to follow, Pace was adamant. "No, Rena. Matt, keep her here."

With that, Pace led Dani and Travis into the darkness.

Matt swung down from his horse and stood beside Rena. Neither moved or spoke for what seemed like an eternity. Matt ached to pull her close and hold her. He hungered for the taste of her lips, longed for the fire her touch always ignited in him.

But he stood beside her, not touching her, for she

hadn't invited his touch. Not since the trip home from Mexico.

"I'm scared, Matt," she suddenly whispered.

He couldn't see the expression in her eyes, for the clouds had caught up with the moon. But he heard the quiver of fear in her voice. Fear of what could happen if the warriors attacked the fort, and some other fear he detected but couldn't define, some personal fear.

He gave up his struggle to stay away from her and slipped an arm around her shoulders. "So am I." He pulled her close and felt her stiffen against him. "So am I."

Serena felt her heart pound, and prayed Matt couldn't hear it. For days she had ached for his touch, despite her decision to stay away from him. Now he was touching her. Knowing she should pull away, she wanted nothing more than to melt against him. *Matt, Matt, how do I get you out of my heart?*

With a forefinger, he tipped her face up to his. "Tell me what you're afraid of."

She tried not to meet his gaze, but couldn't help it. She tried not to shiver at the sound of his low, intimate whisper, but that, too, was beyond her.

"Rena?"

She ducked her head. "The fighting," she managed. "I'm afraid there'll be fighting."

"So am I, but let's give Dani a chance before we worry too much. What else are you afraid of?"

You, me, she thought frantically. *Of what we're doing to our family.* But she couldn't say the words. She merely shook her head and kept her gaze lowered.

The shock of his lips on hers took her by surprise.

"This?" He nibbled at the corner of her mouth. "Are you afraid of this?"

331

She should tell him yes. Instead, she tilted her head back to better meet his kiss. "You know I'm not."

His arms came around her and pulled her flush against his chest. Serena wanted to weep at the exquisite beauty and pleasure of his embrace, of his deepening kiss.

Then came the soft scuff of feet along the hard ground.

Serena jerked from Matt's arms, terrified of letting anyone see her kissing him. The family had more than enough to handle without her adding to the problems. Now was not the time to stir up the animosity that would be directed at Matt.

"Rena?" Matt's hand brushed her arm.

"No." She stepped away.

In the next instant, several figures emerged from the darkness: her parents and Pace. The larger shadow following Pace explained why Serena had been able to hear anyone approaching. It wasn't her brother or their parents who'd made the noise, but Pace's horse.

Then another figure emerged. A squat, dark-skinned man with a barrel chest and powerful shoulders. Her mother's old enemy, Golthlay.

But no, Serena reminded herself, he didn't go by that name any longer. He was now known far and wide by the name given to him by the Mexicans years ago, for reasons known only to them: Geronimo.

To say that he and her parents shared a mutual respect would be stretching credibility. But the three did share what Travis sarcastically referred to as mutual tolerance.

Against the usual Apache custom of starting a meeting with a great deal of polite small talk, Daniella turned to Geronimo and struck immediately at the heart of the matter. "You *must* call off your warriors."

In the darkness, one black brow on Geronimo's forehead arched. "For a white woman, you are either uncommonly brave, or uncommonly stupid," he said in a mixture of Spanish and Apache.

Serena saw her father clench his fists. She held her breath.

Her mother shrugged. "So I've been told. But surely you know that to attack the fort is suicide."

Geronimo folded his arms across his massive chest. "Better to die an honorable death in battle than to let them starve us, take away our dignity, kill our holy men."

"Honorable," Daniella said with a hiss in her voice. "What is honorable about fighting an enemy who cowers behind his closed doors?" She waved a hand in the direction of the fort. "Look there. They won't come out to fight you. You've already defeated them."

Geronimo narrowed his eyes. "Not while they still live."

"The only way they'll fight you is if you show yourselves out in the open. And they'll kill you. All of you. Either right now, tonight, or tomorrow, when they call in more troops. More troops than you have ever seen. What honor is there in throwing your lives away and leaving your women and children to the mercy of these enemies? Don't the old men teach young boys it is better to live to fight another day than to die uselessly?"

Geronimo was silent a long time while he stared at Daniella. Serena let out her breath, then drew in another and held it. Tension stretched her nerves taut.

"What makes you think," Geronimo said, "that we need you to come tell us these things? Does Woman of Magic not think us smart enough to know the things of which she speaks?"

"I *know* you're smart enough," Daniella said. "But you are angry — justifiably so — over what happened today. I came to speak because I feared that in your rage you might forget you are surrounded by troops. Forgive me if I've been presumptuous."

Geronimo chuckled and shook his head. "No more presumptuous than usual, Woman of Magic. No more presumptuous than this young pup of yours." He took a playful swipe at Pace's head.

Serena let out her breath. Geronimo was not angry with her mother. Not that he would dare lay a hand on her, but Serena knew her mother didn't like to anger him.

"Go now," Geronimo said, including Pace in his look. "Many here tonight are not my men, but I will talk to them. We shall see what will be." He turned to go, then paused. "And Woman of Magic? I am glad you still care what happens to us."

With that, he disappeared into the shadows.

Pace let out an audible breath. "Damn, Mother, I've never heard him say anything like that before. You must have really impressed him."

Serena rushed forward, Matt on her heels, in time to see her mother's wry grin. "Either that," Daniella said, "or he finally realizes I *do* care."

"Come on," Travis said. "We've done all we can. Let's get out of here."

When they were mounted, Matt asked, "Where to?"

Travis looked hard at Pace. "Down the river a ways, where we can camp for the night. The canyon, maybe. Then I want an explanation for that telegram."

"I know it's impossible," Pace cried. "But I know what I saw, damn it. I was there."

"Just what *did* you see?" Daniella asked.

Pace closed his eyes and leaned his head back. "It was around noon," he said. "And hot. Hot enough to send heat waves rippling from the ground. The old man sprinkled *tádídín* in the air and started singing."

Serena's heart pounded. "Nocadelklinny?"

Pace nodded. "He called on all the dead warriors, the Chidikáágu', the Mashgalén, the Coyoteros, warriors from all the Apache tribes, to rise up from Where the Cottonwoods Stand in Line. He beseeched them to come back to this life and fight to rid the land of white men. Over and over he sang the words. His voice was the only sound. The creek, the birds, the wind—all were silent."

Serena could picture it in her mind, could feel her heart pound harder, even knowing what Pace claimed could not be.

"He chanted for hours without end. Late in the afternoon, with that strange silence still hovering, the heat waves along the creek bank started changing."

When Pace paused, Travis urged him on. "Changing?"

"The waves turned darker, reached higher. Tall shapes formed and shimmered away, then formed again."

Pace opened his eyes and gave each of them a level look. His gaze finally settled on Daniella. "I saw my grandfather standing before me."

"Pace," Matt said.

"Next to him stood Uncle Tahza, then Mangas Coloradas. I *saw* them."

"Pace, damn it," Matt said.

Pace turned his gaze on Matt. Serena expected Pace to be angry at Matt's skepticism. Instead, her twin gave Matt a look of . . . sorrow.

"I saw Hal-Say, Matt."

From across the small campfire, Serena saw Matt pale at the mention of his long-lost "second father."

335

"You didn't," Matt said. "You couldn't. It's impossible."

Pace jumped to his feet, hands clenched into fists. Here was the anger Serena had expected.

"Of course it's impossible," Pace cried. "It's impossible for me to have known there was trouble here. It's impossible for a woman to be struck by lightning and live to tell of it," he cried, reminding them all of what had happened to Daniella years before. "It's impossible for Mother to have visions. It's impossible for Rena and me to know each other's thoughts. At least we used to be able to," he added with fury. "Until you decided to seduce your *sister*."

"Pace," Serena cried. The stab of pain to her heart nearly took her breath away. "Pace, no!"

"She is *not my sister*."

"I notice you don't deny seducing her, you filthy, stinking—"

"That's enough!" Daniella shouted. "Not one more word."

Matt opened his mouth.

"Not *one*."

Oh, God, Serena thought, her stomach churning. It was starting again, this ripping apart of the family, before the last rends had even had a chance to mend. *What am I going to do?*

Long after the fire was out Matt lay awake on his blanket, too troubled to sleep. Being furious with Pace wasn't keeping him awake. Hell, he'd been furious with Pace for weeks.

No, it was thoughts of Serena that wouldn't let him sleep. She was blaming herself for the trouble between him and Pace, between him and his father. She was beating herself up, letting guilt dim the glow in her eyes. And Matt wasn't sure what to do about it.

He should not have let Dani shut him up earlier. He should have had it out then and there with Pace and his father, set them straight once and for all.

But then, he thought he'd done that already, more than once, on the trail from Mexico. Fat lot of good it had done.

His father, he felt sure, would come around in time. Matt thought he could leave that up to Dani. Pace seemed to be a different story. Matt would give him until they got back to the ranch. If Pace hadn't stopped spouting off by then, Matt would take him out behind the barn and "discuss" the matter.

It hurt, this censure from the two men he loved most in the world. But he would be damned if he let either of them keep him away from Rena.

With his determination firmly in place, and word having come more than an hour ago that the warriors had left the fort without attacking, Matt settled down for some much needed sleep. Just as he dozed off, a duck quacked nearby.

A duck? In the middle of the desert?

He nearly laughed out loud. With a swift kick, he tossed his blanket aside and tugged on his boots, then stood and waited. A moment later, the duck quacked again. The sound was as out of place in that part of the country as a bull moose in church. But this time Matt caught the direction from which it had come.

Still fighting laughter, he left camp and made his way quietly beyond the surrounding scrub and rocks. The clouds had blown away, leaving ample light from the quarter moon. Matt had no trouble locating the spot from which the "duck" had "quacked."

"So it's true," came a voice from his left. "A white man cannot find his way in the dark."

Matt grinned. "You moved."

Chee grinned back. "I did."

The two men, friends since childhood, embraced heartily. A lump rose in Matt's throat for all the years he had spent away from The People, his family. His friend.

He cleared his throat. "So, how is it with you? How is your family?"

Chee's grin died in the moonlight. "Our lives, yours and mine, seem to parallel one another."

Unease rippled down Matt's arms. "Meaning?"

Chee closed his eyes briefly. His thick chest expanded on a deep breath. "I, too, must now raise my daughter alone."

Matt felt a sickness in his gut. "Maria?"

"Malaria. Last summer."

"Ah, damn, Chee."

"Yes," Chee said softly, solemnly. "Damn."

Matt wished there were something he could say to ease the pain in Chee's eyes, but he knew from experience nothing would help. Chee had worshipped the beautiful Mexican slave he had taken as his wife. Nothing could ease the pain of her loss. Only time. And, he thought, a persistent stepsister. But then, Chee didn't have a stepsister. He did, however, still have a daughter. "LaRisa?" Matt asked.

Some of the sadness left Chee's face, to be replaced by smiling pride. "She's five now. A more beautiful child you have never seen."

"Oh, I don't know," Matt said. "I've never seen one as beautiful as Joanna."

"And smart, too," Chee said, ignoring him.

The two men grinned, then laughed. "It's good to see

you again, my friend," Matt said.

"I feel the same. Next time, don't wait for trouble before you come to visit."

Matt sobered. "I assume you were at the creek this afternoon when the troops came."

With a sigh, Chee said, "Yes, I was there."

"What happened?" Matt asked. "Pace told us some cock-and-bull—"

"It wasn't bull. If he told of seeing dead ones walk the earth again, he spoke the truth."

Matt couldn't conceive of such words coming from one of the most intelligent, most practical men he'd ever known. Whatever had taken place at Cibecue Creek that afternoon, both Chee and Pace, and obviously hundreds of others, firmly believed they'd seen Nocadelklinny raise the dead.

Matt shook his head. "And after? That business at Fort Apache?"

"I was there, too. And before you ask, no, I did not think it wise. I went, along with others, to try to prevent an all-out battle. But yes, if it had come to that, I would have fought beside my brothers."

Matt nodded. "I cannot fault you for that." Because of his education, received mostly at the Triple C in his youth, Chee knew better than perhaps any other Apache what insurmountable odds the tribe was up against when they fought the whites. Yet Matt could not blame him for choosing to stand with The People against those who lied to, cheated, and starved them. In Chee's place, Matt knew he would do the same.

"So, what happens now?" Matt asked.

Chee heaved another sigh and looked at the sky. "Now, my friend, we go on from here. We grit our teeth and pray to Yúúsń that the troops pull back and let us breathe."

***

Before leaving the reservation, Travis wanted to stop at the San Carlos Agency headquarters. Matt chafed at the delay, but after seeing how few cattle remained at the agency, he agreed with his father that there wasn't enough beef to last until the November Triple C herd was due.

Travis coerced the agent into taking the next Triple C beef shipment at the end of September instead of in mid-November, as previously planned.

"Something else I'd like you to consider," he told Matheson.

"What's that?"

"Let me take the herd and split it up among the Apaches. Deliver it directly to them."

Matt held his breath. This was an idea his father had tried with every successive agent at San Carlos. Not one of them had ever gone for it. Because of the Coltons' close ties with the Chiricahua, agents in the past had been reluctant to trust any of them. Most took particular dislike to Pace and Serena, feeling the two half-breeds should be confined to the reservation.

Matheson had, thus far, followed in his predecessors' footsteps in his dealings with the Coltons.

"The hell, you say," Matheson cried. "Why the devil would I agree to such an outrageous idea?"

If Travis's smile tightened, along with the muscle along his jaw, Matheson didn't seem to notice.

"Think about it," Travis urged. "With more and more troops showing up every day, the Apaches are understandably nervous. Especially after that business yesterday up on Cibecue Creek. They need something to do. You've tried to turn them into farmers. They're not farmers, never have been."

Travis looked the man right in the eye. "Even if they were," he said, "you and I both know the land around this agency won't grow anything but dirt, and most of that blows away. Taking care of cattle would give The People something to do, keep them occupied."

Matheson spat in the dirt and scratched one sideburn with a finger whose tip was missing. "Keep them occupied, yeah. And keep them away from the agency so I wouldn't know what they were up to."

"True, but if you're really concerned about them breaking out, think how much harder it would be for them if they had cattle to take, or leave behind."

A sharp gleam came to the agent's eyes. "Yeah . . . yeah. Maybe I'll think about it."

"You do that. I'll see you at the end of the month."

When they rode out, Matt thought, maybe — maybe this time it would work. But he wasn't optimistic enough to let the subject occupy his mind.

Serena had not spoken to him, had not even looked at him, all morning.

That occupied his mind.

Twenty-two

While in the study catching up on ranch bookkeeping, Serena heard the door to the room close. She jerked and looked up from her ledger. Her breath caught.

Matt.

He seemed to fill the room and suck up all the air. A huge yearning ache squeezed her chest. With the exception of family meals, this was the closest she'd been to Matt since that night the warriors had nearly attacked Fort Apache, when he'd held her in his arms.

Against her will, she drank in the sight of him. No wonder she hadn't heard him walk in. He had removed his boots—they had probably been caked with manure, for she knew he'd been in the corral, working with the newest herd of mustangs.

His brown pants were tight and dusty, with a small tear at one knee. Serena envied the pants for the way they hugged his lean hips.

Sweat streaked the chest, arms, and probably the back of his light blue shirt. It looked ready to split apart under the strain of those wide shoulders of his, shoulders she hadn't touched, hadn't leaned against in ages. Shoulders she had slept against only once, in Mexico. That time in the cave seemed like another life.

Slowly she raised her gaze past his throat to his tanned face. The heat in his dark eyes stirred an answering warmth in her blood. She fought against it.

He stood a scant inch from the front of the desk. "I've missed you."

His nearness, his deep, quiet voice, the longing it revealed in him and generated in her, sent panic ricocheting through her veins. Visions of her father and Pace glaring at Matt, shouting at him, accusing him, ate at her.

With quick, jerky movements, she shoved her chair away from the desk and escaped to the window across the room. She turned her back to Matt and folded her arms across her chest. Maybe that way he wouldn't notice her shaking.

"Rena?"

"Don't be silly," she said with a nervous chuckle. "How could you miss me? We've seen each other every day."

She felt more than heard him move closer. "Only when you couldn't find someplace to hide. You've been avoiding me."

"Of course I haven't."

He put his hands—those big, strong, gentle hands— on her shoulders. Her knees nearly buckled.

"Then why won't you turn around and look at me?"

She shrugged his hands away and stepped closer to the window. "Be sensible," she said. "The house is full of people. Anyone could walk in."

This time she heard his stockinged feet pound the floor as he made his way to the door. She also thought she heard a muttered curse. The next sound she expected was that of the door opening so he could leave. Instead, the grating of the key in the lock raised the hair along her arms.

She spun in time to see him pull the key out and toss it carelessly toward the desk. It hit, slid across the surface, and took two sheets of paper with it on its way to the floor.

"What are you doing?" she cried.

"That's my question. In Tombstone, you couldn't keep your hands off me. Don't blush, damn it, I'm not complaining. In Mexico, before the folks showed up, you were all over me. Hell, I was all over you. You said . . . Rena, goddamn it, you said you loved me."

Oh, God. Tell him you lied. Tell him, you coward. It's the easiest way, the only way now. But her breath caught in her throat and her tongue stuck to the roof of her mouth. The lie wouldn't come.

"What was I, some kind of experiment? Did you think because it was me, I was safe? You could tease me, make me want you, just to learn the rules before you went out after bigger game?"

Serena stiffened. The lie on her tongue wouldn't come, but maybe his way was better. A swift, sharp argument. Like a knife to the heart. Quick. Final. She raised her chin a notch. "I don't know what you're talking about."

"And pigs have wings." He stepped closer.

She backed away.

"No." He grasped her shoulders again. "You asked me on the way back from Mexico what my feelings for you were. I said I didn't know. That wasn't exactly true."

"Matt, don't –"

"Let me finish. I knew even before then what I felt for

344

you, but it came as such a shock, I don't think I let myself recognize it. I never expected to feel this way about a woman again, Rena. I'm not sure I've ever felt *just* this way before. I love you."

Serena's heart did a flip-flop. Her eyes burned.

"Not as a brother loves a sister," Matt said earnestly. "I love you the way a man loves a woman. *His* woman. And you're backing away from me, keeping me at a distance. Why, Rena? Why? If you're trying to convince me you don't love me, it won't work. I see how you feel about me. It's in your eyes every time you think I'm not looking. God, do you know what it does to me inside to see you look at me that way, then watch you turn away? Talk to me, damn it. Talk to me."

She opened her mouth, not knowing what to say, but he cut her off.

"Then again, don't talk." He pulled her close and lowered his head. "This is better." Then his mouth took hers.

It wasn't a gentle brushing of lips. Not this. This was hunger, deep and raw. It was anger, confusion. Pain. His, and hers. Serena couldn't stop herself from clinging to him, answering the need she felt rippling through him, responding with everything she had. She pushed her hands around his neck and into his thick hair.

He wrapped his arms around her tight and pulled her flush against his sweat-dampened chest. She didn't care about the damp. Didn't care about anything but holding him, tasting him, feeling the heat in him raise an answering heat in her this one last time. For if she was wise, if she didn't want to end up destroying him, she would make certain this was the last time he got near enough to kiss her.

But God, how would she ever let him go?

In the end, it was Matt who let her go. With a deep

groan, he tore his lips from hers and pushed her away until he could see her face. "I love you," he said, his chest heaving. "Look me in the eye and tell me you don't feel the same."

She couldn't. She knew she couldn't. She squeezed her eyes shut and fought the sting of tears.

"You can't do it, can you?" Anger mixed with triumph in his voice. "You can't tell me you don't love me because it isn't true. You do love me . . . don't you." There was no question in his tone, only certainty.

When she didn't answer—dear God, she couldn't—he squeezed her shoulders. "Don't you?" he demanded.

"Yes," she cried. She forced her eyes open and felt a tear streak loose. "Yes, I love you. Yes, I want you. But it can't work, Matt, don't you see? This is all my fault. I've made Daddy and Pace hate you. Daddy and Mama are barely speaking. Mama's snapping at everybody. This whole family is tearing itself apart, all because I couldn't keep my feelings for you to myself. If this keeps up, you're going to end up hating me. I couldn't stand that, Matt. I *couldn't*. They want—"

"I said it once as a joke," Matt said fiercely, cutting her off. "This time I'm not joking. To hell with them, Serena. I don't care *what* they want."

"We're talking about Mama and Daddy and Pace. You can't ignore them," she cried.

"I *can*. I can ignore them and what they want. I've got wants of my own. I want to be able to walk up to you and touch you whenever I want. I want to hold you and kiss you right out in the open and not give a damn who's watching."

His words made her pulse pound. He pulled her close again, until his chest almost, *almost,* brushed her

346

breasts. The intensity in his eyes took her breath away. And his voice, so strong and sure, filled her heart to near bursting.

"I want you beside me," he said, "to hear Joanna's prayers. I want you next to me every night in my bed. I want your arms around me in the dark. I want to be able to lay my head on your breast and know you'll always be there for me, the way I'll be there for you. I want to make love to you, bury myself so deep inside you we can't tell where one of us starts and the other stops. I want to wake up every morning with your hair streaming across my chest."

Ruthlessly, Serena ignored the longings evoked by his impassioned words. "And do you want to face your father and my brother every morning over breakfast and have them glare their disapproval at you for the next twenty years?"

"No," he said calmly. "I want to marry you."

On a sharp intake of breath, Serena closed her eyes and watched her dream come true. And then watched it crumble around her.

"Think of what we could have, Rena."

Her eyes flew open. "I *am* thinking of what we could have," she cried. "We could have our whole family torn apart. *Forever.* I could have you hating me for coming between you and them."

The pain that flashed across his eyes cut her to the quick. In an emotionless voice, he said, "So I'm just supposed to let you go, is that it? I'm supposed to forget that for a few weeks, I actually felt something inside me besides pain, something other than that great, black emptiness that nearly swallowed me? I'm supposed to forget what it feels like to have you touch me, forget your taste, forget the way you flew apart in my arms that night in

347

Mexico? I'm supposed to forget you love me, that I love you?"

Serena trembled violently, knowing this was the end. The end of everything. Another tear slipped past her guard. "Yes," she whispered. "For both our sakes."

Without another word, Matt turned and walked to the door. It was locked. He took a deep breath and crossed the room, rounded the desk, and retrieved the key from the floor. As he put it in the lock and opened the door, he turned back and looked at her. "I won't forget. Not any of it. Neither will you, Rena. You know where to find me when you change your mind."

As he left, he closed the door softly behind him.

With careful steps, Serena relocked the door and returned to her chair behind the desk. There, she sat and leaned her head against the back of the chair and let the tears come.

Matt braced both arms against the corral fence and let his head droop between his shoulders. He was in hell. He'd been there before, spent three whole years there. Now, here he was, back again, only this time it was different. This time, instead of dying inside with the knowledge that he would never again see the woman he loved, the pain came when he *did* see her. Different woman, different reason, different pain. But just as sharp.

He and Serena lived under the same roof, for God's sake. How was he supposed to survive like this? Seeing her every day, but not touching her. Hearing her voice but not her laughter. Catching a whiff of that sweet mixture of wildflowers and some unique fragrance that was strictly Serena, yet not tasting her. Thinking of her, but not being able to hold her.

Damn, but he was losing his mind.

He tugged off his gloves and tucked them under his belt. With his grimy bandana, he wiped the sweat from his face and neck.

He was going to lose more than his mind if he wasn't careful. He'd done smarter things in his life than climb atop a wild mustang when his mind was elsewhere. That dun who'd just bucked him off had come a shade closer than comfort to giving Matt a broken neck.

"Losin' your touch, old man?" Pace taunted from the shade of the barn.

"Cram it, kid."

Pace hooted and sneered.

That was another little problem Matt didn't know how to deal with. According to Rena's logic, his dad and Pace should have backed off Matt by now. They'd had plenty of time to see he hadn't been anywhere near Serena in weeks.

But they hadn't let up. Especially Pace. The censure, the disapproving glares were as strong as ever.

Even more so since Dani had left last week for the Sanchezes'. The minute she'd kissed his dad goodbye and headed down the valley to help Señora Sanchez with her new baby, Pace and Travis had dropped all restraints.

Matt cursed Señor Sanchez for his untimely disappearance. Dani wouldn't normally have stayed more than a few days at the Sanchez ranch, but the *señora* had six other children and no one to help her. Dani wasn't expected home for another week or two at the soonest.

And Dani was the only one who could come close to controlling Travis and Pace. Matt figured he'd just about had all he was going to take from the two of them.

As Pace sauntered toward him, Matt ground his teeth.

"Whatsa matter, Matthew? If I didn't know better, I'd swear you went and lost your sense of humor. What happened? Did little sister cut big brother off?"

Fury, sweet and hot, burst through Matt's brain. With one hand he grabbed Pace by the shirtfront and slammed him up against the corral fence. "If you *ever* talk about your sister like that again," he spat while Pace's feet, a good six inches off the ground, kicked his shins, "I'll beat you to a bloody pulp."

Matt gave Pace a final shake for good measure, then let go and turned to walk off, before he did something he might really be sorry for.

"You and what army, you piece of shit?" Pace taunted.

Before Matt took another step, he found himself face-down in the dirt with Pace punching him in the kidneys. His breath left him in a hard *oomph*. By the time he could suck in air again, Pace was all over him and the dust was thick enough to eat.

Matt spat to clear his mouth of grit, wincing and grunting with each blow. "Goddamn." He heaved, trying to toss Pace's weight off his back. Pace didn't have Matt's bulk, but he was damn sure heavy enough. Matt heaved again and Pace fell off.

The two rolled in the dirt, Pace reining blows, Matt trying to protect himself. "Goddamn," he said again. Where the hell had the kid learned to fight? "Back off, Pace."

Pace landed a solid blow to Matt's jaw. Pain exploded.

"I mean it," Matt said harshly.

Pace ignored him and swung again.

Chest heaving, breath rasping in his throat, Matt finally landed a punch of his own to Pace's gut. "I said back off, damn it!"

"Go to hell." Pace caught Matt in the eye with a left jab.

More pain. And rage. He was scrambling around in the dirt letting his kid brother beat the crap out of him. To hell with it. He lunged and wrapped both arms around Pace and held on.

A pair of dusty boots appeared next to his nose. *Damn. Dad.*

"What in blue blazes do you think you're doing?" Travis bellowed. He then made the mistake of trying to break up the fight.

Matt and Pace both gained their feet. Their father tried to keep them apart. In the ensuing struggle, boots kicked, fists punched, elbows jabbed. And curses flew like chaff on the wind.

Serena gave her hair a final swipe with the brush and braced herself for another ordeal — the nightly torture of facing Matt at supper.

Nothing was going as planned. Her father and Pace should have stopped treating Matt like an outsider by now. He hadn't been near her in weeks. In that time, nothing more personal than "Pass the potatoes" had gone between them.

Yet every day, the tension and animosity still vibrated with every look, every word her father or Pace uttered to or about Matt. If possible, things seemed even worse since her mother had left for the Sanchez spread.

Why, why wouldn't Pace and Daddy leave Matt alone? Why did they insist on blaming him for what was her fault?

Oh, she had tried talking with them, but neither had listened. Pace acted as though she had lost her mind, and her father treated her like a bird with a broken wing. A mentally impaired bird, no less.

351

"It doesn't matter what you did or didn't do, Princess," her father had said. "You're a sweet, innocent young girl. Matt is a grown man. He should know better."

Serena twisted her hair into a knot at her nape and tried not to grind her teeth at the memory. She'd been grinding her teeth so much lately her jaw was developing a permanent ache.

How much longer, she wondered, would it take for her father and Pace to accept Matt again? To stop blaming him for something that never really happened anyway?

How much longer before she would be able to see Matt, hear his deep voice, watch those hard yet gentle hands smooth his daughter's hair, without this piercing ache in her belly?

She'd been a fool to think she could live in the same house with him. It wasn't working, would never work. Every time she thought about what the two of them could have, were it not for family interference, she died a little inside. Soon, there would be so many little dead pieces floating around, there would be no part of her left alive.

Oh, Matt, what am I going to do?

But she couldn't back down — not now. By refusing to marry him, she had hurt him, hurt him something awful. He barely looked at her these days. Which was just as well, because whenever she got near him, she had all she could do to keep from throwing herself against that broad chest and begging him to love her again.

Whatever he had felt for her, however, had died that day in the office. And it was her fault. She had killed it.

She gave her hair a final pat, then took a deep breath. It was time to face him across the table again. Time to pretend she could be that close to him and actually swallow food and not have it sit like a rock in the pit of her stomach.

Time to pretend she didn't want him any longer, didn't love him.

God, help me.

Travis, Matt, and Pace were the last to arrive at supper. Serena kept her gaze stuck firmly on her plate. She prayed the sight of the gravy covering her mashed potatoes wouldn't make her sick, but she would not, *could* not, look at Matt. Not without giving away all her feelings.

Boot steps thudded along the floor; chairs scraped.

"There you three are," Jessica said. "I was beginning to wonder . . ."

Serena forced down a bite of fresh bread.

"Good heavens," Jessie whispered. "What the devil—"

"Watch your language," Matt warned. His voice sounded funny. Muffled.

Curious, Serena looked up. The first thing she saw was his hand resting beside his plate. She winced at the sight of the skinned, swollen knuckles.

"Daddy," Joanna cried, "what happened to your face?"

Serena raised her gaze higher. "Oh, my God."

Matt's face was covered with bruises and scratches, his upper lip was puffy, and his left eye was swollen shut. Serena felt her stomach roll over.

His right eye glared at her. The message written there was plain. *Shut up, Rena. Don't say a word.*

Fighting tears and outrage at the beating he had taken, Serena ignored his glare.

It had to be Pace. Pace was responsible for Matt's condition; she knew it. *Oh, God, what is happening to this family?* She shot a look to her twin. "How dare—"

She swallowed the rest of her words. If anything, Pace looked worse than Matt. She pressed her fingers to her lips to hold back a cry.

Where had her father been during this fight? Why hadn't he stopped it?

She turned to demand an answer, but choked on the words. He sported a cut lip and a swollen cheek.

Serena jumped from her chair. "Damn you," she cried. "Damn all of you!"

She covered her mouth with her hands, aghast at both her words and her tears. It was over. Her sure and certain plan to smooth things between Matt and the others wasn't going to work. All her pain and Matt's for the past weeks had been for nothing.

For she knew now she had to leave. She could not stay here and be the cause of any more fighting.

"Damn you all," she whispered as she fled the room.

Matt closed his eyes — or rather, one eye, for the other felt permanently closed, thanks to Pace's left jab. He fought the urge to swear.

"Daddy?" Joanna said tentatively.

He opened his eye and gave her a crooked smile — all he was capable of until the swelling went down in his lip. "It's all right, sweetie." He slid his chair back. "I need to talk to Aunt Rena. I'll be right back."

Travis slapped both hands flat against the table. Silver and china rattled. "No!" He glared at Matt. "You sit in that chair and leave that girl alone. You've done enough damage."

Matt nearly choked on the words he refused to utter. He would not cause a scene at supper. Dani might not be there, but she would never forgive him, just the same.

354

But it galled him something fierce to have his father come down on him like he was still a kid. Goddamn, it galled him.

It took Matt a full three days to calm down enough to talk to his father. During those three days he had done a lot of hard thinking. And he'd decided, finally, to put an end to everyone's problems. He waited until he was alone with his dad and Pace before telling them his plans.

"I'll be leaving as soon as you get back from delivering the cattle to San Carlos. Joanna and me."

"Leaving?" Travis lowered the latest edition of *The Daily* out of Tucson. "Why? Where are you going?"

Matt shrugged, hoping he didn't look as tense as he felt. "Thought I'd look up some of my New Orleans cousins."

"New Orleans? You haven't been there in twenty years." Travis tossed his paper aside. "What's this all about?"

Matt eyed his father steadily. They both knew exactly what this was about. But Matt tried to keep things polite. "I want Joanna to know about that side of her family."

"How long'll you be gone?" Pace asked, looking and sounding so damned pleased about Matt's leaving that Matt felt like stuffing him in a hole.

"Awhile," was all he said.

"I've never heard you mention wanting to contact your mother's people before," Travis said. "I find it hard to believe you've developed a sudden interest in them at this late date."

"Don't be dense, Dad," Pace said. "Let him go. The sooner, the farther away from Serena, the better."

Matt got mad. "That's it, Pace. Don't let's tiptoe

355

around the issue. Let's bring the whole friggin' mess out in the open and discuss it. Again. And again and again."

"Just glad to see you're finally getting the message," Pace taunted.

"I'll give you a message, you little asshole. If it was just me, I'd say to hell with it and I'd clean your clock. Say anything you want to me, I don't care. But it's not just me. Have you got any idea how your sister feels about all this?"

"Serena knows you're leaving?" Travis asked.

"No, damn it, and I don't want her to. Not yet. And just for the record, I'm not leaving because of the way the two of you treat me. I'm leaving because the way you treat me is killing Rena. Don't you know what it does to her to see the three of us at each other's throats every day? Jesus, you're thick-headed, the two of you."

From down the hall, Serena heard deep, angry voices booming through the closed study door. As she neared, the voices grew clear and sharp. Her stomach clenched. They were arguing again, Daddy, Matt, and Pace. Arguing about her.

"My leaving is the only thing now that will take that look out of her eyes," Matt claimed.

Leaving? Matt's leaving? Serena stifled a cry. *No! He can't leave.*

"What look is that?" Pace taunted from inside the study.

"The look she never had until the two of you started treating her like a brainless idiot who doesn't know her own mind, and me like a molester of little girls."

"So you're going to pack Joanna off and take her to New Orleans," Travis said. "Have you told Dani?"

Serena's lips quivered and her eyes stung. *New Orleans?*

356

"No," Matt answered Travis. "If she's not back by the time you get home from San Carlos, I'll ride down to Sanchez's and tell her. After that, I'm gone."

He sounded tired, Serena thought with an ache. Bone-tired.

"Maybe then Rena can have some peace," Matt added.

Nearly blinded by tears, Serena turned and stumbled back down the hall. Matt was leaving. He'd barely been home at all, and he was leaving. Because of her.

Oh God, why did I ever let him know how I felt?

Matt slammed out of the study, furious with himself, with his dad and Pace. It seemed no matter how good his intentions, he couldn't have a decent conversation with either of them, much less both of them at once. Damn them and their stubbornness.

He wandered out to the courtyard, hoping the fresh air would clear his head and calm him. Maybe then he would find the inspiration he needed to explain to Joanna why he was taking her away. Maybe he'd find the courage to tell Serena.

Inside her bedroom, Serena leaned against the door and pressed the heels of her hands to her temples. The whole world had gone crazy. She had, for certain. Matt, too, and Pace and Daddy. Everyone. Crazy. And it had to stop. She couldn't let Matt be driven from home.

Squaring her jaw and her shoulders, Serena pulled away from the door, opened it, and marched down the hall. By the time she got to the open door of the study where the men were, her footsteps, and her courage, were faltering. Yet she couldn't stop.

With a deep breath, she stepped into the room. It was

357

with both relief and disappointment that she realized Pace and their father were alone. Her father sat at the desk, staring blankly at the folded newspaper there, a troubled crease on his brow. Pace sprawled on the sofa, his face deliberately blank. His Apache look. Unreadable.

"Where's Matt?" she asked.

Pace's eyes narrowed. Travis flinched and looked away. Neither man answered.

"He's leaving. I . . . overheard."

"You shouldn't listen in at keyholes," Pace said harshly.

"That'll be enough," Travis told him.

Serena glared at both of them. "Daddy, I don't need you to defend me against Pace. When are you going to stop acting like I'm a brainless idiot—"

"You sure got that right," Pace taunted.

"Pace," Travis barked.

"Stop telling people how to talk to me," Serena cried. "Stop telling people how to act around me, how to treat me, Daddy. I'm a woman, not a helpless child. I can defend myself."

Travis's expression closed, but not before she saw the hurt flash through his eyes. "I'm sorry," he said shortly. Then he heaved a sigh. "No matter how old you get, you'll still be my child, Rena."

"What about Matt?" she asked him. "He's more your child than I am, yet you're treating him like some kind of monster. Are you going to let him leave just because you can't think of me as a grown woman who knows her own mind? You're driving him away from his home," she cried. "And for no good reason. Whatever there might have been between Matt and me ended weeks ago. If you weren't so busy blaming him for something he didn't do, and jumping to your own conclusions, you might have noticed for yourself."

Travis rubbed his face with both hands in a gesture of weariness. Then he let his hands drop to lie on the newspaper on his desk. "I don't know what to do anymore, Rena. No, I don't want Matt to leave. He's my firstborn son. But I can't sit still and watch him hurt you like this."

"*Him* hurt me?" she cried. "Matt has never hurt me. He wouldn't. I don't think he could. It's *you*. You and Pace, and the way you treat him. That's what hurts me. Even he told you that just a few minutes ago, and he was right."

Travis closed his eyes and shook his head. "I can't think what to do anymore."

"Talk to him, Daddy," she pleaded softly. "Don't let him leave."

She watched the painful struggle on his face as he wrestled with the opposing needs of protecting her and not driving Matt away.

Finally he took a deep breath and rose. "I'll . . . talk to him."

As he left the room, she breathed a prayer of thanks and a sigh of relief.

"You should have left well enough alone."

The coldness in Pace's voice shocked her. He'd never spoken to her like that. Not ever. She turned slowly toward him. "Pace?"

"Let him go, Rena. Get him out of your life and stop this craziness."

"Oh." She raised a brow. "So you admit perhaps I actually have something to do with this, that I'm not some innocent bystander being ravaged by some ravening beast?"

Pace rolled his eyes in disgust.

"Look at me," she asked quietly. When he complied, she said, "Why have you been acting this way?"

He straightened from his slouch and leaned toward her. "Because what's been going on between the two of you is wrong. Dead wrong. Brother and sister, for crying out loud!"

"Don't start with that. That's a convenient excuse for you to throw out, but you know as well as anyone it's not valid."

"It *is* valid, damn you. The two of you have been raised as brother and sister in this house. Among The People, that bond is sacred, blood or no blood."

"Is *that* what all your objections are about? You're worried what The People will say?"

"And you should be, too," he cried. "You're just as much Chidikáágu' as I am."

"And you're just as white as I am," she answered.

"No," he said, shaking his head slowly. "I don't think I am. I could never ignore such a serious taboo as you seem willing to."

Serena narrowed her gaze and advanced on him. "You use your Apache blood as a convenience, to do or not do whatever suits you."

"You know better than that."

Serena hung her head, feeling sick to her stomach. He was right. She did know better. Pace had always taken the ways of The People more to heart than she had.

She lifted her head and pleaded with her eyes. "I'm sorry. What I said was unfair. But Pace, no two people on earth have been closer than you and me. We shared the same womb, rode side by side in the same cradleboard—"

"*Ts'al,*" he cried. "It's not a cradleboard, it's a *ts'al*. Can you not even use the Apache word for it?"

He was hurting, Serena realized with dawning wonder. All this anger radiating from him was from pain. "What is it, Pace? What's wrong?"

His expression closed off instantly. "I don't know what you're talking about."

"Something's eating you alive, I can tell. God, I can feel it. But what? What, Pace? We've always known each other's heart and mind. Always."

"Until lately," he said with a snarl.

Serena jerked as if he'd slapped her. Dear God. Could he be jealous? Did he feel Matt coming between them and breaking their bond? Did he resent her for growing away from him?

His pain was deep and sharp. The sudden opening he gave her into himself left her gasping for breath. He felt her loss as though a part of himself were being hacked away.

The glimpse he'd given her closed as swiftly as it had opened, but not before she felt the resentment. She squeezed her eyes shut, because this time the pain was hers. He resented her because she hadn't felt lost from him, the way he felt lost from her. And he resented her for the loss of his brother, for he knew as well as she that his relationship with Matt would never be the same.

The sickness in her stomach rolled.

No more words were necessary between them. He knew what she'd seen and felt inside him. For that, too, he resented her. She swallowed and tried to clear her vision. "No matter what happens, *shilghúkéne,*" she said, honoring his feelings by using the Chiricahua word for "brother", "I love you. I will always love you."

With an ache the size of a fist in her chest, she fled the room, and the pain in his eyes. She stumbled down the hall and out into the courtyard, desperate for a breath of healing night air.

Dear God, how could she ever have been so selfish? How much more pain could she cause the people she loved? How many more ways could she hurt them?

Matt drank in the sight of her. The moon highlighted the white streak in her hair and made her yellow dress glow against the green bougainvillea leaves and their profusion of purple bracts beside her. The picture she made standing with her head bowed and shoulders slumped made him ache inside.

He must have made a sound, or maybe she merely sensed his presence, for she straightened and jerked her head toward him. He heard her sharp intake of breath.

He knew exactly how she felt. Aside from sitting across from each other at the table, they hadn't been this close since the day he'd asked her to marry him. The day she refused.

"I'm sorry," she said. "I didn't know anyone was here."

He stood and turned away toward the back gate, sure he couldn't stand to brush near her to enter the house. He couldn't get that close and not touch her. Not in the moonlight. Not with the fragrance of honeysuckle wafting from the trellis beside him. Not when she looked at him with pain in her eyes. "I'll go."

"No," she said softly, her voice shaking. "Don't go."

He paused. "I think I should."

"Matt."

The rustle of petticoats and the slight scrape of slippers on flagstone made the hair on the back of his neck stand up.

"I . . . I overheard you in the study."

Damn. Matt squeezed his eyes shut. How many more ways was he going to hurt her?

"You don't really want to go to New Orleans, do you?"

He slowly turned and faced her. "Dad was just here, trying to talk me out of it. It doesn't matter. I can't stay here and watch you tear yourself apart. I can't, Rena, I won't."

"Don't do it," she pleaded. "Don't leave because of me. Please, Matt."

He meant to keep the words locked in his heart, but . . . "Come with me."

Ah, damn. She looked on the verge of tears. If she cried, he wouldn't be able to stand it.

"Come with you and do what?" she asked with a quiver in her voice. "Give up our home? Hide from the family the rest of our lives?"

He fought the pain of futility and tried again to convince her. "Come with me and marry me."

Moonlight caught the lone tear slipping down her cheek. "You're asking me to choose between you and them?"

On top of his earlier conversation with his father and Pace, Serena's accusation was too much. He clenched his fists to keep from shaking her. "You already chose, didn't you? Sorry, for a minute there I forgot. You chose them."

"Matt, I—"

"You did, Rena. You chose them. Now you tell me I shouldn't leave? What do you want from me? I can't go back to being your big brother, damn it. And I can't face you every day and see that whipped-puppy look in your eyes. Either you love me or you don't. Marry me. We can go or stay, I don't care. But if you don't love me enough

363

to marry me, don't expect me to stay."

"Don't love you enough?" she cried. "How can you say that? You know I love you."

"I thought you did, but damn it, when a woman loves a man and he asks her to marry him, she usually says yes. This is it for me, Rena. If you don't want me, Joanna and I will leave as soon as Dad gets back from San Carlos next week. Either marry me or let me go. It's up to you. I can't take any more."

She reached out for him.

Matt stepped back quickly. If she touched him, he'd be lost. He would have her in his arms, his lips on hers so fast and fierce she wouldn't know what hit her.

Maybe that's what he should do anyway, beat down her resistance. Woo her. Seduce her. It's what he'd been accused of for weeks, wasn't it? Why not —

"No," he said. "Not unless you mean it."

"Don't do this, Matt."

Her whispered plea nearly drove him to his knees. But he couldn't back down. For his own sake and hers, he wouldn't. "You know where to find me if you change your mind."

Twenty-three

Serena tugged on the tie of her wrapper and paced the width of her bedroom for surely the hundredth time since dressing for bed. She barely noticed the difference between the soft rag rug next to her bed and the smooth oak flooring that stretched from the edge of the rug to the door as she padded back and forth barefoot. Preoccupied with Matt's plan to leave the ranch, she barely noticed anything.

Tomorrow her father would take the herd to San Carlos. He'd be back in a week. Then Matt and Joanna would leave.

It was so *unfair*. Matt shouldn't have to leave the ranch. He loved it there; it was his home, his birthright.

Serena stopped in the middle of the bare floor. She couldn't let him leave. If anyone had to go, it should be her.

At the thought of giving up her home and family — everything she held dear — pain stabbed deep and swift into her chest. But she would go if she had to. Why should Matt be the one to suffer for what was her fault?

Surely, surely there was another answer, some way to

make things right again. If she and Matt talked — really talked — surely they could figure out *something.*

She clenched her fists in determination. There was no time like the present. With everyone in bed for the night, she and Matt could talk without interruption.

And if he's in bed?

Heat flooded her at the thought. Then she scolded herself. She would ignore the heat and ask Matt to meet her in the salon.

She turned toward the door, then caught a glimpse of her reflection in the mirror. With a grimace, she changed directions and walked to the dresser. If she intended to sneak into Matt's room late at night to talk, there was no point in looking like a hag while she did it.

Her hands shook while she brushed the snarls from her hair. What would she say to him?

She paused and stared at herself as her mind went blank. She had no idea what to say to him, but surely she would think of something.

She took a final glance in the mirror. Refusing to look into her own eyes for fear of the uncertainty she would find, she pinched some color into her cheeks, then turned out the lamp and made her way to the door in darkness.

Amazing, she thought, how her hands could suddenly be so steady while her knees shook like jelly. What if Matt didn't want to talk? How would she make him listen?

I don't know, she admitted, terrified he would tell her to leave. *I don't know, but I have to try.*

She eased out of her room and across the hall to Matt's. The thin strip of light beneath his door told her he was still awake, but if she knocked, someone other than Matt was sure to hear.

God, her palms were sweaty. She swiped them down the sides of her wrapper. The trembling spread from her knees to her whole body. She took a deep breath and opened his door.

She must have make a sound, for when she closed the door behind her, he turned slowly from the boot jack next to the wardrobe at the foot of his bed. His boots stood beside the jack; socks dangled from the fingers of one hand.

But it was the four-inch strip of skin revealed by his unbuttoned shirt that made her gasp. Brilliant variations of yellow, green, and purple spread in splotches across his chest and stomach. The fading bruises exactly matched those around his eye.

Serena reached out a hand toward him. "What did they do to you?" she cried softly. She raced across the floor and pushed his shirt aside.

At her touch, he flinched.

"Did I hurt you?" Her gaze shot to his face.

His eyes revealed a pain so deep she nearly backed away. He ignored her question. "Why are you here?"

She didn't know what to say. She lightly stroked another bruise.

"Don't," he said harshly. "Please, Rena. Don't touch me unless you mean it."

Serena closed her eyes to hold back tears. With the feel of his warm skin beneath her fingers, she forgot she had come to talk. Just then, touching him seemed much, much more important. "I've never meant anything more in my life."

"Open your eyes and look at me."

Slowly, Serena complied.

"Are you sure?" he asked? "Really sure?"

She met his gaze head on and let him see everything

in her eyes. "I love you, Matt Colton. I love you more than anything."

Matt felt her words clear through to his soul. On a ragged breath, he hauled her into his arms and covered her gasp with his mouth, letting her taste his pain of the past weeks, the fierce hunger for her that had nearly starved him, the love he hadn't been allowed to give her.

She was here. He couldn't believe she was really here in his arms. "Rena, Rena," he whispered against her lips. "I love you, need you. God, how I've missed you."

She trembled against him.

He couldn't blame her. He was none too steady himself, and that stunned him.

"Love me, Matt, love me."

"I do, Rena, you know I do."

"Show me. Show me now."

Her whispered plea sent fire shooting through him and nearly cost him his control. He couldn't lose control. Not this time. She might think she knew what she was asking for, after what he'd shown her of loving in Mexico, but she was still innocent, still a virgin. He had to take care. He would cut out his eyes before he knowingly hurt her by his own impatience.

He kissed her again, this time savoring her taste slowly, carefully, before pulling back. When she bent her neck and pressed her lips to his shoulder, a quiver ripped through him.

Serena felt his reaction but was too distressed over the bruise beneath her lips, and the dozen or so other bruises that marked his flesh, to take much pleasure in making him shiver. "I can't believe they did this to you. I'm so sorry." She kissed her way from bruise to bruise across his wide chest.

"Don't be. It wasn't your fault."

Serena raised her head to argue, but he covered her lips with a callused index finger.

"No," he said softly. "It was my fault, Pace's, maybe Dad's. But not yours. I'd hoped by your coming in here like this, it meant you'd finally stopped blaming yourself."

She squeezed her eyes shut, and he wondered at the fierce pain in her expression.

"I'll never stop blaming myself," she whispered.

"Not tonight." He kissed her forehead, then her nose. "No blame tonight, Rena. Say it." He kissed her cheek, her lips. "Say it."

"No . . ."

He kissed her again. "Say it. No blame."

"No . . . blame."

"Now say, I love you."

She smiled against his lips. "That one's easy. I love you."

Her fingers threading through the hair on his chest made his muscles twitch with excitement.

"I love you," she said again.

Matt was too distracted by the realization that she was pushing his shirt over his shoulders and down his arms to be able to answer. He shook free of the shirt and tried to pull her back into his arms.

She resisted and stepped back.

Before he could wonder if she'd changed her mind, she tossed her wrapper to the floor beside his shirt. Then her slender fingers gripped her gown and pulled it over her head. It landed in a soft heap alongside the wrapper.

She stood before him, proud and more beautiful than a woman had a right to be. Her skin glowed pale copper in the lamplight. Her long black hair sleeked itself down her back nearly to her hips, with that streak of white teasing him to sink his fingers into it.

But he resisted, for the call of her firm, round breasts, narrow waist, and slender hips lured him just as strongly. So many temptations, enough to lose himself in for a lifetime. Temptations he had no desire nor strength nor will to resist. And she was deliberately, boldly offering them to him.

Then she said the words again, those words he could never get enough of. "I love you."

With a low growl, he swept her up in his arms and carried her to the bed. "And I love you," he told her, his gaze locked on hers. "I adore you. I want you. God, how I need you."

She wrapped her silky arms around his neck as her lips reached for his. "I'm right here, and I need you, too."

Arms trembling with the strain of holding back, Matt lowered her to the bed. As he straightened to stand over her, their lips clung until the last possible second. Frantic, afraid she might disappear if he took too long, he shucked his pants and lay down beside her.

The feather tick sagged with his weight, rolling Serena against him. Right where she longed to be; where she belonged.

Was she doing the right thing, giving herself to him while so much was left unsettled?

Even as the question tore at her heart, his hands and lips and tongue burned it from her mind. There was only Matt. His gentleness, the need that made his hands shake, stirring a hot quaking deep inside her.

This was right. Too right to question, to worry over. Now, here in his bed, he was hers. She would worry about tomorrow when it came. And it would come soon enough, she knew. Too soon.

"You look . . . sad. Tell me why, Rena," he coaxed.

She buried her face against his neck and shivered. "We've wasted so much time apart."

He cradled her, stroked the hair from her face with such tenderness she felt tears form.

It was all Matt could do to keep from crushing her in his arms hard enough to ensure they could never be apart again. "No more," he told her. "No more blame, no more waste."

Her skin felt like silk beneath his touch. With every kiss he trailed down her neck her breath came faster, and so did his. Whatever sadness she might feel, Matt vowed he would burn it to cinders with the fire she ignited in him.

Needs and wants, so many different kinds, tore at him until he nearly groaned aloud at their fierceness.

Slow, he reminded himself. He had to go slow. But it was hard. *He* was hard. Yet just knowing she would answer his breathless need gave him a miraculous sense of peace. Peace, in the middle of the raging storm brewing inside him.

He cupped her breast in his palm and met it with his lips. Her sharp intake of breath gratified him. He laved and nipped and suckled on the sweet, sweet taste as the bud pearled beneath his tongue.

The skin he crossed on his way to her other nipple was just as soft, just as sweet as the rest of her. He fed hungrily, starved for every taste of her.

If he had thought, he might have worried about her being shy this first time of loving. He would have been wrong. Her hands greedily clung to him. Her legs slid restlessly against his. He shook with the need to plunge

371

himself into her and ease the hot torment in his loins. He ached to take her hard and fast, yet yearned to give her tenderness.

His name came from her lips on a sigh that went straight to his heart. Somehow, the whispery sound of it eased his urgency and gave him the strength to slow his own driving need as he built hers.

But Serena didn't want him to go slow. She was on fire, and it was glorious. Never had she dreamed such intensity existed. As Matt's heated kisses trailed from her breasts down across her stomach, a throbbing emptiness opened inside her and begged to be filled. By him. By Matt.

His hand slid up her thigh to the center of the flames consuming her and did shattering things that made her quake with need. Then his mouth replaced his fingers. All on their own, her hips thrust to meet his searching, shocking tongue.

Suddenly her world tilted and went black. Streaks of white burst through her mind as the wave of release shook her.

Her climax tore through Matt's restraint, ripped away his control. He slid up her soft, supple body and positioned himself at her entrance, resisting, with his last ounce of strength, the urge to plunge inside with one wild, driving thrust.

Instead, he eased into her, and she welcomed him, still in the grip of her climax. God, but the very rightness of being inside her shook him. He had never felt so alive in his life.

It had been so long since he'd known the pleasure of a woman's body, the sweet surrender of a woman's love.

Yes, the feelings were familiar, but at the same time new. As if he'd never loved before. Serena's welcoming arms healed the hurts inside him had he thought were gone.

Breathless, the heat of urgency searing him, he moved inside her. Her answering gasp of pleasure stirred a primal rhythm in his blood. He surrendered to it and gave her everything he had.

He drove into her again and again, feeling her answering urgency, holding back now, waiting for her to come again. When she did, he let himself go. His release was shattering. All-consuming. A miracle.

With no words between them, Matt and Serena lay wrapped in each other's arms, letting their bodies cool, their hearts slow. Then they loved again, slower this time, yet deeper. It was even more shattering than before.

And then they did it again. And again.

Finally, Matt rested his head against Serena's breast and whispered, "I love you. We'll be married as soon as Dani gets home."

Serena lay perfectly still, too shocked to even breathe. *My God, what have I done?* Instead of talking to him, trying to find a way to solve their problems, she had let him believe she would marry him!

And now, incredibly, after those startling words, he was asleep, as if uttering them released his hold on consciousness.

She couldn't marry him! No matter what it cost her, no matter how desperately she longed to do just that, she couldn't give in and be the cause of his total alienation from the family.

My God, what have I done?

And the next question — *What do I do now?*

Yet even as a huge lump formed in her throat, she knew what she had to do.

Matt woke well before dawn. Alone. For one panicky moment he was afraid he'd dreamed his hours in Serena's arms. Then he buried his face in the pillow next to his and smelled wildflowers.

No. He hadn't dreamed her. She had been there. She had loved him and let him love her. He got hard just remembering.

With a lightness he hadn't felt in years, he kicked the sheet aside and splashed cold water from the nightstand pitcher onto his face. Not that he needed the bracer to wake him . . . thinking about last night sent his blood racing, his heart pounding. He needed the cold water a hell of a lot lower than his face. He couldn't leave his room in his present condition.

How many times had they made love last night before drifting off to sleep in each other's arms? Three? Four? He grinned into the towel. Who cared how many? This was only the beginning for them, the beginning of a lifetime of love.

He couldn't wait to see her. He laughed ruefully as he dressed. Sitting across the breakfast table from her without letting everything they'd shared last night show on his face was going to take some doing.

Then he frowned. What had wakened her so early? Why hadn't she roused him and told him she was leaving?

It didn't matter. He knew she had to return to her own room before anyone found out where she'd spent the night. Jesus, Matt's own father would string him up from the nearest tree if he had any idea . . .

Matt closed his eyes and took a deep breath. Whatever happened, it was worth it. Anything was worth last night. Anything. The urge to see her, despite the lack of privacy they would have, drove him to dress in a hurry.

Except for Rena, he was the last to arrive at breakfast.

"Good morning, Pumpkin." He kissed Joanna's nose and took his usual seat next to hers.

"Morning, Daddy. Where's Aunt Rena?"

Matt forced a casual shrug and poured himself a steaming cup of coffee. "Maybe she decided to sleep in."

"Serena?" Spence scoffed. "She gets up before the roosters."

Not when she's been awake all night, Matt thought with a secret grin. She was probably exhausted, especially after that last time, when she had pushed him to his back and straddled his hips.

Heat gathered in his loins. He forced his mind to search for something else to think about before he embarrassed himself. He finally settled on that ornery string of mustangs he had yet to break. He and the dun still hadn't come to an understanding. Today they would.

Today, Matt could do anything. Give him a battle, he would fight it. Give him a war, he would win. Hell, give him the world and he could conquer it with one hand. One devil of a range-wild mustang didn't stand a chance against him. Not today.

By the time Matt finished his ham and eggs, Rena still hadn't shown up, but Matt wasn't concerned. After last night, she would probably sleep 'til noon.

Pace apparently had other ideas. As he stood, his chair scraped across the floor. "I'm going to check on Serena," he said. "It's not like her to sleep this late."

Matt tried for nonchalance and settled for speed as he followed Pace down the hall. "Why don't you leave her alone? She's been working extra hard, with Dani gone this long."

"Why don't you go to hell?" Pace banged his fist on Serena's door.

Matt winced. Personally, he'd never appreciated being awakened by a fist on his door. He didn't imagine Rena would, either. But he knew he couldn't be standing in the hall when she answered the knock. Not if he expected to be able to keep from hauling her into his arms at the first sight of her sleep-flushed face, Pace be damned.

"Serena?" Pace called. "You all right?"

Matt rolled his eyes and turned toward his own room.

"Serena?"

Tired of waiting, Pace pushed open Serena's door.

Matt frowned. That crap was going to have to stop. Pace couldn't just walk in on his sister whenever the hell he felt like it. Good God, what if he'd decided to do that last night? Not finding her, would he have walked into Matt's room unannounced?

"Sonofa*bitch*."

At Pace's sharp cry, Matt stepped back into the hall. "What's wrong?"

"Damn her."

Matt crossed the hall to Serena's door. She wasn't there.

"The only goddamn reason I stayed home from the drive was to keep you away from her, and now this." With obvious disgust, Pace wadded up a piece of paper and threw it at the wall.

"What's your problem? She's probably gone to the kitchen or somewhere."

"She's *not* gone to the kitchen, you asshole, she's gone with Dad."

Matt blinked. A cold stillness settled in his stomach. "She's *what?*"

"You mean she didn't tell you, either?" Pace said with a smirk. "Well, that's something. Guess maybe she's not as crazy about you as you thought, huh?"

With the coldness in his gut starting to heat and churn, Matt picked up the crumpled note that had rolled to a stop beside Serena's dresser.

There had to be some mistake. She would not have simply taken off on the cattle drive. Not now. Not after last night, for God's sake.

A sudden memory of that sadness he'd seen in her eyes last night haunted him. But no, that couldn't have anything to do with this. This had to be some sort of mistake.

His hands shook as he smoothed out the note. As he read it, his skin tightened. She was gone on the cattle drive, and asked, no, *demanded* that no one come after her.

A sharp thud hit him in the breastbone from inside. The note crumpled in his fists.

Why? Why, damn it?

Twenty-four

Thick clouds of dust swirled high, tossed skyward by five hundred sets of hooves. Cattle bawled; cow ponies darted after escaping steers; drovers whistled, coaxed, waved, and cursed the herd down the trail.

Travis rode a half-mile in front of the herd. With a tug on the brim of his hat, he squinted against the glare of the sun and frowned. Up ahead, a rider waited beside the trail, pack mule in tow. What fool would sit there in the burning sun that way instead of making tracks for wherever he was headed? If it was rest he was after, there was shade not a hundred yards south.

Yet the rider sat in the sun. And waited.

The closer Travis drew, the more he was convinced this wasn't a stranger, but someone he knew.

Behind him, Travis knew the old moss-horned steer led the herd straight down the trail. Bonehead wasn't a very flattering name for an animal as valuable as the Triple C's best lead steer, but Jessie had named him when he was still a calf, and the name had stuck.

The point riders were a mere formality with Bonehead in the lead. The old longhorn would know the way to the San Carlos Agency blindfolded.

Travis kept his mount to a walk until he finally identified the rider up ahead. Recognition had him digging in his spurs in surprise.

"What the hell?" he said, drawing to a halt before Serena.

Serena took a deep breath for courage. "Hi, Daddy. Mind if I ride along with you?"

"You know I don't, but what's all this?" he said, with a nod to her laden pack mule.

She swallowed hard and forced herself to exhale the breath she had unconsciously held. *Here I go.* "I'm taking a little trip."

Travis braced both hands on his saddle horn. "What's going on? What's happened? Is it Matt? If he's done something to send you running—"

"Daddy, no!" Serena squeezed her eyes shut briefly. "Please, *please* stop blaming him. It's *me,* damn it—"

"Watch your language, little girl."

"I won't," Serena cried. "I told you before, I'm not a little girl anymore, Dad. You've got to understand that. That's what all this trouble between you and Matt, and Pace and Matt, is all about. You're thinking of me as a child, and him as, as I don't know what."

"Rena, honey . . ."

"It's *me.* I'm the one who started all this. Anything that has ever happened between Matt and me has been *my* idea. I've started it. *Me.* Do you hear? Me, not Matt."

Her father's lips stiffened. "Just what, exactly, is it you've started? What *has* happened between you and him?"

"Nothing too terrible, I assure you." She gave him a sad little smile and looked off down the trail toward the herd. "He asked me to marry him."

"He *what?*" Travis roared, rising up in his stirrups.

"Oh, don't worry. I told him no."

Travis dropped back to his saddle in shock. "You . . . you told him no? I thought . . . that is, Pace and your mother said you . . . you thought you were in love with him."

"I am," she managed around the sudden lump in her throat.

"Then why would you tell him no?"

"Because I can't live with tearing the family apart like this."

The pain in her face rocked him. Travis ached for her. Dani's words from a few weeks ago haunted him. *If she has to choose between you and Matt, love, it will break her heart.*

Dear God, he hadn't meant to make her choose. But then, he hadn't really believed Serena was in love with Matt. Hadn't wanted to admit she was old enough to understand her own heart.

Looking at her now, he could no longer deny what had been right in front of him for weeks. What she herself had been telling him. His baby girl, the daughter of his heart if not his loins, was a woman. A woman in love. A woman in pain.

A woman leaving home.

"So you're going away, just like that?"

"It's best for everyone, I think."

"What does Matt think?"

"I don't know. I didn't tell anyone. I just left a note on my bed, and one in your room for Mama."

Travis wanted to groan. Instead, he arched a brow. "You snuck out?"

She gave him a wry grin. "In the middle of the night."

"Like a coward?"

380

Serena stiffened. Her father could have no idea what strength and courage it took for her to leave home, to leave Matt — especially after last night.

She couldn't let him know about last night, God help her. He would drag her home by the hair. If he didn't shoot Matt on sight, he would at the very least force them to marry.

And he would never, ever forgive Matt. All Serena's efforts, the pain she had caused both herself and Matt, would have been for nothing. For the family would still tear itself apart, and Matt would hate her.

Like a coward? How could he think that?

Instead of arguing, she merely looked at him. "It was the only way."

She'd left him. Matt couldn't believe it.

Sure, she'd run out on him in Tombstone, but he'd driven her away. When she'd headed for Tucson — and got herself kidnapped — it was because Joanna had hurt her, and he had . . . hell, *he* had hurt her. She had needed time to herself.

But damn it, he hadn't pushed her away the night before the cattle drive. He hadn't driven her off, and he'd stake his life on the certainty that he hadn't scared her. *She* had come to *him,* for Christsake. Knowing exactly what he wanted, what would happen, making him think she meant to marry him. Telling him how much she loved him. Giving herself to him so sweetly.

Then she had crawled out of his bed while he slept and disappeared into the night.

God, it hurt.

His first instinct upon reading that damn note was to ride after her. But no. If she had meant any of the things she'd said to him the previous night, she wouldn't have left.

Trouble was, he'd been so sure she had meant it when she said she loved him. A part of him still believed it.

Fool. To hell with her.

Yeah. Sure.

He nursed his anger, fed it all week. Nothing helped. The string of mustangs he'd been breaking, wild and woolly though they were, hadn't been enough of a challenge to calm him. Nothing was. He wanted to break something, all right, but had forced himself not to take his frustrations out on the horses.

Driving the cattle to San Carlos would take four days. A day or two there, then two for the ride home. The way Matt figured, the crew should be home any day.

Question was, would Serena be with them?

Bayliss Matheson, registered agent for the San Carlos Agency of the White Mountain Apache Indian Reservation, watched Travis Colton and his half-breed daughter ride in to the agency from along the river, where they'd bedded down their herd the night before.

Look at that girl. Shameful, the way she wore a man's britches under her skirt and rode astride like that. But then, that was a half-breed for you. Damn redskins had no sense of what was right and wrong.

Matheson didn't have time for the girl or her meddling old man. He was grateful that fire-eating twin brother of hers wasn't around, though. All hell was about to break loose — all hell, and Geronimo, if something wasn't done. Pace Colton would only have compounded the problems.

And the agent knew, sure as spit, that if Geronimo broke out, the Army was gonna blame him, Bayliss Matheson. Just like they'd blamed him for that set-to up on Cibecue Creek last month. All he'd done was warn the fort of a possible uprising. Far as he was concerned, any time redskins got together and talked about killing white folks, that was uprising enough for him.

Could he help it if Carr and those damn misfit troopers of his had ridden down on an unarmed old man? And what difference did it make, would somebody please tell him, if one less Apache walked the earth? This one had been stirring up trouble. They were all better off without him.

Now more trouble was coming. Matheson could feel it. More troops coming in. Rumors about arresting Geronimo and some of the more outspoken Apaches.

Now, Bayliss didn't have what he'd call a real affection for the Apaches, but after the fiasco the last time Colonel Carr took his men right into their camp, he'd thought maybe the Army would back off a bit. Instead, more troops were lining up by the day. They were either going to have to make their damned arrests or ease back, give the Apaches a chance to calm down.

Otherwise, as he'd been thinking for days, all hell was going to break loose. And who would the Army blame? Matheson, of course. He spat at the lizard crawling along the base of the water trough and missed.

Both times he was up to his ass in trouble, and he had to stop and deal with thorn-in-the-side Colton.

Both times.

Matheson paused in the process of scratching his side whiskers.

It was true. Seemed like anytime there was serious trouble involving the Chiricahua, members of the Colton clan had been nearby. Could they be stirring the pot more than he knew? Would they come along now and help Geronimo escape?

Not if Bayliss Matheson had any say.

Daniella tucked the last of the older Sanchez children into bed and made her way to the front room. Alone, finally.

With the fire burning low, she plumped a throw pillow on the horsehair sofa, straightened the braided rug on the bare plank floor, then lowered herself to the rocker and heaved a sigh. After nearly three weeks, Rosa was ready to take care of things on her own. Daniella could leave for home tomorrow.

She worried about what had been happening while she was gone. Were Travis and Pace still hounding Matt? Was Serena still walking around looking like a wounded fawn?

If things hadn't improved by the time Daniella got home, she didn't know what she was going to do. It wasn't like Matt to take such treatment from anyone, even his father. What had happened to him those three years he'd been gone? Although he'd never been a troublemaker — on the contrary, Matt had grown to be one of the finest men Daniella had ever known — he'd never hesitated to stand up for himself before.

And Serena! Daniella wanted to grab her by the shoulders and shake her until her teeth rattled. What in heaven's name was wrong with that girl? Serena had *never* been the docile type. She thought her own thoughts and went her own way. Why the devil hadn't she told her father and Pace to drop dead?

Unless, of course, Serena was having second thoughts about her feelings for Matt.

That was why Daniella had spent so much time biting her own tongue those past weeks before leaving to help Rosa. If Matt and Serena weren't sure enough of their feelings to stand up for themselves and take what they wanted, family be damned, then Daniella did not want to interfere.

With another weary sigh, she dropped her head against the back of the rocker and stared blindly across the room. She was exhausted. How Rosa had managed before the baby came, Daniella could only guess. How she would manage now, with a baby to care for in addition to the other children, was beyond Daniella's imagination. She herself had always had plenty of household help, and a husband who loved and cared for her.

And where was Jesus Sanchez? Off looking for land in California, of all things.

Daniella wouldn't blame Rosa one bit if she met him at the door with a loaded shotgun when he finally decided to come home.

The lamp on the mantel seemed brighter than usual. Daniella knew she should get up and turn down the flame. The idea of moving even an inch, much less across the room, made her groan. What she should do was turn *out* the flame and go to bed.

In a minute. She would get up and turn in in a minute. She couldn't remember the last time she'd been so tired. But then, those six Sanchez children — seven, counting the baby — were more than a handful.

The flame in the lamp flickered, drawing her gaze.

Oh God, it was happening again. She tried to look away, but couldn't. Another vision. She hated them. They terrified her. Never had they shown her anything good or pleasant. Only trouble. Always trouble.

This time was no different. Her hands turned to ice as Travis's face formed before her eyes. *Oh, my God.*

* * *

To Serena, it was like child's play. In fact, she had learned it, this game of slipping undetected from shadow to shadow, as a child. Cochise and both his sons, Tahza and Naiche, had taught Pace and her at an early age how to move secretly, like a spirit in the night, how to become invisible on the open desert in broad daylight.

She hadn't needed the skills in years, and was a little rusty, but they hadn't deserted her. Then, too, she wasn't trying to sneak past Apaches, either. That made the game ridiculously easy.

Despite the seriousness of the situation, Serena grinned smugly, careful to keep her lips covering her teeth, her eyes downcast, so nothing white would show in the dark. She could have moved an entire army of blind four-year-olds past the lazy, inept guards Matheson had posted around the agency.

She slipped up beside the guardhouse and crouched in the shadows, waiting, her gaze lowered. Ten feet away stood the only guard at this end of the compound.

At the far end of the row of buildings a match flared, lighting Jorge's face and drawing the guard's attention. Carlos, purposely reeking of whiskey, staggered toward Jorge and the guard as planned.

Serena slid silently around the corner to the solid door with iron bars covering the window. She whispered, "Daddy?"

"What the devil are you doing here?" he answered, his voice just as low. "I thought I told you to get home."

"I couldn't just ride out and leave you in jail," she hissed. "I sent Benito home. Here. I brought you some things."

Furious over her father's arrest, Serena had watched the guardhouse all day and noted no one had brought him so much as a cup of water. She had not been allowed near him. Now she passed him two small pouches, one of food, the other of water.

"Thanks," he said. "As long as you're here, tell me what's happening. Any trouble?"

"Plenty. Sometime within the next half-hour, the San Carlos Agency is going to be shy a few hundred Apaches."

"Damn. So much for Matheson's theory about averting trouble by keeping me away. A few hundred? Geronimo?"

"And Naiche, Juh, Chato."

"Women and children?"

"Nearly half. What should I do, Dad? Do you want me to break you out of here?"

Travis gripped the bars between them. "No! Don't even think it. I want you to go home, right now. Don't wait for daylight — just go."

Serena pursed her lips. She had no intention of going home and leaving her father locked up like a common criminal. Matheson had no authority to jail a civilian. Neither did the Army. Serena would kick and scream and cause a ruckus like this territory had never seen. She'd have citizens and politicians, even the governor, in such an uproar they'd *have* to let her father go. Damn that Matheson. He would pay, the bastard.

But she didn't say any of this to her father. To him, she was still a little girl to be protected from trouble, not a woman capable of dealing with it. "What about the cattle?"

Travis swore under his breath.

Serena smiled. Did he think she'd be shocked if he said a dirty word loud enough for her to hear?

"The cattle stay. Take two or three men to see you home. Leave the others with the herd. I'll deal with it when I get out of this cell."

387

"Leave the herd? And let Matheson and the Army get their hands on it? You know good and well The People will never see so much as a mouthful of beef once that happens."

"They will," Travis insisted. "Especially now. Matheson knows this is illegal. I'll have him and the Army over a barrel. The People will have full bellies this winter, Rena, I promise."

Maybe, she thought. If anyone could do it, her father could. But that didn't help the ones who left tonight. They were The People, too. And Triple C cattle were meant for them as well as the ones who'd stayed on the reservation.

A plan, bold and probably foolhardy, formed in her mind.

"What are you thinking?" Travis demanded.

"Nothing," she said quickly. "I better go. Carlos and Jorge can't keep the guards distracted forever. You'll hear from me tomorrow. And Daddy? I love you."

"I love you, too, Princess. Get out of here. Go home."

"Tomorrow," she repeated.

If he chose to interpret her final word as agreement to his wishes rather than a repetition of her earlier promise to get word to him tomorrow, well, they could straighten it out later.

Matt knew trouble when he saw it. When Dani and Benito thundered in from opposite directions on lathered horses, spouting something about breakouts and Geronimo, Travis, jail, and Serena, Matt's stomach clenched.

Dani had obviously had another of her visions. Matt would be the last to scoff at what she saw in the flames.

He'd seen it happen too many times, and she was never wrong.

But Benito had ridden with the herd. While he confirmed what Dani's vision had told her, that Travis had been locked in the San Carlos guardhouse, what Benito told them about Serena made Matt's blood chill.

Twenty-five

Two months late, but eagerly welcomed by the sun-baked ground, the August rains came. To Serena they were both a blessing and a curse.

The curse was, she was damned uncomfortable draped head to toe in a poncho, and the rain cut down her visibility, at times to mere yards. Riding out ahead of the herd as she was, not being able to see very far ahead was dangerous.

On the other hand, the rain had brought the Army's pursuit of Geronimo to a standstill. It shouldn't have. It wasn't raining *that* hard. But the first patrol she spotted had made it less than halfway down Sulphur Springs Valley before stopping. Serena and her crew had passed them hours ago. There they had sat, huddled in their tents, waiting for the rain to stop.

Obviously they weren't in much of a hurry to catch up with Geronimo. By the time they stirred themselves, he would be across the border.

Serena was glad she hadn't told her father what she planned. He'd have forbidden her to halve their crew, cut out a couple hundred head of cattle, including old Bone-head, and follow Geronimo into Mexico.

Her father would have more than forbidden it. He would have convinced Matheson to lock her up, too.

When Matt found out — no. She wouldn't think of Matt. She couldn't.

The men behind her with the herd had volunteered to come with her. Not that they were particularly happy about it, but they were loyal in the extreme to the Triple C and the family.

Jorge had argued strenuously against her plan. Only by threatening to ride to Globe and hire men on her own was she able to get him and the others to agree.

They had hit the trail more than an hour before sunup, and another argument had immediately erupted when the men realized she planned to ride out ahead herself.

"It's not safe. Your father, not to mention your mother and brothers, will practice every known Apache torture on all of us if anything happens to you," Carlos claimed.

"Nothing will happen to me," Serena told them. "That's why I have to ride ahead. If we catch up with Geronimo, if he's got men guarding his back trail, any one of you would be killed on sight. They'll recognize me."

She had won that argument, too.

That afternoon, as they neared the cutoff to Tombstone, which lay ten miles west of the trail they followed, the drizzle turned into a torrent. Serena smiled grimly. Geronimo's trail, until then plainly visible, would be wiped out.

She rode back to the herd to help with the cattle. Booming thunder made them nervous. Not to mention the effect of the lightning dancing off nearby rocks.

"Keep them moving," she shouted to the men.

Personally, she wouldn't mind a bit if the herd stampeded, as long as they ran south.

391

The rain pounded all afternoon with no letup. One of the men riding drag caught up with her.

"My horse picked up a rock, so I had to drop back for a spell. Saw riders, more than thirty of 'em, coming out of Antelope Pass."

Serena frowned. Through Antelope Pass lay the trail to Tombstone. "Which way did they head?" She had to shout to be heard over the driving rain.

"Headed this way," he shouted back. "Front rider was Clum. Recognized Virgil Earp and his brothers, plus some men from the sheriff's office."

"You're sure?"

Hodges nodded. "I spend a lot of my time off in Tombstone. I'm sure."

Serena grimaced. She did not want to encounter a vigilante posse from Tombstone. "Keep the herd moving south. The faster the better."

Before full dark, Serena passed three more cavalry companies camped along the trail. She didn't stop to chat, and they were too busy trying to keep dry to notice a lone rider. What they thought when the herd passed them, she had no idea.

She and her men ate in the saddle, a miserable meal, since their food got soaked on its way to their mouths.

Just before it got too dark to see, Serena reluctantly rode back to the herd. Unless the rain quit and the moon came out, they couldn't go farther that night.

Exhausted as she was, as she knew the men and animals must be, she prayed for a strong wind to blow the storm on east.

Sometime around midnight her prayer was answered. Under an innocent canopy of stars and brilliant moonlight, they hit the trail again. Less than two hours after daybreak, they crossed into Mexico.

* * *

"You let her do *what?*" Matt roared.

"I didn't *let* her do anything," Travis bellowed back, his fists clenched. He stomped back and forth across the porch of the agency headquarters. "I didn't know what the hell she was doing until a half-hour ago, when that sorry s.o.b. let me out of jail."

"One small woman," Matt said, glaring at his father and the remainder of the Triple C crew. "One small woman, and the lot of you can't even get her to sit still long enough to blink."

"You're a fine one to talk," Travis answered. "You couldn't even get her to marry you."

Matt felt like he'd been punched in the gut.

Twin gasps, one of surprise, one of outrage, came from Dani and Pace.

"You couldn't even get her to stay home," Travis went on relentlessly, something odd about the anger in his voice. "She didn't just up and decide to go on a stinking cattle drive. She had half or more of her worldly goods strapped to the back of a pack mule."

Another punch to Matt's gut.

"Serena was leaving home?" Pace cried. "Running away?" He whirled on Matt. "What did you do to her, goddamn it?"

Matt kept his gaze glued on his father.

"It wasn't Matt," Travis said tiredly. "It was me. And you," he told Pace.

Matt shook his head. "No, it was her. She decided to leave, so she left. That's all there is to it. But to take a herd of cattle and chase after Geronimo into Mexico, that's got to take the cake."

"You're going after her, aren't you?" Travis demanded.

"Of course," Matt said instantly.

"And you're bringing her home," Dani added.

Matt sighed and closed his eyes briefly. The ache in the region of his heart stabbed sharper with each mention of Serena's name, each thought of her. Bring her home? "No."

"No?" Travis bellowed again. "You're not bringing her home? She seems to be under the impression you're in love with her. Is she that wrong? Have I been right the whole time?"

Matt clenched his jaw to keep the words in, but they came out anyway. "No, goddamn it, you *haven't* been right. I do love her, more than I thought I could ever love a woman again. I'd kill for her. Hell, I'd die for her. I would even," he said softly, with pain, "fight *you* for her. But I will not bring her back. She made her choice. If she changes her mind, she knows the way home."

"You just said you were going after her," Travis said.

"To make sure she's safe, that she has everything she needs. Not to drag her home like some runaway child. She knows if she comes home, I'll take Joanna and leave."

"Matt, no," Dani whispered.

"It's the only way, you know that. Serena and I can't be brother and sister again. I doubt we can even be friends, under the circumstances." He stared directly into his father's eyes. "I won't stay on the ranch and watch her tear herself apart trying to choose between you and me."

Travis gave him a sad smile. "Bring her home, Matt. Tell her . . . tell her I'm sorry. And I am, you know, for everything. You're a man, you can take care of yourself. I was just . . . trying to protect my little girl. Tell her . . . tell her I'll give the bride away."

A strong whisper could have blown Matt over.

Pace nearly strangled on a curse.

Before Matt could think to savor the sweet victory of having his father's permission to marry Serena, Dani gripped Matt's arm. "Don't you tell her any such thing."

God, another punch to his gut. He looked at Dani, bewildered.

"This is exactly why I've kept my mouth shut and my opinions to myself all this time," Dani told Matt. "I could have tried to get your father and Pace to see reason, or at least calm down and think, but I didn't. I kept waiting for you and Serena to make them back off."

"Dani . . ." Travis said.

"Oh, you tried," Dani told Matt, "I'll give you that. But Serena didn't. Not really. And if she's not prepared to fight for you, to stand up to her father and brother, then she's not the woman for you, Matt."

"Dani!" Travis cried in outrage.

She glared at her husband. "And if it takes your own daughter leaving home to make you open your eyes, then I don't think I've got much use for you, either."

"I thought I was protecting her," Travis cried. "She's our baby. Our firstborn daughter."

"Yes, she's our daughter. Which means you should have known all along Matt was the best thing that could ever happen to her. You keep talking about protecting her from getting hurt, but what about Matt? Do you think this hasn't hurt him? Are you that blind? He's your firstborn son, Travis. He's in love with her."

"Save your breath, Dani," Matt said. "None of it matters. You're right about her not fighting for me. Frankly, though, I think I'd take her any way I could get her. But I won't drag her home. I won't hurt her any more than she's already been hurt, and watching you and Dad argue over us would kill her. I won't put *myself* through the pain of watching her leave me again."

"Well," Pace said with disgust, "while you're all standing here deciding Serena's future, she's running around the Mexican desert, probably getting herself shot at, or worse."

"Is she all right?" Dani asked Pace. "Can you hear her? Do you feel anything?"

Pace flexed his jaw and shook his head while glaring at Matt. "She doesn't speak to me anymore — since *him*. I can't hear her, but I know she's out there. I'm going after her."

"Matt's going after her," Travis said emphatically.

"Let him come," Matt said. "It may take both of us. Knowing Rena, we may have to split up to find her."

"Pa-Gotzin-Kay," Dani said. "She'll be at Pa-Gotzin-Kay."

"That's right," Travis said.

"That's where we'd all expect her to be," Matt admitted. "It's what she would expect us to think. Which is why she won't be there."

But she *would* be at Pa-Gotzin-Kay. Matt felt it in every bone. Serena was just clever enough to make them all think she wouldn't go there because it was her most obvious destination. She would have them crawling all over the Sierra Madres looking for her while she sat snug as a bug in the ancient stronghold.

She would go to Pa-Gotzin-Kay. She had friends there. Nod-ah-Sti, Dee-O-Det, and others. And right now she needed a friend or two. For her sake, Matt hoped she realized that.

What he would do once he found her, Matt had no idea.

What he wanted was to make sure she was safe, make sure she knew she could come home if she wanted and he wouldn't bother her. Then he wanted to turn his back on her and ride away.

What he feared was that when he found her, he'd end up groveling at her feet and begging her to come home with him.

His pride told him not to even tell her his father would cause no more problems. Dani had struck a cord when she'd said Serena should want to fight for him. But pride would be cold comfort for the ache in his chest. The thought of spending the rest of his life without Serena left him feeling hollow inside.

Regardless, he had to find her first.

No. That was second. First, he had to ditch Pace.

Then, when he found Serena, he had to remind himself not to strangle her on first sight. What a damn fool stunt, taking off for Mexico with Geronimo on the loose, half the Army chasing after him, and vigilante groups from all over joining in the hunt. The mere thought of any one of more than a dozen things that could happen to her sent ice through his veins.

He and Pace were less than two days behind her, but when it came to Serena's safety, two days seemed like a lifetime.

The trail she'd left with the herd through the lush grass of Sulphur Springs Valley was clear and wide. She had pushed the men and animals harder than any trail boss would have dared. He and Pace were almost to Mexico, and there'd been no sign of the herd bedding down for the night. Serena had driven them straight through.

There were other tracks, too. Serena had driven the herd past at least three different army patrols. Then there were those tracks from Tombstone. Between thirty and forty riders had come out of Antelope Pass and picked up the trail. Serena had managed, so far, to stay ahead of them.

"I hear Chee is riding with Geronimo," Pace said as he and Matt rode side-by-side under a sun that wouldn't admit summer had faded to autumn.

"Looks that way," Matt said.

"Since he lost Maria, he should find a new wife."

"Probably."

"He'd make Serena a good husband."

Matt clenched his fists around the reins. Rena and Chee? Could she fall for Chee? She'd known him all her life. He was one of the best men Matt had ever met. Honest, strong, smart.

And he's on the run.

"Is that what you want for your sister? Life on an Apache war trail, with armies from two countries chasing her?"

"Maybe Chee'll want to go back to the reservation."

"Oh, yeah, that's a hell of a lot better. You'd have Rena living in that disease-ridden place, going hungry all the time, watching her children die before they had a chance to grow?"

Pace gigged his horse and rode on ahead.

Matt let him go. But he wouldn't, he decided then and there, let Serena go.

It wasn't the hardships a life with Chee or any other Apache would bring her that made up his mind. No, he wasn't that selfless. It was the ball of sickness in his stomach that churned at the thought of Serena in another man's arms. Serena as another man's wife. Serena bearing another man's children.

No.

Serena was *his*. He didn't care who he had to fight to get

her back. Even if he had to fight *her*. He would not let her go.

A half-day below the border, Matt and Pace located a small group of warriors who'd broken off the reservation with Geronimo. Yes, they had seen Serena and her cattle. She had replaced her men with Apaches who'd volunteered to help her distribute the beef among the different hideouts. She had, the warriors stated, sent the Triple C riders back north by a different route, to keep them from running into the bluecoats. If the brothers wished to find her, they should go to Cos-codee.

Matt chafed at the delay. He knew she would be long gone by now, but Pace seemed to think otherwise. If Matt made too much of looking elsewhere for her, Pace would surely follow. And Matt did not want Pace anywhere near when he found Serena.

So against his will, Matt rode with Pace for Cos-codee. As they wound their way across the ancient lava bed and through stands of cactus, they saw no sign that another human existed within a thousand miles. Silently, Pace cut between the guardian boulders at the entrance to the canyon. Matt followed, and still all was quiet, until they reached the canyon floor.

There, men shouted, children shrieked and laughed, horses whinnied, and cattle bawled.

"Hear those cattle?" Pace asked. "I told you Serena was here."

"So you did," Matt answered. And so she had been. But that didn't mean she was still there.

When they reached the encampment, Matt had a bit of luck. It was about time something went his way.

Chee was there. Chee, and more than a hundred

Apaches from San Carlos, along with a small herd of cattle Serena had left for them. As Matt had known, Serena had been and gone.

Pace was itching to follow her trail, but this time Matt objected. With Chee to help him, Matt secretly orchestrated a celebration and made sure Pace was included. By sundown Pace was as drunk as any of the other men in camp, except Matt and Chee.

After making arrangements with Chee that Pace would not sober up for several days, Matt waited until Pace and a few others passed out, then he mounted up.

The quickest way to Pa-Gotzin-Kay was the Cos-codee pass along the cedar ledge at the south end of the canyon. But Matt didn't want anyone telling Pace he'd gone that route. Pace would catch up eventually, but Matt preferred to delay that as long as possible.

When he left the canyon, he didn't bother following Serena's trail. She'd have had to zigzag all across northeastern Sonora to deliver cattle to the various strongholds. A second trail stretched before him, longer than by way of the pass, shorter than Rena's trail, but leading directly for Pa-Gotzin-Kay. Here, outside the canyon, there were no eyes to see which way he went, and his tracks would be lost among dozens of others.

He took the trail that led for Pa-Gotzin-Kay. And his last chance with Serena.

On the rocky ledge of ancient lava overlooking the entrance to Cos-codee, a man crouched in hiding. Sweat rolled into his one good eye and made him blink. Frustrated, with madness nipping at the outer edges of his sanity, Caleb Miller Scott wiped the sweat off his brow with the back of a scarred hand.

He knew he didn't have much time left. Every day his spells of lucidness grew shorter and shorter. Each time the darkness took over his mind, he had no idea what happened. He only knew that hours, maybe days later, he would suddenly find himself miles from where he'd been, having no idea how he'd gotten there, how long it had taken him, or even where he was.

But for now, he was sane. Too sane, even in his hatred, to try to kill Colton with so damn many Apaches nearby. Not only would he not get to Colton before the Apaches got him, but *when* they got him, they'd do to him what Colton did to Abe. His blood turned cold at the thought.

Then, of course, there was the small matter of no weapon.

Well, he had a weapon, but he'd pumped the last slug from the little derringer smack between the eyes of that damn cat.

He shivered in the killing heat just remembering the way that she-devil had looked at his leg and licked her chops.

After clawing his way out of that cave, he hadn't really expected to last the day, much less run across Colton again. Not out here in the Mexican desert. And he was still in Mexico, he knew that much. He couldn't remember when or why, but he'd been to this spot before.

In frustrated rage, he ground his teeth and watched his quarry ride off. Then he smiled grimly. Matt Colton was riding off alone.

What the hell difference does that make? he wondered. Caleb was on foot. He'd never be able to keep up.

A loud snuffling startled him. The sound came from somewhere below in the rocks. He waited, breath held. Had he somehow given his position away? Had one of the Apaches snuck from the hideout to trap him?

Terror gripped him. Would he end up staked out in the sun, like Abe?

No, by God, he wouldn't.

The noise grew closer.

Caleb chanced a peek over the boulder before him, prepared to end it right there. If someone was going to kill him, Caleb would make damn sure it was quick. No slow Apache torture for him, by God.

A loud scraping sound, then a huge snort.

Caleb flinched and ducked behind the rock.

More shuffling. A low growl.

What the hell? He peeked again, then wilted with relief. It was only a damn bear. Dangerous enough, but Caleb didn't intend to provoke the huge, walking rug.

He watched, curious, as the bear climbed down from the rocks. It took its time sniffing the ground, then, as if knowing exactly what it was doing, it followed Matt Colton's trail like a hound on a fox.

Caleb's heart thudded. First he grinned, one-sided though it was because of his scars. Then it came, a deep chuckle at first, turning into full-blown laughter. He raised his face to the scorching sun and let the laughter fill him.

The sound of it echoed along the ridge. It carried with it the chill of madness.

Twenty-six

A week and a half after setting out for Mexico, Serena left Bonehead and the remainder of the herd at the foot of the narrow winding trail to Pa-Gotzin-Kay with the Apaches who had been helping her. She would let those in the stronghold decide how to get cattle with five-to-seven-foot horns up a trail that in places narrowed to barely three feet. On one side rose a wall of sheer rock. The other boasted a dropoff of sometimes a thousand feet.

Simply riding up the trail made her heart lodge in her throat. The pack mule was all the additional trouble she needed. If she had to worry about Bonehead trying to fit his long horns around those hairpin turns, knowing one single misstep would send him plunging to his death, she might never have made it up the trail.

But she did make it up. Pa-Gotzin-Kay was the Apaches' ancient Mountain of Paradise stronghold. Here the earth was red and fertile. An abundance of water, trees, and rich grass supported plenty of deer, bighorn sheep, turkeys, and rabbits, as well as the wilder side of life, bears, cougars, even skunks.

The air sang of solitude and should have soothed Serena's troubled soul. That was why she had come here.

For the peace, the privacy. The people here were a quiet people. She had always felt secure at Pa-Gotzin-Kay. She hoped she would this time, too.

There was only one camp, near the center of the *rancheria*. Everyone lived there. As Serena neared, children came out to greet her, then adults. She wound her way through the twenty or so wickiups until she reached the center of camp.

Standing just outside the ring of sacred stones surrounding his wickiup, a wrinkled old man closed his eyes, listened to the wind, and smiled. Then his snapping black eyes opened wide, as did his welcoming arms. *"Shke',"* he cried. *"Bizááyén."* Child. Little One.

Serena slipped from her saddle and ran to embrace him. "Dee-O-Det, my friend, my friend." A lump rose in her throat. It had been so long since she had seen him, had benefitted from his timeless wisdom, his sharp wit. "I have missed you."

"And I you, Child of Magic."

His strong arms held her tight, belying his more than eighty years. After a moment, he pushed her back and looked her over from head to toe. "I guess you are not really a child any longer, are you?"

She smiled. "Sometimes I still feel like one."

His grin widened. "Only sometimes?"

Then his gaze sharpened. He looked off toward the trail that had brought her to camp and tilted his gray head. "Where is Bear Killer?"

Serena flinched. Why would he ask about Matt? What did he know? No one could have told him anything of her troubles, but then, no one needed to. Dee-O-Det had always learned his secrets from the wind. That was his Power.

But Serena was not prepared to talk about Matt. She

managed what she hoped was a nonchalant shrug. "Home, I guess, or at San Carlos, getting my father out of jail."

If she had hoped to distract the old shaman, she had underestimated him, and that was never wise. She should have remembered. Besides, Geronimo and others had already been to Pa-Gotzin-Kay and left. They probably told him all they knew of what had happened.

Regardless, Dee-O-Det refused the provocative bait. Instead, he asked again about Matt. "Why is he not with you? He is your mate, is he not?"

Heat flooded her face. "No," she cried. No matter how she had reminded herself of Dee-O-Det's Power, it still came as a shock to realize he knew so much.

"Of course he is," the old man said firmly. "The wind has told me so. The wind does not lie."

She searched his face for the disapproval Pace had warned her of, but all she saw was acceptance and affection. Thank God.

But if Dee-O-Det knew about her and Matt . . . "Did the wind not tell you of my father and brother?"

"The Yellow Hair and Fire Seeker? What have they to do with you and Bear Killer?"

"It's a long story, my friend, and I have ridden far."

"Then you will probably be tired by the time you have told me everything," he said calmly.

With a few sharp hand gestures, Dee-O-Det had her horse and mule cared for, her belongings stored in one of the extra wickiups the *ranchería* sported for its frequent visitors. A word to one of the men made certain her cattle would be brought up the mountain tomorrow, with someone to stay below with Bonehead.

Serena only managed a brief hug of greeting with her dear friend Nod-ah-Sti before Dee-O-Det tugged her through the low doorway into his wickiup.

Once they settled on blankets around the blackened remains of a small fire in the center, the old man waved his
arm in a graceful arc encompassing several leather
pouches and clay jugs. "You may eat, you may drink, you
may recline and rest to your heart's desire. But you will
talk."

When Dee-O-Det took that tone, Serena knew she
would do as he commanded. If not, he would badger and
pester her until she gave in. With a weary sigh, she told
him all—well, nearly all—that had happened to her since
she went to Matt in Tombstone.

Long before she finished her tale, the air chilled with
evening coolness. Dee-O-Det built a small fire and urged
her to continue. By the time she finished, it was late and
the camp was quiet.

A gnarled but gentle hand wiped at the tears on her
cheeks. "Why do you cry?" Dee-O-Det asked. "Is it because you are sorry Bear Killer is not worth fighting for?"

Serena's head snapped up.

The shaman merely arched a brow.

"You would have me fight my own family?"

"You would rather fight your own destiny? Cut out
your own heart and condemn Bear Killer to a life of loneliness?"

"Dee-O-Det, you don't understand."

"I understand, my child. I wonder if you do. Go to bed
now. Sleep. Tomorrow, perhaps the wind will speak to
you."

The hay beneath her blanket gave her a softer bed than
she'd had since leaving home, but still Serena could not
sleep. Dee-O-Det's words haunted her. How dare he think

Matt wasn't worth fighting for. Of course he was worth it. He was worth anything. Everything.

So why did you leave him?

Serena rolled to her other side and tried to block out her own thoughts.

Her father's words on the cattle drive rang in her ears. *You snuck out . . . like a coward?*

And Matt. *I love you. I adore you. God, how I need you.*

Serena stifled a cry and covered her face with both hands.

She hadn't *wanted* to leave Matt. Didn't anyone understand? Didn't they realize leaving him was the hardest thing she had ever done in her life? The pain had nearly killed her, and hadn't lessened in the days since she'd left. Dee-O-Det had been right about one thing: she did feel as though she had cut out her own heart.

It was so unfair! Why couldn't her father and Pace see how much she and Matt loved each other, how right they were together?

Maybe, that damned voice in her head shouted, *because you never really tried to make them see.*

Stunned, Serena sat up. Was it true? Had she not tried?

She thought back to the day the family had arrived at the canyon in Mexico, to when all the trouble had started.

"Oh, my God."

It came to her, sharp and clear. When she had meant to explain her feelings for Matt, defend his feelings for her, what had she done? She had popped off with that stupid, outrageous statement about how she had stripped off her clothes and tried to tempt him.

She couldn't even give herself credit for trying to ease the situation. She'd thought she'd tried, more than once, to make Pace and her father see reason. Hindsight told her otherwise. Her puny efforts had been ineffectual at best. Until she'd met her dad on the cattle trail, she had never even told him how she felt about Matt. All those weeks, and she'd kept quiet.

She laughed sadly. "Oh, Matt, I've really messed things up, haven't I?"

If she went home, would he be able to forgive her? Twice he'd asked her to marry him. Twice she'd refused. She had hurt him. Badly. Then, that last night, he had assumed . . .

But going home and agreeing to marry him, if he would even still have her, would not solve the problems with her father and Pace.

"*. . . Bear Killer is not worth fighting for?*"

Serena's pulse quickened.

Could she? Could she fight for him? Could she possibly win? She would not only have to fight the rest of the family, but now, because of the way she had left him, she would probably have to fight Matt, too.

Could she do it?

A gust of wind whispered down through the smokehole above her. *You are a woman. You are Apache. A Child of Magic. Were you not born to fight?*

Serena jerked her head up. Dee-O-Det?

She tossed off her blanket, scrambled to the door, and pushed aside the rawhide flap. The camp was dark and deserted. Not even a shadow moved.

Slowly, she lowered the flap into place and returned to her bed.

Were you not born to fight?

She smiled in the darkness and felt the pressure in her chest ease. Stranger things had happened than hearing an old man's voice on the night wind.

Her heart started thudding sure and strong in her chest.

Matt, not worth fighting for?

"The hell you say, my friend." If Matt Colton wasn't worth fighting for, then Serena might as well just curl up right where she was and wait to die.

He *was* worth it. She *would* fight, by damn. No longer would she let her father and Pace call the shots. Tomorrow, as soon as the cattle were brought up, Serena would leave for home . . . and Matt.

A quiver of anticipation raced alongside two equally strong ones of fear and regret.

"Oh, Matt, can you ever forgive me for being so foolish? For being such a coward?"

Rena, Rena, I love you.

She prayed to God he still did.

Serena had hoped to be able to leave Pa-Gotzin-Kay by midday, but bringing the cattle up the treacherous trail proved slow work. By the time the herd was up and the trail was passable, it was late afternoon.

"Stay tonight," Nod-ah-Sti urged. "Let us thank you properly for the cattle. We will celebrate. You can leave at first light."

Because it would be rude to refuse, Serena agreed to stay one more night. She told herself her staying had nothing to do with trepidation over facing Matt and her family again. Nothing at all.

"Besides," Dee-O-Det told her, "the wind is speaking. There is no need to leave tonight."

Serena pursed her lips. "Are you going to tell me what that means?"

The shaman grinned. "No."

At dusk, he said the words again. "The wind is speaking."

409

"Dee-O-Det —"

"Look."

She looked where he pointed. Her heart jumped to her throat and stuck there. *Matt!*

Matt saw her instantly; his pulse leaped. With gloved fists, he gripped his reins so tight his horse halted.

God, she was beautiful. He drank in the sight of her like a man dying of thirst. What was that look in her eyes? Caution? Fear? He forced his hands to relax and nudged his horse forward.

Maybe not fear, but definitely caution.

He didn't know what to do.

What he wanted to do was sweep her up in his arms and carry her off. He wanted to kiss her until they were both breathless, wanted to bury himself so deep inside her he'd never find his way out, wanted to love her until she couldn't possibly live without him.

But a man got gun-shy after being shot down three times. Maybe he should stick to his original plan. He had agreed to come and make sure she was safe. She looked safe enough to him. She looked tired, though. The trip had been hard on her. Yet despite the dark circles below her eyes, she still took his breath away.

He wanted to grab her and hold her and kiss her senseless.

He wanted to run from the pain she was capable of inflicting.

But a man could do neither. Not now, not here. Running away would be the supreme act of rudeness to The People. Grabbing her and kissing her would be scandalous. Among the Apaches, single men and women simply did not do such things. Not even married ones. Not in public.

In the end, he dismounted and stood before her, unable

410

to do anything but look his fill and try his damnedest not to show his pain, his indecision.

But Serena read both on his face. "Hello, Matt."

After a long silence, he took off his hat and whacked it against his thigh. "I promised Dad I'd make sure you were safe."

Serena quailed. Was that the only reason he had come? Because he'd promised Dad? "Is he . . . did he get out?"

"Just before Pace and Dani and I got there. He finally scared Matheson so much about bringing the governor down on him for arresting a civilian, Matheson let him go."

"I'm glad." It was hard, so hard, to pretend casualness with Dee-O-Det, Nod-ah-Sti, and others looking on, listening to every word, even though no one understood the English she and Matt were speaking.

Dee-O-Det relieved the silence. In Apache, he said to Matt, "I expected you yesterday."

"Why?"

Dee-O-Det rolled his eyes to the sky that was by now turning dark. "Stubborn. Both of you."

Matt eyed Serena, then Dee-O-Det. "Would you care to explain?"

"No," the old man said bluntly. "Niño," he called to Nod-ah-Sti's son. "Take care of Bear Killer's horse."

Serena clenched her fists at her sides. This was it. She couldn't afford to pass up such a perfect opportunity, no matter how hard her insides quaked. As she reached for the reins, her hands shook. "Never mind, Niño, I'll take care of it."

Nod-ah-Sti gave her a look of stunned amazement. Dee-O-Det merely nodded as though he had expected such an action from Serena.

Matt's eyes widened in shock, then narrowed with

411

suspicion. "What are you up to, Serena?"

Serena took a deep breath. What she was doing was bold beyond convention. When an Apache maiden cared for a warrior's horse, she signified she was accepting his proposal of marriage. Her next step would be to carry the man's belongings into her wickiup. He would follow her, and they would spend the night, which meant, in the eyes of the tribe, they were married.

The only tiny little problem here was, Matt had not proposed. Not since the last time, when she had told him no.

He had not given the horse to her father, who would have tied it to the wickiup to await his daughter's decision.

Serena didn't care, just then, about convention. This was her chance, and she was going to take it. If her knees didn't collapse. She studied the sky a moment. Stars were popping out one by one.

With a deep breath, she looked back at Matt and answered his question with one of her own. "What does it look like I'm up to?"

Matt's face went carefully, deliberately blank. Light from the huge central campfire a few yards away danced along the planes of his face. "I didn't come here for this," he said in English.

"I know. You came to see if I was safe. I'm not safe, Matt. I'm not happy. And up until this minute, I haven't even been very smart. I'm trying to change that."

Matt felt every muscle in his body stiffen to ward off another emotional blow. He knew what her actions with the horse represented. But then, he had thought he'd known what her coming to his room that night had meant. The pain of that particular misconception had nearly killed him. Did he dare trust her that she really meant to change things this time?

412

"How?" he demanded harshly. "By teasing me again? By deliberately making me think you mean it this time?"

He saw the effect of his words in the way her face paled.

"I was wrong, Matt," she whispered.

The trembling in her lips made his eyes sting.

"I was a fool. I thought . . . I thought I was doing what was best for you, for both of us."

"So what's changed?" Matt demanded.

A lot had changed, he admitted to himself. His father had offered to give the bride away if Serena would come home. But Serena didn't know that.

His heart started pounding. She didn't know! She didn't know his father would no longer object. Yet still she offered . . . offered what? To marry him? Not knowing things at home would be all right?

He remembered Dani saying Serena should fight for him. Would she? Could he expect her to fight her own father and brother?

Yes, damn it, he did expect it. He wanted it, craved it. He needed to know he was the most important person in her life, the way she was in his. If that was selfish and petty . . .

What do you mean, "if"?

Still, he needed to know. "What's changed?" he asked again.

"I have." Serena straightened her shoulders and, her insides shaking, met his look of challenge. "I have changed, Matt. I've realized what's important to me and what's not. Yes, I love my father and brother. But I love you, too. If you still feel the same, I swear to you I won't let them come between us. Not ever again."

"Do you realize what you're doing here?" he asked with a tug on the reins that she, too, held.

Her heart thundered. "Yes."

He merely stood there, his eyes impossible to read, a muscle twitching along his jaw.

Serena's knees shook. "I know you haven't asked me again, but this is my answer. I love you. If you'll have me, I would be proud . . ." She had to stop and swallow past the lump in her throat. "I would be proud to be your wife. I'll spend the rest of my life trying to make up for hurting you the way I have."

Unable to speak past the sudden mixture of love, fear, and euphoria in his chest, Matt closed his eyes. God, he wanted her, loved her. *Needed* her.

But could he trust her?

He felt her tug on the reins. He opened his eyes and met her gaze, a gaze that nearly took his breath away, so full of love was it. A shudder ripped through him.

She tugged on the reins again, and they slipped from his fingers.

Numb with the dreamlike quality of what was happening, Matt watched her lead his horse to a wickiup. She wrapped the ends of the reins around a supporting pole, then proceeded to strip the horse of its gear.

A bony hand gave him a sturdy slap on the shoulder that nearly sent him staggering. Dee-O-Det cackled. "A husband should smile on his wedding night."

Matt took a deep breath and voiced his fear. "If I'm still a husband this time tomorrow, *then* I'll smile."

The old man turned and left, trailing laughter in his wake.

Matt didn't watch him go. He couldn't take his eyes off Serena. She carried his gear into the wickiup, then came out and started grooming his horse. The Apache maiden's acceptance of a man's marriage proposal.

He swallowed. Hard.

After rubbing down the horse, she pulled the reins

from their anchor and led the gelding off into the darkness, in the direction of the stream.

Matt didn't realize he'd taken two steps to follow until he felt the tug on his shirtsleeve.

"You mustn't," Nod-ah-Sti told him with a smile. "Have patience, Bear Killer, she will be back soon."

Would she? Or would she simply jump onto his horse's back and ride out?

Dee-O-Det returned and stood by his side. Matt held his breath and kept his gaze glued to the spot where his hopes had disappeared into the night.

An eternity later, Serena reappeared with one arm cradling a bundle of hay, the other tugging the horse behind her.

Matt felt some of the tension melt from his muscles. But only some.

"Núuká," Dee-O-Det said. Come.

With a feeling of unreality, Matt followed the old man across the compound to where Serena had retied his horse. She turned toward them and stood waiting, eyes downcast, as was proper for a modest Chiricahua maiden.

Matt fought the sudden grin that threatened. No maiden she, he thought. And damn near the most *im*-modest female who could still rightfully call herself a lady. It was one of the things he loved most about her.

The thought of love sobered him. Yes, he loved her. She said she loved him, too. She'd been saying it for weeks and weeks. The hell of it was, he knew she meant it. But would she stick with him this time, or end up ripping his soul to shreds?

Twenty-seven

Matt stood before her, searching her face for an answer, finding only those downcast eyes. With her face fully lit by the big fire, he noticed again the dark circles beneath them.

"What is happening here," Dee-O-Det said from beside Matt, "is right and proper for you to do. In the eyes of The People, you will now become man and wife."

Matt waited for the realization of her actions to sink in, to show on her face. Yet still, her gaze remained lowered. He wanted to see her eyes, damn it. He had to look into them and know, *know* she really meant it this time.

"But for your mother," Dee-O-Det continued wryly, "so she will not skin me alive and tack my hide to her door, you must have the words, you must have the scars. You white people do love your ceremonies. *Núuká.*"

Side-by-side, but without looking at each other, without speaking, without touching, Matt and Serena followed Dee-O-Det past the central campfire to the huge log beside his wickiup. The dozen or so people around the fire, nearly a third of the entire population of the *ranchería,* quieted and stared.

416

Matt barely noticed. He stopped beside Serena, before the shaman's ceremonial log, and waited. Waited for Serena to change her mind. Waited for her to call a halt.

Behind them, someone started a rhythm on a drum.

Matt chanced a glance at Serena. Nothing but calm showed on her face. Those damned eyes still looked toward the ground.

Dee-O-Det cleared his throat and drew Matt's gaze, but not his attention. Matt was suddenly remembering the last time he had stood before this shaman's ceremonial log. Serena had been there that time, too. But not at his side. That spot had been held by Angela. Eyes Like Summer Leaves, The People had called her.

Would she understand Matt's feelings for Serena? He searched his heart for that warm spot Angela still occupied, the spot that had been a yawning black hole of torture until Serena had taught him acceptance. For a moment, he panicked — he couldn't find her.

But should he even be searching for the comfort of his first wife when he was about to take a second?

Then he felt it: Warmth . . . comfort . . . approval.

Matt's senses sharpened as the feelings enveloped him. Yet they didn't surround only him, he realized. The love — Angela's love — encircled them all. Matt, Serena, and Dee-O-Det. With a certainty that astounded him, Matt knew beyond a doubt that Angela, wherever she was, wholeheartedly approved of his union with Serena.

He wondered if Serena knew, if she felt it, too. Or was she remembering the way she had stood at Angela's side some ten years ago and translated the wedding ceremony for his bride? Did she remember that Pace had stood at his right hand that night?

417

In comparison, tonight's events must seem bleak to a young woman embarking on marriage. Angela had been clothed in fringed beaded doeskin as soft as butter, Matt in his finest buckskin. More than a hundred people had gathered to celebrate their union. A huge feast had followed.

Tonight, however, Matt stood in dusty denims, his boots scuffed, shirt sweat-stained. Serena wore a plain skirt and blouse showing signs of wear. Most of the people in the compound were already rolled up in their blankets for the night.

Did Rena feel the difference? Did it hurt her?

Damn, but he wanted to see into her eyes.

A sharp sting on the inside of his wrist jerked Matt's attention. He looked down and realized he'd nearly daydreamed his way through the ceremony. The drumbeat had stopped. Sprinkles of sacred pollen dusted his sleeve. Dee-O-Det had already made the matching cuts in Matt's and Serena's wrists.

Serena stared at the small trickle of blood oozing from the shallow cut on her wrist, then the matching one on Matt's. She couldn't help but remember the last time she had seen this ceremony performed. Couldn't help but notice the faint remains of Matt's first wedding scar.

Was he thinking of Angela, as she was? How could he not? Her presence was everywhere around them. But oddly — or, knowing Angela, not so odd after all — her presence comforted rather than saddened. Serena prayed Matt felt that comfort, too. She prayed he felt the rightness of what they were doing. She prayed . . . God, how she prayed he wouldn't regret loving her.

Dee-O-Det pressed Matt's bleeding wrist over hers, forcing their blood to mingle, and bound them together with a strip of cloth. "You have two bodies," he said, "but now only one blood. You are one."

The words sent Serena's pulse racing.

With a flourish, Dee-O-Det flipped the binding from their wrists. *"Nzhú!"* he cried. "It is good!"

Matt ducked and followed Serena into the wickiup. The rawhide flap dropped into place behind him and sealed out the cheering well-wishers. A small fire in the center of the dirt floor sent an orange glow across his gear that lay next to Serena's along the far side. To the right, their blankets, his and hers, covered a thick pile of hay.

And Serena stood with her back to him.

Matt felt the tension in his shoulders tighten, felt the blood pound in his loins. He clenched his fists at his sides. What were they doing, standing there like two strangers, silent, wary, not touching. Why wouldn't she look at him?

"Rena?"

Slowly she turned, but her gaze remained lowered.

"Damn it, look at me," he cried.

Serena flinched at the rawness in his voice and lost the struggle to keep her breathing slow and even. As she raised her gaze to his, her chest heaved.

"I have one question," he said.

Serena nodded.

"Do you mean to stay with me this time?"

She heard the uncertainty, the vulnerability in his voice and nearly cried out. *Oh, Matt, what have I done to you?* Instead, she met his gaze and leveled her chin. "Yes. I mean to stay. I don't blame you for not trusting me, but I'll prove I mean it every day for the rest of my life." She stepped toward him and placed her hand on his arm. "I swear it, Matt."

Matt jerked at her touch, unprepared for the sudden warmth of her trembling fingers through his shirt. But there was one more question he had to ask. "What changed your mind?"

She dropped her hand from his arm and gave him a sad smile. "I'd like to say I simply got smart, but it wouldn't be true. It took a little jabbing from our old friend out there," she said, with a nod toward camp.

She was talking about Dee-O-Det, Matt knew. Defeat tasted sour on his tongue. She hadn't decided on her own that they belonged together. The old man had probably stirred his ashes, listened to the wind, whatever he did to predict the future. Serena had needed a guarantee that things would work out for them.

He didn't know why that should bother him. She had apparently received whatever assurance she had needed. He should be satisfied with that.

"He said something that made me realize what a fool I'd been," Serena said.

Matt didn't know why he was holding back. It didn't matter why she had changed her mind. She was here, they were married, and he loved her more than a man had a right to love a woman. Loved her more than was wise. "What did he say?" he asked.

"He was surprised you hadn't come with me, told me essentially I was an idiot. Of course, I already knew that. When I explained about the situation at home with Daddy and Pace, he said . . . he said it was a shame you weren't worth fighting for."

Matt felt his heart leap behind his breastbone.

"He was wrong, Matt. I was wrong. You *are* worth fighting for, and so am I. That was something else I realized last night. I've been too busy trying to take care of everyone else's needs."

"Whose needs?" he asked, almost afraid to breathe.

"Everyone's," she said. "Dad needed me to be his little girl, so I tried. Pace needed his sister. You . . ."

"What was it you thought I needed?"

"You needed home, family. Peace."

I needed you, he thought. But he said, "What about your needs?"

She took a deep breath. "That's what I asked myself last night. I thought I needed to make everyone else happy. I was wrong. If you can't forgive me, if you don't . . . trust me, I'll understand. But I won't stop loving you."

"What do you need?" he asked again. *Say it, Rena, say it.*

"I need you. Just you. Always."

Relief, sweet and sharp, rushed through him. "God, Rena." He held out his arms, and she was there, wrapping herself around him, trembling against him, whispering his name.

He knew he was nearly crushing her, but he couldn't help it. He needed to feel her pressed against him so hard, so close, nothing could ever come between them again. Fiercely, hungrily, he took her mouth with his, praying she would understand the need that shook him.

Serena did understand his need, for it was the same as hers, to hold him tight, drink in the taste of him, feel his hardness against her.

With their hands and mouths and bodies, they healed all the old hurts and built fires of longing that would not be denied. Heat raged, urgency rose.

The shudder that shook Matt broke their lips apart. He buried his face in the crook of her neck. "I love you," he whispered harshly. "I love you."

Frantic hands, his and hers, tore at clothing until flesh met flesh. Serena nearly cried out with sheer pleasure. The world spun, and it took her a moment to realize Matt had picked her up and carried her to the blankets. He half covered her with his body, and she felt the hardness of his need press against her thigh. She pressed back.

Matt groaned. "Easy, easy," he whispered. "I want you so much I'm ready to explode."

His words made her already pounding heart pound harder. "Then don't wait." She gripped his arousal and shifted until he lay between her legs, where she guided him home.

Her touch destroyed his control. Matt sank into her welcoming warmth. She was so hot, so wet, so ready for him. He knew he must be dying. Dying from pleasure, dying from love. He didn't care.

Fire and rhythm took over. He thrust hard and fast, and she met him each time, taking all of him, giving all of herself, until the world exploded in sparks of light, red and gold and brilliant white.

This time when Matt woke after a long night of loving to realize dawn had come, he wasn't alone. Rena slept half draped across his chest, one leg thrown over his. He closed his eyes again. *Thank you, God.*

She was here. She hadn't left him. And deep in his heart and gut, he knew now she never would. She was his, and he was hers, as surely as the sun rose and set.

The slender fingers splayed across his chest flexed.

Matt's breath caught.

The knee against his groin shifted.

He hardened.

She opened sleepy eyes and regarded him with seriousness.

He ran his hand up and down the silken skin of her back. "What is it?"

She lowered her gaze briefly. "Am I . . . forgiven?"

"Ah, damn, Rena." He wrapped both arms around her and held her tight. Didn't she know by now? "There's nothing to forgive, sweetheart. I love you."

"Does that mean . . . you trust me again?"

He didn't even have to think about it. "With my life." With a forefinger to her chin, he made her look at him. "With my life."

They shared a long, slow kiss that tasted sweet and new, and grew hot and desperate so fast Matt felt his head spin.

Rena broke away and smiled at him, a purely feminine smile that sent his pulse pounding low and hard. Her fingers roamed lower and lower down his chest, past his navel. He grinned. No one expected newlyweds to get up early anyway.

It was three days before Matt and Serena could bring themselves to turn loose of each other long enough to dress, say their goodbyes, and start for home, with Bonehead trailing along like a devoted puppy.

Their last night in Mexico they camped near a running creek below a manzanita-covered ridge just south of Nogales. While Matt set up camp, Serena followed the game path through the greasewood and mesquite to the creek swollen fat with the August rains that hadn't come until October.

The day had been warm, but the night would be cool. Serena wanted to get a quick bath before the chill settled.

She knelt beside the water and grinned. Who was she kidding? No night with Matt would ever be cool. One look from those gold-flecked brown eyes and her blood heated. She trembled with the knowledge that she could do the same to him.

From the direction of camp, she heard a deep grumble. Startled, she froze. A few yards downstream, Bonehead jerked his face from the water and splashed awkwardly across the creek.

Serena laughed. Matt and his damn bears. Bonehead wouldn't go far. He was almost used to bears by now . . . almost. This was the third one they'd encountered since leaving Pa-Gotzin-Kay. Serena shook her head and laughed again, picturing Matt shooing the bear from camp.

Hurrying now, eager to get back to her husband— *her husband*—she splashed water on her face, then stripped to her underwear and washed as best she could in the muddy water.

Halfway back to camp, she smelled the tangy smoke from Matt's fire. He was burning mesquite roots. She was so hungry she could almost taste the flavor the pungent smoke would add to the rabbit Matt had killed an hour ago.

She followed the path around a final stand of greasewood. "I swear," she said, "I can already taste—"

Her words ended in a strangled gasp. Her world reeled. Her heart clenched.

"Well, well, if it ain't little sister."

"Caleb!"

He stood profiled against the red glow of sunset, his silhouette sharp and black and menacing. Serena felt her heart climb up to her throat. *He's supposed to be*

424

dead.

Yet dead he wasn't. He stood with legs braced. One arm hung loosely at his side. The other stretched out to Matt. In that hand, Caleb Scott held Serena's derringer pressed directly between Matt's eyes.

A violent, icy shudder tore through her. *Think. Think,* she ordered herself.

The gun in his hand held only two shots. He had fired one in the shack when he and Matt had fought. Unless he had found more ammunition somewhere in the vast desert, Caleb had only one bullet left.

Why the *hell* had she left her Colt and Winchester in camp?

Stupid. And a potentially deadly mistake on her part.

"Come on over here, little sister," Caleb called. "Come watch me kill your brother."

Shaking like she'd never shaken before, Serena stepped cautiously closer. Her goal was her holster Matt had tossed onto the blankets laid out next to the fire. She had to pass it to get near Caleb. Would he notice?

"I wouldn't try for the gun, sis. I can't possibly miss him at this range, now, can I?"

"You can't possibly expect me not to kill you if you pull that trigger," she warned him. And she meant it.

"Won't matter much to me if you do," he said casually. "I came here to kill Matt Colton. That's all that matters now."

"You're willing to die to do it?"

Caleb shrugged. "If that's what it takes."

"Get out of here, Rena," Matt said harshly.

"Ah, hell, Colton, I want her to watch."

This couldn't be happening. It had to be a nightmare.

425

She would wake and Matt would hold her and it would all disappear. Yet the coppery taste of terror in her mouth told her she was wrong. This was real. Too real.

Stalling for time, desperate to keep from diving for her Colt too soon, Serena took another cautious step in that direction. "How did you find us? For that matter, how did you live through that fire?"

Caleb's laughter sent a chill down her spine.

"Finding you was easy, once I thought about it. Colton's friends led me straight here."

Serena sidled a few inches closer to the bedroll. "His friends?"

Caleb shook his head at Matt in mock chagrin. "You and your bears. All I had to do was follow their tracks. You wouldn't want to tell me how they always know where to find you, would you? Before I kill you, I mean."

Serena saw Matt's jaw bunch. She prayed he would stand still and silent until she could help. If he made a move on his own, he'd be dead. "What about the fire in the shack?" she said to forestall anything Matt might say. "How did you survive?"

For the first time, Caleb turned his head toward her. "Who says I survived?"

Serena couldn't hold back her gasp of horror.

"Pretty sight, huh, sis?"

Her stomach lurched. Nearly half his face was . . . gone. The raw red scar that replaced it started at the top of his head, where the hair used to grow. It covered the whole side of his face and head, melting his features — eye, cheek, ear, everything — into a blob not recognizable as human flesh. The hideous scar disappeared beneath the neck of his shirt. Remembering the way the flames had engulfed him, Serena knew it must also

426

cover his chest, back, and arm. "My God," she whispered.

"Yeah. My God," he echoed. "So you see, you kill me and you'll just be doing me a favor. But first I'm going to do what I came to this goddamn territory to do."

Matt waited, every nerve screaming at him to move. Each muscle strained to hold him still. If he moved, he was dead. No two ways about it.

Damn it, why the hell hadn't Rena run when he told her to?

And why the *hell* hadn't he checked that damn crevice where the cat tracks had led him? That one oversight looked like it was going to cost him his life.

Bitterness burned the back of his throat. His mouth went dry while sweat soaked his back. Was this it, then? Was he to die here at the hands of this madman? And Caleb was mad. It was plain in his one remaining eye.

Matt wasn't ready to die. Not now. Not when he'd only begun to live again.

His only consolation was that this time, the woman he loved would not pay for loving him with her life. He knew Serena. The instant Caleb pulled the trigger, she would grab for her Colt and kill the bastard.

Matt didn't want her to have to live with that. Didn't want her to blame herself for the rest of her life for not being able to save him.

And he didn't, by God, want to die. So he waited, and watched for an opening. When it came, he nearly missed it.

"No," Serena said thoughtfully. "I don't think I'll kill you after all."

Caleb shifted, but kept the damn derringer pressed between Matt's eyes.

"I think I'll just wing you," she said seriously. "My

427

Uncle Naiche—he's Cochise's son, did I tell you that? He's only a day's ride behind us, with Geronimo. If you kill Matt, he'll want to get his hands on you. Then there's Matt's best friend, Chee. He's with Naiche and Geronimo. You did know that over three hundred Apaches broke out of the reservation, didn't you?"

Matt couldn't miss the sheer terror in Caleb's eye. The man shifted his grip on the derringer and jerked his horrified gaze to Serena.

When he did, Matt flung an arm up and knocked the two-shot pistol aside.

Caleb cried out in shock. He stumbled for an instant, then swung the gun back toward Matt's head.

Serena dove for her pistol.

Matt reached for his at his hip.

Together, they fired, their two shots sounding as one.

The impact of two .45 slugs knocked Caleb back three feet before he fell to the dirt. One lone tear trailed from his startled eye. He gave a grunt of pain, then smiled. And died.

Before Matt could holster his gun and hold out his arms, Serena flung herself at his chest. He couldn't tell which of them shook the hardest. It had been close. Too damn close.

Or so he thought, until later, after he'd buried Caleb and retrieved the derringer.

Both chambers in the little pistol were empty.

Caleb Scott hadn't come to kill; he had come to die.

Matt would have to think about it awhile before deciding whether or not to tell Rena. Right now, all he wanted to do was hold her. So he did. Hard and tight, all night long.

Twenty-eight

As the sun dropped behind the mountains the next day, Matt and Serena bypassed Tucson. "If you don't mind riding after dark, we could be home in another couple of hours," he said.

Serena gave him a look from the corner of her eye. "Home?"

"Yep."

"With real food?"

His lips twitched. "Yep."

"With a real bed?"

He grinned. "Yep."

"And all those people?"

He frowned and looked at her. "You're not worried about that, are you? About what kind of reception we'll get?"

Serena shook her head. "No," she replied honestly. Whatever came, she could handle it. She gave him a slow smile. "Not worried. Just selfish."

The smile she expected didn't come. There was something in his eyes . . .

They made camp two hours shy of home. Bonehead,

however, had other plans. With a snort, a bawl, and a shake of his long horns, he trotted off over the rise in search of his fellow bovines.

Matt and Serena ate the last of the jerky they had each carried from home, along with the last of Nod-ah-Sti's ashcakes. There would be enough coffee, but nothing else, left for breakfast. As close as they were to home, it didn't matter.

All evening Matt tried to search Rena's eyes. Was she worried about his dad's and Pace's reaction to the news of their marriage? How could she not be worried? Matt hadn't told her about Travis's change of heart.

He should have, he knew. But it was so sweet to know she was willing to fight for him.

Asshole.

He'd left her to worry over their arrival home so he could feed his own damned ego.

He waited until they were curled up beneath their blankets and he had both his arms wrapped tight around her before he said anything. When he told her the truth, she was liable to get mad and stomp off. This way he could at least hold on to her.

"Rena?"

She slid on top of him and settled her hips between his legs. His blood rushed to meet her. With hooded eyes and a teasing smile at the hardening she couldn't help but notice, she lowered her stomach, her chest, her breasts, one heart-stopping inch at a time. Her hot gaze devoured him, snared him, thrilled him, burned him.

What . . . there was something he'd meant to say. She was destroying his concentration. Her hands did incredible things beneath his shirt.

God, he was glad they hadn't gone home yet.

Home. Family. Oh, yeah. "Rena?"

She unbuttoned his shirt and pressed her warm lips to the center of his chest. "Hush. I'm busy."

So was he. Busy falling apart. But he had to tell her. "You're—" Ah, what her mouth was doing to his skin. "You're not worried about facing Dad and Pace, are you?"

She trailed a path to one nipple and flicked her tongue. Matt gasped.

"No." She blew on his nipple. Her teeth tugged, her tongue laved.

Matt squeezed his eyes shut and sucked in his breath. "God, what are you doing?"

"I told you. I'm busy." She kissed her way to the other side of his chest and started over again.

"Busy killing me," he said with a moan.

"No. Busy loving you."

"Rena, I need to tell you—" His words ended in a sharp gasp when her hips rocked against his. "Damn, Rena, this is important."

Her hand snaked down and gripped him. "Yes. This is important."

Sweat beaded his face. "I don't think I can take much more of this."

"I can," she whispered. "I can take it all."

Fire shot through his loins and left him gasping for breath. Whatever he'd been trying to tell her couldn't possibly matter. Nothing mattered but the way she freed him from the confines of his pants, the way she hitched up her skirt and straddled his hips. "Then take it," he managed on a ragged breath. "Take it all."

But still she teased him with her clever, clever fingers. "I will," she promised.

He was about to explode. "When?"

431

"Just as soon," she said leaning up to nip at his jaw, "as you stop talking."

He didn't utter another word. Not a coherent one, anyway. Not until she lowered herself on his aching flesh and took him straight into oblivion. Even then, all he could manage was her name. He whispered it over and over, until at last, he exploded deep inside her and her name ripped itself from his throat and flew into the night.

It was just past dawn and the barn was deserted when Matt lifted Serena down from her saddle. They shared a slow, soft kiss, then walked hand-in-hand for the house.

Matt had had ample opportunity to tell Rena his father would no longer cause them trouble, but on the ride to the ranch he had decided to hold his tongue. Suppose Dad had changed his mind? He'd been so worried about Serena, he might have said anything to get Matt to bring her home.

Please God, for Rena's sake, let Dad have meant it.

They went in through the courtyard.

"Nervous?" he asked.

Rena smiled up at him. "About Dad and Pace? No. By the way, I would have thought Pace would have come with you to Pa-Gotzin-Kay. Where is he?"

Matt shifted his weight and studied the toes of his boots. "I, uh, don't think you want to know."

She laughed. "Maybe you're right."

The smell of coffee and hot biscuits lured them to the dining room, where Joanna, Jessie, and Spence were the only ones present.

With a glad cry, Joanna slipped from her chair and threw herself at Matt. "Daddy! Daddy! You came home." Egg yolk dripped onto the tiled floor from the fork clutched in her small fist.

Matt hugged her tight. "I came home, Pumpkin. We both came home."

"Aunt Rena!" Joanna reached for her, and Matt relinquished his hold as Rena knelt to hug her.

Matt knew he had the perfect opportunity, one he couldn't afford to let pass. "I guess she's not really your aunt anymore, Pumpkin."

Joanna's big green eyes widened. She stared at Rena, then at her father. "Did you do it? Did you marry her? Is she my new mama now?"

A look of uncertainty crossed Rena's face. "I'm your stepmother, Jo."

Matt placed his hand on Rena's shoulder. He knew what she was thinking. He could read it in her eyes. She feared he'd be hurt if Angela's daughter called her Mama. "It's all right, Rena. Jo was so young, she can't possibly remember much about her mother. She can call you whatever you're comfortable with."

Still holding Joanna's hand, Rena rose. "I won't let her forget Angela, Matt. It wouldn't be fair, not to Jo, not to Angela. But I swear I'll be the best mother I know how."

He couldn't help himself. He pulled her into his arms and kissed her, long and slow.

Three voices sounded in the room. Two young and female, tittering. One adolescent male, groaning in mock disgust.

Then a fourth voice. Male, adult, and roaring with rage.

Matt raised his head in time to see Pace fly across the room at him.

"Get your stinking hands off her!"

433

Before Matt could blink, Pace grabbed him by the arm and jerked him from Rena's embrace.

"Pace," Rena cried.

Pace swung.

Matt ducked, but not in time. The blow to his chin sent him staggering backward. To keep from landing on Joanna and crushing her, Matt ended up on his tail on the floor.

A childish shriek pierced the stunned silence.

With her fork still clutched tight in her fist, Joanna attacked Pace's back. "Don't you hit my daddy, Uncle Pace! Don't you hit him, you hear?" Her fork stabbed him in the rear.

Pace howled.

Joanna screamed and jumped away, leaving the fork stuck in Pace's left hind cheek.

"What the devil is going on in here?" Travis bellowed, Dani rushing in beside him.

"She stuck me," Pace cried in shock. "The little brat stabbed me with her fork!"

Matt lunged to his feet.

Serena held a sobbing Joanna in her arms and glared at Pace.

Matt strained to keep from reaching for Pace's throat. "Don't you ever, *ever* call her that again."

"He hit my daddy, Rena," Joanna cried. "Uncle Pace hit my daddy and knocked him down!"

"I know, sweetheart, I know. Here, dry your eyes. Would you feel better if I hit Uncle Pace for you and knocked *him* down?"

"Serena," Dani warned, "don't make things worse."

Serena stood, feeling the fire in her veins. "Oh, I'll make things worse, all right," she said between clenched teeth, her gaze locked on Pace as he yanked the fork from

434

his hip. "I'll beat him until he's black and blue if he ever so much as raises his voice to my stepdaughter or my husband again. I'm damn sick and tired of him trying to—"

"Your *what?*" Pace roared.

"You're married?" Travis asked.

"Yes, Dad," Serena told him firmly. "Matt and I are married." She turned to Pace. "Didn't you go to Pa-Got-zin-Kay?"

"Of course I did, but I was too late, wasn't I, thanks to *him,*" he said with a glare at Matt, "and his friends and his goddamn whiskey. By the time I got there, the two of you were already gone."

Friends? Whiskey? Serena blinked. She would have to ask Matt. Later. Of Pace, she asked, "Didn't Dee-O-Det tell you?" She showed him the healing cut on her wrist.

"No, that sorry son of a—"

"Pace, I've heard just about enough of your name-calling for one day," Daniella said sharply.

"Matt and I are married, Pace." Serena reached for her twin brother, begging him to understand. "Can't you be happy for us?"

With a snarl, Pace shoved her hand aside. "Happy? Happy that my brother has married my sister?"

The look of rage in his eyes took Serena's breath away. Then she saw the pain, the betrayal he felt. "Pace—"

He turned on Matt and flung Joanna's fork against the wall. "You'll pay for this, *shik'is.*" He spat the Chiricahua word for brother out as if it left a bad taste in his mouth. "One day I'll make you pay for what you've done."

Matt met him glare for glare until Pace, with another roar of rage, fled from the room, blood staining the hip of his pants.

An instant later the front door slammed hard enough to rattle the windows in the sturdy adobe house.

Serena rushed to Matt's side. "Are you all right? Did he hurt you?"

Selfish as it was, Matt reveled in her attention. She had done it. She had stood toe-to-toe with Pace and fought for her husband, for their right to love each other. He pulled her into his arms and laid his cheek against her hair. "I'm fine. I love you."

"Oh, no," Spence said with a groan, "They're gonna kiss again."

Serena stiffened. But instead of harsh words from her father, she heard his laughter. "They are, huh?" he said.

Serena pulled herself from Matt's arms and turned to face her father. "Daddy?"

Travis looked to Matt, curious. "You didn't tell her?"

Matt smirked. "To come home and find out you hadn't meant it? Not on your life."

"Tell me what?" Serena asked.

Travis opened his arms wide. "Tell you I'm sorry. For everything. Come here, Princess, and tell your old man you forgive him."

With a glad cry Serena fell into her father's embrace. "Oh, Daddy, thank you, thank you. I love him so much."

"I know you do, Princess."

Serena pulled the sheet and blanket up to her chest and let out a contented sigh. "Ah, a real bed."

Matt shucked his pants and tossed them to the floor beside the rest of his clothes. "Don't get too comfortable in there alone, woman."

"Never." She threw back the covers and held her arms up. "Not without you."

Matt let her pull him down against her soft warmth, savoring the feel of her arms, her love surrounding him.

"Do you mind about the big wedding Mama's got her heart set on?" she asked.

He let his gaze roam over her face, soft and golden in the dim lamplight. "I would stand beside you before the whole world," he said. "I'll be proud to marry you again."

He tasted the sweetness of her lips. "I'm sorry about Pace," he told her softly.

She gave him a sad smile. "Me, too."

"He'll come around soon, you'll see."

"I know." She kissed his chin. "What's the real reason you didn't tell me Dad had changed his mind about us?"

Matt stiffened, then let out a sigh. "They say confession's good for the soul. I did try to tell you, last night on the trail. You, uh . . ."

"Distracted you?"

"Boy, did you ever."

"Are you going to answer my question?"

Matt sighed and leaned over her so he could look into her eyes. "Pure selfishness. I wanted to know — *needed* to know — you loved me enough to fight for me, to stand up to Dad and Pace, to stop hiding what we felt for each other."

"Oh, Matt." She pulled him down and kissed him. "I'm sorry it took me so long. I wasted so much time. Time we could have spent together."

"Like this?" he asked with a kiss to her neck.

She arched for him, giving him better access. "Yes," she whispered. "Like this."

He nibbled on her neck and sent hot tingles shooting to her toes. His hand rested boldly on her bare stomach. Right over her womb.

"Matt?"

He kissed and nipped his way toward her breast. "Hush. I'm busy."

437

She grinned. She'd never known having her own words turned back on her could be so thrilling. "Busy doing what?"

"If you can't tell," he said between nibbles, "then I'm in big trouble."

Just as he reached for her nipple, Serena grasped his face in her hands. Once he kissed her there she wouldn't be able to talk, or think. "There's something . . . something we've never talked about."

He turned his face to kiss her palm. The hot stroke of his tongue made her shiver.

"Is it important?" he asked, gold flecks heating his dark eyes.

"I was just wondering . . ." He was kissing his way down the inside of her arm. She lost her train of thought.

"I was just kissing," he said.

Yes. "So I noticed." He was just kissing. Just stealing her breath. Just driving her crazy with wanting him.

What had she been . . . oh, yes. "I just wondered how you and Joanna would feel about —" His lips left her arm and landed on her stomach.

He moved over her and nudged her thighs apart. After settling himself there, he resumed the trail of fire down her belly.

"About?" he asked.

She could hear the smile in his voice. "You're teasing me."

"I'm trying. But you keep interrupting me."

"I was wondering how you and Joanna would feel about . . . a baby brother or sister."

Matt's heart gave a giant thud. Slowly, he raised his head and searched her eyes. "Are you —"

"It's too soon to know."

He swallowed. "But you could be." He placed his hand

gently on her stomach, not the least surprised to find himself trembling. *A baby.* The thought of watching Serena grow big and heavy with his child took his breath away. "You could be carrying my child right now."

"How would you feel about that?"

He met her gaze. "Proud. Humbled. Honored."

Her eyes glistened with gathering tears. Her lips trembled on a tender smile that stopped his heart and brought a lump to his throat. "I love you," he told her, the words coming from deep in his soul.

"And I love you."

Need rose up in him. The need to feel her trembling lips against his. The need to drink her up, swallow her whole. To give her his life.

They shared a long, searching kiss that soon grew heated and fierce. But Matt wanted to slow down. They were married now, man and wife. Instead of hard, bare ground, they had a soft bed beneath them. He wanted to take his time, to drive her crazy the way she had him the night before. He wanted to feel her writhe beneath him.

He tore his mouth from hers and buried his face between her breasts.

His sudden silence left Serena anxious. "So a brother or sister would be all right?" she asked.

Instead of answering, he laved his tongue across her nipple. Serena sucked in a sharp breath. Fire shot to her abdomen and lower.

"Actually," he said, his lips and teeth toying with her. "I've got more brothers and sisters than I know what to do with already."

"Matt."

He kissed his way down one breast and up the other. The tug of his mouth there brought on a throbbing deep

439

and low. "Now, Joanna," he said. "I'm sure she'd love a brother or sister all her own."

Serena arched beneath him, feeling her breasts swell. "That's . . . good. Matt, hurry."

"There's no hurry. We've got all night. We've got a lifetime." He kissed his way back up her neck.

Serena grinned. He was going to pay her back for last night. That was fine with her. She tried to relax and let him take his time, but his lips, his hands, built a fierce urgency in her that made her breath come in sharp little pants.

"You know what the Apaches believe about making babies, don't you?" she asked.

He grinned against her throat. "That they're made one part at a time?"

"Don't you think . . . we ought to make sure ours . . . has all his parts?"

Matt made his way slowly to her ear. "What did you have in mind?"

God, his mouth was burning her, devouring her, making her lose her mind. "Well," she managed between gasps. "There hasn't been much time for us to make too many parts. I thought . . ." God, he was at her breast again.

"You thought?"

"I thought maybe . . . maybe we should get to work on the rest of him."

"Yeah," Matt said, feeling his control slipping. "I agree." Still, he took his time. She was ready, he knew. But he wanted her more than ready. He wanted her desperate. As desperate as he was.

"You . . . agree?"

"Oh, yes," he whispered against her nipple. "He's going to need all those other parts."

"Then shouldn't we . . . get . . . started?"

"We should. We have to make sure he's got every muscle, every single bone, every hair on his head. Wouldn't want a bald baby, now, would we?"

"No," she said with a gasp as he stroked the curls between her legs. "Shouldn't we . . . shouldn't you . . ."

He teased her silken folds with fingers that trembled with eagerness. "Get started?"

"Yes," she cried.

She arched beneath his touch, driving him wild with heat and want and need. His game had backfired. Now he was the one who was desperate. He positioned his hard, aching flesh. "Yes."

"When?" she cried.

"Just as soon," he whispered against her lips, "as you stop talking."

She didn't say another word. Not a coherent one. Not until much, much later.

When Matt could think again, could breathe, he let out a satisfied sigh and gently kissed the spot on Rena's temple where the white streak began.

"I love you," she whispered.

"And I love you." Matt gazed into her eyes while he kissed her lips. "I don't think I ever told you how glad I am you came to Tombstone."

She smiled. "That must be hindsight speaking. You were definitely not pleased at the time."

"You scared the hell out of me. You made me feel things I told myself were wrong. You tempted me, drove me crazy."

"You held out fairly well for a long time."

Matt smiled softly. "Not long. I needed you. I still do. I always will."

Serena pressed her lips to his. Her heart swelled to near bursting. "I'll always be here for you. Always. I'll never hide my love for you from anyone again. We can touch and kiss whenever we want, right out in the open, and not care who's watching."

The warm, loving glow in Matt's eyes pulled the rest of the words she wanted to say straight from her heart.

"I'll be beside you to hear Joanna's prayers. I'll lie next to you every night in your bed. I'll wrap my arms around you in the dark, and you can lay your head on my breast and know I'll always be here for you, the way I know you'll be here for me. I will take you so deep inside me . . ."

"Rena . . ."

"And every morning when you wake, I will spread my hair—"

Matt stole the rest of her pledge with his kiss. "Just love me, Rena, that's all I ask."

"I do. I will. Forever."

Author's Note

Geronimo's escape from the reservation in 1881, as witnessed by the Coltons, was neither his first break-out nor his last. During the next four years, he returned, then left, several times.

General George Crook is quoted as saying the Indian trouble in Arizona was due to "greed and avarice on the part of the whites." It was a radical statement for a United States military officer of his time, and one that left him unpopular, to say the least.

Although he was never captured, despite having 10,000 troops from two countries chasing him and his handful of followers during his last years of freedom, Geronimo surrendered for the last time in 1886. The Chiricahua scouts, without whom the Army would have had little or no effect in convincing Geronimo to surrender, were betrayed by the Army and sent to Bowie, Arizona, with the renegades.

At Bowie, they were put on a train bound for prison in Florida. As they boarded, the irony of the band playing "Auld Lang Syne" was surely lost on the Chiricahua.

It was not lost, however, on one witness. Jessica

Colton watched in stunned horror as her brother, Pace, beaten and in chains, was loaded onto the train with Geronimo, headed for a swampy Florida prison. Determined to follow and free her brother, Jessie doesn't realize army officer Blake Renard has been ordered to see that she . . .

Ah, but that's another story. In a few months, we'll share another cup of coffee, you and I, over another campfire late at night, and I'll tell you the story of Jessica and Blake, the story of a legacy of deceit and betrayal, a legacy of truth and courage and pride, an *Apache Legacy*.

Janis Reams Hudson
Oklahoma City, Oklahoma

DISCOVER DEANA JAMES!

CAPTIVE ANGEL   (2524, $4.50/$5.50)
Abandoned, penniless, and suddenly responsible for the biggest tobacco plantation in Colleton County, distraught Caroline Gillard had no time to dissolve into tears. By day the willowy redhead labored to exhaustion beside her slaves . . . but each night left her restless with longing for her wayward husband. She'd make the sea captain regret his betrayal until he begged her to take him back!

MASQUE OF SAPPHIRE   (2885, $4.50/$5.50)
Judith Talbot-Harrow left England with a heavy heart. She was going to America to join a father she despised and a sister she distrusted. She was certainly in no mood to put up with the insulting actions of the arrogant Yankee privateer who boarded her ship, ransacked her things, then "apologized" with an indecent, brazen kiss! She vowed that someday he'd pay dearly for the liberties he had taken and the desires he had awakened.

SPEAK ONLY LOVE   (3439, $4.95/$5.95)
Long ago, the shock of her mother's death had robbed Vivian Marleigh of the power of speech. Now she was being forced to marry a bitter man with brandy on his breath. But she could not say what was in her heart. It was up to the viscount to spark the fires that would melt her icy reserve.

WILD TEXAS HEART   (3205, $4.95/$5.95)
Fan Breckenridge was terrified when the stranger found her near-naked and shivering beneath the Texas stars. Unable to remember who she was or what had happened, all she had in the world was the deed to a patch of land that might yield oil . . . and the fierce loving of this wildcatter who called himself Irons.

Available wherever paperbacks are sold, or order direct from the Publisher. Send cover price plus 50¢ per copy for mailing and handling to Zebra Books, Dept. 4289, 475 Park Avenue South, New York, N.Y. 10016. Residents of New York and Tennessee must include sales tax. DO NOT SEND CASH. For a free Zebra/Pinnacle catalog please write to the above address.